"Your crew's got a good reputation. Discreet, thorough, and never caught with your pants down. Is it true Ames is psychic?"

Anna kept her gaze steady. "We don't talk about that."

Greaser's piglike eyes widened fractionally. His grin followed a second later. It didn't improve his looks any.

Greaser reached into his jacket and pulled out the obligatory manila envelope, the motion quick enough that Anna didn't have to spend more than half a second wondering if he was going to take out a gun and shoot her right here. "Fifty thousand," he said, and he tossed the envelope on the table. "Now, the object? Unless you want to sit here and count the cash first."

She reached under the table, produced the bag, and plopped it down in front of her. Greaser unrolled the top and looked inside.

"Charming," he said. He slid the bag out of the way, close to the wall, and produced another envelope. It was a large envelope, fat with papers. "Here's the job," he said, pushing it across the table.

"Job?"

"Yeah. Did you think I was here for the conversation?"

"What if we don't want it?"

The big guy shrugged. "Don't take it. You guys are good, but for two million dollars, I can get 'good' lined up all the way down the block."

Anna's mouth fell open. She knew she looked like a complete amateur, but she couldn't help it.

"I'll be in touch," Greaser said, and he got up to leave. Anna was still speechless as he took the paper bag and crossed the room. He didn't even look back, just opened the door and walked out.

PREMONITIONS

Jamie Schultz

A ROC BOOK

ROC
Published by the Penguin Group
Penguin Group (USA) LLC, 375 Hudson Street,
New York, New York 10014

USA | Canada | UK | Ireland | Australia | New Zealand | India | South Africa | China
penguin.com
A Penguin Random House Company

First published by Roc, an imprint of New American Library,
a division of Penguin Group (USA) LLC

First Printing, July 2014

REGISTERED TRADEMARK—MARCA REGISTRADA

ISBN 978-0-451-46744-7

Printed in the United States of America
10 9 8 7 6 5 4 3 2 1

For Mom, who encouraged me to read all kinds of grossly age-inappropriate material when I was a kid. That has made all the difference.

For Dad, who taught me how to work hard and how to swear. That, too, has made all the difference.

ACKNOWLEDGMENTS

Lots of people contributed to the writing and publication of this book, and without any one of them, you'd likely be reading a much inferior book or no book at all. My heartfelt thanks to each of these folks:

Evan Grantham-Brown, who reads every last damn thing I write and makes each one better.

Janet Sked and Conrad Zero, who offered great feedback on the first draft of this novel. Their input and encouragement helped give me the momentum I needed to spin first-draft straw into final-draft, um, spun straw.

Rose Fox, for invaluable editorial advice and for expressing some thoughts that changed how I look at publication and the cultural role of an author. Rose went above and beyond the call of duty and changed the course of this book's life for the better, for which I can't express enough gratitude.

Lindsay Ribar, for editorial suggestions, answering naïve author questions beyond number, and generally representin' the living hell out of this book.

Jessica Wade, for taking the book on to begin with, for her editorial wisdom and vision, and for getting me to think about the wider picture.

Isabel Farhi, Ms. Wade's assistant, for handling a thousand details that I know of and probably a million more that I don't.

Lastly, my wife, Jenny, who gave me unflagging moral support throughout the writing of this book and every book.

Thank you.

Chapter 1

"Where the fuck is it?" Anna whispered.

Karyn shrugged, at a loss for a response. The damn thing was supposed to be right here, on display in the stupidly cavernous room ahead of them, but even as they huddled at the mouth of the hall in near darkness, she could see that it was gone. The glass case was right where it should be in the center of the room, but nothing rested inside. *So much for recon,* she thought. "He must have moved it. We're going to have to search the place."

"I don't even know what a severed rhino dick is supposed to look like."

"Like a severed elephant dick, only smaller," Tommy put in.

Anna snorted laughter. The sound was barely loud enough to be heard a couple of feet away, but to Karyn it seemed to set the silence humming with its echo.

"C'mon, guys," Anna said, "let's pretend to be professionals here." Karyn watched her eyes, the only part of her face visible behind the balaclava, as they flicked from Tommy to Karyn and back. "Any ideas?"

Karyn looked around the room one more time. It looked more like a gallery in a museum than somebody's living room. Polished wood floor. Sparse white walls broken up with abstract paintings, some with low spotlights on them even at this hour. A couple of couches for sitting back and staring at the walls. The empty glass case.

"You getting anything?" Anna asked.

"You know it doesn't work like that," Karyn said.

"Doesn't hurt to ask."

Tommy's low laughter sounded near Karyn's ear. "Come on, now. If you were a fifty-eight-year-old man, and you had a two-thousand-year-old virility charm—"

Karyn touched the radio at her hip. "Nail, where's the master bedroom?" she whispered.

Nail's voice fired up in her earpiece instantly. "Say again?"

"The master bedroom," she said as loudly as she dared. "Where is it?"

"Upstairs. Southwest corner."

"Roger." She nodded at the others. "That way." She took a step into the gallery and froze as she saw a shadowy shape emerge from the hallway across the room. It crouched, bringing up its hands into a firing position. They jerked twice, as though shooting a soundless gun.

Karyn glanced at Anna, who regarded her with a puzzled expression. *She doesn't see that.* Ergo, it wasn't happening—not yet, anyway. "Back down the hall, go!"

Anna and Tommy rushed back away from the room, Karyn close behind them. They ducked into the nearest doorway. Moments later, clicking footfalls echoed to them from the gallery.

The footfalls faded.

"Clear?" Anna asked.

Karyn listened for another few seconds. "Think so. Just a security guard. Armed, though, I'm pretty sure."

Anna frowned. "I thought they didn't carry guns."

"They didn't, yesterday."

"Should we bail?"

Karyn peered toward the gallery. She saw nothing alarming, and while she wasn't going to bank on that or get cocky about it, it was reassuring. Her hallucinations weren't exactly reliable, but they tended to be up-front about anything that was going to clean her clock in the immediate future. "No, I think we're OK."

"Lead on."

Karyn paused at the end of the hall again, searching the gallery. Nothing moved, real or imagined. She strode quickly across the floor to the doorway in the right-hand wall, then through and up the stairs beyond.

On the second floor, heavy carpeting muffled the already faint noise of her steps. There was less light, too, which she regarded as a mixed blessing. Running around here waving flashlights was to be avoided if at all possible, especially if the guards were carrying guns now.

She put her hand on the wall to her left and used it as a guide while her eyes adjusted. The only light came through closed curtains—not much, but enough to give her a sense of the things in the room. Looked like a little living room/kitchen suite up here, decorated in what she'd come to think of as Rich Guy Standard. Leather furniture lined the walls, thousand-dollar barstools sat in front of the bar. Anna elbowed her and pointed. A huge painting hung above the couch. "Original?" Anna whispered.

It was impossible to make out, but Karyn nodded. "Of course."

The two women relaxed somewhat, and Karyn knew Anna was smiling. She felt the same relief. There was nothing weird here, just the trappings of a garden-variety investment banker. *Thank God.* For once, they hadn't wandered into the lair of some kind of cult leader, underworld magician, or sexual pervert. By all appearances, the pudgy, balding, middle-aged man who owned the place was just a pudgy, balding, middle-aged man who'd accidentally stumbled across the wrong family heirloom.

Karyn crossed the room, turning toward a door off the kitchen. She pressed her ear to it, heard nothing, tried the knob. Locked.

She stepped aside and nodded to Anna.

As Anna approached the knob, lockpicks at the ready, orange-and-yellow light flared up from behind the door, blazing through every crack and seam.

Karyn's heart clenched like a spasming fist, and she threw up a hand to block the light. She squinted through the glare. Anna, unperturbed, started to fiddle with the lock, but Tommy looked at her with worry in his eyes.

"Everything cool?"

"Yeah." She lowered her hands. "It's cool."

Now Anna looked up. "You want me to open this or what?"

Karyn squatted to get a better look at the light coming from beneath the door. Orange, yellow, red, screamingly bright in the gloom. It flickered like it was blinking, too regular to be flame. *What is that all about?* she wondered. She had no idea. It didn't look like an overt threat, but who could tell?

"Yeah," she said. "Carefully."

Anna turned the knob and slowly pulled the door open, taking care to keep the door itself between herself and the opening. Rays of brilliant golden light, shot through with red, poured from the room, and once again Karyn held up a hand against the worst of it.

"There," she said. "On the table."

Tommy stared into the room. "What table? I can't see a thing in there."

"Come on," Karyn said. She ducked into the room, waited for the others to follow, then shut the door with a quiet click. She didn't know what the others saw, but for her the whole room was lit up with a bloody golden radiance, emanating from a table near the head of a nondescript king-sized bed. The red light pulsed, alternately letting the gold shine and blocking it out.

"Light?" Anna asked.

"Go ahead."

Anna flicked on a flashlight, which presumably helped her and Tommy out quite a bit. Karyn couldn't even tell it was on except by the way Anna held it in front of her.

The three of them approached the table.

"That's nasty," Anna said.

Karyn nodded. The rhinoceros penis, she presumed, sat in the center of the table, a wrinkled tube of desiccated skin about the size of her forearm, with a weird kink in the middle. Symbols written in silver paint covered its length.

"I thought it was the horn that was supposed to have magic powers," Tommy said. "I mean, you know. Not that I've really looked into it."

"I don't know," Karyn said. She suddenly realized

what the flashing red among the gold reminded her of—an alarm, or maybe the flashing red light of a police car. "Don't touch it."

"Huh?"

"Somebody's messing with us."

"How do you mean?"

Karyn studied the object on the table. Interpreting her visions wasn't always straightforward, but a red strobe that only she could see was pretty suggestive. "I mean—I think that thing is trapped. Some kind of magic alarm or something. Can you check?"

Tommy pulled a piece of paper and a little packet from his pocket. Anna held the flashlight for him while he sketched a quick diagram on the paper. He poured a handful of gray sand grains onto the diagram and spoke a few low words.

Karyn glanced back toward the door. Nothing.

Tommy held the paper over the table, shaking it gently from side to side so that the sand sprinkled from the diagram onto the table. He watched the sand fall, waited, and then shrugged. "Nothing here."

"Try it again."

"I don't think—"

"Just do it."

Scowling, Tommy went through the whole process again. He took a little longer this time, seeming to take more care enunciating the stream of mangled Latin- and Greek-sounding phrases that fell from his lips. This time, the moment he poured the sand onto the table, the red-gold light winked out. The room around Karyn fell into darkness, with only the beacon of Anna's small flashlight illuminating the scene before her.

"Damn," Tommy said. "There's something here, all right. It's subtle, though. Really good work. Pick that thing up from the table, and it'll be like a fire alarm goes off in here."

"But you can undo it," Karyn said. She thought that's what the vanishing light meant. Either they'd get the alarm disengaged, or they'd leave the item here.

"I'm not sure there's any point."

"What do you mean?"

Tommy took Anna's flashlight and pointed it at the dried penis. "It's alarmed out the wazoo, but I'd bet my share of the score that the object itself is inert."

"What?" Anna said.

Karyn nodded. "I told you. Somebody's messing with us."

"It's a fake?"

She thought about that. It didn't add up. Their recon and everything about the place said the owner didn't know a thing about real magic. Sure, he probably thought the penis held some kind of charm, and the ultimate buyer certainly did, but that didn't mean anything. All around the edges of the occult underworld were hangers-on, collectors, wannabes, and grifters, most of whom weren't plugged into the real scene at all. They still paid up, happy to trade green for their delusions. Most of the crap the crew was hired to steal didn't have so much as a scrap of magic clinging to it as best as Tommy could tell, and this job had all the hallmarks of another one in that vein. Except for the alarm.

"I don't know," Karyn said. "Screw it. Let's grab this thing, and if the buyer's got a problem with it, tell him he needs to be more discreet next time. I swear, somebody knew we were coming."

"Okay," Tommy said. "Gimme a few minutes." He frowned down at the table, his fingers wriggling like they did when he was thinking hard.

Karyn turned back to the door. "I've got a bad feeling about this."

Anna moved to her side. "A *feeling* feeling?"

Karyn smiled weakly. "No, just a regular bad feeling."

"It's not too late to ditch, if it's that bad," Anna said.

"No, I—"

A brief crackle, and then Nail's voice in their earpieces: *"Party's over, guys. Our man's home early, and it looks like he brought a date."*

"Where is he?"

"Car just pulled into the garage."

At the table, Tommy had gotten out a short dagger and was in the process of opening the skin of his palm. The cut looked deep, a grinning black slash in the blue-white beam of the flashlight, and Karyn winced. "How much longer?"

Tommy didn't look up. "Ten minutes. Fifteen at the outside." Blood trickled from his hand to the table, a drop here, a drop there. "Please don't interrupt me."

Maybe if the couple stopped downstairs for a chat, that might be enough, Karyn thought. Maybe—

More blood splashed to the table, a flood of it coming from a sudden hole in the side of Tommy's head. Before Karyn could scream, it was gone, leaving his face pristine, unblemished.

Jesus. We need to get out of here.

"New plan," Karyn said. "Grab the table and let's get the hell out of here."

"Take the whole table?" Anna said.

"Tommy, you said if we pick the item up off the table, the alarm goes, right?"

"Uh, yeah. I think so."

"So we take the table. *Now.*"

The table was a glorified nightstand, big enough for a lamp and a few books. Anna picked up one end as Tommy lifted the other. "Go," Anna said.

Karyn moved to the bedroom door, listened, and opened it for the other two. Once they were through, she moved as quickly as she could to the stairs. A glance down revealed nothing. "Come on," she said, starting down the stairs. "Be careful."

She thought she glimpsed the faintest flash of white as Anna rolled her eyes, but she ignored it. She reached the bottom of the stairs and peered around the corner into the main gallery. A light flicked on in a room across the way, and distant, ghostly snatches of conversation drifted across the space to her.

Anna and Tommy reached the landing behind her, and she waved them forward frantically. *Go, go, go!* Any second now, a half-drunk couple or a security guard was going to come walking through here, and then they'd be screwed.

The three of them scurried across the gallery floor like roaches heading for cover, every breath and scrape of shoe ringing in Karyn's ears. The conversation in the far room ebbed, and a woman giggled. Something fell, clattering to the floor. Anna and Tommy moved faster.

Another low exchange came from the lighted room, and Karyn swore she heard the word "upstairs" clearly above the rest.

Then they were in the hall they'd come in from. The front door was just after a little jog in the hall. A clatter of drunken footsteps came from behind them as Anna and Tommy hustled the table around the bend and out of sight.

"Quickly," Karyn said. "That guy's gonna be really pissed in another minute or so."

"We go right out the front door, I suppose?" Tommy asked.

Anna nodded. "You know it. Just give me a sec." She set down her end of the table and crossed the short foyer to the front door, wood with a gleaming oval of translucent stained glass. A shadow fell across the window.

Anna held her eye to the tiny peephole in the center. Ten seconds passed. Twenty.

"Not a lot of time here," Karyn said.

Karyn saw the set of Anna's shoulders stiffen for a fraction of a second, and then Anna moved. She threw the door open with her left hand while her right moved in a blur from her hip, arcing upward. Before Karyn could even register what was happening, the security guard on the front stair spun around and caught a blast of pepper spray in the face. He threw his hands to his eyes and Anna planted a foot in his crotch. As he fell, she stepped casually forward and plucked the gun from his belt, then his radio.

She leaned down over his huddled form and whispered something. Whatever it was, the man huddled into a ball and whimpered.

Karyn was already moving to take Anna's place at the

table. She and Tommy crossed the threshold, and then the cry went up from inside, inarticulate shouting echoing down the stairs and through the gallery.

Anna closed the door, and Tommy and Karyn carried the table across the lawn, as quickly as they were able, to where Nail was waiting in the van.

Chapter 2

Anna eased into a slick leather booth with a clear view of the door, slid a rolled-up paper bag under the table, and tried not to make eye contact with the waiter. No luck. He came over, frowned at the way she was dressed, and pretty much demanded she order something just by the way he was standing. She sent him running for a twelve-dollar beer, the cheapest thing on the menu. This place was a lot more upscale than the kind of shithole she liked to hang out at on her own time, but most of her clients didn't want to be seen walking into *that* kind of establishment, and Clive Durante was no exception.

She was fifteen minutes early, as usual. Clive was a good client, reliable and unlikely to pull any bullshit, but that wasn't a reason to get sloppy. She pushed into the corner, put a foot up on the bench, and scoped out the room. Not too crowded at this late hour, but busy enough that a low murmur of talk and faint, repetitive techno piped through overhead speakers made it hard to eavesdrop, if you kept your voice low. Lots of white and silver tablecloths, standing out against a backdrop of black tables and black leather cushions. She'd already managed to put a dusty gray footprint on one of the latter, but that didn't matter. They wouldn't throw her out for that. Wouldn't want to make a scene.

She drank her beer and fought down a nagging unease about the swag. It had taken a hell of a lot more than ten or fifteen minutes for Tommy to kill the alarm on the object, and they'd ended up having to take the whole mess—table and all—back to Tommy's creepy basement workshop. When it was done, Tommy'd run a shaking hand over the field of stubble on his head. Then he'd crossed his arms, wiry and tattooed in the white tank top undershirt he always wore, and shrugged. The actual object didn't have any more mystical powers than his gym socks, Tommy had said, but that didn't mean it wasn't valuable. Maybe that was why it had been all magicked up. He hadn't said it with much conviction, though.

It wouldn't be the first time Clive had put in an order for something that didn't live up to its billing, and he hadn't minded in the past, but Anna worried anyway. He'd been real good to Karyn's crew over the last few years, and Anna would hate to burn him, or the relationship. He wasn't the kind of connection you could replace overnight.

At nine p.m. on the dot, the restaurant door swung open. Anna got one good look at the man who walked in, and she swore under her breath. The guy's name was Gresser, so naturally everybody called him Greaser, at least when he wasn't around. He had a face that looked like it had been pushed in by an enormous fist, a two-thousand-dollar suit, and an attitude that could make a hyena run off to look for better company. Rooms cleared when he walked in, because anybody who recognized him suddenly remembered somewhere they had to be. People on his bad side got out to avoid getting damaged, and people on his good side made themselves scarce so that he wouldn't be tempted to ask them any favors. It was an open question whether it was better to be in his good graces than not.

Curiously, Anna had never heard a story about Greaser so much as laying a finger on anyone. He didn't have to. When you were Enoch Sobell's strong right arm, fate went out of its way to smite your enemies for you.

She'd seen him once across a crowded room, just as that room started to become miraculously uncrowded.

She'd been smart enough to go with the flow and ease out the nearest exit at the time, but that wasn't an option this time, not unless she wanted to spend the next few days trying to track down Clive Durante and do some heavy-duty explaining. She pushed against the wall and sank down in her seat, looking away from the door.

In her peripheral vision, the big man's shape just got bigger. Silence, surrounding him like a cloud, approached— and then he sat on the bench across the table from her. She looked up, meeting a pair of small, piercing eyes.

"Anna Ruiz," Greaser said. His voice was soft, and Anna found herself sitting up and leaning forward to make sure she heard everything. "Expecting someone?"

"Yeah," she said. "You ain't him."

"You run with Karyn Ames's crew."

"Vice President of Business Development," she said, trotting out the same joke she always used. It seemed a lot more tired today than usual.

"That's good," Greaser said. "Clever. You know who I am."

It didn't sound like a question, but Anna nodded just to be on the safe side. She wished the guy would break eye contact for a second. Blink, even.

"You know who I work for."

Another nod, this one more emphatic. *Let's make sure there's no misunderstandings here,* Anna thought. She was surprised to note a thread of excitement in her anxiety. He was looking for her, specifically. Everybody said Greaser was bad news, but if the crew got in with him, this meeting could open a lot of doors.

Could also fuck us nine ways to Sunday if we screw it up, she reminded herself. She glanced toward the door. Was Durante coming or what?

"Good. Then you know not to jerk me around."

"Sure."

"Your crew's got a good reputation. Discreet, thorough, and never caught with your pants down. Is it true Ames is psychic?"

Anna kept her gaze steady. "We don't talk about that."

Greaser's piglike eyes widened fractionally. His grin followed a second later. It didn't improve his looks any. "Good. I like that." He paused. "You have something for me?"

Anna's heart sped up a notch. "For you? No."

"Mr. Durante is no longer a buyer. Seems he lost interest."

Anna ran the options. Could be a bluff, in which case she should hold out for Durante's arrival. But Greaser knew the client's name, knew where he was supposed to be. Most likely, then, Durante had been run off. That wasn't gonna be good for future business. Anna steeled herself. "Price hasn't changed."

Greaser reached into his jacket and pulled out a manila envelope, the motion quick enough that Anna didn't have to spend more than half a second wondering if he was going to take out a gun and shoot her right there. "Fifty thousand," he said, and he tossed the envelope on the table. "Now, the object? Unless you want to sit here and count the cash first."

Durante she trusted not to fuck her over, but not this guy. Still, she didn't want to count fifty thousand dollars in the middle of a restaurant, in full view of the handful of people left in the room. She reached under the table, produced the bag, and plopped it down in front of her. Greaser unrolled the top and looked inside.

"Charming," he said. He slid the bag out of the way, close to the wall, and produced another envelope. It was large, fat with papers. "Here's the job," he said, pushing it across the table.

"Job?"

"Yeah. Did you think I was here for the conversation?"

"What if we don't want it?"

The big guy shrugged. "Don't take it. You guys are good, but for two million dollars, I can get 'good' lined up all the way down the block."

Anna's mouth fell open. She knew she looked like a complete amateur, but she couldn't help it.

"I'll be in touch," Greaser said, and he got up to leave. Anna was still speechless as he took the paper bag and walked away. He didn't even look back, just opened the door and walked out.

As the door swung slowly shut behind him, she saw him dump the paper bag in the trash.

Chapter 3

When Anna came out of her room, satchel in hand, Nail felt his face shape itself into a grin. *Payday,* he thought, and not a single day too soon. Hard not to feel good about that.

"There you go," Anna said, dropping the satchel on the table. "That's what you get for all that clean living."

He couldn't miss the anticipation in the air, but nobody moved.

The satchel sat in the middle of the cheap card table that was practically the only furniture in the living room of the cheap apartment Karyn and Anna shared. The place was a testament to just how little *stuff* a couple of people could live with. There was the table, a handful of folding chairs, and, lonely in the corner, a black leather beanbag chair. The door to Anna's room on the left, Karyn's on the right, and only the stained gray carpet in the middle. The two women had lived like this as long as Nail had known them, going on eight years now. Karyn said it was so there was less stuff to pack if they had to leave in a hurry, and he supposed that was part of the story. She didn't like to go into a lot of detail about her gift, but he'd seen it in action enough times to understand some of the basics. She saw things, usually things that were gonna happen in some way, and it wasn't hard to see why she might want to keep things around her simple. Less confusing that way. Less worry about what's real or not.

Around the table, everyone stood behind one of the folding chairs. This was part of it, a piece of the odd ritual that had developed over years of working together. Anna was at the place to Nail's right, one hand on the back of her chair, thin as a bundle of sticks but one of the toughest people he'd ever met. Black hair fell in lazy waves just past her chin, and her dark eyes darted around the room, scanning everything, never stopping, not even here where he'd have thought she was as safe as anywhere. To Nail's left stood Tommy, restless as always, nearly bouncing as he shifted his weight back and forth. He was like a scrappy little dog who'd never figured out that he wasn't as big as the other dogs, but that didn't stop him from trying. Nail had given him a raftload of shit a couple of years back when he'd taken to shaving his head, just like Nail himself, probably because he thought it would make him look tough. The result wasn't pretty. Nail took that shit seriously—there was not a trace of stubble on the dark skin of his scalp—but Tommy half-assed it, so that his pink head was covered in very short, patchy growth, like a lawn mowed by a careless drunk. Tommy took all Nail's ribbing in stride, and he never did let his hair grow back out. Every week he at least ran some clippers over his skull.

Across from Nail, Karyn studied the satchel, arms crossed in front of her. It had been only the last year or so Nail had noticed the faint lines at the corners of her eyes, the filaments of gray in the brown bundle of her tied-back hair. Nothing surprising about that—none of them were twenty years old anymore, and he himself had dots of white stubble cropping up on his chin on the rare occasions he let that go more than a day—but lately it was more than just getting a little older. Her eyes seemed like they peered out from dark hollows, and she was jumpier than she used to be. Every time he really let it register, it made him uneasy. She was the rock, the pillar that held this whole thing up, and he wondered about the strain she was under.

All eyes were on Karyn, waiting. This part was as immutable as Thanksgiving dinner now. Anna always made the drop—sometimes alone, sometimes not, depending on the client—and always brought back the cash, but Karyn gave the word.

"Everything go OK?" Karyn asked.

"We got paid, if that's what you mean. Not by Durante, though."

"By who?"

"Joe Gresser."

Karyn frowned. Nail vaguely recognized the name, but couldn't quite remember from where.

"What did he want?" Karyn asked.

"We can talk about that later. Just . . . you know. I don't trust the guy, so you might wanna look at this one extra hard."

Karyn studied the satchel for another moment. Nail was never sure what she was looking for at this point. The job was done and the money was here, so if they were going to get fucked somehow, that fucking would already be in motion. What would the money tell her?

She opened the bag and poured out the contents. Five thick stacks of hundred-dollar bills, rubber-banded together, fell out. No scorpions, snakes, demons, or razor blades fell out with them, at least not that Nail could see. Karyn's face was impossible to read as she stared at the pile.

"All right," she said. Everyone in the room let out a slight breath. Nail smiled broadly.

"Everybody got their accountant hat on?" Karyn pulled out a chair and sat, and the others followed, crowding around the table. She divided the money up into four roughly equal stacks and handed them out. A few moments later, the counting was over. Nail had a hundred too much, Anna was a hundred short, so they straightened that out. "All right. Pass 'em to the left." An unnecessary part of the ritual these days, Nail thought, even though it had been his suggestion way back when. He took his stack from Anna and pocketed it without counting. Only Tommy ever bothered to go through the motions of double-checking anymore, and that only because he liked counting up his riches so much.

"Celebration time," Tommy said, grinning. "Who's got the cards?"

"I'm done. I'm done! Hell with you guys," Tommy said, throwing his cards down.

The game had been going for hours, and thousands of dollars had moved across the table one way, then another. It was hard to tell who was up how much, but Nail didn't need to see the dwindling stack of bills in front of Tommy to know *his* luck had been for shit all night— he'd seen it in operation, one lousy hand after another. "I keep this up, I'll be out my whole share," he said.

"You didn't do shit anyway," Anna shot back.

"Fuck that noise. You guys would be lost without my mad occult skills."

Laughter all around, but Tommy had kicked off the wind-down, and the others started taking their cash off the table. The last shots were tossed back, the last dregs of beer drained. Even Anna, usually the last woman standing at these postscore parties, rubbed her eyes and yawned. Nail thought she had the right idea. He was worn down, too, and because he'd needed to be mindful of his cash, the game hadn't been as much fun as usual. It would be good to get home.

"You see," Tommy said, "this is why you don't play poker with a—"

"Shut up, Tommy," Anna said.

Karyn opened her mouth to laugh, then froze. It was just a moment, the pause between one movement of the second hand and the next, but Nail didn't miss it. Neither did Anna, who turned in the direction Karyn had been looking.

Karyn's expression had gone wary, already recovered from a brief moment of shock, but the pleasant buzz Nail had on vanished, and he found himself standing, pistol in hand.

"You OK?" he asked.

Karyn swallowed. "Yeah. Yeah. Just—hey, can you have a look outside? See if you see anything weird?"

He went to the window, peeked through the blinds.

Then he turned the dead bolt, slipped off the chain, and cracked open the door. The sounds of traffic filtered into the room, along with the shouting of the couple in 221—still at it, even at three in the morning. The stairwell was empty. Nail walked to the balcony, saw nothing unusual below, and walked back.

"Looks clear," he said.

"It's late," Karyn said, shaking her head. "I must be overtired."

"You sure?" Nail asked.

"Yeah. You guys be careful going home, though. If you see anything weird—well, just be careful."

Nail gave her a long questioning look, but finally he put his gun back in the waistband of his cargo pants. He trusted her to know her business better than he did.

"All right. Catch you later."

"Hey, wait up," Tommy said. He grabbed his backpack of questionable implements and followed Nail out.

The noise of an ambulance siren swelled, screamed by, and diminished—probably one of fifteen tonight, Nail figured, but now *he* was jumpy. He descended the stairs slowly, checking left and right as he did. There was nobody out here. A sloppy-looking party had spilled out of one of the units across the courtyard, but it mostly looked like a handful of really smashed couples slow dancing, bizarrely enough, to Metallica. *Really smashed.*

Probably just a false alarm. It had certainly happened before.

"Hey, uh, that was a pretty good game in there, huh?" Tommy said.

"It was all right."

Tommy scratched nervously at the side of his neck. Blue-white light from the outdoor floodlights lit up the left side of his face, but the shadow of the building slashed across, leaving the other half nearly invisible. "Yeah, well, I was wondering—I kinda went a little nuts in there, you know, and I could really use a few hundred bucks. Just for a week or so. You know?"

Nail didn't have to do any counting—he knew exactly how much cash he had in his wallet. He put a heavy hand on Tommy's shoulder. "I'm sorry, man. This ain't a good time."

"Your brother?"

"Yeah. If we hadn't got paid today . . ."

"He'd be fucked. Again."

The whining edge in Tommy's voice was a little too far, especially talking about Nail's family. "Careful."

"Sorry. I'm sorry."

"It's cool." *And, yeah. "Again" is right.* "But I show up a few hundred short, somebody gonna get hurt. Maybe DeWayne, maybe a lot of other people." More likely, his fool brother DeWayne *and* a lot of other people. "I still don't know what the fuck I'm gonna do about next month."

"Shit."

"How bad you off?"

Tommy put his hands in his pockets. "It's not that bad, I guess. I'll get by."

"You and me both."

Once the two men had made their exit, Karyn's nerves toned down their jangling some, if not all the way. Nothing had happened, nothing had gone wrong. For a moment, she had seen a flash of—something. Blood, she thought, spattered all over Tommy's face. Then it was gone so quickly she wasn't sure she'd actually seen it. Even the memory of the vision was already beginning to fade. *Probably just a false alarm.* That happened sometimes, particularly when her stash was low and the images started crowding around, possibilities overlapping with certainties overlapping with reality in a jumbled, confusing mess.

Anna sat in the chair to Karyn's left and leaned forward, elbows on her knees. Her hair hung in her eyes as she looked up at Karyn. "What was that about?"

"Thought I saw something."

"And?"

"It went away."

"Mm-hmm." Anna's mouth tightened. "And how's your stash holding up?"

"Let's just say it's a good thing we got paid today."

Anna straightened, crossing her arms like an irate mother. "You're out."

"See, this is the problem. You've known me way too long."

"Oh, *that's* the problem."

Karyn managed a slight smile. "It *is* time to see Adelaide," she admitted.

"Great," Anna said, baring her teeth and doing a lousy job of hiding her lack of enthusiasm. "When?"

Karyn gave a half-embarrassed shrug. "Tonight would be good."

"I'll get my keys."

"Not yet. First, give me the lowdown. What was the deal with the drop? With Joe Gresser? What happened?"

Anna pulled out one of the chairs, reversed it, and sat with her arms draped over the back. Karyn leaned back against the wall, swigging from a bottle of Old Milwaukee, and listened while Anna related the story.

"Two million dollars," Karyn said, once Anna had finished. "That's a lot of scratch."

"Yep." Anna looked in her eyes, briefly searching for something on Karyn's face, then back down at the floor. She was nervous about the offer, Karyn could tell, or maybe about the job itself. That was enough to give Karyn pause by itself. Anna wasn't nervous about much.

"Got any details?"

The worn jean jacket Anna had been wearing since forever was hung over the back of her chair. Anna reached into the inside pocket and pulled out a thick envelope. She held the envelope out to Karyn. "I haven't looked yet."

Karyn took the envelope but didn't open it, instead watching Anna's face. It had gone still, frozen and expressionless—her robot face, Karyn called it, and she'd learned that nothing else was as reliable an indicator of Anna's anxiety as that locked-down nonexpression. Some people smoked, tapped their fingers, or, like Karyn herself, chewed their nails. Anna shut down all nonverbal cues whatsoever, a tic that Karyn had only slowly learned to identify as a nonverbal cue of its own. "You haven't even looked yet, and you're this worried about it?"

"I ain't worried."

"Uh-huh. You know something I don't?"

"Ha." Anna reached for her own bottle of beer. It was empty, as far as Karyn could tell, but Anna rolled it between her palms and eyeballed it like she was ready to drain the dregs. "You ain't the only one with the occasional bad feeling, that's all. It's one thing when we're talking ten or fifty large, but when you show up with your hand out for *this* kind of money, it starts to look a lot cheaper for the buyer to just shoot you in the head and find an out-of-the-way place for the corpse."

"You think it's risky."

"Yeah."

"Five hundred thousand each," Karyn reminded her.

"Yeah." Anna nodded, but she didn't take her eyes from the bottle. "It also means getting in with Enoch Sobell."

"Might be a good thing. Lots more work."

"I hear getting out again ain't so easy."

"Five hundred thousand dollars," Karyn said again. "You seriously think we ought to pass on that?"

A long breath escaped Anna, the whispering of wind over a dry, empty place. "Maybe," she said, the word so quiet Karyn almost didn't hear it over her own breath.

Maybe it was the hour, or the remnants of the booze sloshing its way through her system, but a low anger flared up inside her. "Yeah, *you* can walk away from half a million dollars," she said, the words spilling out before she'd really understood what she was about to say.

Anna flicked a wary glance in her direction. "What's that supposed to mean?"

"It means . . . It means you can walk away from this shit. One day, you're going to get it all out of your system, go find a nice office job, shack up with some nice girl, and adopt an army of kids. And me"—she shrugged, trying to look noncommittal—"I'll still be here, shifting cursed necklaces and crap like that for the terminally insane."

"I don't like nice girls," Anna said.

Karyn looked toward the window. Why had she even opened her mouth? She'd known for a long time that she'd never have what you'd call a normal life—her condition and the constant need for serious amounts of cash wouldn't allow it. There would be no career, no SUV, no house in the suburbs, no husband to come home to and trade boring work stories. She was OK with that, or at least had come to terms with it. It was only during the latest of nights she got maudlin like this and ended up thinking about how Anna didn't need this crap, how she surely wouldn't put up with this forever. Even the best of friends drifted apart eventually; that was just part of life. People moved on, sent the occasional Christmas card, and called every year or two. One day, Anna would move on. That was a fact, and Karyn did her best not to let it get to her, tried not to wonder how she'd keep her life, such as it was, together afterward. And she for damn sure didn't talk about it.

After a long moment, Anna made an exasperated noise. "I'm not going anywhere. And if I ever did, you could walk, too."

Karyn mustered a sad smile. "Not really," she said. "I've got a *very* expensive habit—and I can't even drive myself to my dealer."

"True that," Anna said. Then, a speculative sound in her voice: "Half a million dollars."

"That'll keep your average hallucinatory precognitive in blind for a good long time."

Anna snorted. "There are no average hallucinatory whatevers. There's you, and there's Adelaide."

"Well, it'll keep *me* in the present tense for a good long while, then."

"Plus we could move out of this shitty apartment."

"Let's see what we've got here," Karyn said, and she opened the envelope.

Chapter 4

"You are a demon." Even with slitted eyes, one hand held out to a chair to steady himself, Enoch Sobell was able to expertly knot his tie. It looked immaculate. Gresser had seen this done maybe two dozen times, and it still impressed him.

"Sir?"

"No decent human being would wake me up at this hour. Ergo . . ."

"Your instructions, sir."

"Even so." Tie finished, Sobell pulled on a sock, wobbling on one foot. "Jesus Christ, did somebody order up extra sun this morning?"

Gresser looked out across L.A. through the huge floor-to-ceiling windows. Around him, the detritus from the previous night's debauchery lay in broken piles. Smashed glasses twinkled in the morning sun, a heavy leather couch had been knocked back onto the marble floor during God knew what kind of nocturnal calisthenics, and a line of alternating panties and boxers had been laid out along the entire length of the bar. All that was missing were the people, who had, in accordance with custom, presumably been rounded up and shooed out at some pitch-black hour before Mr. Sobell awoke. "No, I think this is standard issue."

"Fuck." Sobell put a hand to his head and cracked open his eyes a little further. "Fuck." He cupped his hand in front of his face, exhaled loudly, inhaled, and grimaced. "Fuck." He straightened, tottering just a bit. "Seems I'm still drunk, Mr. Gresser. Thus, a little hair of the dog is in order. Would you mind?"

Gresser shrugged. "Which dog?"

"That goddamned vodka-and-tonic mongrel should do nicely."

Gresser walked around the bar and found a glass. This wasn't the first time he'd found Mr. Sobell like this, nor even the twentieth, and he still wasn't sure how much of it was an act. That some of it was an act was indisputable. One evening about five years back, Sobell had been playing the Merry Drunkard at some godforsaken dive he enjoyed when he was slumming, and some creep had tried to roll him in the bathroom. Gresser had walked in just in time to see Sobell sober up in a shocking hurry and bury a letter opener four inches into the guy's eye. Sobell's cheerful, drunken half smile was gone, his eyes hard and clear for one short moment—and then he'd gone right back to it. "Got a bit of a problem here, Mr. Gresser," he'd said, and he'd hiccuped for good effect afterward.

This morning, Sobell hobbled about looking for his other sock while Gresser poured. Ice, vodka, more vodka, open the bottle of tonic and pour some down the sink, and presto! A vodka and tonic the way Enoch Sobell liked it.

Socks found, donned, and held in place by a couple of thousand-dollar shoes, Sobell made his way to the bar. Half the vodka went down in one toxic slug, and Sobell's face brightened. And, just like that long-ago night in a men's room in a shitty part of town, all at once he looked alarmingly sober.

"Ms. Ames and company? I assume they're on board."

Gresser put both hands on the bar and shook his head. "Not yet. They wanted to think about it. They did deliver the, um, object."

"Fine work, that." Another gulp of vodka. "What did you do with it?"

"Dropped it in the first trash can I found. Fucking disgusting."

"Too right." Sobell cocked the glass, pausing before downing the last of it. "So, she wants to sleep on it. Not a lot of time for that, but it could be worse. Anything happen afterward?"

"Met with her crew. Partied. Ruiz and Ames headed out at about three."

"Oh?"

"Yeah. Went to just about the worst part of town I can think of. Looks like Ames's got a connection down there." He tapped the crook of his elbow with two fingers.

Sobell's brow tightened fractionally. "Where, exactly?"

"You want an address?"

"Yes. That's exactly what I want."

"Uh, Norton Street? East of LaBrea, somewhere in the two hundred block."

"Hmm," Sobell said, nodding. His eyes narrowed; with his body backlit by the rising sun, they looked like black slits. "Adelaide." Gresser could have sworn that the fearless Enoch Sobell actually shuddered.

"I don't know where that is."

"Not where—who. If Ames is visiting that charming young nut job, she's almost certainly the real deal. That's a good thing." He didn't look like he thought that was a good thing. He looked like he thought it was on par with eating a handful of lye.

Gresser hesitated before speaking his next words. He hadn't gotten into Enoch Sobell's good graces by accident, or by being careless, and it wasn't his style to extend himself much. But, still—two million dollars? For *Ames*? That was dumb. "Maybe we can leave her out of this," he suggested. "Me and a few of the boys can—"

"No." Sobell put the glass on the bar with a dry, precise click. "For every job, there is an appropriate tool. Karyn Ames and her crew have a few rather specialized skills. And, frankly, you have a different role to play in this absurd comedy."

Gresser nodded. He'd learned long ago that many of his questions would be answered in time, as long as he was patient.

Sobell pulled his jacket off the nearest barstool and put it on. "I assume the car is waiting?"

Sobell paused before the warehouse door, a dingy little side door next to the big overheads, and stepped aside. Gresser obligingly turned the knob and opened the door for him. He walked into the dimly lit space and stepped through the heavy, hunched shadows cast by obscure machinery rusting in the dark. Blue-white fluorescent lights flickered and buzzed, spitting feeble illumination into the vast volume. Gresser shut the door with a clang and quickly caught up.

"All has been quiet here, I assume?" Sobell asked.

"Yes, sir."

Sobell nodded. He wasn't looking forward to this next piece of work at all, but he couldn't put it off much longer. Any day now, Mendelsohn's pet may very well escape and vanish beyond Sobell's reach, or—rather more likely, he thought—escape, kill every living thing in Mendelsohn's home and a hundred-yard radius, and then vanish beyond his reach. Ames and company needed to cooperate, and Sobell needed to get his preparation under way, which meant taking care of the nasty business at hand. He would have much preferred to deal with Mendelsohn's creature without having to mess with the entity he was on his way to meet, but it simply wouldn't do to show up without payment, and he couldn't think of a better way to get it. Had, in fact, worked a small miracle or two to arrange this ... meeting.

He surveyed the darkness, unable to clear the self-satisfied smile from his lips. "Lead on, Mr. Gresser."

Gresser edged around him and took a sharp right at the next clear spot between shelves of inscrutable equipment. Sobell stepped over some kind of winch and narrowly avoided twisting his ankle on something that looked like a giant ball bearing—not that he'd know a ball bearing from a socket wrench, if it came down to it. His talents had always lain in other areas.

"Charming place," he said. "Union shop?"

Gresser grunted a short laugh. "Through here." The

heavy overhanging shelf of his brow wrinkled in a question. "Ready?"

"Of course."

Gresser pushed open a door covered in flaking paint, a green so dark it was nearly black in the fluorescents. Soft silver light poured from the room.

Sobell squinted. "Bit shiny, eh?" Gresser had already stepped aside, outside the room. His face was an expressionless mask, though Sobell could see the tight bunching of muscles at his jaw. He didn't like this one bit. Probably time to throw him a bonus, then. Good help, and all that.

Sobell brushed past his discomfited lieutenant and went through the doorway. The room beyond, perhaps once a small storage room, was now quite plainly a cell. It had been emptied by some of Gresser's gorillas, but the thousands of glyphs and symbols that lined the walls had been drawn on the panels by Sobell himself before they were installed. It was not the kind of work one left up to lackeys.

In the corner of the room stood the source of the silver light. Man-sized and roughly man-shaped, it still wasn't something you could call a proper human being. It was more like a department store mannequin of unearthly beauty, a form that suggested a thousand shapes rather than actually taking one itself. It didn't even have eyes or a mouth that Sobell could see, merely indentations that implied some, and as it turned its head to acknowledge him, the pattern of light and shadow shifted to suggest disdain.

You are the architect of my imprisonment, then.

The mouth didn't move, exactly, but it didn't *not* move either, simply suggesting movement in a manner that was one of the most unsettling things Sobell had seen in a long life of unsettling things.

"Architect of your imprisonment? That's not bad. Style's a shade overblown, perhaps, but I think I might keep the phrase around for later use. If you don't mind." He straightened his suit jacket. His pulse was pounding so hard he could hear it in his ears, and it helped to concentrate on something mundane for a moment.

I have nothing for you.

"A blatant untruth, as it happens. As you can probably tell at a glance, I am a man with rapidly dwindling prospects for continued existence on this plane."

You're dying.

"If you must be crude, yes. And, as you can also probably tell, when I snuff it, I will be tipped rather unceremoniously into the basement furnace, so to speak, having done my soul a fair amount of damage by dabbling in what the uncultured so stubbornly refer to as witchcraft."

I have nothing for you.

Not the sharpest conversationalist, but the force of its presence—and that disturbing moving/not moving trick—made Sobell feel like he was losing the argument anyway. He couldn't remember the last time he'd been in that position.

"Of course you do. As it happens, I need some of your blood."

A pause, and a real motion this time. The being's head cocked slightly, and the features gave an impression of simultaneous disdain and unwitting curiosity.

I do not bleed.

Again, the words were delivered with such power that for a moment Sobell doubted himself. For one instant he thought, *Shit, of course it doesn't. I should just leave. This was foolish.* But he seized control of himself and forced a smile.

He reached into the inside pocket of his jacket and pulled out a cross-shaped object, dull in the silver light from the creature, one end wrapped in a heavily warded black leather sheath. Sobell grasped the hilt and pulled the sheath away, revealing a rust-pitted length of scrap metal that had broken off about six inches above the crossguard.

The scion's blade.

"St. George's sword. It doesn't look like much, but

I've seen it cut through two inches of solid steel in a single swipe, and I'm told it'll do for you as well."

I bleed for no one.

"Now, see, this is progress. A minute ago, you didn't bleed at all. Let's be reasonable about this. I need, say, a couple tablespoons of your blood—basically as currency, to treat with a rather stubborn sort of creature who can help me with my problem. You give me the blood and your word that neither you nor yours will seek any vengeance, and I'll let you walk out of here with little more than a paper cut to show for it."

The being seemed to grow, looming over him and filling the small room with blinding light. Sobell squinted. Sweat popped out in beads all over his forehead.

"Parlor tricks aren't going to get you anywhere," he said, more firmly than he felt. "You and I both know your balls are clipped in here." *Unless I fucked up,* he thought, and he jammed the treacherous thought back down as hard as he could.

The creature was ten feet tall now, nearly touching the ceiling—a neat trick, given that Sobell was pretty sure the room had an eight-foot ceiling to begin with.

I will swear no such thing.

"It's you or me, my friend, and I'm simply not going down that easy."

Lay a finger on me, and you will be cursed, your soul shriven, your fortunes driven to ruin, your line doomed to produce the misshapen and monstrous until—

Sobell swung the fragment of sword. It was an awkward swing—he wasn't practiced in swordsmanship, and the balance of the broken sword was pretty terrible besides—but that didn't matter. The creature's flesh parted like paper where the weapon touched it. Sobell sliced it from the left shoulder down through the torso, meeting no more resistance than if he'd been swinging the sword in an empty room, and shining light leaped forth.

The creature didn't even scream. It fell back against the wall and slumped, sliding to the floor as far as its shackles would allow. Blazing light from its chest scoured the room.

Sobell held up an arm to shield his face, produced a small vial, and edged in next to the corpse. He held the vial to the creature's body, and was momentarily nonplussed when he realized there was no liquid coming from the wound. *It really doesn't bleed—oh.* Maybe it didn't bleed liquid, but the light itself was pooling somehow in the vial. *That should do nicely.*

He filled the vial and was ready to leave, when an awful thought occurred to him.

"I'm going to Hell for this," he said, and he gave a grim laugh. Then he readied the sword and started cutting.

A few minutes later, he emerged from the room. His suit jacket was in one hand, wrapped in a tight bundle. Fierce white light leaked from the seams.

Gresser looked at the bundle with badly disguised alarm. "Get everything you need?"

"Yes. Burn this building down. Then go through the ashes and burn them."

Gresser nodded. The two men walked rapidly away from the little room. Sobell could hardly stop himself from running, could barely keep from looking back.

Gresser paused at the door to the outside. He wore a pained expression, and Sobell could tell that he was forcing his words out not because he wanted to but because he felt driven to. That wasn't a natural state for Mr. Joseph Gresser—he asked questions only when he really needed to know something. "Was that thing really an angel?"

"You mean like in a theological sense?"

"Yeah."

"Who the fuck cares?" Sobell jammed his trembling hand in his pocket and walked outside.

Chapter 5

"Let me get this straight," Anna said. "He wants us to steal a piece of a god." It had been a long time since she'd gotten such a bad vibe off a job, and this was not helping.

Nail nodded. "Sounds like it."

"It's not a god." All eyes turned to Tommy. "What? It's not. I mean, I'm pretty sure."

Anna folded her arms. The four thieves sat in the living room of the house Tommy lived in, shrouded in the thin tatters of gray light that managed to make their way past the perpetually closed blinds. Dust swam in the air. The whole place made Anna's skin itch every time she came in, and she had no idea whether that was from the general uncleanliness or because the basement she was standing over creeped her out so badly. The things Tommy did were damn handy, but there was a nasty stink about them. You had to wonder about any kind of work that needed so much blood, and maybe you had to wonder a little bit about the kind of man doing it, too. Tommy was a good guy, trustworthy and reliable, but she'd walked in on him gutting a cat one time, and you didn't forget that sort of thing real soon. Tommy swore it was a spell of some kind, something that had to do with divining the future, but all Anna knew was that it was gross, and that the cat had still been weakly mewling when she came in.

"Look, the Brotherhood of Zagam is just a low-rent cult," Tommy said, waving a hand at the papers and photos spread out on the table. "Maybe a medium-rent cult. But they don't have a line on a god, or even a piece of one. Believe me."

"They'd better have a line on *something*," Anna said. "Because I get the impression Enoch Sobell is smart enough not to pay a couple million dollars for a bone with a few stars painted on it."

Nail frowned. "Could be a bunch of things." He ticked them off on the fingers of his left hand. "A fake. Some kind of weird-ass heirloom. Some other kind of magic bullshit. Or a piece of a god."

"Not a god," Tommy said again. "A demon, if anything."

Nail pushed his chair back, leaning dangerously. "I don't believe this shit."

Tommy grinned. "Fucking skeptics, man. Which shit, exactly, do you not believe?"

"Who's skeptical? I don't care if it's the pope's goddamn hat or if it will give you a bad case of the clap on sight. I don't see what we're arguing about. Two million is two million."

Anna glanced toward Karyn, who was listening without saying anything. Typical. If she hadn't gotten signs from beyond—or wherever—that the gig was an outright bad idea, Karyn usually sat back and let them decide. No help there.

That left it up to Anna. "All right. Start with the easy stuff. What is the Brotherhood of Zagam?"

Tommy sighed. "Like I said, they're a cut-rate cult. They claim deceit is the cornerstone of human civilization and worship a thing—"

"A god," Nail interjected.

"—a *demon* called Zagam. I've seen the name dropped here and there in some of the literature. As reliable as *that* shit usually is," he added with a shrug and a wry smile. "Depending what medieval crackhead authority you believe, Zagam is the demon of deceit."

Nail, unable to hide the grin that said he was now openly enjoying fucking with Tommy, raised a hand. "Wouldn't that be Satan? Prince of lies and all that?"

"How the hell should I know? Demon hierarchies are like the family trees of inbred seventeenth-century aristocrats. Not to mention they all contradict each other."

"That's great," Nail said, rolling his head around his shoulders as if he were warming up for a prize fight. "Two million dollars. For taking a jawbone off some backwoods motherfuckers who think they broke a piece off the devil. Sign me the fuck up."

Karyn stirred, and Anna felt everyone in the room pause before she spoke. That pause, it seemed, could have gone on for minutes before anybody interrupted it. Even Nail held still. "What's it do?" Karyn asked.

Tommy bit his lip and squinched up his face. "Um . . ."

"Cures constipation," Nail said, before Tommy could answer.

"Ah . . ."

"Guarantees you a parking space downtown."

"Well . . ."

"Actually, it's cursed—it'll give you venereal warts."

"Only if you rub it on your crotch, dickhead," Tommy finally managed. He punched Nail on the shoulder, then shook his head. "I don't have a clue, actually. Not a clue."

"It makes two million dollars appear," Nail said. "I say we do it."

Tommy nodded. "Yeah."

Anna studied each of them in turn. This wasn't a democracy, exactly, but nobody *had* to participate. So far, they'd been all in or all out as a group—either a job looked good, or something about it smelled so bad that nobody wanted a piece of it. Or Karyn killed it before they even had the discussion. Anna wished she knew what was making her uneasy about this job, wished she could just let it go and get down to business. *Probably just the money. It's a lot of money.*

She glanced at Karyn again. Common sense told her this job was more than they could handle, or maybe just more than she wanted to get into, but the intense look on Karyn's face was tough to deny. *You can walk away from half a million dollars,* she'd said, and while that stung, it was true. That money meant a lot to Karyn. Anna'd been with her at the beginning, and during the few times they'd run too short on cash to pick up more blind, and it had been some scary shit every time. Karyn came wholly unmoored from reality, a ship drifting on imaginary seas, and watching her react to the invisible things she saw in the world around her filled Anna with sick horror. She couldn't imagine what that was like, and couldn't dream of turning Karyn over to that fate. Had, in fact, done a few very desperate things to help Karyn out of those situations in the past.

No, she couldn't deny Karyn this on a gut feeling. She nodded.

Everybody looked to Karyn. Karyn looked right back, and it seemed to Anna that she lingered a long time on Tommy's face, searching for something.

"All right," Karyn said. "Let's line it up."

"I hate this," Anna said. "This isn't how we do business."

Tommy glanced at her sidelong, his eyes darting briefly away from the spot just ahead of his feet he'd been inspecting so carefully since they got the news. "I said I'm sorry, OK?"

"Not your fault," Karyn said. "I get the feeling we'd be saddled with this regardless."

Anna bounced a pebble off the cracked dirt. It ricocheted, rolled, and came up against a crushed Pepsi can. "It's still bullshit."

The four of them waited in the depths of a junkyard, a favorite spot for conducting iffy encounters. Ranks of cars surrounded them, all bleached to the same dead gray by years of sun and scouring grit. Here, toward the middle of the auto graveyard, the mechanical corpses were piled high, leaving narrow canyons between. Anything that happened in here was hidden from the eyes of passersby, and with some Hells Angels Anna knew keeping watch on the outside, nobody armed or unexpected could get in. Karyn's crew would be in complete control.

As much as possible, anyway, Karyn thought. They'd only just accepted the job, and "control" was already tenuous. Had been right from the first phone call. Gresser had picked up, listened to the news, and then proceeded to tell Anna how it was going to be, as Karyn sat and quietly listened on speakerphone. *Boss says you messed up the Durante job,* Gresser had said. *Your boy missed one of the alarms.* Not talking about physical alarms, Karyn knew. *These aren't guys that lightweights can handle, so we're gonna send you some help. A pro.*

That's all right, Anna had said. *We'll manage.*

No can do. Your, ah, "specialist," according to the boss, doesn't have the mojo to pop a zit. You'll take the help, and you'll say thank you. It's not too late to find somebody more cooperative.

Anna had flushed an angry red and her eyes had bulged as if she were going to pop, and the inevitable "Fuck you" was already on her lips when Karyn had pressed the mute button on the phone.

This is bullshit, Anna had said—the first time, with many more to come. *Tommy knows his shit. I'm not going to sit here and listen to this.*

It's not about Tommy, and he's not going to just let it drop, Karyn had told her. *Of course they're going to want to have a babysitter on us for a job this size. I'm not ready to walk away over that.*

Anna had almost argued, but something had stopped her—maybe something in Karyn's determined expression, maybe something internal. *Okay,* she'd said, and that was that. They'd given Greaser the location and time and ended the call.

"This guy better show," Anna said.

Karyn only nodded and chewed her fingernail, wishing for a cigarette. She'd traded one disgusting habit for another, she thought as she peeled away a thin, crescent-shaped strip of nail. Seemed like everywhere she went, she left little curls of herself in trash cans or occasionally on the floor. Tommy had told her a dozen times that that was a bad, bad idea—his ilk could apparently work all kinds of havoc with a few hairs or other pieces of human detritus—but she figured it beat the hell out of two packs of Marlboro reds every day. Most days.

"Ten more minutes, and I say we bail."

"He'll show," Karyn said.

"That your professional opinion?"

She suppressed a sigh. That was the problem with being the local oracle—nearly every remark was treated as though it might be a divine pronouncement. "Just a guess."

No sooner had she said the words than the soft crunch of footfalls on gravel reached her ears. Tommy grinned as though Karyn had been playing a little joke on them. The others crossed their arms and waited.

A woman emerged from the gap between the stacks of dead cars, and Karyn fought to keep her lip from curling up in a sneer, or maybe a growl. Every once in a great while, Karyn met somebody she took an instant, intense dislike to for no good reason, and Sobell's lackey somehow managed to push that button without saying a word. It wasn't the woman's cocky swagger, though that didn't help. Neither did her appearance. She had short, spiky hair dyed a caustic shade of red, sported black tattoos in ugly abstract patterns down the length of her arms, and had what looked to be about a pound and a half of metal hanging in her face: dozens of piercings in her ears, lips, eyebrows, nose, and even cheeks. Dressed all in black, of course. All signs that screamed *Look at me!* as far as Karyn was concerned, or maybe *My mama didn't love me enough.* As somebody who'd spent most of her life trying not to attract any undue attention, the spectacle was faintly sickening—which still didn't quite explain the instantaneous hatred that seized her.

Some people just rub you the wrong way, she thought. *Pheromones or something.*

The woman walked into the clearing, trailing her fingers along the dusty side of an ancient red and white Plymouth Fury. "You Sobell's crew?" she asked. Her mouth pulled into a fuck-you grin that made Karyn's fist ball up of its own accord.

"No," Karyn said. "This is my crew. You Sobell's . . . specialist?"

"Independent contractor. But, yeah. He's paying the bill this time."

Independent contractor, my ass. "I'm Karyn."

"I figured. Genevieve Lyle." She stopped ten feet away, still smirking.

Tommy coughed, shuffled his feet. His eyes were practically bugging out of his head, and an idiotic smile had affixed itself to his face. "Tommy, I'm Tommy."

"Nail." The big guy crossed his arms, face unreadable behind dark sunglasses.

"And you?" Genevieve asked, turning to Anna.

Oh Jesus Christ, Karyn thought in disgust. Anna's eyes had gone a little too wide, too, and a slight flush darkened her cheeks. *Always the bad girls. Just great.* At least she didn't try on a stupid grin to match Tommy's, though she did hold Genevieve's gaze longer than seemed strictly necessary. And, if Karyn wasn't reading things wrong, Genevieve's grin widened the longer the moment strung out.

"Anna."

"Great. We're all friends now. Wanna fill me in?"

Anna and Nail both looked to Karyn, who waited a second and then gave a reluctant nod. Regardless of Karyn's personal distaste, there wasn't anything obvious coming off Genevieve to set her alarms ringing.

"All right," Nail said. "Gather round, folks." He turned to the hood of an ancient Buick that might have been lime green in some forgotten year, and started spreading photos out on the hood. Genevieve, Karyn noted, took the opportunity to snuggle in right next to Anna, and Tommy wasted no time coming around to Genevieve's other side.

Jesus, she thought again, and turned to the photos.

Nail had done a simple drive-by earlier and taken the snapshots—nothing complicated, not yet, but he'd gotten the important stuff. Nathan Mendelsohn's estate, in glorious digital color. Gently rolling hills, shaded in strategic spots by towering palm trees. Lush grass, the only thing green in L.A. County in the dry heat of August. A wide, immaculate driveway stretching out languorously at the feet of a white stucco manse. And a high brick wall topped with mile after flashing mile of concertina wire.

"That's what we got," Nail said. "Up in Topanga Canyon, right up against the state park. Middle of fucking nowhere."

Anna leaned over the pictures, shuffling a few around to get a better look.

"Where are the cameras?" Anna asked.

"Where *aren't* there cameras?" Nail pointed out half a dozen spots, index finger jumping from one picture to the next. "Here, here, here, and here. And here. And those are just the obvious ones. Pretty sure some are hidden."

Genevieve shifted, leaning in next at Anna's left, causing Anna to take one small, shuffling step away. *Sobell's screwing with you,* Karyn thought, trying to project the thought over to Anna. *He's done his homework, and he knows your type. Tommy's too, apparently.*

Yeah, Tommy's too. Even now, Genevieve was brushing her hand across Tommy's under the guise of reaching for one of the photos. He was hyper, too, and simply would not shut up.

"Check this out," he said, pointing to a symbol carved in the bricks on either side of the main gate. "Warding?"

Genevieve lifted an eyebrow. "Fleur-de-lis."

"Oh. I mean, shit yeah. I'm looking at it upside down."

Anna glanced at Karyn to share an eye-rolling "Would you believe this?" moment, but Karyn's mouth was set in a line. *This shit is not funny.*

"Not a hundred percent sure, but I think this"—Nail pointed to an indistinct white smudge on one of the photos, then another—"and this might be actual guardhouses, if you can believe that shit. Fucker's got the place locked down."

"He would," Genevieve said, mouth twisting into a moue of disgust. It was the first emotion Karyn had seen on her face that didn't carry a hint of mockery.

"You know him?" Anna asked.

"Yeah."

"Well, don't make us beg—spill it. What do you know?"

All eyes were on Genevieve, and this time she seemed discomfited by it rather than combative. She didn't step away from the car, but she leaned back like she wanted to. "Mostly the same shit you can get off the Internet. He owns an investment firm. Used to sit on L.A. city council. Makes the gossip rags sometimes, depending on who he's banging at the moment."

"And?"

"And what?"

Anna opened her mouth to reply, but Karyn spoke first. "Get out."

"What?" Genevieve's diffidence was gone now, and a low tension started building in the yard, like a deep hum that was rising in pitch moment by moment. Tommy looked from Karyn to Genevieve and back, eyes wide, mouth tiny and afraid.

"If you're not going to be straight with us, get lost. You've got an ax to grind with this guy, and I don't need some personal vendetta messing up an otherwise professional job. So spill it, or get out."

"You can't fire me."

Karyn didn't blink. "Okay," she said. She slid her tongue along her teeth. "Nail, please shoot her."

Nail reached for his pistol. Tommy grabbed his arm. Genevieve and Anna both threw up their hands. Lots of people started talking at once.

"Whoa! Hold on!"

"Hold up there, big guy."

"Wait a sec!"

Anna put a hand on Karyn's shoulder. "Look, you were the one who said we gotta do it his way. Remember?"

"That was before she started withholding important information." She shot a poisonous glare back at Genevieve. "You're either all the way in or all the way out."

Genevieve said nothing. The tension ratcheted up, and Tommy began casting nervous glances around at everybody as the silence dragged out.

"Karyn's right," Anna said softly. "We either put all job-related stuff on the table, or this is hopeless."

Now Genevieve did step back. She waited with everyone staring at her for a long time before finally nodding.

"I did some work for Mendelsohn a while back. He screwed me over."

"That's pretty much how all these stories start," Karyn said. "Keep talking."

"He's in charge of that stupid cult—wants to be a big man in the occult world more than just about anything. But he's shit. Can't even nail the basics." She made a sour face. "But he does have money."

"So he pays people like you to do the magic stuff for him," Anna said.

Genevieve put her hands in her pockets and gave a halfhearted shrug. "It's a living. Or was, until the cult thing got too weird."

"So you left?" Tommy asked.

"I sort of left, they sort of shut me out. I wouldn't do some work Nate wanted; he got pissed. It wasn't all that friendly a departure."

"What kind of work?" Anna asked.

Genevieve shook her head. "Doesn't have any bearing on the job. You can either trust me on that, or we can all start shooting at each other."

"So this *is* a personal vendetta," Karyn said.

"Well, yeah. But it's not like I'm on some kind of kamikaze kill-him-or-die-trying trip. We steal the bone, it'll fuck him up and humiliate him. And I'll make a lot of money. That all works for me just fine."

"Sobell knows?"

Genevieve stared flatly back at Karyn. "Sobell knows *everything*. I thought you'd have that figured out by now."

"Don't suppose he knows the gate code," Nail said dourly.

"The gate code is the least of our concerns, big guy," Genevieve said. "It's been a while since I spent any quality time with Nate, but even back then he had guards out the ass. I can't imagine the army he surrounds himself with now."

Nate? Anna mouthed to Karyn. Karyn just shrugged.

"So. More recon," Nail said.

"Always more recon," Anna said. She thought back to

their last gig and added, "It'd be nice to be sure the damn thing is even there, too."

Karyn said nothing, merely stood with arms crossed, watching Genevieve through narrowed eyes.

"That good enough for you?" Genevieve asked. "We all gonna play nice now, or you still want to shoot me?"

Karyn forced a humorless smile. "Let's get to work."

Early evening, and the light had a strange yellow-red quality to it. Tall, dry grass rippled in a slight breeze — maybe beautiful, but Nail just thought it looked like the kind of place where wildfires got started and burned down a third of California before finally dying. From back here, though, up a slight rise, he could see to the other side of Mendelsohn's wall. Wet green grass sparkled in an unbroken carpet all the way to the trees, past which he couldn't see anything.

Five steps down the hill and all that vanished, leaving him, Tommy, and Genevieve in an arid wasteland. This side of the wall, even the trees were stunted, twisted things barely worthy of the name.

"Ha!" Tommy said. He sprang forward to the side of the road and squatted. "Jackpot!" He pulled on a pair of latex gloves and picked up what looked like a foil gum wrapper with his thumb and forefinger. After a moment of proud inspection, he put it in a paper grocery bag.

"Good start," he said, beaming. "I feel lucky today."

Nail couldn't help smiling back a little, and even Genevieve laughed. Tommy was a funny little guy, and it was hard not to get caught up in his enthusiasm.

"He always this excited about trash detail?" Genevieve asked.

"It's like a treasure hunt to him. Can't say he's wrong, either — he's worked miracles with this kind of shit before."

Genevieve nodded. "I don't doubt it. I just wouldn't have thought this was the exciting part."

"You want to see a happy white boy, you get him ten minutes with the man's Dumpster."

Nail stopped walking and stared at the wall again. It

was maybe two hundred feet from where he stood on the shoulder of the road, stone, ten feet high and curving away into the distance. How much did it cost to cart that much fucking stone out into the middle of nowhere? "Motherfucker sure likes his privacy," Nail muttered.

"Yeah," Genevieve said. "More than ever, I hear."

"What's that mean?"

"I hear he doesn't come out anymore. Stopped going to council meetings, never leaves the grounds. Real Howard Hughes shit, you know?" She pushed aside a clump of crackling brown grass to reveal a sun-bleached Pepsi can. "This?"

"Nah. Too old."

She let the grass go. It didn't even spring back to its former position, just sort of lay pushed to the side, broken. "He was getting pretty flaky back before I took off, but I guess it's gotten way worse." She shrugged. "Crazy zillionaires, right?"

Nail resumed walking. They were far enough back that there shouldn't be much scrutiny—even the most paranoid zillionaire didn't keep cameras watching every swath of land hundreds of feet out from a mile-long wall—but he'd feel better if they kept moving. Get this done as soon as possible, just in case.

"Oh my God," Tommy said. "Check that out." He was pointing ahead, to where Mendelsohn's driveway joined the gravel road. Nail squinted. Looked like there was a white ... something over in the drainage culvert. Nail's eyes were pretty good, but the light was for shit. How Tommy could make it out, he had no idea.

Tommy bounded ahead, cackling. "McDonald's bag!"

Genevieve laughed again, and Nail shook his head. "Maybe he thinks he's gonna find a cheeseburger." He glanced to the gate. Nobody. The place might have been deserted, if the lawn weren't so perfect.

They walked on, Genevieve making a decent attempt at searching the weeds for trash and Nail focusing more on studying the wall than garbage recon. His commitment to the job hadn't faltered—the prospect of paying off Clarence and getting DeWayne out of that shit for good was enough to ensure that—but the shine was off it. This shit was even weirder than their usual gig. He liked the challenge, but there was every reason to make sure they checked all the boxes on this one, and then went back and checked them again.

They were still fifty feet or so back from Tommy when Genevieve spoke. "So, uh, Karyn. She doesn't like me much."

"Doesn't trust you. It's not the same thing."

"She doesn't like me, either."

"I guess that's true, but that ain't the important thing. Give you some advice?"

"Yeah. I mean, please."

"Just do a good job. Do what you say you're gonna do, and do a good job. I know she ain't Enoch Sobell, but you get in good with Karyn, and you might get a good thing going."

Genevieve's expression was guarded, but by the way she waited, considering his words, Nail thought he'd made an impression.

"We're all on the same side here," she said after a moment.

"Then you got nothing to worry about." He paused, then decided to go ahead. "I'll tell you this, though. If you change your mind, think maybe it starts to look like a good idea to pull something funny, you might do some checking first. You ask the right people, and Karyn's got a rep."

"I've heard. She's psychic, or something."

"I don't know about that. But I guarantee, you start thinking about fucking us over, she will see that shit coming before you even make up your mind."

There was a pause. Then: "What about Anna?"

"What about her?"

Genevieve's expression held nothing of guile, but it was a little too flat to be real. "Just, you know. How's she fit into all this?"

"Have to ask her."

Genevieve smiled. "I might just do that."

Nail grunted and kept walking. A plastic food wrapper

of some kind, trapped under a stick, fluttered in the breeze. Nail went down the embankment, put on a glove, and picked up the wrapper. His thumb slid across congealed orange grease, and he had to wonder why the fuck any rich guy would ever eat a nasty two-dollar microwave burrito. Ants ran up his hand onto his wrist, and he sighed. There were parts of every job that sucked, he knew, but trash detail was about the worst part of this one.

Behind him, Genevieve rustled through more of the high weeds.

"So," she said, "how'd you get into all this?"

He looked back, still holding the burrito wrapper. "You ever stop talking?"

She only smiled more. "It passes the time."

"You're too fuckin' friendly—you know that?"

"Come on, spill it."

That wasn't going to happen, and he felt a bright spike of anger that she'd even pushed him on it. He hadn't shared that story with *anyone*, not even Tommy. Anna and Karyn had been there, helped him and his world-class fuckup brother out of a bad spot when nobody else in the world would, and as far as he was concerned nobody else in the world ever needed to know about it.

"All you need to know is that those two women are like my sisters. I'd do anything for them, and I mean literally fucking anything. Got that?"

"Yeah. Yeah, I got it."

They went back to picking through the weeds, and Nail picked up the pace some, leaving Genevieve behind. Too damn many questions. It didn't take him long to catch up to Tommy.

"Burrito wrapper," Nail said, holding up his prize.

Tommy opened the bag. "In it goes." He stepped close to Nail and glanced meaningfully back at Genevieve. "What do you think?" he whispered. "I got a shot?"

"You gotta be fuckin' kidding me," Nail said. "Hurry up and let's get this over with."

Karyn turned on the kitchen faucet, waited for the water to cool down to room temperature, and filled a glass. She took a sip, wrinkling her nose at the chlorine. Though she kept meaning to get a water filter, somehow it never happened.

The dead bolt on the front door turned with a scraping sound, and Anna let herself in. "How about a beer?" Anna asked.

"Hey, shut the door—huh." It was already shut.

Anna put her elbows on the peeling Formica counter that separated the entry from the kitchen. "How about two beers?"

"That good, huh?"

"None of the usual suspects are giving me anything. I hear Tommy and—"

The dead bolt on the front door turned with a scraping sound, and Anna let herself in.

The other Anna kept right on talking. "—Nail got some good stuff but—"

"How about a beer?" the new Anna asked.

"—gonna need some prep time—"

"How about two beers?"

Karyn closed her eyes. *Go away. Please go away.* When she opened them again, both Annas were leaning on the counter, moving and talking out of sync with each other. The sound wasn't much worse than two people talking over each other, but looking at them made Karyn feel dizzy. They were superimposed, but not like double-exposed film, where one or both seemed somewhat insubstantial—both were perfectly solid, and the resulting amalgam had a distorted figure, arms that were unnaturally wide where one Anna had moved slightly with respect to the other, twenty fingers, and a face that could have inspired either Picasso or Hieronymus Bosch.

The dead bolt on the front door turned with a scraping sound—

Karyn nearly ran for her bedroom. She crossed the living room in half a dozen rapid strides, closed the bedroom door, and paused with her hand on the knob, listening. The chatter from the other side faded, but that didn't make her feel better. Her heart slammed in her chest, so forceful she could hear the hissing swell of blood rush through her ears, and she wondered for a moment if she might pass out.

I can't do this. I can't have this now.

She pressed her ear to the door. The thin material, barely better than cardboard, let everything through, and she heard what might have been a fourth voice joined to the others.

If they come in here, I'll scream, I swear.

Without turning her back to the door, she crossed the small room to the dresser, pulled open the top drawer, and took out a plastic zipper bag.

From outside, the voices quieted until Karyn couldn't hear them anymore. Maybe the Annas had gone. Maybe they were all out there having a beer together. Karyn knew they weren't real, and she was even fairly sure they were harmless, but she couldn't make herself check if they were still out there.

After what felt like a long time, she sat on the edge of the bed, staring at the zipper bag and running her thumbs over its contents.

"I hate you," she said.

In truth, she wasn't sure what she hated more—the necessity of the bitter concoction, or the undeniable fact that there was noticeably less in the bag than there should have been. She'd gone to see Adelaide—when? Four days ago? Something like that. Ten thousand dollars down the tube for a stash that ought to have lasted six weeks, or a month at the least, and at the rate she was going she'd be out again in a little over a week. Three years ago, ten grand would have lasted all summer. Where did that trend end up? Would the stuff eventually stop working entirely? Sick dread, a coil of barbed wire, twisted in her belly. She'd been there before, visions crowding on top of each other until they drew an opaque veil over reality entirely. Going back to that was unthinkable.

She took a chunk out of the bag and, grimacing, put it on her tongue. The bitter, oily taste that flooded her mouth as she crushed the fragment between her molars nearly made her gag, but she washed it down with a long slug of gross chemical water.

There. That'll get me through tonight.

"Hey!" Anna's voice—singular, thank God—from the living room. "You home? How about a beer?"

Karyn stowed the blind back in its drawer and swallowed a couple of times to try to clear the taste from her mouth, then went out. With no Karyn to talk to, Anna had gone directly to the refrigerator. She held up a bottle.

"You drinking?"

"Yeah. How'd it go?"

"None of the usual suspects are giving me anything."

Karyn suppressed a groan.

Anna popped the top off one of the bottles and put it on the counter. "I hear Tommy and Nail got some good stuff, but Tommy's gonna need some prep time with it. He'll probably hit you up tomorrow to help him do that creepy thing he does. The rest of us are thinking about checking out the cult members—Mendelsohn's place is pretty locked down." She opened the other bottle and put the bottle opener on the counter. "Hey, are you o—"

"Don't." That endless, hated question, and Anna knew better than to ask it: *Are you OK?* The question was, in fact, the source of one of only a handful of bitter arguments they'd had over the years. *Are you OK?* Anna, like most everybody else, regarded it as a simple expression of concern, but Karyn had heard it so many times it had lost meaning and become something slippery and indistinct, and somehow insidious. What was "OK," anyway? It wasn't good, it wasn't bad—it wasn't anything. It just lived in that damned question, the only function of which was to make the asker feel like they'd discharged their responsibilities just by barfing it up. *Are you OK?* The hell with that. She'd had enough of *Are you OK?* to last her until she died.

Anna made an apologetic grimace. "Sorry."

"I'm just . . . anxious. That's all."

She offered Karyn a bottle. "Yeah. I hear that."

Chapter 6

"Motherfucker," Nail said. He kept his eyes to the binoculars, but a frown creased his face. "These jokers even split up to go to the bathroom?"

Genevieve shook her head. "Nope. First rule of cult conditioning—never leave anyone alone. Cut 'em off from friends and family, and make sure they never have a moment alone to start thinking. Constant reinforcement."

"Great." He set the binoculars down in his lap and drummed on the steering wheel with his fingers. "So quietly disappearing one of them is probably out."

"Yeah," Anna said, piping up from the backseat.

Genevieve echoed that thought. "Not a great idea anyway. It's not unheard-of for somebody to quit and vanish, but if anything looked funny about it, they'd get suspicious. They're a suspicious bunch of assholes."

"Probably goes with belonging to a cult that worships deceit."

"You said it."

Anna leaned against the window, watching half a dozen cultists walk down the sidewalk. They were loaded down with groceries—evidently, demon worshippers needed eggs and milk like everybody else. So far today, Anna, Nail, and Genevieve had trailed the group from a shitty two-bedroom apartment the six of them shared to a basketball court for a long-ass game of three-on-three to the grocery store. Anna hoped Karyn and Tommy were having better luck, because this was going no-where.

"You were in with these clowns?" Anna asked. "Back when you worked for Mendelsohn?"

Genevieve turned around, bringing her legs up and bracing her back against the dash. "Not really. I was never that stupid. Plus," she added, winking, "my brain is just too dirty to wash."

Anna turned back to the window, trying to avoid staring at Genevieve for too long. The woman knew how to push all her buttons without even trying, and every so often the memory of the lingering look Genevieve had given her when they met jumped to mind and caused faint heat to rise to her cheeks. She knew she ought to keep it professional, knowing what Karyn would say. *Don't shit where you eat.* Well, Karyn wouldn't put it like that, but that would be the gist of it. And she was proba-bly right.

"You've gotta know something," she said, trying to drag her focus back to the issue at hand. "The leadership, significant dates, anything."

"It was pretty secretive. If you weren't a part of their thing, they wouldn't say shit to you. Supposedly, once you'd been in a while, there were ceremonies and shit, but I never saw any of that. They're partial to new moons, I think."

"And it's . . . Hell, what's the phase of the moon now?"

Genevieve shrugged. "No idea."

"Truck's loaded," Nail said, inclining his head toward the beat-up Suburban the guys they were watching owned. One of the cultists, a skinny dude with blond dreadlocks who looked like he ought to be whacking on a djembe in a drum circle somewhere, slammed the tailgate and went around the side to get in. The taillights flared red and, moments later, the vehicle pulled away. Genevieve turned around and resituated herself in her seat as Nail followed.

Anna tried to stretch her legs, but the backseat of the Mustang Nail had shown up with that morning wasn't particularly roomy. "As fascinating as these grocery runs are, we're going to have to speed things up here. Don't you know anybody who might still be involved?"

"Everybody I knew got out, or I lost touch. Like I said, they don't exactly encourage you to keep up with your friends."

"Maybe somebody who's out knows somebody who's in, or can at least tell us *something*."

"Yeah, maybe. Might be worth a try."

"Let's go."

"What, now?"

Nail shook his head. "I saw that nimrod with the dreads leave Mendelsohn's place. I say we stick on him. See who he knows, where else he goes."

"It's not gonna take all three of us," Anna said as an idea formed. Part of her thought she didn't have exactly the purest of motives, but she pushed that aside and kept talking. "Genevieve and I will go chase down some of her old friends, and you can stay on Nimrod. Just let us out at the next light."

He glanced up at the rearview mirror, met her eyes there. "Yeah. Okay."

The air was musty and thick with dust, the light from the hanging forty-watt bulb dim, and the dimensions of the room oppressive. The ceiling hung just high enough that Karyn was in no danger of hitting her head but low enough that she felt a constant need to duck. It wasn't even really a ceiling, just bare joists supporting the floor overhead. At the far corner of the basement hulked a heap of trash taller than she was. Scrap metal, chair legs, what looked like a vacuum cleaner from a bygone era, and a mess of less identifiable crap all heaped up indiscriminately in a precarious pile. Every time she turned away from it, she swore something squirmed or wriggled in there.

Anna had remarked in the past on the creepiness of Tommy's basement workroom, and Karyn agreed completely.

Tommy cleared a space on his workbench—an old pool

table with the felt torn away, revealing the gray slate underneath—and upended a paper grocery bag onto the
surface. A handful of oddities fell out. There was an
empty, grease-stained remnant of a McDonald's bag, a
toothpick, a couple of wadded-up napkins, a filthy sock,
a burrito wrapper, and a hairbrush.

"That's all fairly disgusting," Karyn said.

"Tools of the trade, I'm sorry to say." Tommy didn't
look all that sorry. He poked through the mess with an
expression of avid curiosity, absently rubbing a hand
over the stubble on the back of his head.

He looked up from the mess at Karyn, and she froze.
His eye sockets were empty, a pair of vacant black holes
that poured blood down his face. A meaty red-black
chunk rolled down from the ruins of his left eye socket,
left a trail across his cheek, and hit the workbench with
a quiet splat.

"Hey, what's wrong?" he asked. "You OK? You look . . .
pale."

What the hell? Karyn thought back to the morning.
Had she taken the day's dose of blind or not? Maybe
she'd skipped it and then forgot it in the routine . . . No.
She clearly remembered making coffee that morning,
and she only ever drank coffee because, as bitter and
nasty as it tasted, it covered up the acrid taste of blind
better than anything else she'd tried.

Then maybe Tommy was in danger?

She blinked, or maybe he did, and his eyes were back.
The blood trail down his cheek remained, but Karyn
thought she could ignore that.

Is he in trouble or not? She remembered the last time
she'd seen something go wrong with Tommy, that brief
flash of blood just after the last score. Nothing had happened that night. Maybe it was something that would
happen much later, or maybe . . .

Maybe the blind wasn't working as well as it used to.

I can't worry about this right now. We've got work to do.

"I'm good," she said, though in truth she was shaken
and her nerves were amped up way too high. "You
ready?"

"Born that way. You?"

"Yeah." She picked up a pen and was gratified to see that her hand didn't tremble. *See? It wasn't that bad. Garden-variety hallucination.*

"Cool." He grinned at her unself-consciously, and she wondered if he knew these were the only times she ever saw him at ease. Probably not—he was so lost in the work that he never worried about his own frame of mind, which was surely the reason he was at ease in the first place.

He grabbed a dented metal bowl that looked suspiciously like it had been stolen from a local salad place, and he slid it to the edge of the table. From here, Karyn could see that the inside was painted with a collection of incomprehensible glyphs and sigils in a spiral procession from the edge of the bowl to the bottom. Tommy started up a low mumbling and reached over to a coffeepot that had been sitting on a hot plate with a dangerously spliced power cord. He made a few passes over the bowl with one hand, then poured the boiling water in.

Steam roiled off the bowl in a thick white cloud, way more than seemed justified by normal boiling water, and Karyn took a step back. Tommy's eyes lit up as the steam curled around him.

"Here we go," he said. He dropped the toothpick into the bowl.

Immediately, his eyelids started fluttering. Karyn hated this part. Never mind that she had her own built-in occult weirdness, this process always made her uneasy. Bribery was less unnerving, and old-fashioned pounding-the-pavement recon better still, but sometimes those options were too risky. In those cases, Tommy's creepy divination was the right tool for the job.

Still, she wished his eyes would stop that, particularly after her latest vision.

"Inside of a car," he said, and she started writing. "Dashboard lights . . . Ugh, looks like some trouble at home . . . I'd be pissed too if my daughter left the house dressed like that . . . hmm."

This usually went on for a while. Karyn wasn't quite

sure what Tommy was actually doing when he was doing this, and—just to add that little soupçon of eeriness—Tommy claimed not to be very sure about it either. Sometimes he seemed to be seeing through somebody else's eyes, sometimes he seemed to be rifling through their memories, and sometimes he mimicked their movements or spoke with their voice. Usually that last was a simple matter of relaying their words, but on one memorable occasion, *somebody else's* voice had issued from Tommy's throat. Karyn had been so badly frightened she'd dropped her notepad, and she'd been halfway to the stairs before she'd gotten control of herself. She still had no idea if that had actually happened or if she'd hallucinated it, and Tommy couldn't tell her. He rarely remembered anything from these explorations.

"Ugly stretch of Figueroa . . . downtown . . . Oh, good, more driving . . . Hey, fuck you, buddy! Gas pedal's the one on the right! . . . Man, I hope he doesn't bring that creepy fucker with him again. Or, hell, any of the others—they're all gettin' real weird lately . . . home again . . ." Tommy shook his head. "Not this one, it's just his driver. Next." He fumbled around until he found one of the napkins, then dropped that into the bowl.

More steam billowed up from the water. "What do we got here? Buncha dorks in hoods . . . Kimaris! Vacar! Zagam! . . . Oh-ho. *There* you are, you little tramp. One jawbone, slightly used, in the middle of a rally for KKK rejects. Christ, everybody wants to rub up on that thing. Where the hell are we? C'mon, look around a *little* . . ."

Tommy's eyelids were fluttering at a rate that Karyn found just short of nauseating, and his breathing came rapid and shallow. Was it possible he would go into some kind of seizure? It had never happened before, but as his motions grew more exaggerated, she wondered.

"*Not* the frat house. I don't give a damn where you live, let's get back to it, huh?" Tommy frowned. "Okay, back to the show. Sure looks like Mendelsohn's place. Oh, and we're going inside! Greek urn, a sculpture the size of my car—and what's this? Going down. Base-

ment? Couple of turns. Down some more. Walking pretty
fast, walking pretty fast now . . . Don't look over there!
Remember, *never* look over there . . . God, I think I'm
gonna puke." He swallowed twice, convulsively, and
Karyn glanced around the room for something he could
throw up in. There was the bowl, and that was about it.
For a place filled with stuff, there sure wasn't much she
could actually use.

Tommy continued talking, though, and the moment
passed. "Jesus, Fort Knox has nothin' on this place. This
fuckin' basement ever end? Guardroom, one, two, six,
eight guys, and are there some guns? Why, *yes*. Sand-
wiches. Ashtrays. Looks like some of 'em camp here. No
Mendelsohn, but I think that scruffy guy with the crazy
eyes is his second-in-command, and I sure wish he'd stop
lookin' at me. End of the hall, a right turn, and a big ol'
walk-in safe with a place for the guest of honor in the
middle. A pat on the shoulder from Number Two, and
I'ma put this goddamned bone down right here." A
shudder coursed through his body, starting at the knees
and rippling up through his hips and chest.

A moment later, it had passed. Tommy shook his
head. "Aaand . . . that's a wrap on this one. Lessee what
else we got here."

He tossed another napkin in the bowl and went
through another round of rigmarole. This one was more
like the nonevent with the driver, and thankfully his
breathing slowed and blood came back to his cheeks. By
the time he threw the McDonald's bag in, he looked
nearly normal, except for his constant blinking. He went
through another round of useless scavenging.

Karyn figured that was about all there was to learn,
and then he tossed in the hairbrush.

His reaction was immediate. His whole body tensed
up, like an electric current had activated all his muscles
at once. "Ggggg—"

"Tommy!"

"Don't! I swear, I didn't see anything. I didn't!" His
head suddenly jerked to the left, and his face twisted in

a grimace. Then, in a strangled falsetto: "I don't *want* to see anything. Don't take me back down there, please please please, man—AAAAAHH!"

"Tommy, stop this!"

"I just went down to see the relic, I didn't mean to go *there*, don't make me go back—Oh God, it's dark, it's so dark. Who's there? WHO'S THERE? AAAUGH, MY EYES!!!!"

Karyn dropped her notebook and slapped the bowl from Tommy's hands. Tommy fell to the cement floor, landing hard on his ass. The bowl hit the ground with a ringing clash, and warm water splashed everywhere, soaking Karyn's jeans from midcalf on down.

She dropped to her knees next to Tommy, who had curled up on himself and wrapped his arms around his head. "Are you hurt? Tommy, say something."

A moment passed, and then he slowly uncovered his head and pushed himself up on an elbow.

Twin streams of blood trickled from his eyes like gruesome tears. Karyn froze in the act of reaching for him. Was that real? Was that what the vision had been warning her about?

"Fuck me, that was no fun," Tommy said, and he blinked. He pulled up his grimy tank top and wiped the sweat from his forehead and cheeks, smearing blood across his face. "Did we get anything?"

"How many fingers am I holding up?"

"Very funny, Doc. I feel like I just did five grams of coke and ran with the horses at the Kentucky Derby, so tell me we got something."

"Yeah," Karyn said, and her own panicked heartbeat started to slow. "Best I can figure, Mendelsohn keeps the item in the basement of his house, under heavy security. Probably too heavy for us, unless we can figure out something clever."

"That's a shame. I like it better when they keep their priceless artifacts on the living room carpet."

"Yeah, well. He keeps something else in the basement, too, I think."

"What's that?"

Karyn shook her head. Tommy's anguished face from moments ago seemed superimposed over his quizzical expression now. "I don't know. But whatever it is, we need to stay the hell away from it."

Tommy raised a skeptical eyebrow. "That should be no problem, it being right down there next to the thing we're supposed to steal and all."

The cab stopped at a corner. Anna paid the driver and then followed Genevieve out. The flat light of evening fell across a series of Section Eight housing developments, buildings of dusty brown stucco that gave off an impression of exhaustion, like one day soon they might just give up entirely and sink into the earth. Litter dusted the sidewalk, and Chicano rap thumped from a first-floor apartment window.

"C'mon," Genevieve said, and she started walking. Anna was impressed by her energy. It had been a long, tiring, fruitless day, but Genevieve still kept up a happy chatter. Over the course of the day, she'd filled Anna in as much as possible on Mendelsohn and the Brotherhood, but it was mostly the same stuff they'd already discussed with a few colorful but unhelpful details thrown in, like Mendelsohn's obsession with how his laundry got done, who did it, and how often. Aside from that, she'd talked about her favorite horror movies, places to avoid in Hollywood, roadside taco vendors she frequented, and the goddamn Lakers of all things. Anna had enjoyed the easy conversation and found it fun to try to keep up with one erratic subject change after another, and, despite knowing better, she found herself warming to Genevieve even further.

Genevieve had also managed to work in mention of her ex-girlfriend—stressing the *ex*—in a way that Anna knew wasn't accidental. She hadn't just left that door unlocked; she'd hauled it all the way open, jammed a doorstop under it, and put a sign out front. Anna thought maybe that it was simply an unsophisticated way of trying to get in with her and thus the crew, but that didn't feel quite right, in part because it *had* seemed so unso-

phisticated. The directness of that approach gave Genevieve's interest a genuine feel that Anna had a hard time
believing she could fake so well. Anna knew she shouldn't
take it seriously, shouldn't pretend for a moment it was a
real thing, but it felt good all the same. Maybe that was
dangerous, but maybe not. In any case it couldn't hurt to
just enjoy it for now.

Genevieve stopped just after the corner of the building and gave Anna a sheepish grin. "I should probably
warn you—Tina's not gonna be happy to see me."

"Oh. So totally unlike Chad or Susan or Yuan." Anna
rolled her eyes. In between cab rides and conversation,
the two women had spent the afternoon and evening
tracking down the handful of people Genevieve could
find from the cult, and it had been just about useless so
far. Chad had simply refused to let them in, talking only
briefly through the gap between door and frame left by
the security chain. From the smell of some kind of toxic
incense and the sounds of weird recorded chanting drifting out of his apartment, Anna had guessed he'd moved
right on to another fringe religion. In any case, he didn't
have anything to say about his time in the Brotherhood.
Susan had had plenty more to offer—she'd called Genevieve a witch and several more colorful if less accurate
names while threatening to call the cops if Genevieve so
much as opened her mouth to speak. They'd run into
Yuan just as he was leaving his house. He'd gotten one
good look at Genevieve and started running.

"I'm not going back!" he'd shouted. Genevieve had
managed to get him to stop running, but nothing he'd
said after that proved any more enlightening than his
initial statement.

Tina Chen's place was the last stop. According to
Genevieve, there wasn't anybody from the bad old days
left on her list after this. From the look of things, Tina's
fortunes hadn't improved since her days in the cult. The
apartment complex was a pile of shoeboxes left over
from the seventies, painted in classic avocado and orange, which didn't look like it had been touched up since.

Each unit was accessed by its own door from the outside instead of a central stairwell, reminding Anna of a roadside motel, the kind of place you stopped, slept a fitful few hours on stained yellow-white sheets, and then got the hell out in the early-morning hours, hopefully before any parasites moved into your hair.

Genevieve had stopped at the bottom of the stairs to the second floor. "No," she said. "Tina *really* doesn't like me."

"Want me to go first?"

Genevieve stared off into space, weighing the suggestion. "No," she said at last. "If you start talking to her and *then* she sees me, she'll never trust you. Besides, I'd hate for you to take a bullet meant for me."

"Is that a joke?"

A bemused smile. "I'm not sure."

"After you, then."

Genevieve walked up the stairs, hand skimming the rail, and Anna followed. Anna thought she saw the blinds in one of the windows twitch as they approached. Maybe it was just glare, motion from the kids throwing rocks in the courtyard, but she couldn't help slowing her pace some, letting Genevieve get a little farther ahead.

Genevieve stopped, visibly gathered herself, and knocked. The door swung open a crack on the first knock, and she jumped, startled.

"Shit," Anna said. "Get away from the door," she added in a hushed voice. From where she stood, she could see the splintered jamb and the hole where the strike plate had been torn free. She glanced down at the courtyard, turned her body so that nobody down there could see what she was doing, and pulled her gun from the waistband of her jeans.

Genevieve walked straight in. Anna cursed and followed just as Genevieve started to run.

Anna caught no more than a glimpse of the room—furnished in Budget Single Woman, but clean and squared away—when she saw a woman lying on the floor, soaked in blood, fumbling with a smashed cell phone in shaking hands. Blood had leaked in blotches over the beige carpet, and there was a smear of it where the woman had crawled across the floor.

The woman looked up, and the glaze in her eyes cleared. "Gen. You gonna kill me?"

Genevieve was already crossing the room.

"Call nine-one-one," she said. She dropped to her knees next to the woman and pulled up her bloody T-shirt.

Anna ignored the instruction, swung her gun into readiness and pivoted. The kitchen was visible in its entirety from where she stood, and nobody lurked there. She crossed the room quickly and checked the bedroom. Nobody there, or in the closet, or in the small bathroom.

"Nobody's here," she said, returning to the main room.

Genevieve had Tina's head propped up on her lap while she held her hands over a deep gash in Tina's side. "Come on," she was saying. "Hold on, just hold on." She looked up at Anna, her face streaked with blood and mascara. "Call nine-one-one, dammit!"

Anna hesitated.

"Now!" Genevieve said.

Anna dashed across the room and snatched up the phone. Moments later, a 911 operator was asking her, in an entirely too-calm voice, what the nature of her emergency was.

"There's a woman here. She's hurt. She's been . . ." Anna looked to Genevieve.

"Stabbed." Genevieve said quietly.

"Stabbed. She's been stabbed." The operator tried to say something else, jam some more questions in, but Anna gave the address over his protests and hung up.

"I have to go," Anna said. "I don't want to deal with the cops."

Genevieve didn't look at her, just cradled the woman's head in her lap and whispered meaningless reassurances. "Whatever," she said.

"I *have* to go," Anna said, but she didn't move. Genevieve—the bad girl, the one whose very appearance was calculated to deliver the maximum fuck-you to everyone she encountered—held her own hand over a slowly oozing wound and stroked the woman's forehead with her free hand. Somebody who'd hated her passionately, and here she was, staying with her until help came, and never mind how many questions the cops would have when they got here.

It'll be a shitstorm, Anna thought. *She'll never get clear of it. Questions and more questions—and what if we catch the blame somehow?*

And that was it—as soon as she let slip the word "we" in her inner monologue, it was done. "Shit," she said. She went to the balcony adjoining the bedroom, looked down the street, and, as soon as she thought it was clear, she threw her gun across the street into a stand of ragged palms. *This is going to get me fucked somehow. I know it is.*

She went to the kitchen and got a glass of water. When she came back, Tina was staring at Genevieve with a dazed, numbed sort of fear on her face.

"You gonna kill me?" Tina whispered again.

Genevieve brushed a lock of hair from Tina's eyes and Anna was surprised to see a softness in her face, a slight sheen to her eyes as she looked down at the other woman. Anna put the glass down next to her and pressed back into the corner near the kitchen, feeling suddenly like she was in the way.

"No," Genevieve said. "Help is on the way. Hush, now."

"Then you're not with Mendelsohn anymore," Tina said.

"No."

A long silence followed this pronouncement, during which Anna could hear the clock on the wall ticking, the drone of the highway in the distance, and the wail of an ambulance. She felt more than ever that this was not a scene she was supposed to be witness to.

"Drew," Tina said. "You gotta find Drew."

"What? Tell me he's not in the Brotherhood now."

A wide smile lit up Tina's face, made her look almost healthy despite her waxen pallor. "Not anymore." And, just as abruptly, the smile was gone, leaving her expression haunted and grim. "They're looking for him, though. That's why they were here. And . . . they'll find him. When they were cutting me, I . . . I told them things. Names of his friends. They'll get to him."

Genevieve's face hardened. "Not if we can get to him first. Do you know where he is?"

Tina paused. She studied Genevieve's face and narrowed her eyes, searching for something. Anna supposed she must have found it, because she nodded. "Yeah. He doesn't even have a phone number, so you've gotta go to him." She gave an address, nothing that Anna recognized. Genevieve repeated it back, and Anna did her best to commit it to memory.

"Do you know why they want him so bad?" Genevieve asked.

Tina didn't seem to hear the question. "Go find my little brother, huh?"

"Yeah." Genevieve bent over Tina and kissed her on the forehead. Her shoulders hitched once, as though she were holding back a sob.

The sound of approaching sirens wafted in through the open window.

Chapter 7

"The Brotherhood is cleaning up after themselves," Anna said. She sat leaning forward, elbows on the table, looking at each of the others in turn. "It used to be, you left the cult, and that was it. They made a few runs at re-recruiting you, but nothing else." At her left, Genevieve nodded absently. She seemed to Karyn as though she was half-lost in some inner world, but she was evidently following along. Anna continued. "I don't know what changed, but the word is that, in the last three months or so, nobody's gotten out. And lived, anyway."

"Whose word?" Nail asked, saving Karyn the trouble of asking the very same question.

"Tina Chen. Ex–cult member from a year or so back."

"And she knows this how?"

"Up until about three weeks ago, her brother was in. Now he's on the run. Some of Mendelsohn's guys paid her a visit this afternoon to try and find out where he is. They stabbed her four times and left her for dead."

"Did she tell them anything?" Karyn asked.

Genevieve stiffened, showing signs of life for the first time that night. "Fuck yeah, she did. They fucking stabbed her four times."

An awkward silence hung in the air, and Karyn felt like she'd pushed in a direction she shouldn't have. Anna coughed. "She's in the ICU at UCLA. They think she'll be fine."

Genevieve studied her fingernails. "Yeah."

"What else?"

A grin spread across Anna's face. "We got an address for her brother. It's pretty low on the radar, so we might be able to get to him before Mendelsohn's guys—she said all she gave them were some names of people who 'might' know where he is. They'll find him eventually, but we've got a head start."

"How the hell did you manage all that?" Nail asked.

Anna tipped her head toward Genevieve. "Girl's got game. You should've seen her work the cops. They'll want us again for questions, I guess, but once she got done and Tina put in a good word, that was it. She's good."

"Man," Tommy said, shaking his head. And—*boom*— in the space of a blink, his left eye was *gone*, the hole a deep red gouge in his skull surrounded by ragged tatters of skin. He pivoted, pointing the ruined socket right at Karyn. A wet remnant of torn tissue twitched in the hole.

Karyn seized the edge of the table with both hands. *Not real. That's not real.*

"Sorry I missed it," Tommy said. He looked normal again, panting in Genevieve's direction.

What the hell was that? Karyn thought. *I took my blind. I took a* lot *of it. And it wasn't his divination this time. I don't think. Am I finally losing it?*

Nail held out empty hands. "Well, like I told our fearless leader, I ain't got shit."

"Tommy and I got a little," Karyn said. She read her notes aloud and avoided mention of her vision of Tommy, though at the point in her notes where he'd started shouting about his eyes, she found a strange reluctance to look at him—or at Anna.

"So, we figure that tells us a few things," Tommy said. "One, the bone is usually kept in Mendelsohn's basement. Two, he keeps it under heavy guard. It's locked up and there are a mess of human guards at the very least."

"And three," Karyn added, "he brings it out sometimes for important ceremonies."

"Right on," Tommy said. He grinned at Genevieve. "I got a few tricks, too. Wanna compare notes?"

The sharp edges had been worn off Genevieve's smirk,

and all she managed was a tired curl in her upper lip. "Not tonight, Merlin."

Karyn cleared her throat. "Four: There's a big horrible *something* in the basement. I don't know if it's actually a guard or if it just lives down there, or if Mendelsohn keeps it around to eat people who piss him off, but it's really, really bad news." She gave Genevieve a pointed look. "You know anything about that?"

"Yeah. Stay the fuck away from it."

"You didn't think to mention that before? Like, *maybe* that's important?"

"Look, I didn't think it was an issue. It doesn't exactly have the run of the place, you know? Just . . . leave it alone."

"Anything else you might have forgotten to mention? Booby traps? Maybe a giant moat filled with alligators and piranha? Little things like that?"

Genevieve shook her head. "No. Just the thing in the basement. That's all I know about, I promise."

"What is it?"

"It's a monster. What the hell did you think it was? A genetically modified hamster?"

Karyn stifled an urge to snap at Genevieve, or maybe to go over the table after her, but she forced herself to calm down. She waited a moment, breathed out, and asked in a soft voice, "What does he want with it?"

"Honestly? I think he wants to bribe it into giving him the secrets of the universe. Since it's still there, I'm guessing that hasn't worked out too well, and he's moving on to torture. Too bad torture is pretty much the same as foreplay to a thing like that."

Tommy, Karyn was sad to see, was sopping up every word. "What is it?" he asked.

"I told you. It's a monster. An honest-to-God fucking monster. What else do you need to know? Hit points?"

Tommy snickered. "If you know 'em."

"Nobody knows 'em. Sorry."

"Come on, you gotta know something about it. How did it get there? Did you help him conjure it up?"

"No. Kind of. I got some of the stuff together, but that's it."

"It can't get out," Nail said, his low voice injecting a little calm into the room. "That what you mean when you say it doesn't have the run of the place?"

Genevieve nodded. "Yeah. If it could, Mendelsohn would be a pile of guts with a head by now."

"How far can it go?"

She shrugged. "Don't know. Used to be one corner of the basement, but I have no idea what he's done since then. Could be it can move around some now. I kinda doubt that, though—even Mendelsohn's not stupid enough to give that thing any more freedom than he has to."

"All right," Anna said. "We don't have a lot of choice, then. We avoid the basement."

Nail nodded. "Hell yeah. Too hard to do recon, too easy to get lost or trapped, and there's a fuckin' monster down there. That about ties it up."

"So we have to wait until they bring the bone out," Karyn said. "When's that?"

Anna smiled at her. "I bet Tina's brother knows."

"And look," Nail said. "My appointment calendar is wide open."

Chapter 8

Drew Chen's "off-the-grid" hideout was in a run-down area of L.A. near MacArthur Park, a place Karyn had always hated. It was probably her imagination, but everywhere near the lake seemed to stink of piss. Even here, blocks away, she felt smothered in the stench of seagulls and garbage.

Tommy and Nail hung back and watched from an unobtrusive distance while Karyn, Anna, and Genevieve approached the garage that Drew was supposed to be staying in. Some people felt less threatened by women, Karyn and Anna had learned over the years, and that could open doors that might otherwise remain shut. The occasional dimwit felt so unthreatened that they were emboldened to act in stupid ways, but that was rare, and Anna was more than capable of disabusing them of any misapprehensions they had on that score.

The three of them approached slowly with hands in plain view, and Genevieve knocked. A little metal door at eye level slid open. *Who rang that bell?* Karyn thought, and she stifled a grin.

"What do you want?"

"Drew Chen," Genevieve said. "He's in trouble. We need to talk to him. He'll remember me."

The eyes roved up and down Genevieve's body. "*I'd* remember you."

"That's great. Can we talk to Drew?"

"Don't know any Drew. But I'll go check."

The little door slid shut, and Genevieve and Anna shared a *do you believe this idiot* glance. Karyn felt a stab of jealousy. Wouldn't Anna have looked to her just a day or two ago?

Karyn let out a long, controlled breath and put her fists in the pockets of her jeans. She leaned back against the brick wall of the building and concentrated on staring straight ahead. Shrouded forms flickered in her peripheral vision, there and gone so quickly she couldn't be sure they had ever really been there. A dark flag, fluttering to earth. A huge hunched shape pushing a shopping cart. A cloud of smoke boiling up from the gutter. She tightened her fists and tried to focus on the ache in her fingers.

She wished Drew would get his ass out here, if only so she could get the conversation over with and take another hit of blind. Her reality was already getting flaky around the edges, her heart galloping anew after each half-glimpsed oddity or horror. And Anna was giving her that sidelong look, the one that said she was minutes away from asking that unending goddamn question again. *Are you OK?* Screw that. She just needed to talk with this guy, and then it would be time to make all that crap go away. Well past time, too.

A creaking noise as the door swung open, and Anna pivoted toward the sound.

Must be real, then, Karyn thought, and she turned as well.

Skinny guy. Tall and attenuated, like he'd been stretched. Blue jeans, gray sweatshirt with the hood pulled up around his face.

He stepped out of the building, stopped a few feet away, and hooked his thumbs into his pockets. A string trailed from the back of his hand. It seemed to have grown right from the flesh. It dropped to the sidewalk, stretched a few yards behind him, and came to an abrupt end. A matching string came from the hand at his side, and one from the tops of each of his battered sneakers. This was easy, and Karyn welcomed the chance to focus on something useful. This guy had been played. He'd been somebody's tool or puppet, but he'd been cut loose, probably recently. Just the cult, or something else? Did that make him a danger?

He held up his hand in a halfhearted wave, and she realized she'd been staring.

"Yo," he said. "What do you want?" He was close enough now for her to get a decent look at him, and now Karyn saw lines of tension on his face, tightness around the eyes and lips. He was younger than she'd thought, maybe. She had to admit she wasn't seeing everything as clearly as usual right now. But he looked to be just into his twenties. She didn't guess that meant he was fresh-eyed and innocent, though. His nose had been broken at least once in the past, and a long scar trailed its way down the side of his face.

For the first time, she saw a pair of scissors—kids' scissors, with plastic red handles—jammed into his belt. A couple of foot-tall homunculi, miniature thugs in leather jackets, one with a crowbar and one with a pair of brass knuckles, climbed onto his shoulders and began leering at the back of his head. She understood at once.

"You cut your own strings," Karyn said.

"Huh?"

"But they're coming for you anyway."

"I don't know what you're talking about." But his mouth tightened even further.

"Sure," Karyn said. On the rare occasions she volunteered some information, that's what everybody said. *I don't know what you're talking about.* They were always lying. She'd learned to let it go. This wasn't the time, anyway, since the hallucinations were starting to get especially vivid. That meant not a lot of time to screw around. *A few more hours of this, and I'll wish I were insane. Actually, I will* be, *for all practical purposes.* She fought the urge to check her jacket pocket again.

"So," Anna said. "What's the deal?"

"With what?"

Karyn spoke first, her voice hard. "The Brotherhood came for your sister yesterday. Cut her up pretty bad." Genevieve shot her an evil look.

"Bullshit," Drew said.

"Who do you suppose they were looking for?"

"I don't—"

A scatter of silent bullet holes opened up in Drew's torso, and he fell back. Karyn spun, looking for the assailant, but nobody else was moving.

"Uh-oh," Anna said.

"Inside! Now!" Karyn shouted.

Drew still stood, whole but confused. "Wha—"

"Move!"

A white pickup truck crept around the corner of the block, maybe two hundred feet distant. As soon as Drew went for the door, the vehicle leapt forward with a squeal of tires.

Drew pulled the door open, and Karyn, Anna, and Genevieve sprinted after him. As the door closed, bullets tore holes through it. Drew slammed a heavy bolt home.

"Back of the building," Anna said. "Get to the back!"

She was right, Karyn knew. The garage walls were basically corrugated aluminum—they kept out the wind, but they'd be shit for protection against even small arms. As if to underscore the point, a new line of holes opened up in the wall, and bullets spanged against an old cart covered with tools.

The four of them ran. A cinder-block partition separated the front of the garage from other bays in the back, and Karyn was pretty glad to get it between them and their assailants. Two women and the guy who'd answered the door cowered behind the wall.

"Weapons?" Karyn asked. "What do you have for weapons?"

Drew's eyes were wide and white in the gloom. "Nothing, man. What the fuck?"

"Did you think they were going to come tickle you, or what?"

"They weren't supposed to *find* me, but then you come up draggin' 'em behind like they're tied to your ass."

"They were on the way," Genevieve said. "Tina told them . . . a few things."

"Oh, shit. Then—"

"Shh," Karyn said. Gunfire riddled the back door. Then somebody kicked it open. Everybody stared at her, and she understood. "Somebody's going to come around the back. Is that door locked?"

"The door's always locked," one of the women said.

"I don't think it's going to hold them very long."

Genevieve stood. "How long we got?"

"Don't know."

"I'll work fast." She ran over, took a Sharpie from her pocket, and started scrawling on the metal surface of the door.

More gunfire from out front, and, from the way everyone else flinched, Karyn figured it was the real thing.

"Where else can we get out?"

"How many doors do you think we have?" Drew asked. "There's the front and the back."

"No, man," the doorman said. "Some of the windows are boarded up at the east end. We can kick 'em out."

"Go," Karyn said.

Another partition had been set up, turning two-thirds of the large open space into a living area—practically a warren. Flimsy plywood walls and stolen cubicle dividers carved the space into a series of rooms that appeared to have been constructed without regard to any obvious rationale or even convenience. Even more confusing, the dividers seemed to have been pushed around and pressed into service any time somebody needed a new wall for anything or maybe just grew tired of the old arrangement, so what little organization the place had started with was soon buried beneath dozens of ad hoc changes that had never been cleaned up.

Drew pressed in, with Karyn and Anna close behind. Moments later, Genevieve caught them up.

"Don't know if that'll hold 'em, but it'll give 'em one hell of a surprise," she said. She looked around. "Damn. They'll never find us in here."

"Yeah, unless they throw in a match," Anna grumbled. She was right about that, Karyn thought. The floor was littered with trash—fast-food containers, dirty blankets, and pieces of wood—and the walls themselves were all made of materials that would burn readily.

"Not good."

"Come *on*," Drew said.

More gunfire from behind, the distance and direction lost in the confusing echoes from the garage interior and the bewildering maze they found themselves in. A moment later—

BOOM!

It felt like the whole world pressed in on Karyn for one brief moment, then pushed out again. A high-pitched squealing started up in her ears.

"What the hell was that?"

Genevieve grinned. "Back door."

Drew led the group into the last living space and dragged a whiteboard in front of the door. "Better than nothing," he said, and he shrugged. "Help me with the boards."

Sure enough, a large window opening, maybe four feet wide by three tall, had been covered over with heavy-duty plywood.

"Shit," the doorman said. "We ain't kicking *this* out."

He was right, Karyn saw. In the light of Drew's flashlight, she could see that some overzealous carpenter, in an effort to keep the outside out, had screwed the thick plywood to the frame with literally dozens of screws, spaced about every two inches around the whole perimeter.

"Screwdriver?" she asked. "Crowbar? Anything?"

"Yeah," Drew said. "Out in the garage."

Another burst of automatic-weapon fire sounded in the warren behind them, followed by a couple of pops from a slower-firing weapon. Something crashed, alarmingly close by.

Drew bounced himself off the plywood and groaned. The wood was sturdy enough that, if anything had cracked, it was in his shoulder and not the blocked window.

Two more shots, and a strangled wail. The doorman and Drew lined up to ram the window together. Neither looked too happy about the idea.

"Wait," Karyn said. "Who's left out there?"

"Nobody," Drew answered. "We're all here."

"Then—"

The whiteboard flew aside, tipped, and fell, and Nail strode into the room with Tommy just behind.

"We need to go," Nail said. "Right now."

They stepped past three bodies on the way out of the little labyrinth, and saw another slumped in the doorway at the back. *It was us or them,* Anna thought. *They shot first.* Even so, her heart lurched at the sight of each corpse, and she felt as though she were walking on unstable earth that tilted and rocked and threatened to throw her off, spinning and light-headed, into space. At some point, Genevieve's hand crept into hers and gave it a reassuring squeeze. Anna took more strength from it than she would have expected.

For her part, Genevieve's face was set, hard. Maybe she'd seen more of this kind of thing, or maybe she had better luck with the *they shot first* rationale, but she seemed less likely to fall off the earth than to punch something, and Anna envied her.

It wasn't as though Anna had never seen violence. It was fairly commonplace in their line of work, and she'd been on both the giving and receiving sides. Sometimes you got caught by a mark, sometimes you had to fight your way out (or mace a guard), and sometimes an angry cop lost his cool. She'd fired shots in anger twice, but that had been more for the purpose of scaring somebody off than killing them. Nail, she knew, had done worse during his time in the military, and she suspected him of quietly disposing of a fence who'd decided it would be more profitable to blackmail the crew over the theft of an ancient illuminated manuscript than to just shift the goods and keep his mouth shut.

Even so, this wasn't a beatdown in an alley or something that had happened out of sight that she could easily forget. This looked like a war zone. *Would have been four dead squatters, if we hadn't been here,* she reminded herself. It sort of helped.

She caught Karyn's eye as they reached the main

door. Karyn was taking slow, even breaths at a pace so measured it was almost forced, and even with all the horrible shit she'd seen (none of it real, but all of it real enough), her face had gone pale and her lower lip trembled faintly, like she might start crying any moment.

"Us or them," Anna whispered.

Karyn nodded. "Yeah." She glanced back to the body in the doorway. "Shit."

Nail opened the door. He looked like the only one with his shit still together, calm as if he'd just eaten breakfast. "We gotta go. Even in this neighborhood, cops will be along soon."

Everybody filed out. Tommy ducked to one side and threw up his dinner. Anna did her best to ignore it, partly out of respect for Tommy and partly to keep from following his example. The squatters scattered on reaching open air.

"Not you," Nail said, clapping a heavy hand on Drew's shoulder. "You're with us."

Drew's eyes seemed the size of baseballs, and they didn't focus on anything in particular. "I ... don't ... think ..."

"Wasn't a request, homes. Get in the van."

Drew got in the van. The rest followed, and soon Nail was guiding the vehicle slowly along back streets away from the disaster at the garage.

"What's going on?" Anna asked, almost as soon as the garage was out of sight. "What's so important that Mendelsohn's killing anybody who leaves? Why now?"

Drew pulled his gaze from the window. "You think— you think those guys are gonna be OK? I mean, they didn't have to take me in. I wouldn't want ... you know."

"I don't think Mendelsohn's got any problem with them," Anna said, forcing as patient and calming a tone as she could manage. *And anyway, it's not like there's anyone left to talk about them.* She kept her face still, even as her gorge rose at the intruding thought. "Just you. So what's up with that?"

"You know. It's like, deserter policy. Like the army. You know."

"Try again," Karyn said from the front.

Anna tried on a reassuring smile. "She'll know if you're lying. Every time." Maybe not strictly the truth, but who knew? Even Karyn didn't fully understand Karyn's gift.

"I don't know," he mumbled.

Nail shot an evil glance into the rearview mirror. "I just shot two people and stabbed a third to get this information. You think I'm gonna stop now?"

"Hey!" Genevieve said. "I don't want to hear that kind of shit. We're the good guys, remember?"

"There ain't no good guys."

"Look," Genevieve said, ignoring Nail. Drew turned in his seat to see her. "We got in the middle of some severe shit back there. All we want to know is who we've pissed off, how bad, and why." Her tongue fiddled with a stud in her lower lip for a moment. "It might actually be a matter of survival now."

That was smooth, Anna thought. *Didn't play directly on the "you owe us" thing, but came at it indirectly. He'll get there himself, instead of feeling like it's being used as a crowbar on him.* It appeared Genevieve had a few different kinds of tricks in her bag. *Might be a good idea to keep that in mind.*

"It's Mendelsohn," Drew said, his voice suddenly heavy with exhaustion. "And the Brotherhood. You already know that."

"How bad?"

"How bad do you think? There's four dead guys back there, that I know about. It's not like you fucked up their bake sale, you know?"

Anna felt a sudden, intense urge to slap him. She chalked it up to stress and put her hands in her lap.

"Okay," Genevieve said. "Why? Why is it so important that they get rid of you?"

"Ain't just me. There were a couple others, but they're both worm food."

"That's even worse. Tell us why."

Drew kicked the back of Nail's seat, like a five-year-old with nowhere else to vent his frustrations. "I know all their shit. I was *way* in, you know? And they don't like their secrets getting out."

"What secrets?"

"You know. Like, initiation and shit."

Genevieve didn't even dignify that with a question, merely looked at him.

Drew sighed. "It's the goddamn ritual." He lowered his voice, mumbled something that even Anna couldn't make out from right next to him.

"What?" Genevieve asked.

"I said *they're gonna kill somebody*!" Drew shouted. "Kill somebody! A fucking sacrifice, all right?"

Anna glanced at Genevieve, but the other woman didn't look away from Drew for a moment. "Who?"

He shrugged. "Don't know. An 'innocent,' whatever that means."

"Jesus, Drew. What did you get yourself into?"

"You don't get it," he said. "You always sat on the sidelines and laughed at us, but you don't know what it's like to be *in*. It's—it's . . ." Tears glistened in his eyes. "It's the best thing you ever felt. All the time you're surrounded by people who have your back no matter what. It's like you fit somewhere for the first time ever. Don't you get that?"

Silence, then Nail's deep voice: "Yeah. I get that." He paused. "It fucks with your head. Shit you never would have dreamed of before starts to seem normal after a while, because you're tired and everybody else says it's cool."

Drew nodded. "Yeah. Yeah, that's it. That's exactly it."

Nail's lips pulled back from his teeth in a smile as bitter as any Anna had ever seen. "U.S. Marines, First Recon. Four years."

"Damn, dude."

"Yeah."

"So they suck you in a little at a time," Drew said, "talk about the great glory of bringing your god to Earth, and when they start talking about the 'unfortunate necessity of sacrifice,' you don't even blink. And, if they can help it, they don't give you one moment alone. Cut you off from family. Keep you short on sleep, so you're never quite thinking clearly. And people around you are, like, disappearing into a closed room for hours a day, doing weird shit. Some of them never come out, and they're getting weirder and weirder, but you're so damn tired it never registers. And then one day, you're on the shitter getting your two and a half minutes of personal time, and you're like, 'Whoa. Did I agree to *kill* somebody?'" He looked at his hands as though they were already stained with blood. "So then you're all, holy hell, this is fucked. I gotta get out of here."

He rubbed his forehead with both hands. "And then four guys show up to turn you into a hundred and sixty pounds of hamburger meat. And your friends, too, for good measure."

Anna felt for the guy, but that didn't stop her from trading a *very* uneasy glance with Karyn during his monologue. "Um, what was that about 'bringing your god to Earth'?"

"Come on, can't you just let me out here?"

"What, are they gonna kill you deader because you talked to us?"

"*They're* not, no."

Another nervous look toward Karyn. "Who is?"

"I don't know, man. But this is a *god* we're talkin' about. Shit makes me nervous, OK?"

Tommy cleared his throat. "It's not a god."

"Whatever it is, I don't want to mess with it. I just want to hide somewhere and hope nobody ever finds me again."

Nail turned the van, jounced over some potholes. A short acceleration, and they were on the 405. Even at this hour, there was a steady stream of traffic trundling along well below the speed limit.

"Why don't you get out of town?" Anna asked. "Why stay here?"

Drew snorted. "Unlike you high rollers, I got no money. Nowhere to go. And the last people willing to put me up—well, you saw how that went. They won't want anything to do with me now."

Anna hesitated for just a moment, then reached into

her pocket. She came out with a roll of bills. "I think this is about four hundred, maybe four fifty. We just need straight answers to a few questions, and it's yours. After that, we'll take you straight to the bus station, if you like." Hope and suspicion flared to life on Drew's face. Anna couldn't help a sidelong glance to see Genevieve's reaction. She was smiling, a carefree grin that said, *Hell yeah—that's my girl.* Unless that was wishful thinking on Anna's part.

"You're fucking with me."

"It's either this, or Nail pulls your toenails off," Anna said, but her tone was joking and she smiled as she said it. "I know what I'd go with."

"Cash first?" he tried.

"Sure."

Drew took the money gingerly, like it might rear up and sting him with a hidden scorpion tail. Once he was sure it wasn't going to bite him or explode or something, he thumbed through it and stashed the wad in his pants pocket.

"Okay. Shoot. Er, ask."

"This ritual—it uses a jawbone, right?"

Drew nodded nervously, then wiped at his forehead. "Yeah."

"All right. When and where does it go down?"

This time, Drew looked left and right, like a virgin approaching a streetwalker, waiting for cops to jump out of every window and door on the block. But there was only the crew in the van, and nothing for him to see. "Mendelsohn's place. The sixteenth." He made a twitching half shrug. "New moon."

"Who, and how many?"

"Everyone. All of them. Sixty or more, anyway."

Nobody said a word, but Tommy looked like he was going to chew through his bottom lip and Karyn's face had taken on a queasy greenish cast. Anna's stomach flopped over a few times.

"No problem," Nail said, his voice so even that Anna at first thought he was serious. "I'll just get on the horn and call in an air strike. We'll pick the bone out of the rubble." He shook his head. "Shit."

Anna closed the apartment door, locked it, and paused. Karyn stood a few feet away, leaning against the back of one of the chairs and waiting. That was good. They needed to talk. Tension had crackled in the air between them since before dropping Drew off at the bus station.

Anna turned, fighting the urge to lean back against the door. "So."

"So."

How was this supposed to go? In the ten years she'd known Karyn—most of which they'd lived and worked together—there had only been a handful of arguments. Usually Karyn pointed the way and Anna did the dirty work and didn't second-guess her. Shit, she saw the future, right? Nothing to argue about.

Not this time.

Anna leaped into the silence first. "What's going on?"

"I don't know what you're talking about," Karyn said, fixing her with a too-direct stare, almost an *I dare you*.

Anna plowed ahead. "You're jumpy as hell lately," she said. "And it's worse when you're around the guys. It looked like Tommy scared the shit out of you earlier. *Tommy*, of all people. What is going on with you?"

"What's going on with *you*?"

"Huh?"

"Instead of focusing on the job, you spend half your time drooling at the spy Sobell put in our crew. You think that's doing us any good?"

"That don't have anything to do with anything. I ain't dropped a single ball—"

"Just a matter of time."

"Jesus! We wouldn't have *anything* to go on yet if not for Genevieve, and I'm not fucking up." A sort of stealthy, destructive anger welled up in her. "And what about that shit today? That was bad. Worst we've ever seen."

"I know." Karyn's face was still, frozen. Anna recognized the look from long ago, when Karyn had been seventeen years old and fighting with her aunt nonstop. It meant she was dug in, fortified, and nothing short of heavy explosives was going to move her. Anna's mood darkened further.

"Did you see any of that coming?" A cheap shot, but it was out before Anna could stop it.

A pause, and a slight wrinkling of Karyn's brow. "Not . . . not really. Not before I said something." The words didn't have the ring of truth to them, exactly, but they didn't carry the false note of a lie, either. More like . . . confusion? Anna's anger took on an unsettling undercurrent of worry.

"We should get out," Anna said. "We never should have gotten in."

"Have you lost your mind? It's two—" Karyn stopped herself.

"Two million dollars," Anna finished for her. "It's still not worth it."

Karyn shook her head. "You don't get into bed with Enoch Sobell and just walk away with the job unfinished. We have to do this."

"Four people got killed today, Karyn!"

"Yeah, and four people would have gotten killed if we hadn't been there—the wrong four, if you ask me."

"There's four more I'm worried about now."

"Don't you mean five?"

Anna stared into the angry furnace of Karyn's eyes. "Yeah. I suppose I do."

Karyn's smile turned nauseatingly sweet. "Then why don't you ask Genevieve how she feels about bailing out?"

"That's not fair."

"Why, because she's Sobell's lapdog? Funny, that's what I've been trying to tell you." Karyn pushed away from the chair she'd been leaning on. "I'm going to bed. Figure out what you want to do. We'll have it out with everyone in the morning."

She stalked away and disappeared into her bedroom.

Chapter 9

It felt like the *air* was rotten, Nail thought. Everything about Anna and Karyn's apartment put his back up. The two of them wouldn't look at each other, and a couple of times he was pretty sure he saw Anna biting back some kind of bitter, mean-spirited comment. Impossible to tell, sure, but from the sneer that started to form on her lips each time, right before she silenced herself, it wasn't hard to guess.

He squeezed his left fist, held it, then straightened his fingers. Then did the same with his right hand. Off-brand isometrics, but they kept him calm. He knew everybody else thought he was a rock—and fuck it, man, he was—but this was getting to him. Not the firefight, but the rotten rift that seemed to be forming between Karyn and Anna. Back in the service, a couple of guys in his squad got into some bad blood like this, and it had damn near poisoned the whole group's morale. Squad leader thought he'd fix it by letting the guys go out back and beat the shit out of each other. It sort of had. Not that it improved the relationship any—the fight had cemented the original resentment—but one of the guys ended up in the infirmary with a torn ligament in his elbow and pretty much out of commission after that. Squad leader got demoted and the other guy got transferred, so the problem got fixed, anyway.

That kind of solution was no solution, far as Nail was concerned.

"That was some heavy shit yesterday," Anna said, finally breaking the silence. The four of them were gathered around the card table, awaiting Genevieve's arrival. Anna still looked everywhere but at Karyn.

"I have a feeling we're going to see more of that before this is over," Anna continued. "Maybe a lot more." She looked from Tommy to Nail, eyes sliding right past Karyn again. "The money still look worth it?"

Silence. Karyn had pushed her chair a few extra feet back from the table, indicating she was going to sit this one out. Tommy's gaze went from Karyn to Anna to Karyn, and it was obvious the rottenness in the air had got to him, too. He wasn't going to say shit, Nail thought. Not until it was safe, anyway.

Nail put both hands on the table, palms down, and exhaled. He looked Anna in the eyes. "I seen worse. Anybody here expect this to be easy, for the kind of money up for grabs?"

She didn't look away from him, but her face remained frozen, totally unreadable, and she didn't respond.

Tommy's game of eyeball tennis expanded to include Nail. "Enoch Sobell," he said, tongue flicking at the corners of his mouth. "Guy like me could learn a lot from him. Hate to burn the relationship." He scratched at the stubble on his head, then added, seemingly as an afterthought, "Hate to kill anybody else, though."

"Do you want to do this or not?" Anna asked.

Rather than answer, Tommy practically broke his neck in his hurry to look to Nail. Nail was suddenly, uncomfortably aware that he'd become the focus of the room. Karyn watched him from her aloof perch to his left, Tommy looked to him like a drowning man to a rope, and Anna stared, straight and level. Had she blinked in like the last five minutes?

"I need this," Nail said softly. The words hung there, heavy, and he thought he saw Anna's expression flicker to something else for a moment. "I mean, I need something," he hastened to add. "If we don't do this, I gotta line up something else in a fuck of a hurry. And unless it pays real good, something else right after that."

Karyn stirred, shifting in her chair. "Tommy? You want to do this?" It wasn't quite the question Anna had asked, Nail noted.

Before Tommy could answer, somebody knocked on the door. *Go the fuck away!* Nail wanted to shout. Instead, he got up, leaving Tommy pinned under the twin gazes of Karyn and Anna, and walked over to the door. He checked the peephole and let Genevieve in.

Tommy glanced at her, then nodded at Karyn. "Yeah. I do."

"You're late," Karyn said.

"Our employer wanted an update. I miss anything?" Genevieve asked, her trademark smirk already in place. It didn't do much to hide the circles under her eyes, though, or the weariness in her voice. *Guess nobody's sleeping well these days.*

"No," Karyn said. Genevieve came over to the table and put a wooden box on the corner.

"What's in the box?" Tommy asked.

Genevieve gave the box a shove toward the center of the table. "Quarter million dollars."

"Say what?"

That's the first good news I've had in a week, Nail thought. A wide smile spread across his face. This was a straightforward solution to a straightforward problem, one he happened to know exactly how to solve. "The man understands."

"What's that supposed to mean?" Anna asked.

"Go ahead, big guy," Genevieve said. "You got it."

"Next time the bone comes out to play, it's gonna be in a guarded place with a shitload of people around. Means if we're gonna get at it, we're gonna need ordnance. *That* is our expense account—am I right?"

Genevieve nodded.

He leaned back and laced his fingers behind his head, still smiling. "This is my department."

"Wait. 'Ordnance'?" Tommy was sitting straight up, at full attention, but he couldn't seem to take his eyes off the box. "What do you mean, 'ordnance'?"

"I'm thinking tear gas, flashbangs, smoke grenades.

Maybe a fifty-cal." *Probably too heavy,* he thought, amending his list already. *Maybe just an M240.*

"I don't want a slaughter," Karyn said, her voice uncharacteristically hard. Nail didn't miss the relief that softened Anna's face. "We're not butchers."

"And there's the 'innocent,'" Genevieve pointed out.

Nail shrugged. "'Kay. No fifty-cal. The other shit's nonlethal, more or less, and I don't see how we crash that party without it."

Karyn flipped the top of the box open. "Is this an advance?"

"No," Genevieve said, waggling her finger. "Like Nail said, it's an expense account. If that won't do it—I'm not sure I can go back to the well, but I'm not sure I can't, either."

"Christmas in August," Nail said. "Oh man, am I gonna have some phone calls to make."

He surveyed the room. Tommy still hadn't been able to look away from the box, Genevieve was grinning broadly, and Karyn's mouth had set in a line of quiet satisfaction. When he looked at Anna, she gave him a tight-lipped smile and a small, resentful shrug.

"Guess we're all in," Anna said.

"This job's gonna be good for us," Karyn said.

Anna slipped out of the apartment and pulled the door shut behind her. The air outside, hot, sticky, and stinking of exhaust and melting asphalt, felt almost as good as a nice cool swim compared to the place she'd just left. The morning had been endless, the apartment filled with a sullen silence that she had tried to paint over with noisy pop shit on the radio. By midmorning, she had been ready to kick the radio to death, but the complete absence of human voices in the apartment after would have been worse, maybe blowing up into a real screaming match if last night was any indication. When Tommy and Nail had arrived, the situation hadn't improved any, but at least there was something else to focus on. Then Genevieve's surprise delivery had completely changed things. The brief planning session they'd had after that had gone well enough, but now Anna was brimming with questions.

She caught Genevieve just as she descended the stairs.

"Hey," Anna said. "We need to talk."

Genevieve leaned back against the railing and smiled. "Sure. What's on your mind?"

"You want to go for a ride?"

"Is that what you wanted to talk about, or just where you want to talk about it?"

"The second one."

"Let's go."

Genevieve's ride was a Honda Civic that had seen better days, most of them over a decade ago. Anna brushed a fossilized French fry off the passenger seat and sat. Moments later, they were on the main road, noise from passing cars whooshing by as Genevieve drove. She kept it at exactly the speed limit, Anna noted.

"Lay it on me," Genevieve said.

There was no easy or subtle way of going after this, so Anna plunged straight ahead. "What, exactly, is your relationship with Enoch Sobell?"

"About the same as yours," Genevieve said without taking her eyes off the road.

"What's that supposed to mean?"

Genevieve turned right at the next light and eased in next to a parking meter. Amber light from the dash illuminated the crescent of her cheek as she turned to meet Anna's eyes. "It means just that. I don't particularly like him, I don't owe him my firstborn son, and, God help me, I'm not polishing his knob or anything like that. I've got a business relationship with the guy, and honestly, I'm probably never going to get out from under it. Same as you."

"Same as me?"

Genevieve nodded. "Yeah. Once you start working for him, there's really no walking away. If he thinks you're useful, he's gonna keep using you, and there's not a lot you can do about it. Between his money and his connections, he can completely fuck up your life if you piss him off." She shrugged. "He pays well, so it could be worse."

Anna remained silent, considering. A car drove by, bathing Genevieve's face in glaring white light before dropping it into backlit darkness.

"You don't look too surprised," Genevieve said.

"Guess I'm not. I kinda figured this is how it would end up."

"Top of the underworld food chain. That's gotta count for something."

"So, again: What, exactly, is your business relationship with Enoch Sobell? What's the job *you're* getting paid to do here?"

Genevieve twisted her mouth into her standard smirk. "What do you think?"

"So you're his spy."

"I prefer liaison. I mean, come on—it's not like it's a big secret. I do the go-between crap, give the creepy bastard an occasional status update, and I try to make sure the job gets done. Believe it or not, we really are all on the same side here. He dragged me into it because I know Mendelsohn, and because Tommy is in over his head on this one. Don't tell me I haven't been useful."

Anna nodded. "Yeah. I'm just—yeah. Making sure, I guess."

"No harm in that. We squared away?"

"Yeah."

"Got anything else on the agenda for tonight?"

Anna's first instinct was to pounce on that invitation like a cat on a scurrying rodent, but instead she leaned her head back against the window and sighed. "If I don't get back soon, Karyn's gonna rupture a blood vessel. Another time?"

"Sure. If we ever manage to work it into the schedule." Genevieve grinned, washing away the disappointment that had surfaced briefly in her voice. "Home?"

"Home."

The drive back took only a couple of minutes. Anna

got out at the curb, waved, and headed in to the apartment.

Karyn was still sitting at the table, shuffling through snapshots and plans. She looked up when Anna walked in, her face a still, cold mask. "You get everything you need?" she asked.

"Yeah." Anna walked to her bedroom and closed the door. "Absolutely fucking everything," she muttered.

Chapter 10

The crew spent the next ten days in the usual frenzy of strained, tense activity. The hours were filled with tedious recon and surveillance duty, most of which was a total waste of time, yet a moment's glimpse of something might mean life or death later, and since they were preparing for nothing less than an assault on one of the richest men in Los Angeles, constant focus, even on dirt-boring shit, was an absolute necessity. Anna thought she'd never been so tense doing nothing before. It got so bad that she took to driving around the city after her shift was up, unwilling to go home and lie still long enough to fall asleep.

It didn't help that the air hadn't exactly cleared between her and Karyn. They'd had to make another run to Adelaide's, which was worrisome so soon after the last one, but they hadn't engaged in any real conversation during the long, strained trip. And if anything, Karyn had gotten even jumpier after stocking up on her medication. Anna couldn't tell if she was seeing things or just unusually nervous, and she thought there was even some chance that there was nothing odd there at all. Maybe she was reading her own anxiety into Karyn's behavior.

By the tenth day, she had gone past frayed and on to ragged. She stopped by the apartment they were renting as a base of operations, dropped off her notes without a word to Karyn and Nail (who were deep in a discussion full of phrases like "line of sight" and "blast radius"), and shuffled out. She thought about heading home to get a few hours of sleep, and, while she would have welcomed the rest, she knew it would take some time for the day's stress to dissipate. Driving again, then.

At the first landing down the stairs, she met Genevieve coming up. Genevieve grinned, but it was obvious that she, too, was wearing down.

"Hey," Genevieve said.

"Hey. You holding up all right?"

"Good enough. Five more days, and we can all retire, right?"

"Ha. Maybe you can retire on whatever Sobell's paying you, but my financial advisor tells me that half a million won't stretch nearly as far as I might think. Plus it's a down market, you know."

Genevieve blinked, her expression transforming into one of comical shock. "Your—what?"

With an incredible effort, Anna kept her face straight. "Yeah, and then there's the taxes . . ."

That pushed the joke over the edge, and Genevieve grinned and finally laughed, with Anna joining in a moment later. It felt good—and strangely comforting.

"Hey," Anna said, acting on impulse. "You here on pressing business?"

"Not really. Daily update."

"Go do your thing, and let's go get dinner. I'm starving." She realized that was actually true, and the thought seemed to open up a yawning ache in her belly.

"Sold," Genevieve said. "Back in five."

Anna watched Genevieve trot up the stairs and disappear around the corner. Moments later, the sound of a door opening and then closing reached her.

This is dumb, she thought. *This is exactly what Karyn was worried about.*

No. Karyn was worried about a lot of things, and maybe Genevieve was one of them, or maybe Karyn was tired and pissed and scared and clawing at anything that made her more tired or pissed or scared. How much damage could Genevieve really do? Like she'd said herself, everybody knew she was working for Sobell, so it wasn't as though there were any surprises waiting there.

She was in on the planning and had a similar stake in the outcome.

Anna had thought it over since their late-night conversation in the car, and there wasn't really much downside that Anna could see. And there wasn't really any risk of social embarrassment. Even if Anna put Genevieve's holding her hand after the bad scene at the garage in a special box marked STRESS REACTION—DO NOT TAKE INTERNALLY, there had been plenty of other signals, enough that they couldn't be accidental, and the invitation the other night was about as clear as Anna could ask for. Possibly Genevieve was an incorrigible flirt, but Anna didn't think so—or, at least, didn't think that was all of it. The overlong eye contact, knowing grins, and occasional touches on the arm or shoulder weren't mirrored in Genevieve's behavior with any of the others. She teased Tommy a little, but even Tommy had begun to get the idea that it was no more than that.

If Anna had misread that, that was OK; she could accept rejection with good grace. And if she'd read it correctly—well, fuck what Karyn thought. They were both adults, for Christ's sake. This was completely manageable.

She was saved from overthinking it any further by a clatter of footsteps on the stairs above. Genevieve descended the steps in a rush and almost bounced at the bottom. "So," she asked, "what are you in the mood for?"

Anna smiled back. "I was thinking sushi, unless that's not your thing."

"You drive, I'll buy."

"Done."

Genevieve's happy chatter filled the car during the whole short ride to Anna's favorite sushi spot, a jarring—if welcome—change from Karyn's taciturn silence, or even the calm camaraderie from back before everyone had turned into a tight ball of tension.

"For someone sporting full-on Goth style, you're awfully cheerful," Anna remarked as they got out of the car. "Aren't they going to revoke your card or something?"

"Fuck 'em," Genevieve said. "Once you admit that

you and everyone you love are going to die, you might as well lighten up. It's not like you're going to get another chance."

"That's . . . the most screwed-up way of getting happy I've ever heard."

"Ah, but it works like a champ." She opened the door to the restaurant. "After you."

They went inside. The place was decorated in noxious green with white plastic tables, counters, and fixtures, all rounded off in a way that made it seem like kid furniture. Blue-white fluorescents topped off the ghastliness. Anna gestured at the room. "Don't let the hideous decor fool you. This place is great."

"If you're blindfolded."

"Whatever works."

They sat at an open table. Genevieve claimed to be a sushi novice and let Anna order for the both of them. The waiter left and, before an awkward silence had a chance to develop, Genevieve leaned forward.

"So at last I get a chance to get the lowdown on you and your crazy crew of misfit toys, huh?"

"What lowdown do you need?"

"Oh, come on—all the usual dirt. Where did you grow up? What's your favorite color? What's your critical assessment of *Evil Dead II*?"

"Right here, taupe, and I'll have to send you my master's thesis."

"You grew up in a sushi restaurant?"

"It was tough. I smelled like eel all the time. The other kids used to beat me up and roll me in sticky rice."

Genevieve laughed easily, and Anna felt the knot of tension between her shoulders loosen a little. It seemed a long time since she'd just laughed.

"Seriously, though," Genevieve said.

Karyn's suspicions lurched to the forefront of Anna's mind, and she frowned. "Is this recon?"

Hurt flashed in Genevieve's eyes before she masked it with a half smile and a shrug. "Can be if you want. But, no. That wasn't the idea."

"Sorry. I—you know. This is weird."

Genevieve traced circles in the condensation from her water glass. "Only as weird as you make it."

Anna looked to the window, but there was no escape there—ghostly reflections of both her and Genevieve floated on the surface of the glass, and the night beyond was too dark to dispel them. The chatter in the rest of the small restaurant was too low to mask the silence. "I've known Karyn for over ten years," she said, watching Genevieve's reflection in the glass. "Since high school."

"I didn't ask about Karyn."

Anna bit her lip, then turned away from the reflection to look at Genevieve. "You can't know anything about me if you don't know about her. For real."

"Yeah. Okay." Genevieve put a hand on hers. It was cold, wet with droplets of icy water, but welcome. "Let's have it."

Anna fought down the urge to look back at the window. "She was the one that should have gone to college, had a real life. School came pretty natural to her, I think, before ... before. Me, I couldn't make myself focus on that shit. I guess I could have got by, but I never would have been able to pay for it. In and out of foster homes forever, you know?" She swallowed, took a drink of water with her right hand, not wanting to move her left from the warm cradle of Genevieve's palm.

"Anyway, her probation officer at juvie was right across the hall from mine, and she always needed a cigarette when she came out. I always had 'em."

"Nice girls on their way to college don't have probation officers," Genevieve pointed out.

"Yeah, well, one day Karyn lost her shit and attacked a taco vendor. Like, bad. Cut the shit out of him with a piece of a beer bottle. At the hearing, she said she thought he ripped her off. They put her in counseling, gave her ninety days suspended and a year probation." Another sip of water. "She told me she saw the guy beating the hell out of a little kid, and it was only after she went apeshit on the guy that she realized there wasn't any kid there. Only way to stay out of the nuthouse was to go to jail, so she lied. Six days later, the guy went to jail for putting his stepson in the hospital."

"Jesus."

"Yeah. That was pretty early on, before she really understood what was going on. With her, you know. Visions, or whatever you want to call them. By the time I met her, she had a better idea of what was happening to her, but it was getting pretty bad."

Pretty bad didn't really cover it. Anna could still see Karyn on the steps to the civil building, cigarette held between two fingers as she talked calmly about losing her mind. *I'm not really going crazy,* she'd said, *but as far as anybody can tell, it's the same thing. Shit, as far as I can tell, it's the same. It's all starting to smash together, real stuff and—the other stuff. All the time. I don't know what to do. Nobody does.* Anna had been almost hypnotized by Karyn's even tone, her heart nearly destroyed by the wide, frightened look in Karyn's wet brown eyes.

"I fell for her so hard," Anna said, shaking her head. "I knew she was straight, but I didn't care. I would have lain down in traffic for her."

"Been there, sister," Genevieve said. Her usual glib tone was gone, replaced by quiet melancholy.

"I still would." Anna summoned up a slight grin. "Maybe for different reasons now."

Genevieve just nodded.

"So I decided we'd find a way out for her. It was nuts—a seventeen-year-old dyke and a crazy fortune-teller take on the world! Neither one of us had any idea where to start, or any idea of what kind of shit we'd have to get in to make it work. But we fucking did it."

"And she never made it to college."

Anna shook her head. "Nope. After the first job, we were pretty much hooked. Her medication isn't cheap, and I never heard of an insurance plan that covers it, so she needed the cash. And me—well. I was looking at forty years of working the check-out line at the fucking Home Depot, if I was lucky. Can't say I feel like I really missed out on that."

Genevieve's face was sober, her eyes thoughtful. "I think you're right," she said softly.

"Huh?"

"Knowing about your relationship with Karyn tells me a lot about you."

"Is that a problem?"

"No. Not at all." The old smile resurfaced, with a touch less mockery than usual. She squeezed Anna's hand. "It's all good stuff."

The moment was broken up by the arrival of half a dozen types of sashimi, plus the obligatory California roll for the sushi novice. Genevieve ignored the chopsticks in favor of eating with her fingers, and Anna laughed.

"What about you? What's your story, Madame Mysterious?"

Genevieve's eyebrows shot up. "Mysterious? Me? Ha." She licked soy sauce off her thumb. "It's not actually much of a story."

"Why don't I believe that?"

"No, really. I figured out pretty early on that I could do a few tricks, and my dad hooked me up with a guy he knew who could show me the ropes. That got me started, and by the time old Hector . . ." A cloud passed over her face, and her mouth twisted as though she tasted something sour. "By the time he was done, I was hooked into the occult underground in fifteen different ways. And, yeah, by then a career climbing the corporate ladder didn't look all that attractive. I've been working the 'very, very odd jobs' division ever since."

"What happened to your teacher?"

Genevieve sighed and rolled her eyes, like she'd known this question was inevitable. "Demon ate him."

Anna paused in the act of selecting a piece of spider roll. "You're fucking with me, right?"

"Nope." Genevieve lowered her voice to a whisper. "Here's a little secret for you: All real magic involves dicking around with demons. All of it. You do it long enough, and carelessly enough, and eventually they will take so much of you that there's nothing left. Then they just move in and own the place." She shuddered. "They're pretty tough on their meat suits, so they usually get a pretty short run before the body gives out and they go back wherever they came from."

"That's awful."

"But true."

"And Tommy?"

Genevieve nodded. "Dealing with the devil, just like the rest of us. In a manner of speaking. I have to have a talk with him. He's pretty obviously self-taught, and he treats this stuff like a box of toys he found lying around. Dude's practically sending out invitations for something nasty to get its hooks in."

"What about you? You're smart enough to keep that from happening to you?"

A slow, sad shake of the head. "Nobody's that smart. Keep at it long enough, and it *will* happen. These days, I use the stuff as little as possible, but somehow it's just about impossible to leave it alone. One day, I'll be like Hector, walking around with something else at the controls, making me eat my fingers and shit like that." She pulled up a smile. "By then, I'm hoping to be ninety and in a wheelchair. See how the fuckers like that."

Anna dropped her chopsticks and flicked them away with the backs of her fingers. "Why is everybody around me a ticking bomb?"

"Everybody's a ticking bomb, sweetheart."

"Might as well lighten up, then—isn't that right?"

"Yeah."

"Come on, then. Let's get out of here." She threw a couple of twenties on the table, took Genevieve's hand, and headed toward the door.

As the door swung shut behind them, Anna felt a tug on her hand. She turned, and Genevieve was inches away, standing below the silly plastic awning. She wasn't sure if she moved first or Genevieve did, but the space between them was suddenly gone, her lips pressed against Genevieve's, and for a breathless span of moments, everything was all better.

Chapter 11

"Anybody else worried about the essential insanity of this?" Tommy asked as they prepared to leave their makeshift base of operations. He always asked some variant of this question just prior to the moment where turning back would become impossible. *Everybody feel good about this? Anybody want to back out?* It had become tradition.

Karyn didn't look at him. Barely had for days. Mostly he appeared normal, but two more times she'd seen something awful—once his eyes had been burned from his head, and another time his throat had been cut, his tongue lolling obscenely from slack lips. There was never any direct threat in evidence, and each time the gruesome vision had vanished as quickly as it had come. The closest she'd come to saying anything about it was to categorically ban anyone from the basement of Mendelsohn's place. If everything went well, they shouldn't have to go in the house at all, let alone go anywhere near the basement, but based on Tommy's vision and Genevieve's intelligence, it was better to ditch the job than risk a trip downstairs. Since delivering that edict, she hadn't seen anything else—but she hadn't looked all that carefully, either.

Her other visions had gotten more numerous, too, and only a worryingly high dose of blind made them manageable. She was taking so much now that she had real concerns about whether she was crippling herself for this job. What the hell good was a seer who couldn't see? And besides that, she was going to need to visit Adelaide *again*, right after the job was done.

"I'm good," Nail said.

"I can't even tell what's insane or not anymore," Genevieve said.

Anna merely shrugged.

"Just checking," Tommy said. He turned anxiously to Karyn. "We good?"

I don't know. Other than the visions of Tommy, she'd seen nothing useful, but she was at a complete loss to know what that might mean. *And they're tough to interpret anyway. Half the time they don't mean what I think they do.* Maybe Tommy was in danger, but maybe not. In the past, real mortal danger had always revealed itself in the moments before it struck, and she'd always been able to head it off or escape. Even if Tommy was threatened, she could probably make sure he was protected. It would be stupid to abandon a job of this scale, with this much planning and this much payoff, without being sure.

She nodded. "Yeah. We're good. Let's hit it."

Down the stairs and out to the van, and Karyn felt Anna's eyes like a laser beam drilling a hole between her shoulder blades. That felt more wrong than the thing with Tommy. Up to this point, there should have been jokes and late-night bullshit sessions about how they were going to spend the money, and that should have gone double for this much money. They could make some long-term plans for a change. But that had all pretty much gone to shit since the argument. Karyn didn't sleep much now, and Anna didn't sleep at home, and when they spoke it was about precise tactical details of the job at hand and nothing else.

I'll patch it up after the job. One night of work, and we can make this all better. Money, after all, fixed a lot of things. A shitload of money should fix everything, shouldn't it?

Karyn got into her customary seat in the van, right up front where she could see everything. The trip gave her little time to do anything but fidget, and in any case there were no items left to attend to. Nail had planned the assault, as it were, in painstaking detail. Genevieve and Tommy had scoured the surveillance photos and done some scouting besides, and they'd put together a plan to breach the perimeter without triggering any magical defenses or alarms. Tommy had also prepared a box for the bone that ought to keep anything from leaking out or working the kind of mischief that these things sometimes did. Anna and Karyn had little to worry about at this point, other than just making the grab.

They left the close confines of apartment buildings and headed up toward Topanga Canyon. Tenements turned into houses turned into miles of low scrub and dry grass. This was as close to the middle of nowhere as Karyn had been in ages—a very good thing, since they were about to make a whole lot of noise, and the last thing they needed was a premature visit from the neighbors. Or the cops.

Nail parked the van on a side road a short walk from Mendelsohn's estate. The night sky was dark, absent the moon, and Karyn could barely make out the curve of the estate wall a few hundred yards away.

"Ready?" she asked. A chorus of "yeah"s answered her. Anna met her eyes and gave a single authoritative nod.

The five of them poured out of the van. Nail pulled a heavy green canvas duffel bag from the back, and the others came in around him and grabbed small packs containing their equipment.

Tommy grinned. Smoke wafted up from his blackened eye sockets, and blood burbled from his mouth. "This is crazy. It's gonna be *awesome*."

Karyn shouldered her backpack and started walking.

"Are your men ready, Mr. Pullman?" Enoch Sobell stood inside Nathan Mendelsohn's rambling estate, just the other side of one low hill from the house itself. He was surrounded by a half dozen figures clad thoroughly in black. Balaclavas covered their heads, night-vision goggles masked their eyes, and they sported enough hardware to outfit a Central American army. Sobell wasn't sure what all that stuff was, but it certainly looked impressive, and if this whole thing went pear-shaped and it became a question of armament rather than stealth, he felt fairly secure in the outcome.

He felt for a moment, perhaps, a trifle out of place. He'd doffed his jacket for the occasion—and the necktie, sadly—and even rolled up the sleeves of his Burberry London dress shirt, but amid all this gun-toting machismo it was difficult not to feel at something of a manliness disadvantage. He reflected on the fact that he could torch the whole lot of them with a few words and gestures, incinerate them so thoroughly that it would be like they'd never been there, and that cheered him up somewhat.

Of course, that's what got me into this mess in the first place, he thought, and the cheer dissipated.

"Yes, sir."

"Very well, then. Just wait for the screaming to start."

Tommy stopped twenty yards back from the wall. He recited a few words, pricked his thumb with a needle, and pointed his finger. The camera located near the top of the wall, neatly hidden beneath a phony downspout, turned a few degrees to the left.

Nail moved forward quickly, and the others followed in his footsteps as closely as possible.

It's on, Karyn thought. Any moment now, the cry could go up. Maybe nobody'd notice that one camera among dozens had shifted its viewpoint a tiny bit, but maybe somebody would. The clock was officially ticking.

Nail stopped just short of the wall, and Genevieve drew up next to him. She produced a square scrap of paper, presumably the same one she'd spent all afternoon drawing an intricate web of patterns on. She tossed it into the air ahead of her. It caught fire, flared up, and disappeared.

Genevieve stepped to one side and, grinning, made an *after you* bow. Anna came forward, and Nail boosted her up. She stood on his shoulders and leaned against the outside of the wall without actually climbing atop it. She got out some tools, fiddled with something at the top—disabling the pressure sensor, according to the plan—and cut through the razor wire. It coiled up like an angry serpent, and she jerked her head back. Then she hauled herself up.

A quick look around, and she made a *come on* gesture to Nail. He hefted the big duffel bag up to her, and she dragged it to the top. The scrape of canvas against the rough stucco of the wall seemed louder than aircraft taking off, but then the bag was up, and Anna dropped it down the other side. She then dropped a short rope ladder, secured with hooks to the top of the wall.

Nail went up first, then Genevieve, then Tommy. Karyn came last, pausing at the top. She couldn't see the house from here, but a line of parked cars filled the road around the low hill ahead and extended nearly to the front gate. Looked like the party was every bit as big as Drew had said.

She pulled up the ladder, dropped it down the inside of the wall, and climbed down.

From there, if the maps and Google Earth were to be believed, it was a half-mile run to the copse of carefully cultivated palm trees that would provide cover while they regrouped for the main event. This would be the worst part. Nail was pretty sure that, given all the people here tonight, perimeter security would get the most attention, and internal motion sensors and whatnot would likely be down. Genevieve agreed, but there was really no way to be sure. If they got spotted now, the clock would run down a whole lot faster than planned.

Before Karyn could get her thoughts in order, Nail took off. If the sixty pounds of hardware in the duffel bag slowed him down any, it sure didn't show. The others lit out after him, and Karyn ran behind.

Her heart pounded in her ears, and her breath came loud and fast. She saw nothing threatening ahead, real or otherwise, but every hair on her body trembled in anticipation of a shout or a shot, and the faint crunch of footfalls on the trimmed golf course grass seemed a Klaxon blaring for Security's attention.

The crew strung out in a long line. Fifty yards ahead, Nail dropped into a crouch and slipped into the shadows beneath the trees. A low murmur built in Karyn's ears—the rushing sound of blood, she thought, until it took voice. *That's more than sixty,* she thought.

Ahead, Genevieve and Tommy ducked in next to Nail. Karyn joined them moments later as the chorus of voices rose in some perverted variant of "Hallelujah!"

In the time that it had taken Karyn to catch up, Nail had already assembled two mortars and had moved on to the M60, a ridiculously large, tripod-mounted machine gun that he'd acquired from who knew what dubious sources. She knew she must be imagining it, but Nail seemed to be humming with joy as he set up the weapon.

Ahead of her, a truly surreal scene had been assembled. Mendelsohn's house, a sprawling multilevel mess of twenty thousand square feet enclosed by glass panes and the occasional stone wall, choked the space between two shoulderlike hills. The hills narrowed, forming a sort of natural cul-de-sac a couple of hundred yards back in which stood a little guest house. It was surrounded by a wide patio: flagged in stone, encircled by a six-foot retaining wall, and large enough to play soccer on. At one end was an auxiliary swimming pool—evidently, the one nearer the house was wholly inadequate for Mr. Mendelsohn's guests. All the pool furniture—and, if Karyn wasn't mistaken, a large gas grill—had been pushed to one side, clearing most of the patio space. The lights from both the guest house and the main house had been shut off, as well as most of the patio lights, except for the few that cast blue rays up through the swimming pool. Instead of regular illumination, torches lined the retaining wall at intervals of maybe twenty feet.

Over a hundred robed figures crowded around the center of the patio. There were more torches here, enough that Karyn could see what was going on in the middle of the chanting throng.

Goddammit, she thought. *They are gonna kill someone.*

Mendelsohn had spared no expense on the altar. It looked to be a seven-foot-long slab of marble, inlaid with all kinds of vaguely threatening, darkly glittering symbols. A person—a man, Karyn thought, though it was hard to be sure—had been swaddled in white bandages and secured to the slab by chains hooked through eyebolts.

On the slab near the man's head was a grinning crescent shape: the bone.

Eight guards stood at various points around the edges of the ceremony, small submachine guns in full view. They faced inward, not out, and Karyn realized that they were there not to keep intruders from crashing the party, but in case one of the faithful had a sudden change of heart.

At one end of the altar, a hooded figure raised a wavy-bladed knife to the sky. The chanting picked up in speed, the rising pitch lifting the hairs on the back of Karyn's neck. The figure chained to the altar squirmed.

"Hurry up," she whispered.

"We're go!" Nail whispered back. "Get ready!"

Each of them took a moment to put on a respirator and thermal vision goggles, and readied their weapons. Karyn caught a glimpse of Anna's face, cocked in her direction, and gave her a reassuring nod.

"Go!" Nail said.

Anna and Genevieve cut right as Karyn followed Tommy toward the house to the left. Seconds later, Nail fired the first grenade launcher. A loud, heavy *whump* split the air, and a canister of tear gas arced out above the assembled cult members and detonated. Two more followed, then a smoke grenade. White fog choked torches and cultists alike, and the air filled with the sounds of coughing and retching. Ahead of her, Tommy tossed a couple of stun grenades into the fog. The resulting bang nearly deafened Karyn—and, unlike the people below, she'd known it was coming.

Shock and awe, she thought with disgust. And then Nail opened up with the M60. If the night had been loud and frightening before, it must have seemed like Armageddon to the robed figures down there now. Hell, it seemed like the end of the world to Karyn, like she'd been dropped into Baghdad or Darfur with no warning, and even though she knew Nail was firing over their heads, the rounds doing nothing but churning dirt on the opposite hillside, terror squeezed her heart.

She and Tommy reached the spot where the wall tapered down to the patio. He hopped down, and she followed a second later. They stood between the crowd and the main house, where hopefully they'd be able to cut off anybody trying to escape with the bone. Karyn felt irritating drops of tear gas on her exposed skin, but the cloud was invisible through the goggles, the people exposed and clear as if it were midday. A figure emerged from the mob in front of her, and she almost fired, but she held off as she realized it was just a terrified cult member running for safety. The man ran past her and clambered up the wall. Two more followed. Then she saw a fourth figure, a man moving steadily toward her rather than fleeing, and before she even confirmed the presence of his weapon, she pulled the trigger.

The Taser hit him high in the shoulder, and he collapsed not ten feet in front of her. She kicked his gun away as she ran past and tugged at the Taser line. It didn't budge, so she dropped the Taser rather than screw around trying to pull the darts loose and reel them back in.

Another flashbang detonated ahead and the remaining worshippers who weren't stunned into immobility finally gave up and ran. A group of six came out of the tear-gas fog, scrambling over each other in their haste to escape. Karyn sidestepped them and stumbled into a rolling bank of noxious cloud. She gasped. The respirator did its job, mostly, but the air coming through had a noxious tang to it, and her eyes teared up as trace amounts slipped in around the seal of her goggles.

A shape ahead of her moved, light gray against the dark gray of the seething mob behind it. From the bulky headgear, she assumed it was Tommy. Another figure moved past him, running toward the house, arms clutching something to its chest.

The figure was gone in a moment, and Tommy followed.

Karyn started forward after them, then stopped abruptly and fell forward as something snagged the cuff of her pants. Half a second later, searing pain ripped into her calf.

Knife! He's got a knife!

The man she'd Tasered clung to her ankle with one hand and clumsily swung a short survival knife with the other. Her calf was bleeding, the guy was surely going to stab her again, maybe do some real damage, and all she felt was confused surprise coupled with indignation that this was actually happening to her.

What the fuck? I guess I really did take too much.

The men moved at the first explosion, like sprinters leaving the starting blocks. In moments, they had disappeared over the low rise that had masked them from the house. Sobell took a moment to work a small spell that would scramble his appearance on any electronic equipment and ambled after them.

By the time he reached the front door, the two guards that had been posted there were dead, their bodies stuffed into the front coat closet. The low-ranking member of the team had already mopped up the blood trail, and the whole group stood at attention.

"Lead on," Sobell said.

They moved through a short hall and into a spacious living room. Sobell couldn't keep the sneer off his face. Mendelsohn's place was a tasteless hat tip to Frank Lloyd Wright designed by somebody who didn't understand the aesthetic, other than that everything must be squared off and, preferably, feature some kind of ungainly cantilever. Square blocks of uncomfortable-looking furniture lined the room in tiresome rectilinear precision. The room was dark, but Sobell felt certain that all the furnishings were black.

Ought to do good taste a service and burn this place down before we depart, he thought.

Sobell's team flicked on gun-mounted flashlights as

they moved to the basement stairway and began the descent. Sobell cast one last glance at the living room, shook his head, and followed the bobbing lights down. If his intelligence was correct, this level of the basement was carved up into perhaps a dozen rooms housing no fewer than thirty of Mendelsohn's most devoted followers. They would be outside now, awaiting their peculiar version of the Second Coming. And good riddance.

Pullman, the squad leader, had done a good job memorizing the plans. He took two lefts and the next right without hesitation, dropping low just as he turned the last corner. The guardroom ahead was still staffed despite the activity outside—six men playing cards and waiting, guns at the ready.

Pullman wasted no time. He fired, dropping two of the guards immediately before the others scattered. The shots were uncomfortably loud despite the suppressor mounted on the gun barrel, and Sobell covered his ears.

The squad followed Pullman, and Sobell stepped back around the corner to wait until it was finished. An awful lot of shooting got crammed into the next few moments, and chips of concrete flaked off near Sobell as stray shots pounded the wall.

Then everything was quiet.

"Status?" Sobell shouted.

"Enemy's down," Pullman said. "Edgars got hit, but the body armor stopped it. We'll have to move, though, sir. Pretty sure they got off a call to the others."

Sobell walked around the corner, brushing dust from his shirt. "The others should be fairly busy right now. But your point is well taken. Shall we?"

The hall passed through the guardroom and continued around another bend, bringing them up short in front of a curious door. Sobell pushed the barrel of one of the guns up and across, playing the light over the surface. Black cast iron, rough, reminding him of nothing so much as the surface of an old frying pan. Somebody had etched it with a collection of runes and sigils. Probably Genevieve, Sobell figured. It looked like her work.

There was no doorknob or handle of any kind, but

that didn't bother him. He touched the door in three spots, said a few words. A white-hot line flared up around the outer edge of the door, causing the soldiers to step back and cover their eyes. A moment later, the door swung open.

"Don't touch that," Sobell said. "It's hot." He pushed up one sleeve of his shirt where it had unrolled and slid down. "After you."

The stairs turned out to be metal as well, though of a much more utilitarian flavor: rough treads, handrails made of galvanized pipe. The hall below was similarly Spartan. The walls were unadorned cinder block, and the ceiling was left open to the bare structural members and floor above. This level was dark and unguarded. That made sense, Sobell thought. There was, after all, only one way in.

Sobell followed the men. He noticed a faint, odd smell as they started walking—something dead, certainly, but also the foundry smell of scorched metal, something with the acrid chemical tang of paint thinner, and something that was, unless he'd lost his mind, lavender. It turned into a full-on stench within just a few dozen steps. He swallowed roughly once or twice. The men in front of him coughed and rubbed at their eyes.

After about a hundred feet, the corridor turned sharply left, but before they reached that spot, Sobell called a halt.

"Stay here. Don't come around that corner unless you hear me scream bloody murder." He considered. "Actually, don't come then, either. I'll be fucked in that case, and there won't be anything you can do about it. Just stay here and cover my behind. I need some quiet time. No interruptions."

"Yes, sir."

"That's the spirit. Hand me that flashlight, would you?"

One of the men unclipped the light from his gun and handed it over. Sobell took a deep breath and turned the corner.

The light dimmed immediately, the hot white glare

dropping to a feeble orange glow. *There's confirmation for you, if the smell didn't do it.* He stared at the wall to his right until his eyes began to adjust. The only sounds came from his breathing and the quiet rustle of his clothes when he shifted his weight. Nevertheless, he felt a presence in the gloom, felt the will of a conscious *something* concentrated on him as if it were a weight trying to crush him to pulp.

When his eyes had adjusted enough to see the cracks between the cinder blocks in the wall, he turned. This time, he kept his eyes on the floor ahead of him as he moved forward. The sense of *presence* screamed at him, and at the edges of his vision, he saw the unearthly darkness shrouding the end of the hall.

Cold sweat popped from his skin, wet beads down the length of his spine, and it took an intense effort of will to keep putting one foot in front of the other. He passed a hall that led off to the right, the place where—if his intelligence was to be believed—that ridiculous jawbone was kept. He stifled the urge to run down that hall, to get away from that crushing weight.

Three steps more and he stopped at a line of symbols across the floor. His light had dimmed to a tiny red worm of filament, as though the battery had nearly run down, and the faint illumination it emitted ended abruptly at the other side of the line. Hatred, palpable as pummeling fists, surged from the darkness and boiled the air around him. His stomach churned, and terror coursed through his body—and he had the very clear sense that the hate wasn't even directed at him.

Dear God. Genevieve had told the truth, he'd known that all along, but he doubted she knew exactly what was down here. Even garden-variety demons were nothing to fuck around with, but *this* . . . Whoever had conjured this thing up must have been profoundly lucky, and this thing must have been having an unusually stupid day.

He summoned his courage. "Bit cramped, innit?"

Images assailed his mind. A man's head in a vise, eyes bulging and mouth open in a silent scream as somebody turned the crank. A bat with its wings systematically shattered by tiny hammers. Something he caught only a glimpse of but looked like a grown man folded up and jammed into a very small metal box. Before the image was gone, he saw splinters of smashed bone protruding from nearly every bit of exposed flesh. Others crowded in, most gone too fast to register.

"Ah, nonverbal. Rather old school, as they say, but we can work with that." A complete bluff, that, but it was never good to be seen weak or uninformed. Although, the thing could plant images in his mind. Did that mean it could also pull things out? Better not to dwell on that. Better just to get what he needed and get out.

An image of a tattooed skinhead, lips sewn shut with black thread, giving him the finger.

"Subtle. I don't suppose there's any chance you want out of this charming little cell? I mean, it looks cozy and all, but it does seem like it must get awfully dull."

Nothing. No images or sounds, just blackness ahead of him. Waiting. He found himself wondering just how good the wards were.

"As it happens, I need some information. You need out of this hole so you can presumably wreak whatever unspeakable vengeance you've been plotting in there all this time."

Another flurry of horrible images battered his mind, grotesque images that made the man stuffed in the box look like a mural on a nursery wall. They were permutations of the demon's unspeakable vengeance, he was sure. Sour acid rose to the back of his throat. *Fuck, don't vomit here, do* not *vomit.* His mouth flooded with saliva, and he swallowed once, then twice. Then the images were gone. He had a grim feeling that the residue they left behind would stay with him for a long time, probably resurfacing at midnight every night for the next, oh, rest of his life or so.

"Okay, then. In exchange for getting you out of here, I need two things."

A series of barter images rose to mind. A man that looked like a seventeenth-century farmer trading a chicken for a rake. A woman trading a piece of jewelry for a rug. Two dirty, naked children trading marbles. Each image, he noticed, had the participants trading one thing for one other thing.

Fucking demons. Nowhere to go, no way out, and it was determined to stick to some bizarre set of arbitrary rules it had established for itself. He'd never understood it. Demons were creatures of almost pure appetite, and even the oldest and most crafty seemed hard-pressed to resist sating immediate urges in favor of longer-term objectives, but there were strange exceptions to that general rule. It seemed most had an OCD streak, and certain kinds of rules were inviolable, at least as far as Sobell could tell. This one would surely wait if he wouldn't deal. Its patience may not have been limitless, but as far as Sobell knew, its time was. Eventually, the wards would decay just enough, or an earthquake would crack them, or something, and if its terms weren't met, the demon would wait until then, its anger growing fiercer and hotter by the minute.

Still, this wasn't his first demon-wrangling rodeo. He'd come prepared.

"First, I let you out. In exchange for that, you don't hurt me or my men." A stupid thing to have to barter for, but probably necessary. Demons could be unbelievably petty about payment, and this one was likely furious and frustrated beyond measure, itching to wreak hideous violence on the first victims it could find.

A handful of pebbles. The seven of spades. A cluster of seven grapes. The subtext was clear: *That's not one thing, that's seven.*

Sobell sighed. "Fine. You don't hurt me. What you do aside from that is your business."

A handshake, a letter signed in blood.

"Done," Sobell said. "Second, you may have noticed that I am not a healthy man."

A sense of vast dark amusement surrounded him, and his mind swam with images of a horrid demonic feast, chunks being torn off a living body and devoured by laughing monstrosities. The body, he was not surprised to note, was his own.

"Yes, well. The dark arts are *such* a wear and tear on one's soul, and, yes, one day I'll have to deal with that problem, too. But I'm afraid today's issue is merely this vessel of flesh that carts around your future dinner."

Merlin. Methuselah. A thousand-year-old man crumbling to dust, parts breaking off as he took each step toward some invisible goal. And, as if the demon might actually have some kind of sense of humor, a fossil embedded in shale — a skull of some kind, and part of a rib cage.

"Not that old, sadly, though I'm working on it." Sobell licked at dry lips and wished for a glass of water. "I am in a hell of a bind, though. My body dies, and you bastards get my soul. I use much more magic to extend my life, and you bastards get my soul before I even get to vacate the premises. So, I need you to give me another, say, hundred years or so."

A man with his pockets turned inside out, a sheepish look on his face.

"You *can't*? What the hell good are you?"

At first, there was no response. No images at all, though that oppressive sense of hate seemed to gather its focus uncomfortably close to Sobell. Then, a new set of images: A little girl, whispering something into a little boy's ear. High school kids passing notes in class. A phone book. A set of encyclopedias, for God's sake.

Information. It can give me information. Sobell's spirits sank further. What question could he even ask? What information was any good to him now, other than a straight answer on what to do to extend his life?

Ah. There was an obvious answer. A miserable, terrible, degrading obvious answer, dragged up from his past and fraught with every kind of risk he could think of.

"Forcas," he whispered, unable to bring himself to speak the name more loudly.

A new image, that of a wolf, snarling, muzzle stained with blood. It lunged at another, smaller wolf and tore out its throat, spraying red over snow.

Great. Apparently they're not friends. "How do you think *I* feel about it? I'm the guy who fucked it out of a hundred years it never wanted to give me. How I'm going to fuck it out of another hundred is quite beyond me right now." He wouldn't, he knew. There would be a full bargain this time. A bargain, and amends. Probably some kind of gruesome payment with interest.

What choice did he have?

"Can you tell me how to contact it? Or find someone who can?"

A pay phone. A gold-inscribed summoning circle, with candles blazing at the points of a pentacle inside. The meaning was obvious. *Just call it.*

"I don't do that anymore." Sobell sighed. "I *can't* do that anymore. Can't risk it." Summoning was serious business, unbelievably dangerous at the best of times. In his current situation, it would be an open invitation for something nasty to move in. It crossed his mind to subcontract the job—just get somebody else to summon the thing—but he ruled it out immediately. There was nobody he trusted enough to act as an intermediary between him and a demon, and nobody he'd trust with the knowledge of his current vulnerable state. "I just need some information. Some way to get started."

A little boy, maybe five years old, arms crossed and lower lip thrust out, pouting. A slick-looking salesman, leading a woman from one car to a different one.

"There's nothing else I need," Sobell said. "No matter how unpleasant it is for you to send me to one of your rivals, I promise it will be more unpleasant for me. It's this or nothing."

Another long pause. Then, at last, a floating, disembodied Cheshire cat grin.

"I'll take that as a yes." In five minutes, his hopes had sunk from getting his life extended to maybe getting some information on it, to maybe getting some information on whom to talk to to talk to another demon he'd already pissed off once in hopes of reconciling their differences. This was weak indeed, but the sad fact was that he didn't have much left in the way of options. If there had been other avenues remaining, he wouldn't have orchestrated this goddamn foolish episode and be down here in an idiot cult leader's basement, fucking around with a demon. "Very well. Let's do this."

Judas dickering with some Romans. A hand extended, palm up.

"Cute. How's this for payment?" He opened his satchel and pulled out a bundle about the size of a shoebox, wrapped in black cloth. The bottom shone brightly, silver light tearing through every seam. Sobell was surprised to see that the light didn't stop at the runes on the floor, but penetrated into the cloud of darkness beyond. For a split second, he almost looked deeper into the darkness—then he recovered his wits.

A sense of vast, deep hunger enveloped him, and something in the darkness moved. He turned around, rather than risk getting a look at it.

"One angel heart," he called over his shoulder, "for your personal collection. You can eat it, keep it, or fuck it for all I care. In exchange, I need a hundred years."

More images—an empty safe, a penniless beggar.

It had been worth a try. You could never tell when they were just being cheap. "Very well. I need you to tell me what I have to do, who I have to talk to, deal with, or kill, to meet with Forcas *without* having to summon the damned thing."

Bloody fingers held together. A smoldering wax seal smashed onto parchment.

"Done." He took a deep breath, dreading the next few moments. The demon had to keep its bargains, or so he'd been told. Such had been his experience, as well. Nevertheless, how could one really know? Even his vast experience held only a few nuggets of wisdom regarding these creatures, and if the ones he'd dealt with in the past were bound by their word—or merely abided by it because it amused them to do so—who could say whether those rules applied to the incalculably ancient and powerful creature behind the sigils?

He set the heart on the ground. Then he took a small blob of clay out of his satchel, dropped it on the floor, and used his shoe to smear it across one of the runes, filling the carving and, for all practical purposes, erasing it.

Just before his foot crossed the line, he closed his eyes.

Heat engulfed him, seeming to come from inside rather than out, welling up from a tiny core in his belly to burn his body, spreading outward to his shoulders, elbows, knees, out to his fingertips and toes, so intense that he felt he must burst apart as all the fluids in his body reached a boil. A series of images was burned into his mind as he stood there, bewildering in its apparent randomness. A bony, sharp-faced man of middling age with a scruff of patchy beard. When he opened his mouth, it was teeming with slimy white worms. A woman with serpents for arms. Thirteen vultures circling a stone slab. And lots of blood. Of course.

The last image was that of a seedy-looking man in a fedora and a moth-eaten pin-striped suit, holding three dice carved of dull black bone in his hand, and Sobell felt a shock of recognition. He knew that guy, or had years ago.

That was a place to start, then.

The heat dissipated as suddenly as it had come. Down the hall, men screamed.

Sobell opened his eyes. The heart was gone.

Alone in the corridor, he began to laugh.

The goggles were amazing, and Anna would have liked more time to simply marvel at them. The fog and smoke were practically invisible through them, while the screaming and scrambling bodies were lit up like billboards outside a car lot. It took almost no effort to avoid the frightened cult members as they caromed off each other and fell down and crawled away from the sudden eruption of chaos. This was gear they should have sprung for a long time ago.

She turned to grin at Genevieve, but the other woman was already cutting a path toward the altar. Anna picked up speed and followed.

Between the goggles and the respirator, she felt weirdly isolated from the scene, as though she were watching a movie or playing an incredibly realistic video game. The only thing tethering her to reality, it seemed, was the irritation of the exposed areas of her face caused by the clouds of tear gas that still hung in the air. If she could just rinse that away, this would be nothing more than entertainment.

Dangerous way to think, girl. None of that shit.

Ahead, a figure approached Genevieve, whether seeking help or accosting her, Anna couldn't tell. Anna lifted her Taser. Genevieve held out a hand. Nothing happened that Anna could see, but Genevieve's interlocutor fell back, clutching his face.

A moment later, Anna caught up.

"You OK?" she yelled.

"Yeah. Come on!"

Between the shouting, the screaming, and the chattering bursts of Nail's machine gun, the noise was nearly intolerable. Anna grimaced and wished she could put her fingers in her ears, but that wasn't gonna happen. Tough to carry a weapon and fend off the angry hordes of the Brotherhood without using your hands.

Genevieve pushed aside a couple of crouched bodies and moved past to the altar. She looked down at something Anna saw as a huddled gray blob of heat pressed against the stone, then up.

"Shit! Help!"

A second later, Anna joined her. "Is he breathing?" Genevieve shouted, pointing at the body on the slab.

"Jesus, I—oh." It had been hard to tell through the goggles what she was looking at, but the spreading pool of warmth on the surface of the altar told her most of what she needed to know.

"No. He's dead."

"Oh, God."

Jesus Christ, what a mess. Anna moved toward where she thought the house was, stumbling around a couple of downed cult members. Somebody threw a wild punch, and she dodged, getting all tangled up with the guy and turned around. He went down gagging a moment or two later, but by then she had no idea where Genevieve had gotten off to. Fifteen steps through the crowd, and a familiar voice reached her.

"Come on!"

Tommy. And, sure enough, ahead and to her right, a man-shaped warm spot was taking off like hell after another figure, farther in the distance.

She lit out after them.

They had quite a head start, but Tommy was in no great shape, and the guy ahead of him seemed even worse off. By the time the two of them reached the main house, Tommy was slowing and the other guy was practically stumbling, slowing down with every step. Anna put on a surge of speed as the two men went in through the sliding glass door ahead. Her feet slipped in the wet grass, but she flailed and kept her balance. Moments later, she burst into a huge open space with glass on one side and a wall of stone, still radiating warmth from the day, on the other. Her footfalls were harsh slaps on stone as she pounded through the room, nearly catching up with Tommy by the other side.

Tommy tore his respirator off and let it bounce against his chest as he rushed forward. The other man—Mendelsohn, she guessed—was old and slow, and there was only one way this footrace could end.

"Come on!" Anna yelled, and she sped past Tommy.

Everything was dark in here, and roughly the same temperature, and damn near impossible to see. Anna missed a turn and rebounded off a wall, hard. She pulled her goggles and respirator down around her neck. The corridor she was in was dark, but not too dark, swathed in shades of gray, and Mendelsohn ran toward the far end. She rushed forward, caught up, and lunged, just missing the fluttering fabric of Mendelsohn's robe as he pushed off the corner and bounced into a large living space.

Halfway across the room Mendelsohn's foot caught on the edge of the carpet, and he tripped.

Got you! Anna thought, and then a sound like an exploding train, still rushing forward on its tracks, smashed the world open. *Something* burst from a stairwell near the edge of the room, something shrouded in darkness.

Ahead of her, Mendelsohn let loose a scream of terror unlike anything Anna had ever heard, a high-pitched, wavering shriek more like a mortally wounded animal than a human being.

Anna didn't know what the thing in darkness was, but she *felt* it, and the hate radiating from its heart set her body trembling with fear. Her screams joined Mendelsohn's, and she threw herself to the side, back, in any direction at all that would get her away from it.

The fucking bone wasn't worth this. She managed to orient herself and began to flee back to the corridor, just as Tommy rounded the corner and rushed into the room. He took half a dozen halting steps into the room, seeming to stare blankly at the thing in darkness. His goggles blew apart. He fell to his knees, mouth still hanging open.

To Anna's left, the darkness reached out and enveloped Mendelsohn. There was a horrible wet, crunching sound. Incredibly, Mendelsohn's scream grew louder. Across the room, Tommy began clawing at his own face. Anna ran toward him.

Ahead of her, somebody else emerged from the corridor behind Tommy. Whoever it was fired one shot, a brief bright blaze in the darkness, stumbled back and fired again just as Anna reached Tommy.

Warm wet blood sprayed across Anna's arm, and Tommy collapsed to the floor.

Mendelsohn's screams stopped abruptly, and suddenly the darkness and hate were gone.

"Tommy!"

The blood was forgotten as Tommy's screams ripped the air. Anna knelt next to him, mindless of the hot wetness that soaked the knees of her jeans. She pulled out a flashlight and flicked it on.

"Tommy, are you all—" The question fell dead from her lips when she saw the tattered hole in the front of his shirt. For a moment, she could do nothing but stare. Then Tommy's screams tapered off. He curled up, huddled into himself, and shivered.

Genevieve rushed into the room, stopped, and looked around helplessly. She ran past Anna, doing something in the darkness, something that involved a lot of wet, squishing footsteps, but Anna paid no attention.

There was no more time for this. Anna pressed a button by her hip and spoke into her headset. "Tommy's down!" she yelled. "Abort this fucking disaster. Nail, get the van out front. Now!"

Chapter 12

"Fuck! Fuck! Put him down, here. No, here. Christ, not on the ground, put down a blanket or something!" Anna ran her hands through her hair, smearing sweat, blood, and grime across her forehead. "Where's Lau? Where's the fucking doctor?"

They'd fled to the junkyard after the debacle at Mendelsohn's. Anna had stolen one of the cars out front and hauled ass to meet Nail, transferring Tommy to the van outside the estate. Tommy had screamed and cried during the whole ride, but now he was alarmingly quiet.

"He's coming," Nail said. "Fast as he can." Sweat shone on his face, gleaming in the van's headlights. Destroyed cars hulked around them. They seemed to lean inward, grilles spread in grim metal smiles, to watch the bloody spectacle.

"It's gonna be OK, man. You gonna be OK." Nail knelt next to Tommy, holding his head up and trying to give him water. It spilled down his cheeks, and Tommy coughed twice, violently. Dark specks appeared on Nail's skin and glasses.

"OK," Genevieve said. She paced back and forth between the stacks of cars and repeated this pointless bullshit to herself. "OK. OK. It's going to be O-fucking-K. OK." Anna thought she was hyperventilating.

Anna knelt on Tommy's other side, opposite Nail, and pushed like hell on the wadded-up shirt that was holding

Tommy's guts in. It was soaked through already, and her hands were slimy with blood.

"Where's the fucking doctor?" she shouted.

"He's coming! He's coming, goddammit!" Nail said.

"I need more bandages. Now!" She didn't know whether she needed more bandages or not—where was Lau, fucking Lau, the fucking doctor?—but she had to do something.

Nail handed her his shirt. "It's all I got."

She took it. She threw the old, blood-soaked shirt to the side. The light wasn't great, but even so, she gagged at the sight of Tommy's wound. His T-shirt was shredded, a ragged hole blown through it by the bullet that had mushroomed and fragmented as it plowed through his body. A hole big enough for her to put both fists in poured blood from high in his belly.

He coughed again, less violently this time. A thick trickle of black blood ran from his mouth.

"Can't breathe," he said. His voice was barely audible, a low sound like softly tearing paper, but Anna felt a crazy relief. They were the first coherent words he'd said since she and Genevieve had found him. "No air."

Anna crumpled Nail's shirt into a ball and jammed it into the wound, trying to ignore the slippery, squishy feel. *Apply pressure,* she thought. *You're supposed to apply pressure.* Really, though? Were you still supposed to apply pressure when the bandage was going into the guy's stomach cavity, and your hands were going in after it? Was that really how it was supposed to work? She didn't know, nobody knew, and Lau wasn't there and nobody could tell her anything, so she pushed until the wound was packed and her fingers were touching things she didn't want to think about.

Tommy didn't even wince. Anna watched his face for any sign of emotion or engagement, but he'd checked out again since his earlier comment. She hoped he was drifting somewhere without pain.

Anna looked up, past Tommy and Nail. Karyn stood in the center of the clearing. Her face hung slack, seemingly without comprehension, but wetness gleamed in her eyes. By her sides, her fists hung loose, closing and opening in uneven twitches.

Like Tommy's heart, Anna thought.

Nail dropped his hand to Tommy's wrist. "I can't find anything," he said. "Come on, man, give me something here." Worry creased his brow, and his eyes were in constant motion, moving from Tommy to Anna to Karyn.

The twitching in Karyn's hands weakened, then stilled.

"What are you doing?" Anna yelled. "Fucking help us!"

Karyn stepped back, still staring at a spot somewhere past Anna. The sound of her boots grinding the rocky sand was louder than Tommy's breathing. "I don't—"

"Didn't see this coming, did you? You don't think maybe you coulda cracked open the future and looked around for *this*?"

Karyn flinched. "I couldn't, it doesn't—"

"You couldn't what?" Tears mingled with the sweat running down Anna's face. She didn't care. "You couldn't what?"

For the first time, Karyn focused on Anna's face. "You know it's not that easy," she said. A note of pleading had wormed its way into her voice. Anna found herself taking a small, petty satisfaction at that. "You know that."

Nail's voice, low and jagged: "He's not breathing."

Anna pulled her attention back to Tommy. Beads of sweat glistened on his forehead, and blood from his mouth and nose pooled at the base of his neck. His chest didn't move.

Nail closed his eyes. He started to speak, let out a half-strangled syllable, then shook his head.

Anna met Karyn's eyes and summoned every ounce of venom she had. "You were supposed to stop this," she said.

Karyn's gaze lingered on her face for one long breath. Then, without a word, she turned away and started walking.

Chapter 13

The doctor showed up not ten minutes after Tommy's final, anguished breath. Anna sat on the dirty ground, leaning back against the fender of an old Buick, and let Nail deal with him. If there was anything left to wring from her spent emotions, she couldn't find it. The past hour she'd careened from the adrenaline rush of the job to the horror of what happened to Tommy to the bottom of a well of grief so deep she thought she'd never climb all the way back out, and now she was empty.

She thought maybe she ought to feel ashamed of her outburst at Karyn, but she didn't. Maybe Karyn couldn't control what she saw or how, but that was her fucking job—that's what they relied on her for. And then she'd just walked off, leaving Nail and Anna holding Tommy's corpse, Genevieve standing to the side, face white and staring.

Fuck her, Anna thought, but even that thought carried no emotional weight.

Across the small clearing, Nail slipped the doctor a handful of bills. The two of them hoisted Tommy's body and disappeared down the canyon of stacked cars.

That's it. That's the last of Tommy. The last wisecrack, the last magic trick I'll watch him fuck up horribly. One last disappearing act. Guess the joke is on us after all.

She didn't look up as the crunch of footfalls came her way. "Hey," Genevieve said.

"Hey."

Genevieve sat in the dirt next to Anna and took her hand. "He was good people," she said softly.

Anna nodded.

They sat in silence for a long time. Genevieve's hand was warm and dry in Anna's, the bones thin and surely too frail to hold Anna up after this. But there was strength there, and Anna felt it flow into her—not much, a trickle rather than a flood, but enough. If only Karyn had been by her other side . . .

Genevieve shifted. "So, uh, I don't know if this is a good time, but . . ."

Anna lifted her head. "What?"

"Well . . ." Genevieve pulled her backpack into her lap, then pulled out the box she and Tommy had prepared for the job. Black, covered with silver runes as always. The silver handle gleamed faintly yellow in the reflected gloom from L.A.'s skies.

Genevieve unhooked two clasps and opened the box. An old jawbone sat inside like the bottom half of a sinister grin. It looked right at home, yellowed and dry in this desert land. There was something about it that encouraged the eye to linger while making the stomach turn slow, oily circles.

Anna looked up. "What the fuck? How?"

"I found it in what was left of Mendelsohn. I just stashed it when the shit got ugly. Didn't have time to do much else." She closed the box. "What do you want to do?"

"I *want* to ram it so far up Enoch Sobell's ass it'll count as dental work. But we should cash it in. Fuck, we earned it."

"You want to make the call, or should I?"

"I'll do it. But I have to go home first. I need to talk to Karyn."

"Karyn?" Anna called as she entered the apartment.

Nothing.

She stepped inside, closed the door, and swore. Karyn hadn't even gotten home yet, which meant what? That she was out getting hammered? That she'd been ambushed by somebody who'd tailed them from the clusterfuck at Mendelsohn's? Or maybe she'd just taken the long way home, needing to clear her head.

Still, that didn't feel right. Karyn didn't really party, and she didn't spend a lot of time wandering the streets, either—too many possible surprises, too many nasty things she tended to see in the people she moved through.

Anna went into the living room, pulled out a folding chair and leaned forward, hanging her head on the card table. She'd wait for a while, and Karyn would come in, and everything would go back to making sense. Maybe they'd have it out, maybe they'd just grieve together, but everything would be fine.

Goddammit, Karyn. Where are you? She dialed Karyn's number on her cell. It went to voice mail. She put the phone away and stood. Maybe there was a beer in the fridge. Maybe that would take the edge off the mild panic that was threatening to slip its leash and run racing around her head and heart.

The fridge contained the usual condiments and clotted milk, a loaf of bread—kept there so the roaches couldn't find it—and a bundle of asparagus Karyn had gotten excited about for no good reason and brought home shortly before the goddamn job had really taken off and asparagus became the last of anybody's concerns. It had blackened and grown some vegetation of its own.

There were also three bottles of Old Milwaukee. Anna'd almost rather drink horse piss, but Karyn liked the stuff.

Plus, we're fresh out of horse piss, Anna thought as she grabbed a bottle. She stared at the other two for a moment, then grabbed them, too. It wasn't like they were any worse warm.

Anna took her beers and settled into the beanbag chair, the only other piece of "furniture" in the living room besides the folding chairs and table. Almost nothing to show that people actually lived here, but like Karyn said, it was less shit to pack or abandon if they had to leave in a hurry.

Less shit to pack. That phrase kindled up real dread in Anna's belly, and an ugly thought crowded to the front of her mind. She put the beer down and crossed the room to Karyn's bedroom door. Knocked twice, just to be on the safe side. Then she went in.

The top drawer of the dresser hung open, half-empty, and the closet yawned like an opening to Hell. A handful of hangers had fallen on the floor. The black duffel bag—the one that Karyn kept packed in case they had to ditch in a hurry—was gone.

Karyn was gone.

Chapter 14

The phone rang, and Karyn jumped. It was the seventh time that night, or maybe the eighth, that the phone had started up its jingling, nerve-jangling racket, never mind that she'd pulled the cord out of the wall after the third time and smashed the phone to plastic shards and circuit board fragments after the fifth. A dull red ray of neon light slipped through a chink in yellow-and-brown flower-print curtains that hadn't been changed or laundered since Lyndon Johnson was president, illuminated a swath of air thick with dust, and lit upon the wreckage of the motel room's telephone. A few broken pieces of plastic that had landed on the top vibrated as the ringer made its futile plea for attention.

That's not really happening, Karyn reminded herself. The phone was broken, sure, but it wasn't ringing. The plastic wasn't doing a skittering little dance down the top of the machine. The neighbors weren't about to start pounding on the door, demanding that she answer the phone goddammit it's three o'clock in the morning.

She knew it was mostly in her head, though that hadn't stopped her from answering the phone the first couple of times. It had just kept on ringing, of course, because the message it was trying to convey had nothing to do with the actual phone.

She sat on the edge of the motel room's bed, on a cheap comforter that also hadn't been laundered since before she was born, and rested her head in her hands.

It wasn't going to go away. The phone wasn't going to

stop ringing, not unless she gathered up its mortal remains, slipped out of the room, and dumped it in the
swimming pool, or somewhere else out of earshot. And
what would happen then? Either something else would
start up, or maybe, finally, it would stop and leave her in
peace—and she would go on, ignoring the message.

Because it *was* a message, no different from the usual
stream of cryptic quasi-hallucinations that plagued her.
They usually needed quite a bit of interpreting, but she
thought this one was straightforward enough to figure
out.

They were going to come looking for her. Probably
already had. That meant she'd have to face them again,
face Anna's anger and Nail's quiet rage. She'd let them
down—and worse.

*I killed Tommy. Like I shot him myself. For four hun-
dred thousand dollars I'll never see.*

She'd replayed that night so many times she felt as
though she were living in a mental loop of the night's
events. Tommy's charred eye sockets at the beginning of
the evening, the mad run toward the ritual, her encounter
with the guy who'd stabbed her. Little more than a scratch,
really, but enough to separate her from Tommy when he'd
needed her. Tommy had run, and she'd been writhing on
the ground, kicking and fighting, when something had
rushed past her, something vague and terrible. Her at-
tacker had frozen, and she'd had this intense, paranoid
sensation of being the center of some vast, hateful entity's
curiosity. Then the moment had passed and she'd scrambled free. After that, escape and recriminations.

Of course they'd come looking for her. Anna would,
anyway, and once Anna got fixated on something, it
would take the jaws of life to get her to let it go. She'd
run down the taxi companies, find out which drivers
were dispatched in the area earlier tonight, and call
them, one after another, until she found the motel.

Karyn picked up her bag.

Twenty-six bucks. Karyn thumbed through the bills again
and verified that they were all that remained of her cash

reserves. *Probably shouldn't have stopped here,* she thought as she pushed a half-burned French fry around on the plate. *But a girl's gotta eat.* That, and she felt pushed around today, shoved from one place to the next by sinister shapes lurking just at the edge of her vision. Everywhere she went, there was an obvious way to go, an obvious path to avoid. The effect was tearing apart her nerves.

She looked around the diner. From her seat in the corner, she could see the rest of the occupants, the people walking by the big glass window in front, and the door. No surprises, then. Not yet. Behind the counter, plates clattered and a beat-up radio played some ghastly Rod Stewart song.

She put her wallet back in her pocket. Twenty-six bucks. She'd left the motel at four in the morning with every intention of getting out of town, but somehow that hadn't happened. Instead she spent most of her cash on another room, and she'd only managed to wander since then. Besides the gentle, indefinable nudging from the visions, there wasn't far you could get on twenty-six bucks, and once you got there, there wasn't much you could do. And that was the crux of the problem right there, wasn't it? What to do . . .

At the next table over, a cell phone rang, "Für Elise" playing in tinny digitized tones that made Karyn's fillings buzz. The phone's owner ignored it, but he gave Karyn a tight, distracted grin when she looked at him. Then he went back to staring at his plate. The phone kept ringing. At adjacent tables, conversations went on uninterrupted.

Karyn ran through the short list of people who might help her. There was Benny, if she could find him. Crystal and Deke, maybe. If they didn't feel like shooting her instead. There was—

Another phone went off, this one a few tables away. It offered a shrill, out-of-time counterpoint to the nasal Beethoven still coming from the first one.

A woman walked by the front window—thin, rangy, with chin-length dark hair and a faded jean jacket. Anna. Karyn hunkered down in her seat, dropped her head forward, and covered her face. *I can't deal with this. I don't have to deal with this. Why now?* She peeked out between her fingers.

It wasn't Anna at all. Didn't look remotely like her, in fact, other than the jacket. This woman's hair was a stringy blond, her build not as spare.

A third phone started ringing, then a fourth, then several more joined in. It was becoming impossible to hear the voices over the din, yet nobody else seemed bothered.

Karyn closed her eyes and concentrated on slowing down her breathing. Sometimes that helped. *When's the last time I took my medicine?* She ran back the calendar in her head. What was today? Saturday? Hadn't she taken the last of the stuff just the day before yesterday? Could it already be this bad?

No wonder she had somehow failed to leave town. In the back of her mind, the sensible part of her had insisted she keep close to her supplier. Still, that wasn't going to do her any good with twenty-six bucks to her name, less the cost of breakfast. She'd be making snowmen in Hell before Adelaide would spot her on credit.

Another deep breath. The nagging ringtones diminished in volume, though there was something odd about the sound that didn't reassure her at all. The sounds became muffled, swallowed, rather than simply switching off or decreasing in volume.

Karyn opened her eyes.

The whole left side of the room had plunged into sucking darkness. The wall on that side was gone, with only blackness in its place, and the blackness exuded darkness and shadow into the room. Close to it, people became vague and indistinct, turning into shadows themselves.

In the darkness, something writhed.

Panic threatened to close up Karyn's throat, to make her heart squeeze into a bloody fist. *This isn't really happening,* she reminded herself. *It's a warning of some kind, that's all.*

The darkness moved forward, swallowing another table. The ringing sounds from over there diminished as the people seated at the table disappeared into the shadow. A woman turned and cast Karyn a look of hatred so severe it made her flinch before the woman faded away.

The back wall of the diner, the one behind Karyn, sank into blackness. She clutched the edge of the table until her knuckles whitened and her fingers ached.

This isn't happening. This is not happening.

Something—a tentacle, or the wet hand of a rotting cadaver—reached out of the blackness and touched her ankle.

It was too much. Karyn screamed. The shades in the diner leered. She launched herself from her seat, upending the small table. Glass shattered and cutlery flew, and she felt a faint twinge from the shallow cut in her calf, but she ignored it all as she fled for the door.

Shouting and noise came from behind her as she flung the door open and ran out onto the sidewalk. She barely stopped herself before she ran into the street. A quick, panicked look around showed her cars speeding past, people shuffling along in the lunch rush, a cop checking the parking meters. Almost normal, except for the way the radios screamed from the cars as they rolled by, except for the way the inside of the diner had become a black cloud inside the window, like a fish tank full of ink.

A bell jingled, and the door to the diner swung open. Karyn screamed again. Passersby turned to look at her. The women were all Anna, the men all Tommy. He wore the shirt he died in, bloody hole and all.

She turned to run and collided with a man on the sidewalk. He fell back, an irate expression on his face — and she recognized him. It was Drew, the former cult member they'd put on a bus for Seattle.

That's not really him.

He stepped toward her, and Karyn shrank against a parking meter as he approached.

"Hey," he said, "are you OK?"

Nail walked by, flecked in blood from head to toe. Karyn tried not to stare. "Do I look OK?"

He paused, a wry grin on his face. "I've seen okayer."

"Sorry," she said. "I—I get distracted sometimes." *Who the hell is this?* She wished the Drew mask would disappear and she could figure out if this was somebody she should be afraid of, or a genuinely concerned passerby who ought to just move on.

"I got that. The distraction thing, I mean. Are you OK? I mean, do you need some help?"

She didn't know how to answer. Behind the man, the black cloud roiled and boiled inside the diner. It was starting to seep out through the cracks around the door, and her eyes were drawn back to it again and again. She feared that it would burst forth when the next person opened the door. Everybody on the street wore the face of somebody she knew, and the cars racing past blasted radios that screamed at her in a foul, loathsome language she couldn't understand. This was as bad as she'd let it get in years, so, no, she wasn't OK. But who could help her?

Besides Adelaide.

"That's sweet, but—" A woman—another Anna, of course—reached for the door to the diner, and Karyn cut off the thought. She wanted to shout, to lunge forward, slip past Drew, and tackle the woman before she could unleash whatever was behind Door Number One. *But there's nothing there. Nothing. It's all in my head.* Except ... maybe the door was a helpful symbol, and maybe the thing *would* come boiling out and swirl around the Anna-faced woman to engulf Karyn and tear her mind apart. It wasn't real for anyone else, but it might be real enough to her.

The door opened, and a black tide, like an oil gusher bubbling up from Hell, flooded out.

Karyn ran. No pause to think or consider—just pure reaction poured out through her heels.

A screech of tires ripped the air, followed by the hollow *pop* of metal banging together, and Karyn's hip caromed off a car that had barely stopped in time to keep from turning her into a wet smear on the road. She spun, cast a quick look over her shoulder, and kept running. Somebody swore. She didn't care. She hit the sidewalk on the other side of the street and kept going.

Ten steps and she stumbled over an Anna in bag lady drag, hauling a rusted red wagon. Four more and she bounced off a Tommy, blood on his hands up to the elbows, then a Genevieve. She stumbled, pitched forward, and fell to the sidewalk, erasing the skin from her palms—but she caught herself before her face hit.

"Jesus, are you OK?"

She pushed herself to a sitting position and winced as her raw hands scraped the sidewalk. It was Drew. Behind him, no black tide, no Annas or Nails. No Tommys. Something seethed at the mouth of an alley a block or so back, and she shuddered, but it really wasn't so bad.

"You asked me that before," she said, her voice shaking alarmingly. "It depends what you mean by OK."

"It was a stupid question both times. Let's get you to a doctor."

Karyn started to her feet. Drew took her arm and helped pull her up. "I'll be fine."

"Pull the other one."

"Huh?"

"Leg. Pull the other leg."

"Oh. Right." She looked distractedly past him, to the alley, and fought the urge to look behind her again.

Drew sighed. "I don't mean to be a pain, but I'd feel like a complete asshole if I just left you here. You obviously need some kind of help. A doctor, probably. And, you know—you helped me out before, so it must be my turn."

Karyn's shoulders pulled inward, tense, as though she expected something to attack her from behind. She tried to make them relax, but they weren't having any of it. This whole scene was a nightmare, and it was probably going to get a lot worse before it got better—if it ever did get better. It had been years since she'd tried to do this at all, let alone cold turkey.

"Your turn?"

"Um, yeah. Maybe you remember—bad scene at the garage? Guns, fire, all that shit?"

"You're Drew?"

He glanced around them. "You know, I was OK with

the freaking out, but now you're really starting to make me nervous."

"We put you on a bus."

"You put me at a bus station." He shrugged. "I couldn't go. I don't know anywhere else. Tina's my only family, and she's here."

"You're crazy."

"*I'm* crazy?" He twisted his face in a worried, confused half smile. "Look, we need to get you some help."

Her normal inclination would have been to tell him where he could stick his help, but this was out of control and getting worse. "OK," she said, surprising herself a little.

"OK what?"

"OK. Take me to get help."

"Oh." Drew frowned, like he was trying to figure out for the first time exactly what that would entail. "You want to follow me in your car, or what?"

"I don't drive."

He nodded, but, thankfully, didn't offer any commentary. It didn't take much imagination to guess that anybody who screamed at phantoms and ran out into the middle of a busy street for no apparent reason probably shouldn't get behind the wheel of an automobile.

"Well, uh . . ."

"You have a car?"

"Yeah."

"Great. There's somewhere you can take me."

Chapter 15

Anna smoothed out her jacket and tried to slow her breathing. She'd spent all night trying to track down Karyn, with no luck, and finally she'd taken a break. There was other shit that needed doing, even if she couldn't really concentrate on it. She'd made a couple of phone calls, and she'd been invited to come to Sobell's club downtown that evening. It was the kind of club that didn't have a sign out front or flashy lights or even a name, the kind of place you went only when invited—and, if you were smart, you did your best most times not to get invited at all.

Anna had heard all the stories. Sobell practiced black magic here. A virgin was sacrificed once a month. Nightly orgies were the rule, and the mayor showed up every week to indulge in a kink that, depending on which rumor you believed, fell somewhere between mildly bizarre and downright unholy. Anna's idea of a good time was a can of Bud and a roomful of slightly drunk, happy, chattering people—sex parties and blood rituals were, generally speaking, right out.

Yet here she stood. That was the trouble with being the woman who knows somebody who knows somebody. Sometimes the final somebody at the end of the trail of somebodies wanted to meet in person.

The club took up the top two floors of an office building—an outrageous use of prime office space, but Enoch Sobell could do what he pleased. It had a spectacular view of the city, and, as a bonus, the business district was pretty empty at this time of night. Anna supposed that counted as additional privacy for Sobell's guests.

She met a security guard at the loading dock near the building's back entrance. The guy checked her ID against a list, mumbled a few words into a headset, and opened the door.

"Straight back. Take the elevator to forty-eight." He didn't frisk her or anything. Rather than take comfort in that, Anna found it unsettling. The guy probably *knew* she was unarmed, whether through a hidden X-ray scanner in the doorframe or through more occult means. Or maybe he was just relying on Anna's reputation for not being crazy or stupid.

The door clicked shut behind her, and she swallowed thickly. Panic threatened to break loose, and she was suddenly convinced that the door was locked. She pushed the bar and it opened.

The security guard looked at her, annoyed. "What?"

"Uh, is there a bathroom?"

The guy shook his head in the universal *you sad asshole* gesture. "Upstairs. Forty-eighth floor."

"Thanks." Anna let the door shut again. The only light in here came from the white-and-red exit sign hanging above the door and the glowing green buttons of the elevator controls ahead. She fiddled with her jacket again, then crossed the short hall and hit the UP button.

The elevator doors slid open immediately, letting out a flood of low red light. Anna guessed that the inside of the car was originally supposed to be some kind of chic ultracontemporary design, all mirrors and chrome, but the red light edging the top and bottom bathed it in a sick, bloody radiance that turned her stomach. All the reflective surfaces just made it worse.

She got in and pushed the button for forty-eight. The elevator rocketed upward fast enough to upset her already queasy stomach, and she wondered for a moment if she would throw up. *That would look fucking great. Step out into Enoch Sobell's private club with puke on my shirt. Maybe they'd shoot me for lowering the tone.*

Perversely, the thought helped her get control of herself. By the time the car started to slow, she was standing straight and she felt almost steady again. Still, she wished Karyn were there to tell her what to expect, let her know that everything was going to be all right.

Except it's not.

The doors opened.

Anna's heart rate shot up, and she could feel the pounding in her chest, but when she looked out, the only shocking thing was how normal everything seemed. Expensive, yes, but normal. The whole floor was open, affording a nice view of the city from anywhere in the single huge room. White marble covered the floor, and tables so black they looked like holes dotted the space. A round bar area occupied a space just off the room's center.

There was nobody in the whole place.

She stepped out of the elevator and scanned the room again. With nobody in evidence, she decided to head toward the bar and wait. Maybe somebody would come around and get her. *Yeah, and take me up to the forty-ninth floor, where all the black magic and sacrificing takes place.*

The bar was empty, too, so she sat on a stool and spun to look out at the city. No sound disturbed the silence, and after a few minutes alone Anna felt her mind returning to its well-worn track. Where the hell was Karyn? Was she OK? With every passing hour, Anna's anxiety worsened, and the likelihood that Karyn had gotten herself in real trouble increased.

She's not a child, Anna reminded herself. But Anna'd been looking out for her for so long, it was hard to imagine how Karyn would get by alone.

Her thoughts were interrupted by the sound of hard soles clicking on marble. She turned. The lights were low, but the big man in the expensive suit was hard to mistake.

Greaser came over to the bar. He didn't sit.

"Drink?" he asked.

Anna dredged up a halfhearted smile. "I'm on the clock."

Greaser nodded. "Mr. Sobell's used to getting what he wants," he said abruptly, leaving the subject of drinks to die in the dirt. "The way he wants it."

"That's what I'm here about."

"I hired you because you have—had—a reputation for being discreet."

That drink sounded better by the second. "This job was an exception," she admitted. "But we got it done."

Greaser put his hands in his pants pockets and stared down at Anna. "Who do you think recommended you clowns to Mr. Sobell? What idiot put his own reputation on the line getting you this rather lucrative job?"

Anna groaned.

"That's right. You made me look like a fuckup. I probably don't need to tell you how much I hate looking like a fuckup."

"No."

More silence. Greaser's face loomed like a planet, blocking out most of Anna's vision. Sweat trickled down her sides.

"So," Greaser said. "You have it now?"

"Not on me."

A muscle bunched in Greaser's jaw. "No shit. But you do have it."

"Yes."

Greaser got right in Anna's face. The smell coming off him was like hot breath blowing from the den of a waking predator. "You'd better not be fucking with me."

"No."

"Here's the deal, then. Mr. Sobell wants to talk to you. If you're lucky and very good, he'll agree to pay you the original price. What you do with the money after it changes hands is up to you."

"Um, OK."

"You're going to give half of it to me. We'll call it reparations for making me look like a fuckup."

There it was—the sucker punch. Anna sucked in a breath. The others were going to be pissed. But what else could she do?

"OK," she said. And a million dollars evaporated.

"Great. Glad we got that straightened out. Let's go see the boss."

They took the stairs, a set of spiraling black risers that was nearly invisible against the backdrop of the city. The antechamber at the top was a square room paneled in strips of ebony that had been polished to a deep luster. Despite the high ceilings and the room's overall size, the blackness seemed to push in on Anna. She didn't feel any better when she noticed that the ebony had been carved with thousands of symbols—floor, walls, and ceilings— until the room looked like an oversize version of one of Tommy's boxes. She felt a pang, and she wished Tommy were here to explain what the hell all this meant. It could have been anything, she figured, from some kind of awful curse to a glorified burglar alarm to nothing more than a rich man's eccentricities, no more potent than the writing on the side of a cereal box.

Greaser took her through a pair of oversize double doors—twelve feet, if an inch, and yet Anna still felt the urge to duck her head.

The next room surprised her. It was almost a normal office, albeit a large one. Soft white carpet covered the floor, and the walls were lined with a warm, reddish-brown wood. Mahogany, maybe. The only odd note was a series of alcoves along the walls, each with a pedestal on which some strange object had been placed. Anna didn't look too closely, but she saw a heavy, leather-bound book, a chunk of carved stone that looked vaguely Mayan in origin, a dented helm from the Middle Ages, and more. As she walked through the room, she also noticed a total lack of windows.

Toward the far end of the room sat a wooden desk.

Behind the desk sat Enoch Sobell.

Sobell rose as Anna and Greaser approached, extending a hand in greeting. He was a tall, sturdy man with a politician's ersatz smile and hooded black eyes. His dark hair was dusted with silver at the temples. He could have been the CEO of a big company—and was, actually— but he had another vibe entirely, cold and hungry like a snake in a human suit.

Anna took his hand, thinking half-coherently, *This man is the Devil.*

"Please sit, Ms. Ruiz," Sobell said.

Come into my parlor, Anna thought, but she sat.

"I don't meet most of my contractors personally," Sobell began. "I hope you understand the importance I put on this meeting."

Anna thought of the few times she'd been deposed. There was a certain approach to making it through the minefield of a deposition intact, and the biggest rule was *Don't volunteer anything.* If a question was asked, you answered it—and no more. Offering more information than asked for was a good way to get your ass in a sling, often producing whole ugly lines of questioning that never would have come up if you'd just kept your mouth shut. Enoch Sobell was no lawyer, but this seemed like a good time to stick to depo rules anyway.

"Yes, sir," Anna said.

"I hired you to do a straightforward job. Difficult, yes, but not complicated." Anna thought that was bullshit—there'd been nothing straightforward about it—but now did not seem like the time to correct him. Sobell continued. "I also hired you because you have—had—a reputation for discretion." Greaser's words, almost exactly. Not hard to see where he got them from. Sobell's face creased in a slight frown, and he steepled his fingers together in front of him. A heavy ring with an overlarge green stone flashed on his right hand. "Eight dead in a gunfight in the home of one of the city's more prominent citizens does not constitute discretion where I come from."

What the fuck? She didn't remember Mendelsohn's any too clearly, but she would have remembered a firefight. Had Nail accidentally shot half a dozen people? That didn't sound like something he would have screwed up, and no way would he have done it on purpose. And none of the rest of them had been carrying firearms.

"I don't understand," she said. "We didn't kill anybody."

"The papers say eight bodies were found."

She remembered the remains found near Mendelsohn's corpse. Genevieve's monster had gotten Mendelsohn, and maybe somebody else. But surely not that many, unless others had been in the house when it broke loose. "Shot?"

Sobell shrugged. "Our fair city's redoubtable news rags didn't say. They just said eight dead."

"Make it nine," Anna said. The words escaped on their own before she could do anything to stop them. *So much for depo rules.* "We lost one of our own."

Sobell stared at her, waiting.

Anna looked down. Again, the room seemed to crowd in on her, so close it seemed her chest couldn't expand to draw in air. It didn't make sense. A room this large should have felt more like an auditorium than a closet. *Why aren't there any windows in here?* "No," she said finally. Regardless of the body count, the whole thing had been loud and frightening. "We weren't all that discreet."

"The only reason the investigation hasn't branched out into a number of unpalatable directions is that, according to my contacts, they found Nathaniel Mendelsohn's body dismembered and stuffed into a number of plastic filing bins in his office closet."

"What? He's—what?" Hadn't Mendelsohn been pureed and poured all over the floor of his own house by the fucking monster from the basement?

"Apparently, the remains had been decomposing there for some number of weeks, during which time a fellow referred to as the Revered One has been running things. Understandably, the authorities suspect some kind of cult infighting gone out of control. Hopefully they continue to suspect that, in which case this should all blow over nicely."

"Um, good."

He put his hands on the desk in front of him and wove his fingers together. "I'm not prone to making threats, Ms. Ruiz. But I do hope you understand that I'm a somewhat public figure. I can't afford to be tied to any criminal activities."

Translation: I'm going to kill you and your friends if you publicly link me to this clusterfuck. "I understand."

"So. You called me. I assume you have news."

Anna pulled in a long breath against the strange pressure of her claustrophobia. "Yes, sir. We've got the item."

"The jawbone."

It was all Anna could do not to cast a furtive look around the place—she'd long since gotten in the habit of never mentioning swag by name. "Yes, sir." She swallowed. "We'd like to finish the deal."

Sobell didn't smile, but something in his eyes lit up. To Anna, he might as well have been licking his lips.

"Terms?"

"Original terms," Anna said. Then, before she could stop her mouth, "We just want this to be done." *Oops. That was some shitty negotiation.*

Sobell gave her a long, considering look that seemed to peel her flesh off in strips. Anna could feel the negotiation slipping out from under her, the price dropping by the second. She had a moment to wonder if Greaser was going to take a million regardless, or if his fuckup restitution fee was going to stay at half.

"Done," Sobell said. Anna could hardly believe it. "Work out the exchange with Mr. Gresser."

"Yes, sir."

Chapter 16

"We're not gonna find a doctor down here," Drew said. "Even the guys working the homeless clinic won't come down here."

Karyn couldn't argue with that. Tenement buildings loomed over the street, most of their lower windows covered in sheets of graffiti-tagged plywood, and the potholes in the road yawned like bomb craters. The idle, the unemployed, and the unemployable stood around everywhere, smoked cigarettes on every stoop.

"Nope," Karyn said.

"But you're not looking for a doctor, are you?"

A ball rolled out into the street, and a couple of kids ran after it without even checking for traffic. Drew braked with a jolt. "Are you?" he asked again.

"Not exactly."

"Shit. What are you hooked on?" The kids gave him the finger and cleared out, but he didn't move the car forward.

"You want to get going," Karyn said. "You stay still long enough here, somebody'll start stealing parts off your car with you in it."

"Very funny," he said, but he pressed the gas. The car rolled forward at a cautious twenty miles per hour. Drew took his gaze from the road long enough to look at her. She didn't look back. "I get it—the screaming, the shakes. My sister tried to get off the horse cold turkey once, and it didn't look too different."

"I'm not a junkie."

"Well, it isn't your fucking *doctor* that lives down here in the DMZ," Drew said, the note of anger hard and surprising in his voice.

"Depends what you mean by 'doctor.'"

"There's a clinic I know—methadone. I think you can get state help for the fees."

"Maybe you didn't hear me right. *I'm not a junkie.*"

Again, Drew stopped the car. This time, he turned to face Karyn. "Then what *are* we doing here? Tell me we're not here to meet your connection."

"What's it to you?"

"That horse my sister was trying to get off? What do you think pulled her into that stupid fucking cult? Nothing cleans a person up like getting religion." Karyn heard his teeth grind together. Then he spoke again, quietly. "I followed her right in. I'm trying to help, for God's sake, not deliver you to the butcher."

"It's not like that," Karyn said. "Really."

"Then what's it like?"

For one crazy moment, she thought about explaining. *But when has that ever ended well?* Instead, she grabbed the door handle. "It's all right. I'll walk from here." She pushed the door open.

"Whoa!" Drew's hand shot out and grabbed her wrist. "Are you insane? Skinny white girl down here alone? They'll *eat* you before the end of the block."

"Nobody's going to eat me," she said, though she could see things moving in an alley off the other side of the road, and she wondered if that was really true. She didn't get out of the car.

"Come on. Close the door, and I'll get you out of here."

She sat back, but she didn't close the door. She measured Drew with a long, searching look, and finally decided—*What the hell?*

"OK," she said, "I'll be straight with you. I do need to meet my hookup."

Drew opened his mouth, so she continued before he

could stick his foot in it. "But it's not heroin. Really. I've got a . . . condition."

"A condition."

"Yeah. I can keep it under control, but I need a very special, very expensive kind of medicine."

"The kind you won't find in the pharmacy," Drew said.

"That's true, but it's not what you're thinking. There's nothing illegal or dangerous about it. It's just rare and expensive."

"And peddled out of a crack house."

Karyn shrugged. "If you like." She closed the door. "Can we go?"

Drew didn't answer, but he took his foot off the brake, and the car started rolling. "What condition?"

"I don't want to talk about it."

Drew nodded and guided the car around a chasm in the pavement. Karyn saw lines of tension on his face, tightness around the eyes and lips.

"Turn right ahead."

Drew steered the car onto a side street that was, if possible, in even worse repair than the street they'd been on. If Karyn hadn't spent so much time down here, it would have been hard for her to believe this was America, not some bombed-out Eastern European relic of World War Two. Here the idlers were gone for the most part. Only the most desperate of squatters lived in the condemned buildings in this part of town—and the odd person who was so determined to have solitude in the middle of this city that they were willing to live somewhere nobody else would come.

She felt a surprising surge of warmth toward this stranger who'd picked her up and helped her when everything else had turned to shit, and, without really thinking about it, she said, "I hallucinate the future."

"Huh?"

"That's my condition. I hallucinate the future."

She imagined she could see Drew's skin crawling, a wave of goose bumps traveling up his body. Almost everybody had one of two reactions to her "condition"—

outright disbelief, which wasn't so bad, or a bad case of the creeps. Sometimes it passed.

"That's an odd way to put it," Drew said.

"It's the truth. I don't *see* the future, not in any way that makes sense. I get images overlaid on top of images, all smashed in with the regular world. I can't tell any of it apart, except that most of the hallucinations don't make any sense. Even the stuff that does usually needs a lot of interpretation."

Drew grinned. "How come you don't make a killing at the stock market?"

"It's that interpretation bit," Karyn said. "It's a bear. Plus, it's not like I get to know what I want to know about—I just get what I'm given."

"And the medication? Is that for real?"

"Oh, yeah." She watched a stray cat batting at a piece of litter before answering. "My condition gets . . . pretty bad if I don't keep it suppressed."

"The screaming and running into traffic."

"The future's an ugly place." *So's the past.* "Pull over here."

Drew made a face. "Why the hell would somebody dealing in crazy expensive 'medication' live in a crack house?"

"You think my condition's bad, wait till you meet Adelaide."

Drew grimaced as he guided the car over to the side of the road. "Great." He parked two feet away from the curb, but Karyn didn't feel like now was a good time to criticize his parking skills.

"This won't take long," she told him. "You can wait here, if you want."

He looked up and down the street. Nothing moved but the stray cat they'd passed earlier. "There's nobody here. At all. The whole street."

"Adelaide likes her privacy."

"It gives me the creeps. I'm staying with you."

"Up to you."

Karyn got out. Drew turned off the car and followed, his footfalls loud in the empty street.

At the front door of the apartment building, Karyn hesitated. She always met Adelaide here, but she'd never gotten comfortable with it, and it looked like the door had taken a close-range shotgun blast since her last visit. There was a hole clean through it, shreds of veneer surrounding the hole like long teeth. Adelaide wouldn't bother to fix it, Karyn knew. A working front door was the least of her concerns, if she even noticed at all.

Karyn pushed open the door. It swung inward with the slightest touch, hitting the wall and hanging askew on one hinge. A rank, wet smell — mildew and rot and stagnant standing water — belched from the inside of the building.

Drew coughed and covered his mouth. "Ugh. Is she, uh, dangerous?"

Karyn stopped at the threshold. "Very. Whatever you do, don't look directly at her. You'll turn to stone."

"You're joking," Drew said, his eyes wide.

"Yes, actually." Karyn smiled. "Just be polite, and don't talk unless she asks you something. It'll be fine."

She went inside, wrinkling her nose at the smell and shaking her head in astonishment at the ruin. No matter how many times she came here, it was impossible to get used to. Nobody had lived in this building for years, obviously — other than Adelaide. The sheetrock had rotted and fallen off the walls in most places, landing in moldering piles and leaving the skeletal framework of the building exposed and rusting. Grime streaked the floor. Holes gaped in the ceiling like infected wounds.

Karyn made her way down the hall and turned at the end. She pulled open another door, this one heavy and metal.

"The stairwell?" Drew asked, his voice high and anxious. "You sure these stairs will support us?"

"Don't worry. We're not going up."

"That's not better."

She was inclined to agree, but she said nothing as she headed down the stairs. Her calf complained at each step, and her hip joined in as well, angry from her encounter with the car outside the diner. They loosened up as she moved, but she still had the impression she was more hobbling than walking.

The stench worsened during her descent, and it soon became obvious why. Brackish black water covered the floor, coming halfway up the bottom step. Oily rainbows swam on the surface amid floating black lumps and rotting detritus.

Karyn reached the bottom and stepped right in. The water filled her shoe. Her stomach made a noise of complaint.

Ahead of her was a doorway, and beyond that was darkness, lit only by shafts of sickly light coming through the dingy panes of the basement windows.

"Oh, nasty. It's *warm*," Drew said as he stepped into the water behind her.

"Shh."

"You're not going to lure me down here and kill me, are you?" he asked in a whisper.

"Nah. I only do bag ladies."

A pause. Drew's shadow on the bright patch of water ahead of her stopped moving.

"Joking," she said.

"I must be nuts," he said, but he started moving again.

Something pale shifted, flashed in the water ahead of her, and was gone. *Was that actually there?* she wondered. The water wasn't deep enough to harbor much of anything beyond a few frogs and the odd billion or so mosquito larvae, or at least she didn't think so. But if it wasn't really there, what was the message? What was it trying to tell her?

There's a game with no end. Keep walking. Warm water sloshed around her ankles as she moved forward. She could see a room ahead, sun filtering down through the filthy windows and offering a little light, but she knew Adelaide wouldn't be there.

She turned to the right and kept moving. After a dozen steps, only the vaguest of light and dark shapes suggested walls and openings. Karyn held her hands out in front of her to avoid running into anything.

A hand dropped onto her shoulder, and she whirled around.

"Don't want to get separated," Drew said softly.

"No." She'd been here dozens of times over the years, but she still felt glad of Drew's presence. She usually hadn't come alone before, either.

That thought triggered an unwelcome swarm of associations. *Not now.*

Her right hand hit a wall, slid across a slimy surface. She stepped left and through a doorway, wincing as damp spiderwebs trailed over her skin. Not for the first time, she thought she'd scream if a spider ran across her face. This time, that didn't happen.

Behind her, Drew ran into the doorframe and swore.

Ahead and somewhat to the right, a faint flickering lit up the dank basement. It was slight, an orange wash over indistinct humps and walls, but the darkness had been so complete before that it seemed almost as good as huge floodlights. Karyn wasn't sure she wanted to see her surroundings any more clearly than this, anyway.

She walked to where a section of the ceiling had fallen in, leaving a space barely high enough for her to get through without crawling. The light came from beyond. She crouched and shuffled through.

On the other side, a pile of rubble pushed its way up out of the water, providing dry if rocky ground for a space about the size of a big living room. A handful of candles on makeshift stands—a sheared-off girder, an upended cinder block, a stack of swollen and rotting paperbacks— illuminated the room.

In the far corner, a mass of rags undulated.

Karyn stepped out of the water and onto the little island of rubble.

"Go away," a voice said. It shook and cracked, surely coming from a throat at least a thousand years old.

"It's me. Karyn."

"Adelaide knows. But her head hurts so bad. It's full of lizards today, spiders and lizards. Come back tomorrow."

Drew leaned toward Karyn. "She talks about herself in third person?"

"Shh." Karyn took another step forward. The rags shifted. "I need your help."

"Always. You always need Adelaide's help. What do you ever do for her? What do you ever give Adelaide, to ease her conscience for helping you kill your gift?"

"Twenty thousand dollars, last time."

"Twen—" Drew began, and Karyn elbowed him.

"Gone now. Adelaide used it, used it all. Adelaide gave it to the spiders. The spiders and rats. What will you give her this time?"

Karyn crossed her arms, huddling into herself. "I—I don't have anything this time. I just need help." The words sounded pathetic, and she hated them.

The mound of rags erupted, fragments flying every-where—only they weren't rags, and they weren't frag-ments. They were rats, hundreds of them, from lean gray gutter rats to sleek fat albino pets, red eyes shining in the candlelight, and everything in between. They ran in all directions.

Karyn heard the splash as Drew stepped backward into the water.

From the center of the pile of rats, a woman stood. She wore a simple shift, surprisingly white in this dank underworld, and her thin arms poked out like sticks. Her ancient voice must have been a lie or the result of dam-age—Karyn had never figured out which—for her skin was unlined, her eyes clear, and her body moved with a fluid grace.

Karyn had a couple of inches on her, but she shrank back anyway as Adelaide approached.

"Nothing?" The voice was jarring coming from a woman who surely couldn't be thirty yet. "You have nothing for Adelaide? You come *here* with *nothing*?"

"I don't have anything," Karyn said.

"Adelaide isn't a charity."

"Please. I need help."

Adelaide cocked her head as though looking at a par-ticularly curious specimen of insect. Eyes opened and closed all along her forehead, down her cheeks, in her shoulders and chest. *That's* definitely *not real,* Karyn thought, though the effect was no less unsettling. It got worse when mouths started opening beside them.

"I'll owe you," Karyn said.

"Oh, fuck," Drew said, and he reached out a hand to her arm. "Don't—"

She brushed him away. "I need this."

Adelaide's mouths gaped and tittered. Her eyes—her real eyes, the normal two—stared past Karyn, unblinking. "You'll owe Adelaide. A favor?"

"Yeah. Sure."

"One favor for blind."

"Yes."

"Done." She put her hand out, a surprisingly normal gesture in this shadowed otherworld.

Karyn shook it.

"What does somebody like that need with cash? Let alone twenty Gs?" Drew sat on the rubble, leaning against the wall and tapping his hands on his knees. He hadn't stopped the twitchy jitter-and-jive since Adelaide had left an hour or so before.

"I don't know. I'm not sure I want to," Karyn said. She couldn't fault Drew for nerves—she felt more than a twinge of anxiety herself. Adelaide had claimed she didn't have any blind, but that she could get the materials together in short order. *Stay,* she'd said. *You stay and wait for Adelaide, and she will help you.*

That hadn't been that long ago, really, but it felt like forever, and Karyn had developed a sour feeling in her stomach.

The rats made her nervous, for one thing. She looked around the small space, and the shiny black beads of rats' eyes stared back from everywhere. They gnawed on invisible morsels held in their creepy little paws, scuttled along corners, and crouched on ledges and shelves. A few lurked half submerged in the water like crocodiles awaiting prey. Karyn had never seen rats act that way before, and she found it deeply disturbing. If that weren't enough, the hallucinations were coming back. Twice she'd seen—or imagined, whichever was more technically correct here—something large and vague prowling among the rats, there for a fraction of a second in her peripheral vision, then gone. The ceiling had started to leak blood.

She watched Drew carefully for his reactions. In Adelaide's strange place, Karyn was even less sure than usual what was real or not, so she trusted her own perceptions very little. Drew hadn't so much as flinched when blood started dripping onto his pant leg, so Karyn thought it was safe to assume that was in her head.

"Hey," she asked, a worrisome thought having occurred to her, "do you see a bunch of rats?"

"I've never seen so many fucking rats in my whole life."

"Ah. Good."

Drew shifted, hefting a piece of brick in his hand. He appeared to weigh the idea of tossing it at one of the rats, then came to his senses before Karyn had to stop him. "How do you know that, um, person anyway?"

"A friend of mine introduced us." Anna. God, that had been—how long ago? Ten years, at least. Adelaide had been a waiflike teenager at the time, though knowledgeable beyond her years. Karyn had found her frightening even then.

"Some friend."

"What's your problem?" Karyn snapped. The image of Anna kneeling in blood and dirt sprang immediately into her mind. *You don't think maybe you coulda cracked open the future and looked around for this?* Anna had said, and she'd been right.

"Look around, lady. This is some crazy shit you've gotten yourself into. How did this ever seem like a good idea?"

"I didn't ask you to come with me."

"I know."

"So, what *is* your problem?" she asked, gently this time.

"I must be nuts." He put the brick down and rested

his head back against the wall. "Hell, I don't know. Sucker for a damsel in distress, I guess."

"Don't give me that crap."

Drew frowned. "Look, I was just trying to help. Really. Doing my good deed for the week." He paused, rolled the brick away with his hand. "Christ knows I've got some things to make up for."

Part of Karyn wanted to go over and kick the hell out of him for treating her like a charity case, but the sadness in his voice was too sincere, the sentiment too close to home for her to ignore. She went over, sidestepping a couple of rats, and sat next to him. "Yeah. Me, too." She gave him a tight-lipped grin.

Something moved in her peripheral vision, and she turned her head. A man emerged from the low tunnel. Karyn could hear his back crack as he stood to his full height.

He pulled a gun from the waistband of his pants.

Karyn started, adrenaline flooding her system, then froze halfway to her feet. The guy was standing *on* the water. And, now that she looked, he didn't cast a shadow.

"Uh-oh," she said. The man pulled the trigger, but no sound came from the gun, and he disintegrated.

"What?" Drew said.

"We have to go."

"Why?"

"They're coming for us. You or me, I don't know which. Wanna stick around and find out?"

"Hell, no."

"Then come on." She reached a hand down to help Drew stand.

"Wait. What about that shit you need? How do you know you're not just seeing things?"

"Because I never *just* see things. They always mean something, even if I'm too stupid to figure it out. We need to go. *Now.*" She stepped toward the water.

Drew got up behind her. Through some malign magic, he had made a gun appear. It was a short pistol, some kind of semiautomatic. He held it like a man who had maybe fired it twice, once to see if it worked, and once by accident.

"Put that damn thing away before you hurt yourself."

"We might need it," he said, his eyes wide.

"No way." She tipped her head toward the exit. "You go first."

Drew put the gun in his waistband, then looked back at Karyn. "Yeah. All right."

He crouched, heading through the half-collapsed tunnel, and Karyn crowded close behind him. "Faster," she said. How much time did they have?

"Shit!" Drew said from ahead of her in a loud whisper. He turned around. In the light from the candles, the whites of his eyes shone wide and yellow. "I heard somebody coming down the stairs. How do we get out of here?"

Karyn pushed past him out of the tunnel and stood up straight. To the left, the doorway they'd come in through had transformed into a giant mouth, bristling with foul black teeth a foot long and dripping venom.

Karyn pointed to the right. "That way."

They ran into the next room and slipped away from the door opening. Drew started toward the window ahead of them, but Karyn grabbed his wrist and pulled him back. Glorious daylight shone through the window— but blood ran down the glass in viscous red streaks. Clots fell off and plunked in the water. Karyn remembered that the window was visible from the way they'd come in. With her luck, she'd get halfway out the window and somebody'd shoot her in the ass. *They might get me, but I'm not going out that way.*

She pointed to the left, and the two of them started moving.

"Don't splash," she whispered.

"Why'd she rat you out?" Drew asked. "I thought you knew her."

"A little louder, please. They can't follow us as well if you don't speak up." A few more steps, and they went through yet another doorway, this one in a half-rotted wall with pieces of moldering plaster crumbling off it. The doorway slanted precariously to the right. The space beyond was, Karyn thought, a veritable labyrinth, the walls of which were equally dilapidated walls of decaying two-by-fours and plaster. There wasn't shit for light, and the walls made it impossible to tell where—or if—there was a window anywhere in here.

"I don't know," Karyn said softly as they picked their way through. "I don't even know if it's you or me she ratted out. Maybe both. If I had to guess, I'd say she was pissed that I didn't bring her anything, so she went and found somebody who would. She's not my friend any more than any dealer is friends with their clients." Though she had been Karyn's supplier for going on ten years now, so something bad was up. Equally bad—maybe worse, long-term—Karyn had no idea where else to get blind.

She didn't want to think about that just then.

Dim light made its way through the standing wreckage in the room, and Karyn's heart leaped. *Finally!*

Drew sped up. Karyn took a few steps after him and froze.

"What?" he asked.

"We're about to get fucked," Karyn said. A huge shark fin stuck out of the water ahead of them. Behind, flames rained from the ceiling.

"What?"

This was Adelaide's place, and Adelaide had the same *condition* Karyn had, only a thousand times worse from years without treatment. Karyn couldn't begin to imagine what that was like. No wonder Adelaide was insane. But insane or not, she'd also had years of practice at sifting through thousands of overlapping and contradictory images, and she knew better than Karyn how to manage her gift. Adelaide would know where the exits were—and she'd know which ones Karyn would be most likely to take. She'd be waiting ahead, or somebody would, and somebody was already coming from behind.

Back the way they'd come, beyond the sheet of fire, something splashed.

"What?" Drew asked for the third time.

"Somebody's ahead. And somebody's coming from back there."

"What are we going to do?"

Karyn looked around. The light was terrible, barely enough to see the shapes of the walls, but she had an idea.

"Follow me," she said, and rather than go forward or back, she ran straight at the nearest wall.

Rotten wood cracked and moldy sheetrock exploded outward. A nail dragged a bloody line across her cheek, missing her eye by the width of a finger.

Somebody swore, and a shot rang out, sounding like a detonation in the wet basement.

"Go!" a man's voice yelled.

Karyn hit the next wall and bounced off, though she'd felt it give when she hit. Before she could make another go at it, Drew plowed into it with a lowered shoulder. There was a soggy crack, and he went through. She kicked a fragment of two-by-four out of her way and ran after him.

On the other side, light spilled down the stairway like rays from heaven.

Two gunshots punched holes in the wall near Karyn's head, and then she and Drew were charging up the stairs.

They stumbled out into the light moments later. At the curb ahead, Drew's car sat on four flat tires. A white pickup truck with an oversize cab idled right behind it. The truck hunched and growled, and a bulging white eye the size of a basketball peered out at Karyn.

"Gun," she said.

"Um . . ."

"Give me the gun, *now*." Whatever misgivings Drew had crumbled under her glare, and he handed her the gun.

Karyn hurt nearly everywhere, but she forced herself to run to the truck. The locking mechanism clicked just as she reached the door. *Gonna take more than that, buddy,* she thought, and she thumbed the pistol's safety off. The driver's-side window exploded with one shot. The guy inside held up his hands. Glass fragments peppered his hair, and his face bled from a dozen tiny cuts.

"Don't shoot!"

"Out."

A chasm opened in the road outside the guy's door, its mouth wet and sucking. Karyn flinched, but kept from stepping back. "Move!"

The guy got out, and the hole disappeared just before his foot hit the ground.

Karyn pointed with the gun. "Over there." The guy took several large steps backward in his haste to comply.

"Come on," she said, tilting her head toward Drew. "Let's get out of here." She slid into the vehicle, over the driver's seat and into the passenger's. Drew got in behind her. He didn't need to be told what to do—he put the truck in drive and hit the gas as Adelaide's building belched forth a couple of gun-waving goons.

The truck wobbled as Drew got the hang of it, but he kept control and the building receded. The guys got off a couple of shots, and Karyn ducked, but if they hit anything important she couldn't tell.

Moments later, Drew took the vehicle around a corner, cutting off any further shots.

"Don't slow down," Karyn told him.

"Where are we going?"

"Straight, for now."

"OK."

Karyn glanced back and saw no sign of pursuit. She slumped back in her seat, slouching down so her eyes were level with the dash. "Friends of yours?"

"Friends of—no!" Drew took his eyes off the road, and the vehicle swerved as he jerked to look at Karyn. "But, yeah, I think I recognized the driver. One of Mendelsohn's guys."

"Figures. If anybody would know who to sell me out to, it would be Adelaide." Karyn craned her neck, peeking over the dash. Big guys with guns crowded the sidewalk and lined the streets, and seething creatures with giant black claws and multiple yawning mouths sprawled across the street in front of her, to the sides, and behind. The subtext was not hard to figure out—nowhere was safe. Not now.

"We need to get rid of this car," she said.

"Can we get a little more distance from your friend and her new set of borrowed rent-a-thugs first?"

"Yeah. More distance would be good." Karyn peeked over the dash again, then pushed herself lower in her seat. There was nothing out there she wanted to see. "You can ditch me, you know. I won't hold it against you."

Drew made a pained face, but at least this time he kept his eye on the road. "I don't know what good it's going to do me to ditch you. At least one of those guys got a good look at me, which means they know I'm still around. I'm fucked." He considered. "I should have got out of town."

"How much money do you have?"

"Six bucks."

"So Tahiti is out."

Drew nodded, then looked down at the instrument panel. "Hell, there's only a quarter tank in this boat. Santa Monica is out."

Great. No money and no gas meant only one option, as much as Karyn disliked it. "Pull over," she said. "Let's ditch this thing, and I'll take you somewhere safe."

"That's a terrible place to keep your key," Drew said.

Karyn ignored him as she tipped the heavy potted plant up. The plant's dry stalks rustled, and a few desiccated leaves fell to the sidewalk. Under the pot was a small square cobblestone, one of many on this side of the front stoop. She flipped that over, pulled out the house key, and returned stone and plant to their previous positions.

The house was a small, one-story home sheathed in cracked vinyl siding, looking out on a tired yellow lawn. In that respect, it was no different from the other houses lining the street, though there were no abandoned plastic toys here. No one had lived here for a long time.

Karyn unlocked the door. It opened with a creak when she pulled, and a hot, musty smell wafted outward like the dry cough of a very sick person. Karyn wrinkled her nose. They'd need to open the windows if they didn't want to catch something. Or catch fire, for that matter.

Drew gave her a skeptical look, but he'd followed her this far, so she doubted he'd have a change of heart at this point. The two of them had taken the subway as far as they could, and then found a taxi. Karyn had watched the meter until they were down to the last dollar, and then she'd paid the cabbie and walked the rest of the way. Drew had complained, but not overmuch after she'd reminded him he could take his chances on his own. And anyway, the walk had given their clothes some time to dry.

Inside, the place was like she'd left it, sparsely decorated in avocado and orange Old Lady Chic. An uncomfortable green chair sat ramrod-straight in the corner, and a matching couch stretched along the left-hand wall. A person could lie on it, but the dining room table might actually be more comfortable. The TV opposite the couch was a wood-framed seventeen-inch tube that dated from the eighties. Karyn hoped it had died and gone to TV heaven by now. The Virgin Mary, robed in blue, looked down from a picture frame above it. The air in the room was dry and stale.

"So, uh, I guess you're older than you look," Drew said.

"Ha-ha. This is my great-aunt's place."

"'Is'?"

"Yeah," Karyn said. Her aunt Florence, the woman who had basically raised her, was in a home now, but she saw no reason to share that with Drew. The house stayed empty most of the time these days, except on those rare occasions when the crew used it as a safe house. It would have been a great place for Karyn to spend the last couple of days, except that it was surely one of the first places Anna had gone looking for her. Even now, Karyn felt uneasy about staying here, but if it came right down to it, she had bigger problems than Anna and nowhere else to go.

"I don't suppose that means the air-conditioning works?"

"Doubt it. Probably no electricity or phone, either." She moved to the window, unlatched it, and shoved. It opened with a squeal. The air outside was still and stagnant, offering little in the way of cooling, but maybe the heat would make its way out by osmosis or something.

Drew sat on the chair, launching a puff of dust and a trillion or so mold spores into the air. He coughed and waved his hand in front of his face. When the cloud dissipated some, he tried a few experimental bounces on the seat of the chair. "Christ. It's like somebody draped a sheet over a pile of bricks."

"Yep."

The phone—a salmon-colored rotary dial—rang with a hideous clanging of bells. Karyn jumped, but Drew only looked at her curiously. *OK. So it's not actually ringing. Good to know.*

"What now?" Drew asked.

A loud knocking came from the door, and Karyn spun. The noise ratcheted up in speed and intensity to a frenetic banging in seconds, and the door rattled in its frame.

"Please don't freak out on me," Drew said. "Everything's cool, right?"

Karyn scanned the room. The phone's shrill bell still rang, the door jumped and banged, and—what the hell?—a complete three-course dinner had materialized on the coffee table. At least there were no black clouds or shrouded tentacle creatures lurking in the corners.

"Yeah," she said, a little breathlessly. "Everything's cool, for now."

"You wanna lie down?"

"On that?" she asked, glancing at the couch. "No, thanks."

He shrugged. "So. What's next?"

She tried to concentrate through the racket. Nothing threatening, just some noise and some mystery food. So somebody was most likely looking for her again—or still—but maybe they weren't dangerous. And, if the banging at the door meant that they were coming here, well, it was most likely Anna.

She exhaled. *Don't know if I'm ready for that. But I'm running low on options—and, hey, maybe she'll bring food.* Her belly rumbled at the thought.

Drew was watching her, anxiety written all over his face. "Are you OK?" he asked.

"Don't ever ask me that again."

"Sorry."

"But, yeah. I'm OK. As for what's next, well . . . we wait."

That didn't seem to lessen his anxiety any. "For?"

"We just wait."

Chapter 17

"Any luck?" Genevieve asked.

Anna sank down in the soft brown chair in the corner, trying to fight off a sudden, intense feeling of needing to be elsewhere. She usually liked Genevieve's homey little place, but today the contrast between here and the stripped-down apartment she was used to only made her feel Karyn's disappearance that much more. She shook her head.

"You?"

"No." Genevieve sat on the arm of the chair and put a hand on Anna's shoulder.

She shifted, resting her head on Genevieve's thigh. Searching for Karyn had been a total dead end, like she'd known it would be. How do you find somebody who knows everything about what you're going to do? "I'm tired," she said. "I don't know how long I can keep this up."

"That's what happens when you don't sleep for forty-eight hours," Genevieve said, but there was no mockery in it. She rubbed her hand along Anna's neck, working at the stiff spots.

Anna groaned. "There. Right there. *Ow*, Jesus!"

"He's not here."

"Very funny." Anna lifted an arm that seemed weighted down with bricks and scrap lumber. She would have liked to stay here, pressed close against Genevieve, and relax. Talk about inconsequential shit and either drift off to sleep or get naked. She'd been staying here, sure, but there had been so little time while preparing for the job, and they'd been so exhausted at the end of each day that there hadn't been nearly enough time to just be together. To do couple stuff. Not that she really knew what that was all about, but it would have been nice to start figuring it out. But there hadn't been time then, and there wasn't now, either. "We gotta go."

"Five minutes. You'll feel better, I promise."

"I'll fall asleep, is what—*ow!*" She slapped at Genevieve's hand and sat up. "That's about enough of that."

Genevieve smiled. "Not even close."

"No, probably not. But we really gotta go."

"Yeah, yeah. All right." Genevieve got up, and Anna followed her to the table where the box lay.

"One last check, to make sure it didn't run off." Genevieve opened the box. "What the hell?" She reached for the jawbone, then pulled her hand back and wrinkled her nose. "That's gross." Her fingers had something that looked like brownish snot on them. She wiped the goo on her pants. Anna leaned across her body and inspected the bone.

"That *is* gross," she said. The thing was covered in a thin layer of slime, shot through with red veins of blood. But it hadn't been like that before, had it? No way. She remembered thinking it looked like something you'd find in the desert, yellowed and bone-dry.

She and Genevieve shared a nervous glance.

"Let's get rid of this fucking thing," Anna said.

"Amen."

"We ready?" Anna looked at her companions. Genevieve's eyes were bright and she bounced on the balls of her feet, sure signs that she was ready to roll. She cradled the box in her arms. She nodded.

Nail's face remained impassive. "Let's just get this done," he said.

Tommy would have nodded, anxious as a dog waiting for its master to come home—but he wasn't there, of course. Normally, Karyn would say the word now, something short and to the point—but she wasn't there either.

Anna batted the thoughts away. "OK. Places, everyone."

"Hey," Nail said. "You carrying?"

Anna shook her head. It had totally slipped her mind.

"Here." He held out a nickel-plated nine-millimeter, butt first. "In case."

It was as close to a touching gesture as she'd ever seen Nail make. "Thanks."

He turned to his rifle and checked it for the thousandth time.

"OK," she said. "Don't shoot me, all right?"

Nail snorted.

Anna left the room with Genevieve by her side. Down the stairs, out of the decrepit building. Across the way to the parking garage. As long as Anna kept moving, nothing could pile up on her, weigh her down. *Two days. No Karyn.* Like that.

She walked faster.

"I swear this thing's getting heavier," Genevieve said, puzzlement in her voice. "Is that possible?"

"You tell me. I don't even know what it is, really."

"That makes two of us."

Up two flights of stairs, bringing them roughly level with the window Nail was hiding behind across the street. Any bullshit over here, and he'd perforate the motherfuckers from afar. That was the theory, anyway, though she hoped and prayed this wouldn't go down like that. If it did, she didn't know what good the pistol would do her. Still, she appreciated the gesture.

The two of them came out on the landing. Buzzing white fluorescents lit the interior of the garage, beating the shadows down to little stubs. This level of the garage was nearly empty at this time of night. Only a black SUV with dark, tinted windows sat parked near the wall.

"Here we go," Anna said.

They stopped twenty feet or so from the SUV, making sure to leave Nail with a clean shot.

The car doors opened, two on each side of the vehicle. The guys that got out looked ridiculous, like pro linebackers crammed into FBI suits, but Anna bet nobody ever laughed at them. Not more than once, anyway.

Once all four had assembled in a rough, forbidding line, Greaser got out of the car. He carried two aluminum attaché cases, one in each hand.

"Ms. Ruiz," he said. He put one of the cases on the concrete and gave it a hard shove with his foot. It slid a dozen feet and scraped to a stop.

Anna gave Genevieve the nod. She went over to the case and knelt, fiddling with the catch. Anna kept her eyes on Greaser. The big guy looked relaxed, almost amused. That seemed like a good sign.

Genevieve opened the case. To Anna's well-calibrated eyes, there was exactly one metric shitload of cash inside.

"Million bucks," Greaser said. "Want to count it?"

"Yeah," she said. "I do." She nodded at Genevieve, who tightened her lips and turned to the task. Thick stacks of hundred-dollar bills piled up next to her. Greaser grinned, and the other four goons stood motionless and without expression.

"Your crew's looking a little light these days," Greaser said. "Everybody on vacation?"

Anna kept her face still, refusing to give him any satisfaction. "Yeah."

"Rough season."

"Yeah."

The conversation died, leaving everybody to stare at each other until Genevieve finally finished.

"It's all here," she said.

Greaser pointed at her. "The box."

Anna gave Genevieve another nod. Rather than set the box down and kick it, Genevieve walked over and set it down in front of the linebackers. They made no move, and she backed quickly away.

Greaser came forward, knelt, and flicked open the hasps. He lifted the lid. A deep sense of revulsion swept through Anna, and she turned her head away.

It was a long time before Greaser closed the box and stood. When he did, Anna could see a light sheen of sweat across his forehead, and his mouth hung open slightly, like he was panting for air.

He said nothing, but he shoved the other attaché case over. Genevieve cracked it open. "Cash," she said. "Want me to count it?"

Anna shook her head. "Give it back to him, and let's get out of here." Impotent rage boiled up in her as Genevieve kicked the box back. It sucked, but there had never been any question of turning down his shitty deal. Sobell, from what she'd heard, kept Greaser on a pretty slack leash, and if he decided to use that slack and Sobell's resources to hunt them down, he would surely find them. Whatever happened after that—well, Anna was sure that she, personally, would be happy to pay a quarter of a million dollars to escape that fate, only the option wouldn't be open anymore.

"Pleasure doing business with you," Greaser said without any feeling. He still seemed distracted. That was fine with Anna.

"Remember the deal," she said. "You sit tight right here for thirty minutes. After that, you go wherever you please."

He nodded and waved her off.

The two women left.

"What's he doing?" Anna asked.

Nail bent to the scope of his rifle again. "Just took the box and got in the car. Lights on. Started the car. Aaand . . . nothing." He peered over the scope, then back through it. "Don't look like they're going anywhere."

"Good. Fucking *great*." Anna settled into the nearest chair. Now maybe the knots in her shoulders would come out at last. Half this shit cleaned up, and a pile of cash in hand besides. If she could only be sure that Karyn was OK, she'd have liked nothing better than to pack a bag, hop in the car with Genevieve, and get out of town for a while. Find some time to do a couple of things.

She gave Genevieve a thin smile and went back to waiting.

*   *   *

Gresser sat in the rearmost seat by himself. He held the box in his lap, thumbs at the sides of the lid. More than anything, he wanted to open it again. The first time, he'd looked inside expecting one of Sobell's ridiculous relics, dry as dust and about as exciting. A museum piece, in other words, a useless item for a mostly useless collection.

He'd been mistaken, though. The jawbone inside was wet, covered with a spongy brown coating. Little tendrils reached from the bottom side and pressed against the walls of the box. He'd been mildly disgusted, ready to close the box—

And it had whispered to him.

The words were alien, unintelligible, but the sound had been right in his ears, closer than any lover he'd ever had. He'd closed the box, more out of shocked reflex than anything else.

Nobody else had noticed a thing.

Now, his boys—meatheads, the lot of them, but useful meatheads—sat awaiting his orders. They knew better than to make suggestions or ask questions, but he sensed a low anxiety in them anyway. Ruben and Marcus, in the two front seats, exchanged an uneasy glance and probably thought he didn't notice.

He caught a glimpse of the clock. Had they really been sitting here for forty-five minutes? How was that possible?

"Go," he said. *No wonder the guys are nervous. We shoulda been outta here fifteen minutes ago. Weird.*

The SUV bounced some as they made their way over the speed bumps and down out of the garage. Ruben turned the car onto the main thoroughfare, empty at this time of night.

Gresser turned back to the box. The thing inside had whispered to him, and the words clanged and crashed around his head still, as though they were getting louder with every echo and would soon burst out through his forehead.

Leave it, he told himself.

Don't worry. I'm not going to do anything. I just want to have a look.

You didn't get where you are by messing with Mr. Sobell's property.

A small, faint voice, long suppressed: *Look around, Joseph Alan Gresser, and tell me where you're going now.*

He opened the box. In the seat ahead of him, Marty twitched, started to turn around, then shuddered and stopped himself.

The bone was every bit as ugly as it had been before — but, wait. Were those tendril things *moving*?

The bone whispered to him again. The words were different, still wholly foreign and yet tantalizingly close to something he could understand. If he could only hear it a little better . . .

"Slow down," he said.

"I'm going the spee—" Ruben began, but he cut himself off when he checked the mirror and got a good look at Gresser's expression. He slowed the car down. The wind noise dropped considerably.

The whispers reaching Gresser's ears were plain English, clear as if they'd been amplified to rock concert levels.

You're better than this, Joseph, the bone said. It sounded a lot like his old man. *Kicking around Sobell's whipped dogs, hoping you'll get the best table scraps yourself. You're* better *than this.*

He looked up. None of the others had heard, he was sure.

No, he told it. *I'm nothing without Mr. Sobell.*

That's wrong. What does he do? Sit around and give orders. You do all the work, and you know it. He's nothing without you.

Gresser considered. The bone was right, if he really thought about it. What had Enoch Sobell done in the last fifteen years that Gresser himself hadn't handled? Anything? The guy ran his companies and let Gresser do all the real work, all the dangerous and illegal shit that might get a guy thrown in prison. How was that fair?

What do you want me to do about it?

I can help you, but not if you turn me over to His Lordship. I need time.

How?
Kill these men, and let's get out of here.

Gresser frowned in concentration. Sure, these meatheads were about as useless as tits on a bull, but ... ah. What a perfect idea.

"Turn around," he said. "Turn the car around."

"What was that all about?" Genevieve asked. She had been pacing and bouncing and generally being nervous for over an hour now, and the atmosphere of anxiety in the room wasn't doing Anna's head or her back any favors.

"I don't know," she said. "Maybe they were making sure."

"No. Unh-uh. You tell Gresser to sit tight for thirty minutes, he'll be gone in twenty-nine, just to piss you off. They sat there for almost an hour, Anna."

"They behaved. Maybe they took us seriously." That sounded pretty flimsy, even to her, but it was a stupid issue. "Who cares? We have the money. Sobell's got the bone. We're done with this thing, and we're each a quarter million dollars richer." That was the bottom line, right?

"True that," Nail said. He finished unscrewing the last bits of his gun and put them in the case. "Can we get out of here?"

Anna glanced back toward the garage. Nothing unusual there, and Gresser and company were gone.

"Yeah," she said. "Let's go."

Gresser's meatheads drove the car back into the garage without saying much of anything, though Ruben and Marcus exchanged confused looks again.

Probably think the boss is slipping, Gresser thought, and he grinned. *Dumbfucks.*

Ruben guided the car into a parking space—if not the same one they'd been parked in before, then one very near it—and stopped with a jolt.

"Easy on the brake there," Gresser said.

"Yes, sir." Ruben checked the mirror again, met

Gresser's eyes, and looked away. The others sat, facing forward and awaiting orders like obedient dogs.

Gresser set the box on the seat next to him, calmly reached inside his jacket, and pulled out a gun. Marty and Jorge were dead before they could even think about turning around. Marcus managed to get half turned and even one hand on his gun before Gresser shot him three times through the seat.

Only Ruben was smart enough to get out of the car. He ducked as soon as the firing started and pushed the door open, sliding out after it. Gresser pulled the trigger twice, sending bullets into the dashboard and instrument panel.

"Shit." The car was full of blue smoke, enough to make Gresser's eyes water, and his ears rang like an air raid siren. Who knew firing a gun inside a car was so goddamn *loud*?

The window to his left blasted inward, spraying black glass over the inside of the car. He tried to crouch, but he was simply too big to make that effective. He grabbed the box, and keeping as low as possible, made for the nearest door. Bullets tore into the seat behind him and into Marty and Jorge's bodies, and then he was out.

"Ruben, you're making a mistake," he shouted. His own voice sounded weirdly hollow and distant in his ears, like somebody else was talking to him through a long tube.

Ruben may have been a meathead, but he was smart enough not to say anything and give Gresser a read on his location.

OK, smart guy. Let's see how you like this.

Gresser simply walked around the back of the car. The first shot missed him clean. The second dug a blazing furrow in the side of his neck. By then, Ruben was out of chances. He stood ten feet back from the vehicle, gun gripped in both hands and panic in his face.

Gresser shot him in the gut. He dropped, mewling. He tried to get off another shot, but it went wide and ricocheted off the concrete.

"Hey, smart guy," Gresser said, kicking the gun from

Ruben's grasp. "You shoot for the body, not the head. Bigger target." He shook his head. "Didn't I teach you better than that?"

Ruben gasped and clutched his stomach. "Boss . . ."

"Don't you fuckin' 'Boss' me. C'mon." Gresser grabbed the big man by the back of his coat and hauled him back to the SUV. Left a pretty good blood trail, but he didn't figure that'd be a big deal.

More blood pattered down on the concrete, and Gresser's hand went to his neck. He bent down, checking his reflection in the side mirror. The wound was bloody, but he'd had worse. "Shit, that's ugly. Your hands weren't shaking so much, I'd be a dead man, Ruben. How do you like that?"

Ruben didn't have much to say. Looked like he'd gone into shock. Probably better for him that way.

Gresser opened the driver's door and hoisted Ruben inside. Ruben wasn't any too helpful, so it took a bunch of grunting and heaving and swearing, and at the end of it, Gresser's head spun in wide, wobbly circles. He put a hand against the vehicle to steady himself.

After the world stopped trying to buck him off, he took his gun back out of his jacket. It was a nice gun—a nickel-plated, pearl-handled Colt .45 that dated back to God-knew-when. Too bad.

He checked Ruben's breathing. Not much of that, anymore. Ol' Ruben was alive, but not by much. Gresser put the gun in Ruben's waistband. Then he took his rings off—silver pinkie ring on the left, big gold skull on the right—and jammed them on Ruben's fingers.

There. Sobell didn't know how many guys he'd taken with him on this job, and probably couldn't have named more than four or five of Gresser's meatheads out of dozens anyway. Ruben was big enough to pass for Gresser, once enough damage was done to the body.

Gresser popped open the fuel door.

Chapter 18

Enoch Sobell sat facing the window that looked out over the city, though he'd stopped really seeing this view years ago. It may as well have been a mediocre painting, purchased long before and, with all its meager secrets gone, reduced to little more than wallpaper in a fancy frame. He looked over it, past it, his eyes fixed on a spot in the cloudless sky and his mind running pointless laps.

His brand-new lieutenant, a clod who went by the uninspiring name of Brown, clomped into the room. *He's not stupid,* Sobell reminded himself. *But he's a crank-turner, an order-follower. He's never had an original idea, and he never will.*

"About a third of the guys haven't checked in," Brown said. "Nobody knows where they are."

"This is bad, Mr. Brown."

"Yeah."

"The last time I got fucked this thoroughly, it took six whores and twenty thousand dollars, plus extra for hardware and damages. I couldn't walk for four days afterward."

"Um."

"I think I was on a mix of methamphetamine and Darvocet at the time."

"Uh."

"I was considerably happier about that fucking, Mr. Brown."

Brown shuffled his feet. "I, uh, can't say as I blame you. Sir."

"Any word on the body?"

"Which one?"

Which one. Christ. Like any of the others are important. "Gresser's. They're sure it was him?"

"It's kind of a mess. I don't know if there's even enough left to get a match through dental records. The gun, though—well, that was a mess, too, but we're pretty sure it was his."

On the one hand, that was another miserable facet to this five-cornered goatfuck. Gresser could be relied upon to handle disasters like this with virtually no oversight. On the other hand, Sobell was glad the bastards who'd gotten the drop on Gresser hadn't taken him and tortured the fuck out of him or anything like that. He knew *way* too much for safety. *I'd probably have to have gotten rid of him eventually anyway,* Sobell thought with a sigh. *And also, those grapes probably taste like shit.*

"No sign of the, ah, object either," Brown offered.

"That would have been a lot to ask." Sobell sighed again. "I assume you've already pulled the home addresses of Ms. Ames and her merry crew of assholes?"

"Uh, no. They're not exactly in the phone book."

Sobell fixed Brown with a stare hard and pointed enough to nail somebody to a cross. "That's why we have people, Mr. Brown. And money. I assure you, your predecessor had all this information secured." *Probably in his goddamned firebombed skull, which does me exactly no good now.* "If he found it, you can, too."

"I'll get right on it."

"Yesterday would be nice. They're probably all long gone by now. I think one of Gresser's former employees might also have the address of Ames's dealer. You might send someone around there."

"Yes, sir."

"Now, would you be so kind as to get the fuck out of here?"

Brown nodded, did an about-face, and quickly exited the room. Now that he'd been given some direction, he'd keep grinding away until he found the info he needed. It might take him a while, but he'd get there. Why it required a lightning bolt from Heaven to give him the idea in the first place was something Sobell would never understand.

This whole mess was a distraction he did not need. His most trusted lieutenant murdered, a bunch of thieves run off with an artifact that might or might not be useless but certainly had been fairly paid for, and all the while a demon's enigma awaited his attention, if he planned on living much past his next birthday.

"Never mind that for now. There is work to be done," he announced to the empty room. He stood, stretched, and walked to the staircase. Up the stairs, through the antechamber, and into his office. He opened a concealed sliding door behind his desk chair and entered his private chamber.

The room was a mirror image of the office, spare, with only the objects in the alcoves breaking the blankness. Whereas the impressive and expensive were on display in the office, here Sobell kept the real collection. No more than a dozen items, and most of them appeared to be junk. Katherine's gown, for example, was a thin scrap of ancient, nearly transparent rags, and the Babylon Codex had to be encased in glass, lest the slight draft of a person's passage cause it to crumble further. But Sobell had seen the gown cloak a six-foot man in the appearance of a small child, and the one page of the Codex he'd managed to read had scared him so badly he hadn't gone near the case since.

He wasn't sure what he needed today. It would be the height of stupidity to wait for Brown to get this issue resolved himself, so Sobell would have to get dirty, but the right way to do it eluded him. A seeking spell wouldn't work without a bit of hair or blood from the party being sought, so that was no good. A demon would certainly do the job, but his recent encounter had reminded him most firmly why he'd sworn off summoning demons years ago, after one had slipped the leash and gone on a rampage that made the current clusterfuck look about as important as losing a game of Parcheesi.

Demons were squirrelly fuckers—one little mistake in the binding, and a demon would walk through it like the Arc de Triomphe.

No, I won't be doing that again.

He didn't know a spell that would help, so he turned to the collection. Something here had to serve. He'd gladly have burned half the priceless artifacts in the room to get his hands on Ames and make an example of her. Really, what good were the damned things? Take St. George's sword, for instance. It was impressive, ancient, maybe even holy, but how often did one need to cut through steel plate in this day and age?

He walked the perimeter of the room, pausing at each object. This was the largest collection of its kind that he knew of, and even so, he despaired of finding the right tool for this job.

He stopped in front of a black ceramic jar on a simple pedestal. The jar had been sealed with wax, the outside covered with symbols and runes Sobell didn't recognize.

Aha.

There was a creature trapped in the jar, or so Sobell had been told. It was reportedly called a Whisperer Demon or a Whisperer Shade, depending whom you asked. He doubted it was a demon, since it'd be tough to jam a demon of any size into a container no bigger than a pickle jar, but who knew? The capabilities of demons were notoriously variable and not well understood.

The creature in the jar could help him, if even part of what he'd read about it was true. And yet . . .

It's not really *a demon. Probably. And, anyway, I won't be summoning it. I'll be doing the miserable fucker a favor, actually.* I *didn't put it in that jar.*

He almost walked away. Risk was part of what he did for a living, every day, but the uncertainty here made his mouth dry and his breath come short. Behind Door Number One was either the answer to his problems or something that would cheerfully fold him up and stuff *him* in yonder magic pickle jar, size considerations be damned.

But he thought of Gresser, burned beyond recognition. Of two million dollars that had been stolen, like the perpetrators thought they were mugging a helpless grandmother.

Of the bone.

He got out his pocketknife—horn, ivory, and steel—and cut his left palm. He wiped the blood around the lid of the jar, three times in a circle, and spat out the words that were supposed to open the container.

On the third pass, the wax cracked and fell away. There was a faint hiss, as of escaping air, and then the lid popped off and fell to the floor.

When nothing further happened, he looked in the jar. Empty.

I'm going to kill that son of a—

The faint hiss sounded again, this time from behind him.

Enoch Sobell turned slowly around. There was nothing behind him—except, wait. The hiss resolved itself into a distant-sounding chorus of whispers. An area of the wall opposite Sobell was darker than the surrounding walls, and very slightly wavy, as though he viewed it through a nearly invisible, rippling sheet of black gauze.

A word emerged from the whispers: "What?"

That was surprisingly to the point. He paused, considering. It occurred to him that maybe the right thing to do was to set this aside for now, to go straight for the man the demon had shown him. Forget, however briefly, the slaughter of his best employee and the subsequent theft of what was his.

And if the man I'm looking for is on the other side of the world? What then? Well, then, if what he'd learned about the shade was true, it might take months or more to find the man as it essentially went door-to-door chasing rumors across half the globe. Sobell didn't have that kind of time, and his contacts would likely be better, and faster, for that purpose. *The wrong tool for the job, I suppose. Best resolve this current mess before it encourages any sharks to start circling.*

"Karyn Ames. Find out where she is as quickly as you can, then come tell me."

He got no response, but the air ahead of him fluttered once, then brightened.

He searched the room, looking for any telltale sign, finding nothing. He was alone.

That wasn't so bad, he told himself, but a deeper part wondered.

Chapter 19

Two hundred fifty Gs, Nail thought. It was a thought that still wouldn't find a home, just kept roaming around in his head like it couldn't settle in. *Two hundred fifty Gs.* Had to be a good thing, right? Had to be. Enough to get Clarence off his brother's ass for good, take care of his own debts, and stash some away. There ought to be some fuckin' relief in there for somebody, right?

He stopped at the stairs to his apartment. The afternoon was the usual stifling hot, even though the stairway between the buildings was in the shade, and three floors all of a sudden seemed like a hell of a walk. Everything seemed exhausting. Times like this, it usually felt good to hit someone—go out, find the guys responsible, and make it right. Not this time. Tommy was dead, and it wasn't even really anybody's fault. Just a bullshit stray round. Oh, sure, somebody'd pulled the trigger, but Anna had filled him in. Everything had gone crazy by that point. Probably the shooter hadn't even known what he was doing, just firing off a shot out of fear before he got the hell gone, practically a reflex, and Tommy'd been in the wrong spot. Nail had known a guy in Afghanistan who went out like that, only it had been friendly fire that time, some nervous kid named McCarthy behind the gun. Nail had felt equally useless then. What was he going to do, go pound PFC McCarthy into the ground? Guy had been on suicide watch ever since the shot, so it's not like there was any satisfaction to be had there.

So that was Tommy. The situation with Anna and Karyn was no good, either. He'd already hit up a few spots this afternoon on Anna's recommendation, hoping maybe to run across Karyn and talk to her some. Maybe try to mend some fences, or at least make sure she was OK. He'd never got the full story on her weird-ass talent, never wanted to, but he'd heard enough to know she could find herself in a bad way if she wasn't careful, and Anna's panicky voice on the phone had told him everything he needed to know about how serious it was. He'd had no luck, and now he was too damn tired to keep driving around.

He looked around, feeling at a loss for what to do with himself. A dozen or so feet away, four battered old air-conditioning units hummed, and beyond that, a sorry-looking hedge of some ugly damn bush put up a half-hearted screen between him and the street. He thought about going for a run, thought about the air-conditioning, and decided three flights wasn't so far after all.

He hefted his duffel bag—*Two hundred fifty Gs*—and started up the stairs. Once inside, he'd take a shower, pull the curtains closed, and catch a nap. Then maybe try to catch back up with Anna, see if Karyn had turned up, or if there was anything else he could do.

"Hell, no," somebody said from the next flight up. "My fuckin' nephew's too goddamn stupid."

"He ain't that bad. Cut him some slack."

"I told his old man. I says, Denny ain't got the sense . . ." The chatter continued, and Nail's mind was already wandering away from it. He trudged up another few steps, then turned the corner.

There were four guys ambling down the stairs, two of them talking up a storm of bullshit, not ten feet away. Big guys, no-neck bruisers, and dressed way out of season in long coats.

Nail started to back up, hoping to duck back around the corner before they saw him, but it was too late. One of the men, a red-faced guy with a head like a bowling ball, pulled a sawed-off shotgun from his coat.

There was no warning, no "freeze, motherfucker," and

the crazy-eyed grimace on the man's face told Nail there wouldn't be. He threw himself down and forward.

The gun went off just over his shoulder, a clean miss, and he plowed into the red-faced guy's knees. Something popped and the guy howled as the two men fell, rolling down the stairs. After a thumping, bone-jarring ride down half a dozen steps, Nail caught himself. The red-faced guy rolled up a moment later, and before he could get his balance, Nail punched him in the head. Pain exploded in his hand, but the guy fell back down, stunned, and Nail snatched the shotgun from him.

The other three guys stood a little way up the stairs. Two of them had pulled out guns, too, little short-barreled Saturday night specials. Not real accurate, but they were too damn close to dismiss. A .22 and a .32, it looked like. Small, low-velocity bullets, which at least meant not a lot of stopping power. *Might not* go through a human body.

Nail pulled the red-faced guy up in front of him. The guy groaned as he tried to put his weight on his left leg, and he ended up standing on only the right.

"What the fuck?" Nail asked.

"You're a dead man," one of the guys up the stairs said. Tall guy with a crew cut that emphasized his already flat head.

"Yeah, I got that. You wanna tell me what the fuck is going on?"

"You shoulda skipped town after you did Greaser, asshole. Now you're gonna pay."

" 'Did' Greaser? I ain't 'did' no one, man. We made the fuckin' drop."

This was bad. It didn't make any sense for starters, but these didn't look like the kind of guys who worried too much about that. If it weren't for the red-faced sack of shit in front of him, they'd have put a bunch of holes in him already. He wasn't sure they weren't about to try anyway.

"How about you put the gun down and let Teddy go, and we'll go somewhere and talk this out?"

Okay, they were definitely going to shoot him. Crewcut's voice had gone all singsongy, like he was trying to get a mean dog to calm down. He sounded about as sincere as a mob lawyer.

"How about you throw me that bag, and I walk away real slow, and nobody shoots nobody?" Nail tried. He didn't have much hope that that would work, but you never knew. Besides, that was a quarter of a million dollars sitting in a bag next to Crewcut's feet. Had to at least make a little effort for it.

"Nobody's gotta get hurt here," the guy said. "You got something that belongs to Mr. Sobell. You give that to me, and I'll take the money, and *maybe* you'll get a good long head start."

Crewcut had a shit poker face—Tommy would have taken him for a mint—and Nail read the precise moment the man decided to shoot him.

Nail shoved the red-faced guy forward. Crewcut's gun went off, the bang echoing brutally in the stairwell. Nail fired back in his general direction, even as he lunged toward the stair rail. Didn't hit shit that he could see, but at least a couple of the guys tried to get down. Crewcut fired again, wildly, missing, and Nail rolled over the rail.

He landed on his feet, more or less, on the next flight of stairs down. Above him, the red-faced guy was slumped against the wall, bright blood pumping out onto the stairs. The other guys were running down past him.

Nail took off. A firefight in close quarters with these clowns would be a fucking disaster, total chaos, and even if he had a huge edge in training, there was no telling what would happen. Four steps down, he jumped the next rail again, then ran, skipping three steps at a time, all the way to the bottom. A couple more shots were fired. God knew where the bullets ended up, but they didn't hit Nail.

He bolted past the air-conditioning units, hung a sharp left and headed for the parking lot. A glance behind him showed his pursuers huffing and puffing, having finally come around the corner—far enough away he could get some wheels before they could catch up to him. He jumped in his van.

"Hey!" one of the guys shouted. Now, though, there were other people around, maybe half a dozen scattered throughout the parking lot. Lot of witnesses. Maybe that meant something to these assholes and maybe not, but no more shots were fired.

Nail fired up the van. Moments later, he was leaving tracks of melted rubber at the parking lot exit. He took the first left down a narrow alley, then screamed back out on the next street, eyes half on the road and half on his mirrors. Another couple of quick turns and an ignored red light later, he thought he was clear.

He pulled into another alley and reached for his phone. Dialed Anna while staring at his mirrors. Voice mail.

Not good.

He floored it, and the van roared out into the street. Anna and Karyn's apartment was fifteen minutes from here, if traffic didn't fuck him. Fifteen minutes. Karyn was probably safe—she wasn't around and anyway, she was Karyn. Anna, though . . . Had Sobell's guys already gotten to her?

Nail glanced at the speedometer, saw he was doing sixty in a thirty-five. Too bad. If the cops stopped him, he'd tell them there was a murder in progress.

He dialed the phone again. Nothing. Flipped through his numbers, veered around a black Toyota that was lurching down the middle of the road like a wounded animal, and dialed Genevieve. No answer.

Six minutes, and he was almost there. That would be a new record. He dialed the phone again. No answer at Anna's number. No answer at Genevieve's.

He rolled into the parking lot at Anna's place eight minutes after starting out for it. To his surprise, Genevieve was standing out on the fire escape. Her back was pressed to the stucco, and she was slowly edging toward the ladder.

He parked the van, grabbed his newly acquired shotgun—draping a jacket over it as an afterthought—and ran over.

Genevieve caught his eye and put her finger over her lips, telling him to be quiet. Not three feet from her, the window was open. The sound of something smashing came from inside.

Genevieve made it to the ladder and started descending. A moment later, a heavyset guy poked his head out the window.

"Hey!" the guy shouted.

Nail brought up the shotgun. "Hey yourself."

The guy disappeared back into the apartment. Any second now, he'd be back out, waving a fucking gun. Or maybe he'd be smart enough to send a friend around front.

"Come on, girl," Nail said. "We gotta go."

Genevieve dropped to the ground. Sure enough, the guy peeked out around the edge of the window, waving some hardware around. Nail pulled the trigger. Stucco and plaster rained down on the fire escape. Some lady walking her dog yelled at her kids to get inside.

"Nice timing," Genevieve said.

Nail didn't take his eyes from the window. "Where's Anna?"

"She's not here. She's . . ." She looked up at the window. "I'll tell you later. What now?"

"You hear sirens?"

"Yeah."

"Let's get the hell out of here." He threw his keys to Genevieve. She got in behind the wheel of the van.

Nail backed up, keeping the shotgun trained on the window.

"You don't know who you're messing with, asshole!" the guy shouted. *Tough talk from a guy who won't come out where I can see him.*

Nail got into the van and poked the shotgun through the open window. "Gen, get us out of here."

"Right on."

They pulled away. Nail half expected the guy in the window to start blazing away at them once they were halfway down the block, but evidently he wasn't as stupid as he looked.

Nail looked over at her. "You OK?" He flexed his right hand and grimaced.

"Yeah. You?"

"Yeah. Where's Anna?"

"Went looking for Adelaide."

"Who?"

"Long story. What are you doing here?" Genevieve grinned. "Not that I'm complaining."

"Buncha guys came for me, too. I busted my hand on some motherfucker's hard-ass head. First time that's ever happened. You gotta have a *hard*-ass head to break my hand." He moved it again, and again made a pained face. "What are *you* doing here?"

"I could track Karyn if I had a hair or something. I've checked already, but I thought I'd make another run at it, just in case. No luck."

"You don't answer your fucking phone anymore?"

Genevieve grimaced. "I left it on the counter. I heard it ring, but I was hiding from those guys by then. Guess they've got it now."

"Too bad. Any way you can get ahold of Sobell?"

"Why?"

"Greaser's dead, and Sobell didn't get the bone."

Genevieve turned her head sharply toward him. "What?"

"That's what they told me. They were ready to fuck me up because they think we killed Greaser and took the bone and the money."

Genevieve's face, pale to begin with, was nearly white. "Oh, this is not good. Not good at all."

"No shit."

"There," Nail said, pointing at an open spot next to the curb. Genevieve parked and reached for the ignition.

"Don't turn it off," Nail said. "Just in case."

"Sure you don't want some help?"

"I'd rather you kept the car running."

"Okay."

He got out. The sun was edging down below the concrete horizon, and long shadows covered the sidewalk. He walked fast, ignoring the throbbing in his hand. Hopefully he wouldn't need Gen's emergency getaway car service, but after the day's events, it couldn't hurt to have her ready. If there was an open price on their heads, Pete would know, but Nail didn't give it much better than sixty–forty odds that Pete would give him the lowdown rather than try to collect.

He took a quick look up the street, just to be sure, then stepped into Pete's Paradise, a tropical-themed shithole that pretended to its name about as well as Spam pretended to be steak. The door closed behind him with a rattle. One look at the place, and he almost turned around and walked out. There were maybe six people in the whole bar, bartender included, and there was a *bad* vibe here. A couple of guys in the corner had their heads together, muttering, but they stopped and stared at him when he looked their way. Behind the bar, Pete himself suddenly turned his back on a customer who'd been leaning over the bar, close enough to whisper, Nail thought. Even Elly, the woman who regularly hung out in the back corner alone and drank herself to oblivion every night, was talking into a cell phone, one hand covering her mouth and the bottom of the phone.

Nail put his hand on the door to let himself out, and stopped. *They ain't talking about you. Can't be. That's just nerves talking.* He walked to the bar with his head up, and sat at the end of the bar opposite the bartender's buddy.

"How about a Bud?" he asked, overloud. Pete made a show of wiping down a glass first, but he made it to the tap eventually.

"Slow night," somebody said.

Nail gave a start. Some guy was sitting right there next to him at the bar, and he hadn't even seen him. *Guy must have just sat down,* Nail thought uneasily, but part of him knew better. He wasn't the kind of guy you could just sneak up on. On that side of his body, his skin crept, like it was trying to crawl away from the newcomer.

"Yeah," Nail said, his mouth suddenly dry. "Always a slow night in here. Don't know how they stay in business."

He didn't look, but something shifted in his peripheral

vision, and he felt the presence move closer to him, practically leaning against him. He got the impression of a hunched man in a long coat, collar up, some kind of hat pulled down low over his forehead, but he couldn't quite make out any details—not the kind of hat or the color of the coat, or even a single element of the man's face. Was he a white guy? Black? Did he have any facial hair? Did he have brown eyes? Did he have *any* eyes? That thought sent another crazy prickle of gooseflesh rippling along his body.

He decided to not look at the guy. He had a hunch he wouldn't like what he saw.

"Secret for a secret," the guy whispered, the sound like dead leaves blowing over tombstones.

Nail's mouth had gone desert dry, *bone*-dry, and what the fuck was Pete doing? He was clear across the bar, on the goddamn phone.

The guy next to him wasn't the kind of guy you left hanging, though—and wasn't there something else, too? There was a strange pull, an urge to tell what he knew. Distantly he was aware that that was an urge he almost never had, but that didn't seem so important right now.

Nail licked his lips. "OK."

The guy leaned in even closer. Something wispy and insubstantial brushed Nail's ear, and his body convulsed with a racking shudder.

"Enoch Sobell," the guy said.

Maybe this is just the guy I need to talk to. "Yeah?"

"He ain't in charge anymore. His boys are leaving him."

Holy shit. Curiosity overwhelmed fear completely for one moment. "For who?"

"No getting greedy. I gave you one—your turn."

Secret for a secret? Nail suddenly realized he didn't know shit. Wasn't that why he was here?

"Karyn's gone," he said. He wasn't sure where the thought had come from, or why it seemed like an appropriate offering—the words had simply bubbled up and fallen out of his face. It felt like the guy held his breath, though, listening intently to Nail's every word. It was a good feeling. "After the job went bad, she took off. Don't know where. Don't know if she's still in town. She doesn't drive, though, so if she skipped town, it would have to be on a bus or something." His mouth seemed to be running of its own accord, and there were a dozen things jammed behind his teeth, all crowding to get out at the same time. "I don't know how things got so fucked up," he said. "We made the drop. Greaser got the bone and he even took half the money. I swear."

He felt a faint pressure on his shoulder—a hand, probably—and another shudder threatened to ripple through him. Then the voice, closer than ever. "Thanks. And one more thing, for your service . . ."

A cold draft slipped down the side of Nail's face and down his collar as the guy whispered into his ear. "That night at Mendelsohn's."

Nail's spine went rigid. "How do you know about that?"

"Sobell was there. He had business with a demon. The man's got a lot of troubles right now. A lot of enemies."

"Goddammit, how do you—"

The guy was gone.

Nail looked around the room, wide-eyed and still somewhat dazed. The two guys were still huddled in a booth, Elly in the corner. Pete gave him a bitter, bemused smile. "Hear anything interesting?"

Nail didn't know where the whispering guy got his information, but there was no doubt the guy knew some shit he was definitely not supposed to know. The comment about Mendelsohn's place was unsettling, if true, and even if it wasn't, he shouldn't have known Nail had anything to do with it.

Sobell's got a lot of enemies right now, the guy had said, and Nail didn't miss the fact that all of the "secrets" he had offered were Sobell's. Whether the guy was deliberately trying to stir up some shit or not, if he was running around handing out that kind of information, things were about to get ugly. Nail left in a rush.

Chapter 20

Anna had gotten nowhere after revisiting what felt like every last place she and Karyn had spent more than twenty minutes in the last year, and she was about ready to give up. Karyn had apparently scrubbed herself from the face of the earth, at least as far as anybody knew. She had considered casting a wider net, maybe even getting a skip tracer who owed her a favor on the job, but eventually rejected the idea. Surely there was nobody better to go crawling through L.A.'s underbelly, lifting up rocks and asking clever questions of the creepy things that came scuttling out, but Anna didn't want to spread this around. The skip tracer would get the job done, sure, but he'd let something slip—he'd probably have to, to get it done. Anna and Karyn had made enemies over the years, and there were eight or ten parties Anna could think of off the top of her head that would be only too pleased to find out that the two of them were separated, that maybe Karyn had her guard down.

They'd be wrong, of course—Karyn would see them coming from six miles off. Her guard, Anna thought, had probably not been up this far in years. The big worry was that if Karyn wasn't seeing *every* kind of trouble coming by now, she would be soon, and she couldn't run from everything.

That thought had triggered Anna's next logical avenue in a flash of insight that, in retrospect, had taken way too long to arrive. Karyn couldn't stay down forever, or she'd lose her mind. If she wanted to prevent that, there was only one person to go to. Now Anna slowed the car and frowned. Ahead, two cars were parked in front of Adelaide's building. It was tough to be sure from here, but it looked like the one in front was sitting on four flat tires. She turned the ringer off her phone, put it in her pocket, and parked just around the corner.

She approached the parked vehicles warily, looking for any sign of movement. Nothing stirred. Sure enough, though, the front car's tires had been slashed. Whose car? Somebody who'd driven Karyn here? Somebody else entirely? And what about the other car, a blue sedan covered with a film of road dust? Adelaide didn't get a lot of visitors, so the odds that this was somebody else who had just happened by weren't great.

A glance inside the first car didn't give her anything useful. A couple of wadded-up fast-food wrappers told no story worth knowing, and a handful of grimy nickels in the armrest didn't say much, either. The second car was similarly unhelpful. If she wanted to learn anything else, not to mention maybe scoring some blind for Karyn, she'd have to go see if Adelaide was around. She forced down a faint sense of disgust that threatened to swell, but there wasn't much she could do to calm her pounding heart.

She's not dangerous, Anna reminded herself. *She just freaks me out. Some people are freaked out by bugs, I'm freaked out by crazy, basement-dwelling prophets who like rats too much. No shame in that, but there's nothing to be afraid of.*

Plus, she recalled, *I still have Nail's gun.* It was snug in the inside pocket of her jacket, the weight swinging against her body when she walked. That didn't calm her down any, but it helped her summon the will to move.

Adelaide's building was as much of a wreck as ever, about as destroyed as a building could be without a bomb having fallen on it. *One day this goddamn building is going to fall in and kill her, and then I won't have to do this shit anymore.* Or would she? Karyn would have to score blind somewhere, and anyway it was hard to imagine how Adelaide would fail to see a mundane disaster like that coming. Probably she'd just move out the day before the collapse and go find another horrifying building to squat in.

Anna pushed open the door, wincing as the damp smell hit her. There was mold growing in here that science hadn't ever heard of, she was certain. She followed the hall • straight to the back and paused at the top of the stairs. Had she heard a voice? Or had that been the product of her own keyed-up mind? Or Adelaide talking to herself?

She waited, straining to hear anything, but there was nothing. Stepping cautiously so as to make no noise, she turned the corner. One slow step at a time, she descended the staircase.

She had made it about two-thirds of the way down the stairs when she heard something splash beyond the doorway. A moment later, a man's voice reached her, coming from much closer than she would have expected.

Uh-oh. She backed up the stairs as rapidly as she could, keeping her eyes fixed on the doorway the whole way. Once she made it to the top, she thought about running for it, but there really wasn't much of anywhere to run. Her car, maybe, but if whoever it was saw her, she could be in a lot of trouble. Instead, she went up the stairs. The fourth step sagged underfoot, sending a sickening bolt of shock through her stomach, but it didn't give out, and she reached the landing without mishap. She edged around the corner where the stairs switched back. It was dark here, away from even the faint light that came through the first-floor windows, and while that wasn't exactly what she'd call safety, it was reassuring.

"Fucking *move.*" A man's voice again, this time coming from the hall. Anna peeked around the corner. The thin, bedraggled figure in front was Adelaide. A skinny guy with blond dreadlocks walked behind her, shoving her with the barrel of a gun. "Fucking move!" he said again, and Adelaide shuffled forward a little faster. She was laughing now, or maybe talking to herself, bursts of sound at erratic pitches, and the sound made Anna shiver.

Another man, a squat, solid-looking fellow in a T-shirt and jeans, followed the two of them. Anna didn't recognize him, but she had no trouble at all picking out the first as one of the guys from the Brotherhood they'd spent the better part of a day trailing around after, way back at the beginning of the job.

She pulled back behind the corner, cursing under her breath. What could the Brotherhood possibly want with Adelaide? Maybe they'd followed Karyn here, or maybe they'd found her some other way, but no way was this a coincidence. No way.

She heard the creak and scrape of the front door opening, and the low orange light of sunset flooded through the hall, then vanished again.

Shit! They were going to be gone in a few moments, and then what? Maybe Adelaide knew where Karyn was, and even if she didn't, Anna didn't know where else Karyn would be able to get her medication.

There was, she supposed, some chance that Karyn was here, downstairs—but if that was the case, she was already beyond help. Those two guys would have made sure of that.

She went down the stairs and crept out of the building as quickly as she dared. When she emerged from the building, the dusty sedan was already moving away. She let it get almost out of sight at the end of the block before running out to her car.

As she started the car, she took out her phone and dialed Genevieve. No answer.

"Call me," she said, and then she pulled out after the departing vehicle before it disappeared from sight entirely.

They weren't pros. That much was obvious, Anna thought. She was pretty good at tailing by car, but these guys didn't drive like they had even considered the possibility that somebody might follow them. They took a leisurely thirty minutes or so to drive a straight shot to a motel that looked like it had been run-down on the day it was built, forty years ago. They parked, shoved Adelaide across the mostly empty parking lot, and disappeared into a unit across the way.

I don't owe her anything, Anna thought. *I should just get clear of this shit.* And while that was true, the yammering voice of worry was louder, shouting over and over: *Where's Karyn? Where's Karyn? What about her meds?*

The lights were on in the motel room the three people had gone into, and from the shapes moving on the curtains, it looked like there was a whole lot more than three people in there. Who, she wondered, was in charge of this mess? What were they talking about? What was *Adelaide* saying? She wished Nail was here. He had equipment fo. this kind of thing, or knew where to get it. Supersensitive microphones. Lasers you could bounce off windowpanes to pick up sound vibrations. All kinds of shit like that.

Well, there's the old-fashioned way.

She gave it another moment's thought, staring at the window the whole time, and then got out of the car. The room next door to the lighted window was dark, and she approached it as quickly as she could. The place was old, the door locked with actual hardware, and it took her all of fifteen seconds to jimmy the lock. She slipped inside and closed the door.

Nobody was inside, but it looked like the room had been rented out. A weathered backpack lay on one of the beds, a red nylon duffel bag at the foot of the other. Anna hoped the owners wouldn't be back soon. She went around to the right-hand wall, easing around the TV, and pressed her ear to the wallpaper.

The walls were typical of cheap motels, and while the voices were muffled, she could clearly make out the sound of somebody shouting.

"Where is she? *Where is she?*" A man's voice, rising to a shrill note at the end. The sound, Anna thought, of a guy on the verge of completely losing his shit. Somebody gave a quiet answer she couldn't make out. It sounded like a woman's voice.

Dammit, speak up. I can't hear a damn thing.

"TELL ME!"

Then silence. A few moments later, several men began talking in low voices, but again, Anna couldn't make out much. It was just so much maddeningly indistinct mumbling through the plasterboard.

She looked at where the TV sat on a short dresser. *Well . . .* Moving carefully, she pushed the dresser away from the wall, pivoting it on one corner. It was empty, made of cheap fiberboard, and not very heavy. The TV cord stretched out behind it, so she reached down and pulled the plug from the wall. Then she took out her pocketknife, flipped open the blade, and crouched down in the space formerly occupied by the dresser.

If the rooms mirrored each other, as suggested by the doors, this would be a great way of listening in without being observed. The dresser on the other side should block the hole from sight, but there was enough of a gap because of the space needed for the plug that it wouldn't block a lot of sound. It would be almost as good as being in the same room with them.

As long as I'm not too loud. And the dresser is in the same place. Ugh. Yeah. Her knife poking through a visible spot in the wall would invite some unpleasant attention in a hurry. She pulled her pistol from her jacket and put it down next to her where she could get at it quickly.

The first layer of sheetrock was straightforward enough. She slid her knife through and slowly cut a fist-sized piece out. She was pretty sure the sheetrock was thinner than code, which suited her fine. The rasp of the knife against the gypsum seemed loud in her ears, but the voices continued talking, so she kept going slow. White powder covered her fingers and floated to the carpet as she sawed, and at last she pulled the piece away, revealing the narrow gap between the walls and the back of the piece on the other side.

Already the voices were clearer.

". . . wasn't there," a man said, sounding rather defensive. ". . . don't know."

"Did you see *anyone*?" The loud guy again.

More mumbling. Anna put the point of her knife to the wall and slowly began drilling a hole through it.

"... nothing. I mean, the place is a mess, but we couldn't find nothing."

Anna's knife poked through the drywall, and she froze. If the dresser wasn't in the same location on the other side, there would be a quarter inch of shiny metal protruding from a spot about a foot off the floor in the middle of a blank wall on the other side.

A moment passed without outcry, and Anna pulled the knife back. Adelaide's voice drifted through the little hole in the wall, sounding small and scared.

"Home. Adelaide wants to go home. Right now. Her head hurts bad today, so bad. Stuffed with rats."

"It's OK." The man's voice had quieted, dropped to a soothing murmur that was barely audible through the wall. "It's OK. We're going to help you, remember?"

"Adelaide doesn't know. She can't—Adelaide can't *think*."

"You came to us, remember? We can't help you, if you don't help us."

She sold us out. Plain and simple. Goddammit.

"Adelaide needs ... She needs quiet."

Instead of cutting her some slack, the guy raised his voice. "Where is the relic?"

"Adelaide wants to go home!"

"You said you'd bring us Ames. *Where is she?*"

A high, wavering note sounded, an awful plaintive wail that made the hairs stand up on the back of Anna's neck. A moment later there was a crash, then a thud. The cry stopped for a second, then started up again, louder this time.

They knocked her down. Kicked her chair over. Something like that. Anna ground her teeth together and suddenly found herself wondering just how many men were in that room. Were they armed? If not, she could simply walk in, hold them at gunpoint, get Adelaide, and walk out. If they were, though ... she'd have to get the drop on them somehow. And even then ...

You are not just going to walk in there and shoot six or eight people.

No. No, she wasn't. That didn't leave much in the way

of options, though. Just being here was risky enough—a frontal assault on the next room was over the line even for her.

Somebody's phone rang, and Anna moved closer to the hole. She heard a series of grunts and noncommittal responses, followed by a curt good-bye.

"OK," the guy said. His voice was high and nervous. "Revered One?"

"Yes?" The loud guy again.

"That was Brother Sheffield."

"And?"

"The stuff Sobell's guy said checks out. Looks like something blew up at that parking garage. It's surrounded by yellow tape and everything. Ames's crew must have run off with the relic."

Anna listened with mounting unease. She remembered Greaser's car sitting at the drop site for more than an hour and Nail commenting on how strange that was. Greaser had left, in the end, but now the remains of a car that had been blown to hell were parked in the same garage. Probably even the same spot. Which meant— what?

It meant a setup, of course. Her best guess was that Greaser'd torched his own car and run off with the million bucks and the bone, leaving Anna and company as the perfect fall guys for Sobell and the Brotherhood to take their wrath out on.

"Where is Ames?" the loud guy demanded.

Adelaide started humming. Something smashed against the wall.

Chapter 21

The afternoon had passed with a wretched, crawling slowness, each moment dragging reluctantly after the last in a chain broken only by the occasional illusory rap at the door or ring of the phone. Karyn had jumped at nearly every one, triggering a startled reaction from Drew.

"Take a nap or something," she'd told him after the first hour. "You're not helping."

"We're sitting here waiting for what? Somebody to come kick our heads in?"

"Tahiti is out, remember? I don't know what the hell else we'd do besides wait. Unless maybe you've got some new bright ideas?"

"This sucks," he'd said, and then he'd curled up on the chair and turned his back to her. Still jumped a lot, though.

The waiting was bad enough, but as the afternoon wore on, Karyn began noticing other things that were even more worrisome. At first, the knocks merely came with more frequency. Then the phone began ringing virtually nonstop, the racket from the old handset ceasing only long enough for Karyn to let out one tense breath before it began again. Eventually, she'd moved the damn thing into the other room, and when that proved inadequate to stifle its ringing, she'd put it in the oven and closed the door. If the gas had still been connected, she would have been sorely tempted to melt it to slag, but even this way it was quieter.

By evening, she was wondering how she'd ever sleep again. She sat on the couch and put her fingertips to her temples, trying to drive out the noise by raw concentration. Closing her eyes didn't help—it turned out that blocking out all visual stimulus made the noise that much worse—so instead, she stared straight at the wall ahead of her, unblinking as though she were trying to set it on fire with the intensity of her gaze.

Part of the wall turned gray as she focused on it. At first, she thought it was a trick of vision, like when stars would sometimes seem close enough to grab when she stared at them intently enough. She squeezed her eyelids shut for a count of ten and opened them again.

The gray spot had spread.

What the hell?

She got up from the couch and walked across the room, holding one hand out in front of her. *What is that?* The spot was gray, fuzzy, and almost circular in outline, and she had no idea what it was until she reached the wall and leaned in close. A faint, familiar smell came from the spot.

Mold. That's mold. As she watched, the spot expanded to the size of a dinner plate, then a hubcap, then larger, like watching a time-lapse video. The center sank in, leaving a dark hole. She reached out a hand to touch it, but felt only smooth, flat wallpaper.

"What are you doing?" Drew asked.

"This is so w—" she began, turning toward him.

She screamed and jumped back. Drew was gone, and Anna was in his place, a bullet hole slightly off-center in her temple. Blood and worse spattered the couch, the chair, and the wall behind her.

"Whoa! Hold on! Relax, OK? What's going on?" The apparition stood.

Drew. That's Drew. It didn't look like Drew, and it didn't sound like him either. It spoke sort of like he did, but the voice was all Anna. Karyn stared in fascinated horror.

There was a rattle from the front doorknob. The Anna figure disappeared, leaving only a nervous-looking Drew who, this time, jumped at the same moment Karyn did. He froze, leaning toward the back door like he was ready to bolt.

"Oh," she said hoarsely. "Company."

"Don't—" he began.

She took a few steps and opened the door.

Nail stood there, fist cocked back and teeth bared. A moment later, he recognized her, lowered his fist, and grinned.

"God, it's good to see you," he said. Behind him, Genevieve smiled.

"You sure about that?"

"Hell yeah. Anna said she stopped by yesterday, but the place was empty. This is the only *good* surprise I've had in a week."

"Yeah, well. Come on in," Karyn said. As he and Genevieve came in, she looked past them to the street, then shut the door. She gave Genevieve a curt nod. "Where *is* Anna?"

"She said she had an errand to run," Genevieve said.

"What errand?" Karyn asked.

"The kind of errand you ought to give her a big hug and a thank-you for when she gets back," Genevieve said. "You know what I mean."

Karyn's concern bloomed into something approaching panic. "Oh, shit," she said. "Call her. Right now."

Nail shrugged. "Been calling her for half an hour. No answer." He paused, studying Karyn's face. "We cool?" he asked.

Karyn glanced at Drew, who was standing half in the living room doorway looking like he had to pee real bad. "Yeah," she said absently. "But we have to find Anna right now. Where'd you park?"

"Couple blocks down."

"Let's go."

Nail frowned. "That ain't such a hot idea. Sobell's guys are trashing the earth trying to find us."

"Sobell?" Karyn asked. "Why would Sobell be looking for us?"

"We got the bone and made the drop. Now the bone's

gone and Greaser's dead," Nail said. "We don't know what happened, but think about it. If you're Sobell, all the signs point right back to us. He's already sent some guys."

Karyn scowled at Genevieve. "Isn't this your department? Can't you call him up and straighten things out?"

"I wish." Genevieve leaned back against the wall, most of the swagger gone out of her. "Greaser was my contact, for one thing. For another, I know you think me and Sobell are like two peas in a pod, but really, I'm just like you guys—a contractor. If he thinks you fucked him over, he thinks I helped."

Karyn considered this for all of a second. "Too bad. We have to—" She stopped abruptly, a sick feeling in her gut and a horror in front of her. She thought she might have screamed again, or maybe it had just come out in a breathless wheeze.

"What's wrong?" Genevieve asked. It wasn't Genevieve anymore, though—she'd turned into Anna just as Drew had. This time there were six bullet holes, all through her torso, though she was still standing, propped against the wall with eyes half shut. "What's wrong?" the apparition asked.

Karyn closed her eyes and held her hands open in fans by her sides. One breath, then two. This wasn't real. When she opened her eyes, everything would be back to normal.

She opened her eyes.

Nothing was normal. Three Annas stared back at her. Two had been shot, and the third had sustained a blow that had pushed in the corner of her head, distorting her face horribly.

"It's cool," the third Anna said. "It's cool."

"Yeah," another one added. "Everything's fine." Blood pulsed out of a hole in her chest with each word.

"All right," Karyn said, though her heart pounded and it was all she could do to keep herself from hyperventilating. *Not real.* But it was always real, wasn't it? At least, sort of. And she didn't need to be told again.

"We have to go," she said.

"I don't know . . ." the Anna with the crushed head said.

"Anna's going to get killed. We have to go *now*."

One of the Annas—Genevieve, Karyn thought—seemed to turn a shade paler, and alarm filled her voice. "Adelaide?"

"Yeah. That place is crawling with guys from the Brotherhood."

"What?"

"What about him?" The Anna with the broken head pointed to the one behind her. "What the hell is he doing here, anyway?"

"He comes, too," Karyn said. Now was not the time to bother with that second question.

The one behind her started. "Um, I—"

"Can't leave you here," Karyn said. "Sorry. Now, for the last time, we need to fucking *go*. Move it!"

Chapter 22

Enoch Sobell paced his office. He hated it. Pacing was so . . . so *prosaic*. Expectant fathers and anxious boring people of all stripes supposedly paced, and if there was one thing he strived not to be, it was boring.

Anxiety, though, seemed to have a will of its own. Every time Sobell sat, he ended up tapping a foot, then shifting left and right, unable to get comfortable, and before he knew it, he was strolling the length of the office over and over again, shuffling his thoughts into apparently random combinations.

If it worked worth a damn, he might not have minded so much, but he couldn't think of a single instance where he'd actually gotten a useful idea out of pacing. It was always when he stopped thinking of a problem that he found the solution.

Sex would be great right now. It would, too, but these days it took quite a production to get him up to the task, and he'd probably get interrupted in the middle, which would only piss him off further.

Coke? No. That just made him wired and, oddly, amped up his focus, so he'd pace twice as fast and think about the problem twice as hard. *Acid?* It had been decades since he'd used the stuff, but it might do the trick. He couldn't concentrate on shit when he was tripping, best as he could remember, and the hallucinations might even be inspiring.

He shook his head. *Better not.* The problem was

solved, he was sure. The Whisperer Shade would find Ames, and he'd take care of the rest. It wasn't so much that he needed to come up with a solution, he realized—he was simply terrible at waiting.

The intercom buzzed.

"Mr. Sobell, we've got a solution," Brown said through the tiny speaker.

Uh-huh. He rolled his eyes, but he buzzed the man in.

Brown walked in with a suspicious spring in his step, and Sobell scowled. Now was not a good time to be jaunty. He'd goddamn well better have a solution, acting like that.

Brown pulled out a small device, little more than a phone-sized LCD screen with a few buttons at the bottom. He held it with a smile.

"Mr. Brown, what in holy blue fuck is that?"

"GPS."

"Thank Christ. I was afraid I might get lost in here."

"It's not for you, sir."

Sobell drew in a long breath, forcing himself to be patient. "Please tell me what you plan to do with that thing."

Brown's smile grew. "Manny and Carl found the Ames woman's apartment."

"Good. What about the others? Did you find all of Gresser's records?"

The smile faltered. "Um, well. I haven't found any records. I mean, Manny and Carl found the apartment. They were ... confused. Like, they said you told them where to go. They seemed, I dunno. Kind of out of it, honestly."

Sobell found that rather disturbing. He wouldn't have recognized Messrs. Manny and Carl at gunpoint. It was likely he'd never even seen either of them. He filed the fact away for later. "Continue," he said.

"They said they almost caught Genevieve Lyle at Ames's place, but she took off with a guy matching the description of DeShawn 'Doornail' Owens."

"And?" Despite himself, Sobell was getting interested.

"And, Ms. Lyle left her phone." Brown grinned like

he'd delivered the punch line to the world's funniest joke.

Sobell didn't get it. "So?"

"So, the outgoing call record only has four numbers in it. We checked them—all prepaid, so they can't be traced. But we called them. Two are out of service, and one goes to Owens. And the last goes straight to a woman's voice mail. All she says is 'Leave a message,' but we're pretty sure it's Karyn Ames."

"How do you know it's not her favorite fuckbuddy?"

"We don't, I guess. But she's only called those four numbers in the last couple of days, so the safe money's on Ames."

Well, maybe it was and maybe it wasn't, but Sobell nodded, pleased. This was the best work he'd gotten out of Brown yet, and it was definitely worth checking out. "What now?"

"The phone is still on. Nobody's answering it, but we can use the cell towers to track its position." Brown held up a hand. "Let me amend that. We *have* used the cell towers to track its position. Then we send it to this unit." He made a show of reading the GPS. "The phone is in a Motel 6 on Figueroa and Grand."

Sobell nodded again, and this time he felt a grin spread across his face. "That's good work. Let me grab something, and let's go."

"You're coming?"

"Oh, yes. Though I warn you, if we go in there and I end up witnessing Ms. Lyle riding some ugly bastard like she's practicing for the rodeo, I might have to shoot someone on principle."

Brown actually chuckled. There was hope for the guy yet.

Joe Gresser had one hell of a headache. Tension, he thought. There was a lot going on, a lot to keep track of. A lot at stake. It didn't help that he'd run his mouth for what felt like twelve of the last sixteen hours. Maybe that was an exaggeration, but he was still pretty sure he'd done more talking just that day than in all of the preceding two weeks, and it was amazing how much that took out of him.

He turned in his chair, wondering if there was an aspirin in here somewhere.

His temporary base of operations was the office of a third-rate garage and full-time chop shop. The office was small and cramped, crowded with an oversize desk and a mess of filing cabinets. A ten-year-old computer squatted under the desk, hooked to an equally vintage CRT that whined like a swarm of mosquitoes. That was all fine—he wasn't here for the decor. The garage itself was owned by somebody whom Sobell had some leverage over, and it was so tenuously linked to the man that Gresser doubted he even knew it was one of his properties. That would be good, for now. Nobody would come looking for him while he . . . prepared.

Low voices came from just outside the office door. Alvarez, it sounded like. Maybe he had news from the search.

"I ain't goin' in there," Alvarez said.

Werner, the man tasked with guarding the door against interruptions, wasn't having any of it. "Fuck you, then. I ain't doin' it, either," Werner said. "It's your news."

Gresser chuckled and looked down at his left shoulder, down at the creature that now clung to his jacket collar with tiny claws. It was like some kind of grotesque baby, or—he grasped for the word—*fetus*, only with an oversize, weirdly shaped head. The jaw was sized for a normal adult, but the cranium had barely developed, remaining little more than a flat, faintly pulsing mass of flesh. Tiny slitted eyes glared from it.

"It's going to be OK," he assured it. "We got this."

It shifted, making a squishing noise in the brownish slime that had oozed from its body, staining the jacket and Greaser's undershirt, dripping down his belly and into his lap. It wasn't happy, he knew. They were supposed to have an army around them, but something had gone wrong. He wasn't too clear on the details—he wasn't too clear on a lot of things right now. But it was manageable, he knew that. They'd made quite a start already. Alvarez and Werner had been two of Sobell's most loyal, and now they were Gresser's, body and soul. There were over two dozen others who had also found themselves persuaded. There would be more.

He got the impression that his new little buddy was nothing if not opportunistic, which suited him right down to his bones.

"I'll give it to you, and you tell him," Alvarez said.

"Sorry, bro. I'm just the help."

"Don't 'bro' me, asshole."

Gresser gave his little buddy a rueful smile. Buncha pussies they had working for them, but it was all going to be OK. There'd be others, better, when they weren't quite so . . .

Vulnerable.

Yeah, that was it. Vulnerable.

"Yeah, fuck you, too," Alvarez said. A moment later, the door opened. Gresser had a brief view of the garage beyond, a row of half-dismembered auto carcasses, and then Alvarez came in.

"Glad you could make it," Gresser said.

Alvarez pressed himself back against the wall, eyes wide and fixed on Gresser's little buddy. "Urk," was all that came out. His throat worked as though he was trying not to puke.

Gresser shifted in the chair, crossed his legs, and folded his hands in his lap. "So?" he prompted.

"Mr. . . . uh. Gresser?" Alvarez said, face drawn tight in confusion. "I thought . . . Where's . . . ? Mr. Sobell?"

Gresser frowned. His little buddy crawled up a few inches, allowing him to reach into his jacket. He pulled a pistol out and set it on the desk. "You can talk to me," he said.

Alvarez managed to tear his eyes away from Gresser's little buddy and focus on the gun. That seemed to help him gather his thoughts.

"A total zero, sir," he said.

Gresser tipped his head back slightly, looking down his nose at Alvarez. "Really?"

"They knew we were coming," Alvarez said, panic causing his voice to crack on the last syllable.

The creature around Gresser's neck shifted. Its tiny eyes looked up at him, and then it moved its misshapen head and met Alvarez's eyes directly. It chittered, a high-pitched clicking and squeaking noise that sounded to Gresser like laughter. Then it crawled up on Gresser's shoulder and pushed close to him.

He's lying, it said.

That was funny, in a way, and Gresser smiled. "Don't lie to me," he said. "You're way out of your league."

Alvarez nodded. "Maybe they didn't know we were coming, I don't know. But they've all cleared out anyway. And . . . we lost Carl and Manny."

Gresser nodded. Losing those two meatheads wasn't so bad for its own sake, but it was an uneasy reminder of his own vulnerability right now. His little buddy made another gabbling sound, and Alvarez fought a losing battle to keep his disgust off his face.

"Is that all?"

Alvarez didn't answer. Gresser tapped the gun on the desk, and once again Alvarez's attention snapped back to the matter at hand.

"Uh, no. Not really." He made a pained face. "There are . . . rumors. I don't really—my head . . ."

No surprise there. L.A. was boiling over with rumors tonight, and it seemed like nearly every man in Gresser's small army had called in or come by to deliver some piece of weird and often irrelevant news in the last few hours. Not all of it was useless, though, and it was a good practice to keep his finger on the city's pulse.

"Spill it."

"They're all saying you—Mr. Sobell, I mean. They're all saying he's out. Like, out of his building. On the streets."

Gresser checked with his little buddy, who laughed again. "Now, that *is* interesting. We might have an opportunity to move the schedule forward some."

Alvarez said nothing.

"Forget about Ames's crew," Gresser said. "We'll get to them later. Right now I need you to find as many of our guys as you can and send them here." He smiled.

"Tell them Mr. Sobell wants to see them, here. Tell Werner to send 'em back to see me in groups no larger than two."

"Yeah, OK. Sure thing."

"All right. Get on it."

Alvarez reached for the doorknob, and the creature on Gresser's neck chittered.

"Oh, one more thing," Gresser said.

Alvarez hesitated, then slowly turned around.

"As far as you know, you were back here talking to Mr. Sobell himself."

Alvarez's lips peeled back from his teeth in a horrid grimace, and he closed his eyes. His hand went to his temple. A moment later, he relaxed. He opened his eyes and lowered his hand. The confusion clouding his face seemed to diminish.

"Sure thing, Mr. Sobell," Alvarez said.

Chapter 23

The van ride to Adelaide's ranked among the most surreal experiences Karyn had ever had. She ended up in the backseat next to one walking, talking dead Anna, while two more sat up front. She started labeling them in order to hold on to her sanity. To her right was Drew-Anna, the one whose brains were leaking out her head. Genevieve-Anna drove, and Nail-Anna rode shotgun—and held a shotgun, for that matter. Held it in his lap out of sight, but this business with Sobell evidently had him worried pretty badly.

Karyn felt a moment of unaccustomed warmth toward Genevieve when the other woman pressed the pedal to the floor and sent the van blasting forward almost before everybody was sitting down.

"Where?" Genevieve-Anna asked.

"Next left," Karyn said. "Then right on Santo Domingo."

The van careened from side to side around each corner, until even Nail-Anna was telling Genevieve-Anna to slow it down a little, huh? They couldn't do Anna any good if they were all dead or in jail. Karyn shouted directions from the back, trying to focus on the streets and the map in her mind rather than the odd, unreal details that showed up alongside the road—images of decay, mostly, rusted-out vehicles and collapsing buildings. Like the mold in her aunt's place, these weren't visions of tomorrow or the next day, but of some distant future, and she had to continually remind herself they weren't relevant to here and now.

"There," she said. "Adelaide's. Stop up there on the right."

"Anna's car's not here," Genevieve-Anna pointed out. The streetlights here were dark, broken in many cases, but she flicked on the van's high beams. The only car on the street was Drew's, sitting forlornly on its flat tires.

Karyn could feel her pulse pounding in her chest, her neck, even her wrists. Where was Anna? It wasn't simply that she'd come and gone and was safely on her way, or Karyn wouldn't be surrounded by macabre visions of her best friend's walking corpse. "The Brotherhood . . . I don't know."

"Goddammit, you have to know!" Genevieve-Anna yelled, and Karyn's sense of unreality pressed in on her. Was that Genevieve really talking, or was it a vision of Anna herself, pleading for Karyn's help?

Drew-Anna cleared his throat. "Um. I might be able to help."

"I seriously doubt that," Karyn said softly.

"No, I, uh, I might know where she is. I mean, there's really like only one of two places it could be."

There was a moment of shocked silence, then all the Annas started talking at once, the racket threatening to split Karyn's skull. She pressed her hands to her head, as if with enough pressure she could get everything to calm down.

Nail-Anna turned around and stuck his shotgun in Drew-Anna's face over the back of the seat, as he kneeled backward in the passenger seat.

"Start talking," Nail-Anna said.

"Motel 6, Figueroa and Grand."

Genevieve-Anna didn't wait. She pulled the van out with a lurch.

"Good start," Nail-Anna said. "Keep going."

"Or there's an apartment complex, but a bunch of the guys live there. I'm guessing they won't use that unless they have to."

"Keep talking. What else do you know about all this? What the fuck are you even doing here?"

"Look, I didn't want any part of this shit, really. This isn't my fault."

Nail-Anna racked the shotgun. "I would hate to have a *Pulp Fiction* moment in this car, if you know what I'm saying."

"Please don't," Genevieve-Anna said. "Just let the guy talk, huh?"

Karyn studied Drew-Anna. The only message she could pull from her vision was the obvious one—Anna was going to get hurt or killed, if she hadn't already. She saw no signs that might be interpreted as threat or duplicity, and she hadn't the whole brief time she'd known Drew. She'd ignored or misinterpreted signs before, but this wasn't the same—there was nothing here to misinterpret. If she was missing something, it was very subtle indeed.

"Ease up," she said. "I think he's safe."

"Not good enough," Nail-Anna said. "Not this time."

Karyn winced inwardly, but she couldn't fault Nail for that after the way the last job had gone down. She wasn't even sure whether to trust herself.

"Can you at least put that thing away?" Karyn asked. "This isn't Afghanistan. Somebody's going to see you and call the cops."

"OK," Nail-Anna said, pulling a pistol from his jacket. He slid the shotgun down onto the floor, and pointed the new gun at the backseat.

"That's not what I was going for."

The gun didn't waver.

"I don't know what to tell you," Drew-Anna said.

"Anna. Who's got her? How many? What are they going to do with her?"

Drew-Anna squirmed. "Look, they've been working up to this for over a year. They've been told for weeks that their god would come to them in the flesh—"

"It's not a god," Genevieve-Anna said.

"—when the time was right and the ceremony was complete. When you crashed the party and stole the relic, it had to be like Armageddon for 'em. I bet they're goin' *crazy*. Like, some fucking Crusades shit. They will do *anything* to get that thing back. I, uh, I really doubt they'd stop at kidnapping and, uh, torture." He said the last word quietly, as though hoping nobody would hear.

Karyn wrinkled her nose. A ripe rotting smell had begun to fill the car, and now she noticed that the Annas were going through some kind of accelerated decay. Their skin had changed to a yellowed, waxy color, and flies had begun buzzing around them. She cracked the window.

"How many will be there?"

Drew-Anna shrugged. "All of 'em. What did you expect?"

"Shit." Nail-Anna ran a hand over his forehead, dislodging a half dozen flies that flew around erratically before lighting again on his face.

"I told you, they're really pissed. This was supposed to be the big deal, the Brotherhood rising to power at the side of their"—he looked sidelong at Genevieve-Anna— "boss."

"Goddammit," Nail-Anna said. "No wonder Sobell hired us. He didn't want a shitload of nutcases gunning for him, so he hired out the job. That's why he wants to waste us now. With us out of the picture, those crazy fuckers will never know where the bone ended up."

"Those 'crazy fuckers' have a ton of guys, a pile of guns, and I have no idea what else. If they have your friend, they're only going to keep her alive if they think she can deliver the relic or the rest of you. Any idea how you're going to deal with the whole mob of them?"

"No clue," Nail-Anna said.

Conversation died quickly after that. Genevieve-Anna went into her own thoughts and watched the road. Nail-Anna simply stared back, almost without blinking, waiting for an excuse to put more holes in Drew-Anna's corpse.

Karyn watched the others and tried to keep an eye out, but that was rapidly becoming hopeless. Straightforward visions of decay weren't all she saw out there now.

The streets were filling up with monsters, and even the buildings had taken odd new forms. A ziggurat-looking thing had taken the place of what she was fairly certain had been a Conoco last time she'd driven by, and it was by no means the strangest building she saw. She watched them pass with amusement at first, then greater concern. If her symptoms kept getting worse, the world would soon become impossible to navigate. No wonder Adelaide stayed in all the time.

The scene around her was so bizarre it took her a moment to acknowledge the white streaks blazing from a vehicle on a cross street ahead. It ran the light, careening into the intersection ahead of them and drawing angry honks from the cars with the right-of-way.

"Asshole," Genevieve-Anna said.

Karyn spared it a glance. Then the shock hit her—it was a black SUV, and it was on fire.

"Follow them," she said.

"What about the motel?"

"I don't think you'll have to worry about that."

Genevieve-Anna pressed the accelerator and matched speed with the SUV, hanging back half a block or so. Another SUV joined the first from the right, and a third pulled in on the left, speeding to catch up with the other two. White light poured from each, but the flames blazing from the first one burned brighter. As Karyn watched, it exploded, yet somehow kept speeding forward. The windows blew outward on the one on the left.

"Something bad's going to happen to them," Karyn said.

"I can't wait," Nail-Anna muttered.

There had been shouting, the sounds of breaking furniture, and the occasional burst of senseless chatter from Adelaide, but if the Brotherhood and their Revered One were going to get what they wanted, it must have been obvious to them by now that they weren't going to get it from Adelaide.

Unfortunately, it was looking like Anna wasn't going to get anything from her, either. *But I can't leave her with these bastards,* she thought. That sentiment had occupied most of her concentration for the last ten minutes or so, but she couldn't seem to do anything with it. The same situation held—the room was crowded, she was alone, and she couldn't see a way through this that wouldn't end in blood.

I should get out of here. Maybe try to get some help. She pushed back from the little hole she'd cut in the wall—but then somebody in the next room shouted, and she stopped, listening once more.

"Where is she?" the Revered One bellowed. *Oh, come on. You* know *she can't help you. What's another round of this going to do?*

A high keening sound began, then cut off abruptly with a heavy thud.

"Where is she?"

"Adelaide doesn't know!"

"Where is the relic?"

"Adelaide needs—*I* need to go home! I can't think! I can't think here, everything is—everything is everything, all the time! I need—I need to go *home*! You said you could help me, I *saw* that, Adelaide can I can we can—"

"Where is Ames?"

A pause, and then: "She's coming! Coming here!" Adelaide shouted, a note of triumph in her voice.

What?

The sound of the lock turning pulled Anna's attention from the drama next door. For half a second, she thought about dashing back to the closet and hiding, but she knew she'd never make it. She stood and raised her gun just as the door opened.

Two men stood there, staring. The one in front had only his key in hand and no weapons visible. The other had a small revolver jammed into his belt.

"Back the fuck up," she said. "Right now."

"Not good," Genevieve said as she pulled the car up to the curb.

Nail nodded agreement, adding, "Damn," under his breath.

The motel was a two-story building, planned in the shape of a giant U, with faded red doors at regular intervals. Lights glowed through the curtains in a handful of units, but it was obvious that business wasn't so good these days. The small armada of black SUVs that rolled in doubled the number of cars in the parking lot.

Genevieve had kept the car back a ways, hoping the guys in the SUVs wouldn't see them, but that had created another problem for Nail to worry about. "Sobell's guys got here first," he said. "What do we do about that?"

"How many you think there are?" Genevieve asked. She'd started tapping her fingers on the dash again, which made Nail want to tie her hands to her belt or something. That nervous shit spread.

"Dozen. Maybe fifteen. Depends how many guys they jammed into the cars."

"How'd they know to come here?"

"How the hell should I know? Shut up a second, OK?"

Genevieve went back to wearing a hole in the dash while Nail studied the scene. Fifteen of Sobell's thugs on one side, surely armed to the teeth and beyond; a shitload of deranged fanatics on the other side; and Anna in the middle.

"Who's strapped?" he asked.

"I am," Karyn said. Genevieve shook her head, and Drew just looked down.

"Gen, you got any magic tricks ready if we gotta throw down?"

Genevieve shook her head. Nail could see her sweating, her usual cool composure cracked and useless. "I got nothing. Maybe if I'da prepped, but . . ."

"All right. That's what we got, then."

"This is insane," Drew said. "We're outnumbered ten to one."

Nail brushed the comment aside. Wasn't nothing to be done about it anyway. "Which room?" he asked Drew.

"One forty-four. And one forty-five, six, seven, and eight. Maybe others."

"Jesus."

"What's the plan?" Karyn asked.

Nail shook his head. "Ain't got one. Love to hear it if you do."

She didn't say anything, just kept staring across the way, her eyes distant and haunted in that way they got sometimes. Nail checked his weapon rather than look at her. *She's great,* he thought, *love that woman, but sometimes she freaks me right the fuck out.*

Across the courtyard, the SUVs waited, rumbling, exhaust belching from their tailpipes.

"No plan," Nail said. It came out even and calm, despite the adrenaline that coursed through his system. "No time for a plan, and I don't know that I coulda come up with anything even if I had a few hours to work on it. We wait for an opening, that's all."

Nobody said it aloud, but Nail could see it reflected in their eyes and, hell, he thought it himself: *Great. Just great.*

"This place is a shithole," Enoch Sobell announced. To his right, Brown nodded. "I'm half inclined to burn the entire stinking edifice to the ground on principle, Ms. Ames and the bone be damned."

Brown's eyes widened fractionally, and Sobell could see him trying to come up with the whole litany of reasons why that was a bad idea. Unfortunately for him, they all tried to come out at once and got logjammed in his throat. His mouth hung open soundlessly.

So tough to find underlings with a sense of humor these days. I suppose I should let him off the hook. "Not today's job, though," Sobell said. "We must stay on task."

"Yes, sir."

"I don't suppose that gadget of yours will tell us what room?"

"It's accurate to within a meter."

"I don't know a meter from a furlong, Mr. Brown. Will it tell us the room or not?"

"Yes."

"And?"

Brown pointed at a door barely fifty feet away. "There."

"Hm. I would have hoped she'd have better taste. Ah, well. Reconnaissance?"

"None yet. This is the first we've been here."

"Well, then. Let's have a look around. Slow and steady wins the race, eh? One thing, though—I very much need Ames alive. Her companions, well, feel free to kill any or all of them if they're in the way. Just don't hit Ames. It'll piss me off."

"Got it."

"And—oh, hell." Sobell inclined his head toward the door. "Here they come."

The door opened and two men stepped out. They exchanged a couple of words, and one of the guys pointed at the other. Even from here, Sobell could see by the buzzing white light outside the door that the second guy had blood on his face. The guy wiped at it, smearing it around some. Then the other guy pulled out a set of keys and, oddly enough, opened the door to the unit right next door.

"What is—"

"Shh," Sobell said. He leaned forward eagerly. The two men were backing up as a woman emerged from the room, gun in hand. It wasn't Ames, but almost as good. Ruiz might have answers, and she would surely know where Ames was.

Brown frowned. "I don't think those are her friends."

"I concur," Sobell said. "Shoot both of those men."

"Drive!" Karyn yelled.

Genevieve floored it. The car leaped forward with a wail of burning tires.

The two men backed up out of Anna's way, but not before sharing a glance. When they backed up, they moved in opposite directions, apparently figuring that one of them could rush her if she turned far enough to shoot the other. She hoped they wouldn't be stupid enough to try that.

Anna stepped outside. The quartet of black SUVs in the parking lot registered immediately. They didn't belong in this neighborhood.

Oh, shit.

The doors of the SUVs flew open, disgorging a dozen or more men.

The loud, dry crack of a gunshot echoed through the courtyard. One of the guys in front of her staggered and fell.

Out of reflex, she crouched, getting as low as possible. A moment later, it seemed the whole world erupted in gunfire.

"One down! Hit 'em, hit 'em!" Brown shouted. He had a lot of enthusiasm for this kind of work, Sobell noted. He had formerly been part of the army or the marines or some ridiculous, testosterone-laden enterprise like that, if Sobell recalled correctly, and this sort of absurd, unsubtle action must have given him the chance to relive his glory days, however briefly.

He was good at it, Sobell had to admit. And Ruiz had done them a favor and dropped out of the way. The guy on the left had been killed immediately, and the other was still moving, stumbling around but filled with holes. Sobell grinned as the guy pulled a gun from his belt and fired a random shot into the air.

A bullet hole appeared in the windshield of Sobell's vehicle, and the window next to him blew out. He watched, bemused, as the guy fell down and Ruiz started running.

"Well, that's that," he said to himself. "Time to go get—"

Another shot, and one of Brown's bruisers fell backward.

Where did that come from? Sobell wondered, but then he saw a glint of light on a rifle barrel sticking out of a window in the next room over from the one the woman had recently vacated.

Christ, there's another one? That's tiresome.

"Mr. Brown, would you—"

Another motel window exploded, then another. A door swung open. The night came alive with noise and blood. Two more of Brown's men went down before they even started shooting back.

Huh. I think they have more guys than we do, Sobell noted with calm surprise.

He thought it prudent to get down on the floor.

Bullets smashed into the wall behind Anna, shattering glass and punching holes in wood. Nearer to her, the hail of answering gunfire sounded like an entire invading army had just dropped in. Her first instinct was to stay down, no matter what—most of the shooters were aiming high, and maybe she could stay below the exchange and somehow survive this. Then the body in front of her jumped a couple of times as stray slugs pounded into it.

Too close. Time to go! She started moving in a low, fast crouch. The light fixture overhead exploded, showering glass over her.

The screech of wailing tires cut through the sound of the guns.

Anna blinked. At the end of the row of motel units, not a hundred feet away, Nail's van came to a shrieking, juddering stop. The side door flew open.

Karyn was there, beckoning to her.

I've lost my mind, she thought—but she was already running, bent low and staying as close to the wall as she could manage. A bullet hit the sidewalk ahead of her and chips of cement flew. Two steps past that, she stumbled and nearly fell. Somebody to her right shouted.

She ran past a second door, then a third. There were four more before the car, and she thought her heart might burst from an overdose of adrenaline before then, but she ran.

One of the doors opened, and a man jumped out, seizing her by the arm. She pulled and struggled, she kicked at him, but he was much bigger than she was, and he dragged her toward the door.

Karyn watched in horror as one of the Brotherhood grabbed Anna's arm and started hauling her away.

"No!" she screamed—and then she saw. The guy had a bullet wound in his neck.

"Shoot him!" she said.

Nail held his gun, steady as always, but he didn't pull the trigger. "I got no shot! She's in the way!"

"Shoot him!"

Nail's finger tightened, but he still didn't shoot. He shook his head from side to side. Sweat poured down his forehead, down his face. "She—she ain't clear! *I got no shot.*"

"Now!"

He squeezed the trigger. The hammer pulled back.

For the first time ever, Karyn saw Nail's hand tremble.

The guy behind Anna jerked. His hand flew to his neck, where bright blood quickly flowed through his fingers, and he fell.

No sound had come from Nail's gun, and his finger was still frozen on the trigger. He hadn't fired.

He looked at Karyn, eyes wide and spooked. "I woulda hit her. I *know* it."

The hand on her arm abruptly fell away, and Anna ran. The car seemed a thousand yards away, and the war around her went on endlessly, and she ran harder than she ever had. Her legs burned, and the impact of each footfall on the cement traveled up her body and jarred everything loose, but she pushed herself even harder.

A small explosion came from the parking lot, and she flinched as tiny, stinging fragments of metal cut her neck and legs.

Then she was at the car. Karyn reached for her, pulled her into the backseat, and slammed the door shut. Instantly, the war zone became muted, a TV program in the apartment next door instead of lead-filled reality.

"Go!" she yelled, laughing crazily. "Christ, just go!"

Chapter 24

Well. This has gone rather astonishingly sour. Sobell peeked up over the seat. Sure enough, the firefight was still raging. Half of Brown's guys, give or take, were down on the ground, either not moving or moving in a way that suggested their moving days had a very limited time horizon remaining. The others had wisely taken cover behind open vehicle doors or the vehicles themselves. The motel, Sobell noted with some satisfaction, was shot full of holes along a fifty-foot stretch, and more appeared every second. Sadly, the people inside were still shooting back.

Of even more concern, it appeared that the front of the vehicle Sobell was in had caught fire.

That's my cue. He crawled toward the door and slipped awkwardly out, keeping low as he did. Ahead of him, Brown was still returning fire over the burning hood of the vehicle.

He wondered what it took to blow up a car in real life. In the movies, it seemed they'd explode if you sneezed on them particularly violently, but he didn't think it actually worked that way. *How is it that I've never found that out in all my years on earth?*

Now was probably not the time, he reflected.

"Mr. Brown!"

Brown squeezed off two shots, sending one of the enemy ducking below a blown-out window frame. "Sir?"

"A strategic retreat is in order."

"What?"

"We need to go!"

Brown, bless his heart, didn't take much convincing. He made some arcane hand sign for the benefit of any of his men who were looking, shouted for the ones who weren't deaf yet, and began backing up. His guys followed, keeping the bulk of the vehicles between them and the army of maniacs in the motel. Sobell did likewise, taking the extra precaution of keeping the bodies of Brown's men between him and said maniacs.

A few more shots were fired, but even the madmen over there didn't seem to relish the idea of breaking cover and coming after them. Sobell, Brown, and the remaining men backed away to the other side of the motel. One guy took a rifle round in the chest. Sobell picked up the pace while the others fired back at the rifleman. Either they hit him or scared him off, but that was the last they heard from him.

Sobell dashed around the corner of the building. Six men followed, including Brown.

"What the fuck was that?" Brown shouted—not precisely *at* Sobell, but vaguely in his direction. "A handful of cheap thieves, and they have a fucking army now?"

"Put your gun away," Sobell said. "The police will be along shortly, I would imagine, and while I'd like to be long gone by then, we don't need to draw any additional attention."

"More attention than that? I have eight dead guys back there!"

"*I* have eight dead guys back there." Sobell checked the lines of his suit. Not bad, all things considered. "Don't worry—I won't send you a bill."

Brown was a soldier, not really much of a criminal at all, Sobell realized, and when he considered shooting Sobell dead, it might as well have been written on his face in DayGlo magic marker. Sobell merely watched, though, as Brown made his decision.

Soldiers did have the benefit of being predictable.

Brown put his gun in his shoulder holster. "Where did they get all those guys?"

"I suggest we get off the street. They might have cars."

Brown glanced toward the road behind them, satisfied himself that an army of crazed gunmen wasn't driving toward them at that very moment, and nodded.

Sobell walked into the alley adjacent to the motel, Brown by his side.

"It appears I underestimated the number of parties involved in this proposed transaction," he said.

"What? Who else is there?"

"The Brotherhood of Zagam," Sobell said. "It was their damned old bone to begin with."

"I have no idea what you're talking about, sir."

"Sometimes, incredibly, even my reach exceeds my grasp." He considered this. "But probably not this time. We will, however, need to revise our strategy." He pulled his phone from his pocket and dialed his driver.

While the phone rang, he gave Brown a thin smile. "Let's get back to my office and do some planning, shall we?"

"Anybody behind us?" Nail asked as Genevieve pulled the van into a sharp turn, tires shrieking.

Karyn took a stray elbow in the shoulder, and Anna's bony hip dug into her side, but she craned her neck around to look behind them. She couldn't make out anything—the night was a blur of flame and police lights, strange buildings and monstrous shapes, and she had no idea which of it represented current consensus reality. At least everybody in the van had returned to normal, though. No more corpses for the nonce—always a good thing.

"Nothing," Genevieve said, glancing at her mirrors. "No one. Better get back to the 'burbs, though. If anybody survives that mess, you can bet your ass we'll be the top item on their shit list."

"Punch it, then," Nail said. The van surged forward, jostling everybody in back again.

"You guys rule," Anna said. "Incredible timing."

Genevieve glanced up and grinned at the mirror. "That's right, babe."

Next to Karyn, Drew shifted. "Lucky you," he said.

"What the hell is he doing here?"

"I just saved your ass, but don't thank me now."

"Nobody likes a whiner," Anna said, and she laughed. It was an honest, for-real laugh, a loud, rapid flight up the scale that even made Karyn smile.

"Does anybody know where that fuck Greaser is?" Anna asked, the humor abruptly gone from her voice.

Genevieve sighed. "Dead, last I heard."

"Bullshit. He took off with the bone and our money, and he set us up to take the heat."

"I'm glad somebody knows what the hell is going on," Nail said, his voice underscored with sarcasm.

"No, actually, that makes total sense," Genevieve said. Karyn was inclined to agree, but she kept still. Her initial enthusiasm at reuniting with Anna had dimmed, and she couldn't help remembering the last words Anna, hands wet with Tommy's blood, had said to her.

Didn't see this coming, did you?

Except she had, hadn't she? And—

Fuck that noise. None of that now. She looked out the windshield, trying to lose herself in the weird scenery before her, but the only thing that registered was Anna's shoulder, stiff and unyielding next to hers.

"Why else would Sobell be gunning for us?" Genevieve continued. "I thought he was cleaning up the evidence, but that's not really his style. If he didn't get the bone, he thinks we screwed him."

"I don't even know if he wanted the fuckin' bone," Nail said.

"What?" Anna said.

"Somebody told me he was there, at Mendelsohn's, the night all that shit went down. That he had business with a demon. Didn't say nothin' about a jawbone."

"'Somebody'?" Genevieve asked. "Like who?"

Nail shifted. "Like, a guy."

"This guy reliable? How the fuck would he know?"

"I don't know."

"He tell you anything else?"

"Not really."

"There was a demon there, though," Anna said. "Something awful, anyway."

"He wanted the bone," Genevieve said, and though Karyn couldn't read her face in the rearview mirror, her voice had a strained note in it. "I know he did. He had to."

"Watch the road, huh?" Nail said.

"Is Gresser dead or not?"

"That's what I hear," Nail said. "Word is definitely that we killed him and ran off with the goods. Whether he's actually dead or not, who knows? Doesn't really matter at this point."

Genevieve nodded. "So, regardless of what he wants with the bone, Sobell's got reason to be pissed at us."

"Him *and* the Brotherhood," Anna said. "When we make enemies, we don't mess around."

"How'd you end up with *them*?" Nail asked.

Anna crossed her arms. "Adelaide," she said, the word clipped and brittle. Karyn tensed even further, her shoulders drawing in until she had to take short, shallow breaths.

Nail frowned. "Anybody going to explain that?"

"No," Karyn said.

The remainder of the ride passed in uncomfortable near silence, with only the occasional passing car relieving the drone of the engine. Karyn's neck ached, and the wonders and horrors around her had lost their ability to either charm or distract. She closed her eyes and tried not to feel Anna's movements next to her.

The hell of it was, Anna had been right. Right about Tommy, right about Karyn's responsibility, even right to be furious. Soon they'd get to the safe house, and Karyn would have to face her in the light, to look her in the eye and read the recriminations—all true, all accurate, but only all the more painful because of it.

I got Tommy killed, Karyn told herself, as she had a hundred times, either in an effort to accept the idea or, more likely, to flog herself for it. *I'll spend the rest of my life dealing with that.*

Genevieve pulled the van up in front of an empty

house, lights off and the yard bare in the gray-yellow light reflected from the dirty sky.

"No," Karyn said. "Not tonight. If we need to get out in a hurry, I don't want to have to run four blocks to the van. Can you bring it around back of the place?"

"You know something about something?" Nail asked.

"No. Just don't feel good about not having wheels tonight."

"I hear that."

Genevieve took the van down the street and eased it into the narrow alley behind the row of houses. Chain-link fences protected the yards on either side and hemmed in the alley. "Nowhere to park," she said.

"Block the alley. Nobody comes through here at this time of night."

She turned off the van. They got out, and Karyn led them through the back gate. A motion light came on next door, but the houses stayed dark. Karyn stopped in front of the back door, waiting. Had the curtain twitched over there? She tried to remember anything she could about the neighbor, and came up with a total blank.

Who cares if somebody's looking? This is your house, basically. You're stalling. A few more moments, and they'd all be inside, face-to-face, nothing to hide behind and no way to avoid each other. No way to avoid Anna, more to the point.

She squared her shoulders, unlocked the door, and went in.

"Leave the light off," Karyn said just as Anna reached for the switch. "In case the neighbors are nosy."

Anna put her hand in her pocket, feeling like a dumb kid. *Where's my head at? I know better than that.* Low light came through the thin curtains, enough to illuminate the bulk of the couch and coffee table. Nothing had been moved. The safe house looked the same as always, the same as it had a couple of days ago when she'd swung by looking for Karyn, the same as it had the last time she'd scoped it out with Karyn, shortly after they'd moved Karyn's aunt into the home. Years ago, now.

"So what happened?" Genevieve asked, worry in her voice.

"I was looking for Karyn," she said, unable to keep the bite out of her tone as the hours of frustration and worry boiled off as anger. "The phone was dead, and she never came back to the apartment after Tommy, so I settled for the next best thing—her pusher."

"Don't," Karyn said softly.

"Don't what? You bailed on us! You fucking disappeared, and I wouldn't have even known you weren't dead if you hadn't taken your bag from the apartment."

"Anna, don't—" Genevieve began, but Anna cut her off.

"Stay out of this."

Genevieve looked at Anna for a long time, then finally nodded. "Anybody got a Sharpie or something?"

Everybody in the room turned toward her. "What?" she asked. "Whatever else is going on, Enoch Sobell is looking for us, and you can bet he's not staking out random street corners waiting for one of us to walk by. He's breaking heads, and trashing our homes, and he's probably whipping out arcane shit I never even heard of. If he's got so much as a hair off one of our heads, we're screwed. Gimme a couple hours and a marker, and I can hide us." She surveyed the room one more time. "Chalk would be better, but I know enough not to expect miracles."

"Try the junk drawer in the kitchen," Karyn said.

"Yeah. OK." Genevieve turned to Anna. "You sure you're all right?"

Anna nodded. Genevieve studied her face for a long moment, then nodded once in return and left.

"Oh yeah," Nail said. "I could eat a goddamn bear, so I'm gonna check the fridge."

Nobody moved for a moment, and then Nail put a heavy hand on Drew's shoulder. "My boy Drew here is *starving*."

"Uh, yeah. Starving," Drew said.

"We ain't goin' nowhere," Nail said as he walked into the kitchen. "Take your time."

Karyn nodded. "Thanks, guys."

The silence thickened, became something almost perverse. Every sound seemed overloud in Anna's ears, from the clank and rustle of Nail pretending to raid the refrigerator in the next room to the obnoxious chirp of a cricket that had gotten in under the baseboard somehow. And yet she couldn't even hear Karyn breathe.

Anna sat on the chair in the corner, taking a strange sort of comfort in its stubborn uncomfortableness, and watched Karyn across the room on the couch, pressed against the far end like Anna might suddenly leap forward and attack her.

Anna wished she could see Karyn's face. She'd started adjusting to the dimness, but being unable to make out details made any conversation even more difficult. "You sure you don't want a light? Maybe just the hall light or something?"

"I'm sure," Karyn said. Her voice held notes of weariness deeper than Anna had heard in a long time. Maybe ever.

Low murmurs from the kitchen. Distant sound of the highway, a river that slowed but even at this hour never dried up.

"You're all scratched up," Anna said.

"Yeah. Running around in the dark."

"You went to see her."

"Uh-huh."

"She hook you up?"

"No." Karyn's figure slumped, a low heap in the darkness. "I'm . . . I'm totally out. Couple days now." Motion, and Anna thought she might be chewing her fingernails. "Another good reason to keep it dark in here."

Christ. Anna had been with Karyn during a couple of pretty bad episodes, but if she'd really gone through the rest of her blind since their last visit to Adelaide, Anna couldn't imagine what she was going through. What she'd put herself through. She coughed. There was no way to sugarcoat this next bit, and as much as she'd like to forget about it, that wouldn't do Karyn any favors.

"Adelaide sold us out," Anna said. "I'm not sure what they offered her, but she sounded like it was a big deal."

Total silence from Karyn.

"I think they were gonna hold off payment until she could track you down. She was pretty far gone, though. I'm not sure she's going to be any help. I mean, I think they might kill her."

No response.

"How does that even happen? I mean, doesn't she see everything?"

Karyn's voice floated across the darkness in a whisper. "Seeing too much is just as bad as seeing nothing. It gets ... confusing. You know that."

"Yeah. You've told me," Anna said, and bitterness surged within her. "What the hell were you thinking? You know I was looking for you, carrying around a bag with a quarter of a million dollars in it?"

"I don't deserve a cut. I didn't finish the job."

"Doesn't matter. It was in my car, so I guess the fucking Brotherhood's got it now."

Karyn moved again, and this time Anna heard her sigh. "I'm sorry. You shouldn't have come looking for me."

"That's bullshit, Karyn. You don't just walk out on your friends and disappear like that. Not because you fucked up, not for anything."

The murmuring in the next room had gone quiet, or the sound of Anna's breath in her own ears drowned it out. Her eyes had adjusted well enough now that she could see Karyn massaging her temples, eyes closed, expression unreadable from here.

"The guys need you," Anna continued. "This is *your* outfit, for Chrissakes."

"Do you have any idea what it's like?" Karyn said. Her voice was barely louder than a whisper, barely audible over that goddamn cricket. "I didn't ask to be the oracle."

"Cry me a river." Karyn had nothing but a bullshit argument, and Anna was scoring points left and right, so why didn't she feel any better?

"You know I almost got you shot in the head back there? I saw a wound in the guy that grabbed you, a bullet hole, and I *knew* Nail could make that shot. Was going to make that shot. I told him to shoot. He wouldn't do it. Said he'd hit you instead. But, hell, I saw the evidence right in front of me—he *would* make that shot."

Anna shrugged. "He made the shot. What's the problem?"

"He never fired. One of Sobell's guys got the bastard." Karyn opened her eyes, twin gleams of silver faint in the shadows. "Nail would've killed you."

"*Might* have killed me."

"Jesus Christ. You're not listening. Everybody thinks I know the goddamn future—I don't know shit. I have guesses, maybe a little better than average, but everybody takes my word like it came from God or something. I can't take this shit anymore."

"Nail didn't."

"What?"

"Nail didn't take your word like it came from God. You said he could make the shot, he knew better. So he didn't shoot. Yeah, you've got the inside info, but that doesn't mean everybody just puts their brains on automatic and goes with it." She'd made her point, but she couldn't resist going a little further. "Maybe if your head wasn't so fucking huge, you could see that."

That got Karyn to sit up straight. "Which is it? Either my head's so goddamn big we can't all fit in the room with it, or you all really do need my help. You can't have it both ways."

"Why not?"

Karyn's eyes widened, silver slivers opening to ovals. "That's not fair."

"Poor baby."

"So now what? We sit here for another hour and fight while you get off one-liners at my expense?"

Anna felt a pang of guilt at that, as she'd just been thinking much the same thing, yet the urge to get off another one still swelled inside her. She quashed it as best she could. "We can have the whole knock-down, drag-out fight later. For now, I just need to know—are you with us?"

Karyn nodded.

"We'll get this thing with the blind figured out. We'll

find somebody else. Or if all Adelaide wants is the highest bidder, we'll make that happen somehow."

"Sure."

"You all right?"

Another nod, but even in the grayscale shadows of the living room, Anna knew it for a fraud.

Sobell had a good nose for trouble and, flamboyant personality notwithstanding, a good head for avoiding it. You didn't get to be a few hundred years old otherwise, certainly not in his chosen line of work. He liked to keep it mysterious for the peons, but there was really no trick to it—you watched the details. People's eyes told volumes, though they were tricksy buggers, and they lied to you more than you might expect. Not as much as mouths, but even so. When you walked into a room, what did people say? More importantly, how did the manner of their speech change? Even without a whisper of the content, there was much to be gleaned from volume, pitch, timbre—metainformation, he supposed they called it in this day and age, though he'd known those tricks since he was scrabbling for loose change in Amsterdam, literally centuries ago.

Tonight, he had a wealth of details at his disposal, and they added up to nothing good. He'd walked several blocks since the motel debacle, Brown and company his unwieldy entourage, and he'd seen a number of things that set him to worrying. The junkies and the pushers left off their dealings and watched him walk by—not with fear, but with an eerie species of recognition, like not only did they know who he was, but they had been expecting him. One sore-raddled toothless meth addict gave him the very hairiest of eyeballs and appeared to consider jumping him right there on the street. That was offensive enough, but the obvious recognition on that lowly specimen's face, the indication that he knew who Sobell was and dared to think such thoughts anyway, was truly worrisome.

Sobell got the strong sense that, if it hadn't been for the entourage, the guy would have gone for it, too. And he wasn't the only one—Sobell was accreting a thin, straggling tail of lowlifes, too scattered and too short on numbers to be much of a threat right now, but growing.

It was probably nothing to worry about, he reminded himself. Another couple of blocks, and he'd be at the rendezvous, whereupon his driver would pluck him from this shit-filled rat hole and whisk him back to the office. The entourage would have to take a taxi—such was the lot of minions and hangers-on.

He passed a bail bondsman's shop, stepped over a passed-out hooker in front of the police surplus store. A set of footsteps accelerated behind him, and Brown caught him up in front of a seedy music store with heavy-duty bars on the windows.

"It's unusually busy down here tonight," Brown said.

"I'd noticed."

"Employees?"

Sobell raised an incredulous eyebrow. "Of mine? Hardly."

"We need to get out of here. I think this could get ugly."

"Ah, I guess that means we'll need to cut the tour short. Pity."

Brown remained silent. Sobell wondered if he'd hurt the poor man's feelings.

"Don't worry—my driver should be up ahead." He kept an even pace, worried that moving faster would set off some attack instinct in the people behind them.

Ahead, the street was empty save for a cracked plastic Starbucks cup. Sobell checked the signs at the corner as they approached and verified that he was in the right place.

"Hmm," he said. "How long ago did I call?"

"Twenty minutes, at least. Maybe thirty."

"It might be advisable to start worrying. Luis should have been here by now."

"He could have gotten hung up in traffic," Brown said. Sobell gave him a withering glare and offered no further comment. A glance behind them showed maybe two dozen of the area's lost and forgotten strewn down the length of the sidewalk, standing in doorways, and looming in the mouths of alleys. Not one bothered to look away when Sobell looked back.

"Hey, I think that's your car," Brown said, pointing. A pair of headlights turned onto the street a few hundred yards ahead.

It certainly looked like Sobell's car, a long black town car, but the sight of it stirred a faint tickle of fear inside him.

"Too slow," Sobell said. He started crossing the street, away from the approaching car, away from the drugged-out wolf pack behind. He walked quickly now, and Brown jogged to catch up.

"What?"

"Too slow. He's more than ten minutes late and driving less than the speed limit. I don't know who's driving that car, but it's not Luis. He wouldn't dare."

The distant purr of the car kicked up a notch.

"He's speeding up now."

"Run." Sobell followed his own instruction, breaking into an open run with his overcoat flapping behind him. The clacking shoes of the entourage picked up the pace, and the vagrants behind them began cutting across the street, angling toward Sobell.

Sobell turned right and headed for an alley, running full-out now for the first time in years. It was as disagreeable an experience as he'd remembered, and in addition to his rough breathing and the general strain on his knees, he developed a stitch in his side almost immediately.

The sound of screaming tires echoed through the canyon of brick and stone, followed by a sound Sobell had grown exceedingly tired of in the last hour or so—gunshots. Somebody fell. Sobell found reserves of speed he'd been unaware of and dashed forward. Brick exploded on his left, but he made the alley unscathed, Brown close behind with the surviving members of his security detail.

"Fucking *shoot* them!" Sobell snarled. Brown reached for his gun, and Sobell grabbed his wrist. "Not you." He pulled a small folding knife from his pocket and opened it.

"Hold still," he said. "This is going to sting like crazy."

"Are you—ow!" A red gash appeared in Brown's palm, blood flowing heavily forth. He tried to yank away from Sobell's grip, but Sobell squeezed more tightly. Red droplets ran down Brown's fingers and spattered the dirty pavement.

"Hold still," Sobell repeated. Brown seemed to pull together his will and keep from coldcocking Sobell, but it looked like a close thing.

Sobell pulled Brown down to a kneeling position. He drew several quick lines in the dirt, then smeared his finger in the blood running from Brown's palm.

"What the hell are you doing?" Brown asked.

"Shut up for a moment. I need to concentrate." The gunfire was bad enough—tough to tell who was winning, but there was an awful lot of shooting. Again. Sobell dabbed the lines with blood in several spots, returning to his grisly inkwell a couple of times for a refill. Brown watched, either baffled or appalled, but at least he'd stopped complaining.

Sobell finished and stood. "Come on."

Brown pushed the corner of his shirt into his wound and pressed.

"Quickly."

Some of the entourage backed into the mouth of the alley, still firing. They were down to a mere handful now, the others having fallen to bullets or the depredations of the descending horde of low-rent criminals that had taken such sudden interest in the group.

"Guys!" Brown shouted.

"They're fucked," Sobell told him quietly. "It's called sacrificing the rear guard. You can stay here and get violently introduced to the afterlife with them, or you can live. Your call."

Sobell fled down the alley without checking to see if Brown followed. The man was a soldier—he'd understand. If not, he'd go down fighting and be assured a place in Valhalla or whatever. *Not my problem.*

At the alley's end, Sobell crouched to the dirt.

Brown was right behind him, face twisted in grief and anger.

"Are you with me, Mr. Brown, or are you here to exact revenge for your fallen comrades?"

Brown stared at Sobell, glanced over his shoulder, and looked back. Anger turned to disgust, but he nodded. "I'm with you."

"Good. Give me your hand." Another quick sketch, a line across the width of the alley, and a few more dabs of blood.

"Uh-oh," Brown said, and Sobell looked up to see the last of the entourage fall. The alley filled with an angry, weapon-wielding mob. Sobell was surprised to see his driver among them, but he didn't stop to think about it much, as the man started shooting at him.

He shoved Brown out of the alley and followed, ducking around the side of the building. Counted to three, peered back around to see the mob clawing its way toward him. He reached out, pressed his hand against the line in the dirt, and uttered a few words in a long-dead language.

A long stretch of ground convulsed with an enormous cracking and rending sound, heaving up under the feet of the oncoming mob. Shouts of alarm turned to cries as the walls of buildings on either side skewed, slumped, and finally collapsed inward. The air filled with choking black dust.

"Keep moving," Sobell said.

Brown stumbled as he looked back at the wreckage.

Sobell pushed him along. "Careful, you'll turn into a pillar of salt."

"What?"

"Kidding. But move, would you? I doubt I got all of them."

Brown's eyes were wide with a familiar type of shock. Of course, there were rumors about Sobell's occult pastimes, but they were all just stupid stories until you saw him in action. "What did you do?"

"Nothing a stick of dynamite wouldn't have done better. Now come *on*."

The two men ran.

*   *   *

"All done," Genevieve said, wiping her hands as she stood. "It will take a miracle to find us now, unless the devil himself is looking."

"You think he might be?" Nail asked. He wasn't even sure whether he was joking. He raised his voice loud enough to be heard from the living room. "Hey, we cool?"

"Yeah, we're good," Anna said. "Good enough, anyway."

"Cool." Nail went into the living room, pulling a chair after him. He flipped it around so he could lean on the back. Genevieve edged around him and sat, legs folded, on the floor next to Anna's chair. Karyn still sat on the couch, head down and hands over her eyes.

"So," Nail said. "Eventually we're gonna run out of peanut butter. What's the plan?"

Karyn lifted her head, though she still didn't open her eyes. "You didn't eat that, did you? I think it's been in there since I was four." That got a couple dry chuckles from around the room, but it didn't put Nail any more at ease. There was a phony note to it, one that had to be obvious to everybody.

"What about we skip town?" he offered. "Feels like we stick our heads up anywhere around here, we're asking for a world of hurt to come raining down on us."

Anna tapped her fingers on the arm of the chair. "You serious?"

"Dead serious," Nail said. "Enoch Sobell's gunning for us, we know that, and those jackasses from the Brotherhood followed us with an army all the way here from Topanga Canyon. And if Anna's right, Greaser's got his own little thing goin' now, and it'll be a whole lot better for him if we're dead. Ain't nowhere in L.A. safe, except maybe right here. And like I said, we're getting pretty goddamn low on peanut butter."

"I don't know," Anna said. "Took me ten *years* to get in with some of the guys I'm in with. I don't want to do that all over again."

"Beats the hell out of picking your own guts out of your teeth. These guys are maniacs. They scare *me*, and you know I ain't scared of much."

"I don't know if it matters anyway," Genevieve said.

"How's that?"

"You said it yourself—Enoch Sobell's looking for us. You think a little thing like geography is going to make him forget all about us?"

"That all depends on how much geography we're talking about."

Genevieve shook her head. "There's isn't enough," she said, and the despair in her voice surprised him. "They've been to Anna and Karyn's place, so we're fucked. All he needs is a few hairs off somebody's hairbrush, and he can track them to the ends of the goddamn earth."

"The Brotherhood isn't gonna give up, either," Drew added, drawing a stare from everybody in the room. "Like you said, they brought an army after you. You think they're going to pack up and go home when they can't find you in a few days?"

"*How* did you get here, again?" Anna asked. "I get it, you saved my ass, but what the fuck are you still doing here?"

He gave an irritated sigh. "I've been through this with—well, with everyone by now. I couldn't just leave. Tina's the only family I got, and the only people I know are here. So I changed my mind. Thought I'd keep my head down, stick it out. Then I ran into your friend here when she was, uh, having some kind of episode."

Anna stood up and took a step toward him. He backed up, despite having five inches on her. "That so?"

"Yes, it is," Karyn said. "He's cool, really. I can tell."

"Yeah. And Nail might have made that shot. Remember what I said, about not shutting our brains off?"

Drew still held his hands up at about shoulder height, and now he pushed them a little higher. "Damn it, I told these guys where to find you! You think we just showed up by magic?"

"Around here, you never know," Nail muttered.

"I don't know," Anna said. "Seemed like everybody in the goddamn universe turned up there."

"Told you," said Genevieve. "All it takes is a hair."

Anna balled her hands into fists and stared at Drew. "That's great. Well, I'm saved. Karyn's saved. You've done your job well, hero; now how about getting the fuck out of here?"

Drew didn't move. Nobody did.

"Ah, fuck," Nail said. He really didn't want this to be their problem, but . . . "He can't."

"What was that?"

"I said he can't. Think about it. If the Brotherhood saw him, they'll think he's with us. They'll turn him inside out. Besides that, one of Sobell's guys saw him, too. He's *also* gonna think homeboy here is with us."

Drew shrugged, gave an apologetic nod.

"That is not our problem."

"Maybe not, but a little gratitude might be in order," Drew said. A note of frustration had finally worked its way into his voice. "Besides, I know those assholes. I know who they are, how they work, what they want. I can help you."

"It's not like he's coming on a job with us," Genevieve said. "We're all in the same boat, trying to get unfucked together."

Anna held off on the retort Nail expected, closing her mouth tightly and crossing her arms. She stepped forward, almost touching Drew, and glared up at him. Then she turned her head toward Karyn. "He's cool, huh?"

Karyn pressed her hands to her eyes. "Yeah. I mean, I think so. I haven't got a bad vibe off him this whole time."

Anna sighed, and it felt to Nail like half the room's tension bled away in that breath. "All right, then," she said. "What now?"

Chapter 25

"What *are* you?" Brown asked. Sobell regarded that as something of a miracle—the two of them were hustling down back alleys as fast as their tragically unfit flesh could carry them, and Brown wanted to get into philosophy for probably the first time in his life. Sobell ignored him and took the next left, huffing and puffing, and then another right. His shoe slipped in something greasy and unidentifiable, but he kept his footing. He cast a glance behind, saw nothing, and slowed to a walk.

"What are you?" Brown repeated as they emerged onto the sidewalk. The street was moderately busy, filled with passing cars, and a handful of pedestrians, orange in the streetlights, wandered by on their errands.

Sobell took a few deep breaths before replying. "I'm an old man, Mr. Brown, and I lost interest in that question a long time ago." Another lungful of air, sweet despite its rank odor. "I lost interest in *discussing* it even before that, so I recommend you simply think of me as your employer, and leave it at that."

"Back there—what did you do?"

"You already asked me that. Do you think you'll get an answer more to your liking this time?"

Brown looked down at his bloody hand. "This whole thing is fucked up."

"I could not agree with you more. Luis has been my driver for ten years. I've given him Christmas bonuses—sizable ones, I might add—presents for the kids, reasonable working hours and conditions, and I've had nothing but good service from him. Yet I believe he just tried to shoot me dead. Something is rotten in the state of Denmark."

"I don't know about Denmark, but it looks like everybody and his dog is out to waste you."

Sobell nodded. "And more horrifying still, it appears we will have to take a common taxi back to the office. Would you mind?" He raised his eyebrows and gestured toward the road.

Brown gave him a brief, incredulous glance, then stepped wearily to the curb and flagged down a cab. He even opened the door for Sobell when the cab stopped, which Sobell regarded as a thoughtful touch.

Sobell pulled his coat around him and sat. The space was tight, but the cab didn't smell nearly as bad as he would have guessed, and he'd certainly ridden in worse conveyances over the years. It wouldn't do to be *seen* in this thing, but the ride was serviceable enough.

He paid little attention when Brown got in next to him and gave the cabbie the address of the office building. The car jerked forward with Sobell still staring, unseeing, out the window. Over the last couple hundred years, he'd worn a dozen faces, run a thousand scams. He'd been a con man in London, an enterprising snake oil salesman in the American West. Near the turn of the twentieth century, he'd done a brisk trade selling deals with the Devil, and never mind that he'd had to fill in for the part of Old Scratch himself. The trick was convincing the marks that the Devil had run down on his luck and preferred cash instead of souls, at least for the current run of business. Once you'd gotten them to that point, it was amazing how far you could stretch a few cheap tricks. He'd learned, though, that only the most hard done by would readily deal with the Devil, and the most hard done by rarely had the cash to foot a decent bill. He'd changed the horns in for a Bible. In the thirties, he ran a traveling tent revival—a satisfyingly ironic business effort, and a surprisingly lucrative one in a time that had been lucrative for very, very few.

All in all, it had been a life of ups with very few downs, if he didn't count being run out of town on a rail every now and then. The last couple of decades, he'd tired of running scams and finally set to building himself an empire. With the collected wisdom gained from observing a couple hundred years of human nature, it had gone even more smoothly than he'd expected.

Now, though, he worried. It would never show on his face, he was certain of that, but in the still, small, untouchable center of himself that paid no attention to his will or his desires a speck of worry had formed and, like a creeping mold, it grew. Forget the bone. You win some, you lose some, and he'd lost that one, at least temporarily. But then Greaser had gotten, well, greased. And the Brotherhood had risen against him. Surprising, that— he'd read them as essentially spineless—but not the end of the world.

But Luis? And the men he'd had with him? And random, godforsaken street people? A snatch of Bible verse, held over from his tent revival days, ran through his mind.

"And I will set my face against you, and ye shall be slain before your enemies: they that hate you shall reign over you; and ye shall flee when none pursueth you."

"What's that?" Brown asked.

"Leviticus. Chapter twenty-six, verse seventeen. Not the most uplifting book of the Bible, Leviticus, but quite memorable for the quality and thoroughness of its threats. Nobody beats old Jehovah on spite—that's certain."

"Yes, sir."

Ah. Brown had collected enough of his wits to return to soldier automaton. Too bad.

"How's your hand?"

Brown looked at him with poorly veiled suspicion. "Hurts like hell. Why?"

"Just checking. I'd wrap it if I were you—don't want to leave it open. Might get infected."

Brown grunted and turned to the window. Sobell did likewise.

I will set my face against you.

Sobell searched the faces as they passed, looking for recognition, hatred, or some sign he could interpret for an explanation. Nothing, or nearly so. Once in a while, he'd catch a narrow-eyed stare from a punk in a doorway or a woman on a street corner, but on second glance, it was always gone, just a figment of his sudden paranoia.

I will set my face against you.

Maybe they would—maybe He would—but this empire wasn't falling without a bloody fight.

He watched as the low, crumbling buildings gave way to tall structures of gleaming glass and stone, watched the figures moving in pools of light, nearly disappearing between streetlights as though they stopped existing in the darkness. Fewer people walked here at this hour, most of the denizens of the business district having fled to the suburbs at the close of day. Sobell found consolation in the increasing emptiness—it seemed a sign that, here at least, things were as they should be.

His office building loomed ahead, an oasis of brilliant white security lights amid the dingy glow of streetlamps. Usually the illumination gave him a sense of invulnerability, a feeling that he'd see any approaching threat long before it became a real danger, but tonight he felt exposed. Walking through those lights would be like stepping under the shining eye of God and inviting an awful scrutiny he wouldn't be able to withstand.

I will set my face against you, he thought again, and the image of Luis's face, twisted with rage, swam in his mind.

"Go around back," he said while they were still a block off. "To the loading dock."

The cabbie drove past the building, and Sobell watched for any sign that something had gone amiss. Nobody stood in the bright lights out front, and the usual security guard was visible through the glass doors, seated at the desk and watching the monitors. Nothing irregular at all. If it hadn't been for Luis, Sobell would have stopped here and walked right in, just like any other night.

The cab turned to go around the building, and Sobell

had the driver pull over at the corner and let them out there. He tossed the guy a fifty and waved him away without a word, so preoccupied he was with watching the building.

"Everything OK, sir?" Brown asked.

"Everything? Of course not." He took a few steps and looked around the side of the building, back to the dock. Plenty of light here, too, and one guard as always.

"Looks like Sammy's on duty," Brown said. "We should be good to go—I trust Sammy."

Sobell scowled at him. "I don't."

"He's worked here since—"

"So had Luis, and yet he recently decided I'd look good with a few extra orifices in my person."

"You want me to check it out?"

Sobell nodded slowly. "I think that would be an excellent idea. Are you still armed?"

"Yeah."

Brown started down the ramp, and Sobell ducked back around the side of the building, peeking around to watch. The guard saw Brown coming and waved. Brown walked all the way to the bottom, then up the short stairs to the dock. The two men exchanged words, totally inaudible from this distance. Sammy grinned and said something. Brown shook his head. Sammy nodded and inclined his head toward the door.

Sobell leaned around to get a better view—this was moving from conversation to altercation quickly, and he wanted to see everything.

Brown shook his head again and took a step back.

Sammy lunged for him. Startled, Brown fell back. One foot went off the back of the concrete, and one hand shot out and secured itself in Sammy's jacket. Both men pitched off the dock, a shoulder-high concrete platform, and fell to the hard ground below.

Brown hit so hard Sobell heard the air blast out of his lungs, and the man arched his back and writhed like a fish. Sammy recovered faster and got to his feet, though he'd injured something badly—it looked like his right leg wouldn't take any weight.

He stood over Brown and pulled out a gun.

Sobell started running—oddly enough, in Brown's direction. *Should be going the other way,* he thought as his shoes clicked on the cement. It was true that Brown deserved better than to be abandoned and shot down like a dog, but Sobell had left better men to worse fates. *Stressful night, addled my brains,* he thought, but he kept running.

Sammy turned at the sound of Sobell's footsteps, and Brown lashed out with one foot, hitting Sammy's good leg. The leg buckled and Sammy dropped.

Brown went for the gun just as Sammy brought it around. It went off, the sound like a cannon in the concrete echo chamber of the loading dock, and Brown's head jerked to the side. Four hands wrestled for control of the gun now, and the two men rolled and struggled on the ground.

Brown was wounded and tired, though, and Sammy slowly forced the gun back toward him.

Sobell took St. George's sword from his jacket and pulled it clear of the sheath just as he reached the rolling knot of limbs that was Brown and Sammy. The gun went off again, sending a fine gray dust into the air and setting a bell to ringing in Sobell's head. A shout, and a cry, and the two men rolled over yet again.

For a brief moment, Sammy's back was to Sobell.

Sobell reached down and plunged the broken shaft of St. George's sword into the nape of Sammy's neck. There was no resistance whatsoever—he could have been swinging it in air—but the man's head fell forward, and his body went limp.

"Shit!" Brown shouted, pushing away from the dead man. That Sammy was dead was beyond dispute—Sobell's broken sword had left a deep, smooth-edged gash that went halfway through his neck. Blood spread in a widening pool.

"Quickly," Sobell said. He pointed at the thin, transparent coil that spun down from Sammy's ear. "Others will be coming." With exaggerated care, he slipped the sword fragment back into its sheath—as far as he knew, nothing else would hold it. He offered a hand and pulled Brown to his feet.

"Thanks," Brown said, still gasping.

"Let's go."

"One . . . minute."

"We don't have a minute." Sobell turned and began walking rapidly up the ramp.

Moments later, Brown followed. The commotion started behind them just as they rounded the corner. By then, Brown had found his breath, and the two men sped up. They jaywalked across the empty street, jogged rather tiredly down a couple of blocks, and finally Brown grabbed Sobell's elbow.

"Stop, I gotta stop."

Sobell glanced behind them—nothing. "All right," he said, wiping his forehead and dabbing his handkerchief on his cheeks. "I confess I'm thoroughly sick of running myself. Let's get off the street, though."

They stepped into a darkened tavern, the particularly bilious variety known as a sports bar, but this one time Sobell was inclined to put up with it. Televisions squawked and blared eye-splitting color from every direction, and not a single person in the place was looking at anything else.

Without waiting for anybody to greet them, Sobell went to the booth farthest from the front window and sat. Brown scanned the room and then did likewise.

Brown hunched forward. "Sammy wanted to know if I'd seen you yet."

"Lots of people seem to be looking for me right now. What did you tell him?"

"I said no."

"Good."

"Not really," Brown said. "It got real weird after that. He told me I had to come up and see you immediately."

Sobell raised his eyebrows. "Now that," he said, "is quite interesting."

"I told him I'd pass, maybe take care of it in the morning, and then—"

"I saw. He became rather insistent."

The two men stopped talking as a perky waitress showed up at the table to take drink orders. In his current frame of mind, Sobell would rather chew ground glass than interact with the kind of cheerful person who asked questions like "How are we doing tonight?" but he wanted to attract attention even less. Placing an order was the easiest way to get her to go away with no fuss, so he did.

"It appears I have a doppelgänger," Sobell said, once the waitress had gone.

"I don't know what that means."

"It means somebody is pretending to be me, effectively enough to control essentially all of my employees and usurp my very throne, so to speak."

Brown's face took on a skeptical expression. "Who could do that?"

"Only one person I can think of. Your predecessor."

"Mr. Gresser? He's dead."

"Oh, I very much doubt that anymore," Sobell said, mouth set in a grim line. It all made too much sense now, and he saw how much trust—how much *power*—he'd put in his former lieutenant over the last few years. Gresser had the hearts of the troops, he knew all the secret places and codes, and most of the shady side of the business. If anybody had a hope of picking it up, it would be him. But this wasn't Rome—most people wouldn't just accept that Sobell had been deposed by military coup. Not unless . . . "It also means one other thing."

"What's that?"

"It means the bone works."

"I don't—"

Brown broke off as somebody slid into the booth next to Sobell. Sobell reached for the sword's hilt, then paused as he got a good look at the newcomer, or at least as close an approximation as it was possible to get. The figure next to him sat in a heretofore unnoticed confluence of shadows and was strangely hard to see, even at only an arm's length away. It appeared to be a man, or at least the shape of one, draped in a long coat, hat pulled low. Sobell wasn't sure, though, that it had a face, or even a head.

"Ames," it said, a harsh, grating whisper like newspaper tearing.

Ah. The Whisperer De— Shade. Not a demon. A shade.
"Yes?" Sobell's voice wavered. Embarrassing, but Brown had the look of a man who had lost control of his sphincters, so he doubted he'd get any grief for it from that quarter. He did hope Brown's face wouldn't stick like that.

The shade whispered an address. Sobell repeated it in his head a couple of times to keep it fixed in memory.

"Very well," he said. "You're released from service."

The figure lost form and dissolved—coat, hat, and all—right into the seat, sending up a seething fog of cold vapor. Sobell had an urge to move away from the spot, but he was already nearly pressed to the wall.

He surveyed the room. *No, sir, not attracting any attention here,* he thought disgustedly—but, amazingly, they hadn't. The ball game went on undeterred, and the denizens of the establishment kept their slack faces trained on the screens.

"Released from service?" Brown asked.

"Of course," Sobell said. "You're not my only employee. Sometimes, for the tough jobs, it's best to find a good contractor."

"What did it say?"

Ames. That was a useless endeavor now, if his hunch about the new occupant of his office was correct. The takeover of his business operations was irritating enough, but somehow what really galled him was that Gresser had actually moved into his office. The nerve of the man! Hadn't he been treated well over the years? Treated like a king, practically. Hell, Sobell would have given him most of the less savory enterprises in name as well as in practical fact, if he'd asked. For years, he'd been paid handsomely, and Sobell had looked the other way at the occasional graft or bonus extortion Gresser levied on certain associates, reasoning that they were perks suitable for a man in Gresser's position. In fact, Sobell had gotten every dime he was owed, as far as he knew, and he'd done a fair amount of checking. If Gresser had the habit of pushing a little harder and pocketing the difference, that was fine.

But now he's in my office. And not just in the office giving the orders, but sitting on Sobell's collection, too. Not that Gresser'd be able to figure out how to use any of that shit, but he'd done an admirable job of cutting off Sobell's access to it. Sobell inhaled slowly, then let out a long, steady breath, trying to cool the fury building in him. It didn't work. He would gladly have brought his own building crashing down, collapsing it with Gresser in it and sealing it like a tomb, but of course he'd been concerned when he built it about somebody doing the same thing to him, and the girders and foundation were heavily warded. The trick he'd pulled in the alley earlier wouldn't work, nor would anything like it. *Dynamite would, though,* he thought, remembering what he'd told Brown earlier. But, no. Too ostentatious, and too impersonal. He'd like to choke that bastard Gresser to death with his own hands. Plus, dynamite would probably destroy his collection and his documents. And, besides, one didn't generally blow up a major building in this day and age without repercussions. Somehow, it would get tracked back to him and ruin years of work.

"What did it say?" Brown asked again.

"Oh. It divulged the whereabouts of Karyn Ames."

"Karyn . . . ? Oh." Unsurprisingly, Brown seemed unsure of what to do with this information now. Sobell himself wasn't sure what to do with it.

Or, actually . . . most of his resources were held inaccessible in that building, and Ames was a notorious thief. And, if rumor was to believed, psychic.

"Shall we pay her a visit?"

"Um, sure. Can I take a piss first?"

Gresser leaned over Sobell's desk, laboring away at a—at a what? What the hell was this thing? He held a pen in his right hand, and he was tracing out a bizarre series of lines and symbols on a thick sheet of something that seemed closer to leather than paper. Sobell had surrounded himself with this kind of crap, which was his privilege as a crazy old rich bastard, but what did Gresser know about it?

He wished his thoughts weren't so fuzzy. He wished his back didn't hurt so much. There was a weight there, bearing him down and crushing him. His spine cracked and his shoulders screamed as he stretched, and he groaned aloud.

What's bothering you? The voice came from nowhere, but it was very important to answer it.

"I can't—I don't . . ." He closed his eyes tightly shut, searching for some focus. For one desperate moment, his identity thinned out like rotten, unstable boards beneath his feet, and he teetered on the verge of panic.

Who am I? he wondered. *I'm Enoch Sobell—no, that's ridiculous. Well, wait. Everybody talks to me like I'm Enoch Sobell. But I don't remember being Sobell* before. *Before, I was . . .*

Clashing memories spun in his head. For the past— how long? For the past little while, everybody had been calling him Sobell, but he remembered fear on their faces, fear and confusion. Perhaps he frightened them, but he wondered if he'd vandalized his own memories, painted the fear in like graffiti. Maybe they hadn't been afraid at all. Maybe they were always afraid.

Another memory—a young punk, a big kid with a smashed-in face, almost as quick with his mind as with his fists, though nobody ever credited it. A dead man lay at the kid's feet, sprawled out in his own blood, and an older man stood with his hand on the kid's shoulder. The older man was Enoch Sobell, but Gresser couldn't fit himself to that body, to that point of view. No, he suddenly understood. He was the kid in this memory. He was . . .

Joe Gresser. Always had been. But then what was he doing here? And why did his back hurt so much?

What's bothering you? The voice again, and Gresser felt a pain in his neck now, as well as a redoubling of the pain in his shoulders. He ought to look down and see what was going on there. It might be serious.

"Back hurts. Too heavy," he said.

There's nothing on your back. Nothing heavy at all, and no pain. You're strong, Joseph.

"Yeah," he said. "That's right." He straightened up. Bones ground together between his shoulder blades, and the rifle fire of ligaments snapping back in place over knobs of bone cracked and popped. It didn't hurt, though. Wasn't heavy. A crushing fatigue had settled into his muscles, but even that seemed distant now. *I'm strong,* he reminded himself.

To the work, Joseph. Finish the work.

He nodded and bent back to the desk. The drawing was a murderously complex piece of work, or at least it seemed that way, since he had no clear idea of what he was trying to do. The voice guided him, but words gave poor direction for this assembly of curves and lines, symbols and mystical connections, and the task was taking forever. No wonder his neck—no, his neck felt fine.

Perfectly fine.

The phone buzzed, startling him badly enough that he scratched a black line across the paper.

You stupid, worthless fuck!

It was true—he was stupid, he was worthless, and—

Later. Answer the goddamn phone.

He answered the goddamn phone. "What?"

"Sir? Mr., uh, Sobell?" The woman's voice was halting and confused, her words an echo of the swirl of confusion in his own mind.

Wait. Am I Mr. Sobell? I thought I wasn't, but then I was, and now . . . "What?" he repeated, cutting off the bewildering echoes bouncing back and forth in his skull.

"There's been a security incident."

"Take care of it."

Hesitation. "Well, sir, it has been taken care of. We lost a man, though."

"That's too bad," he said, though he felt more irritated by the interruption than sympathetic. "Make the appropriate arrangements. Surely you know how to handle that?"

The woman on the other end of the phone line hesitated again. Who was it? Shouldn't he recognize her?

God, his head was a mess. "It's not that. It's—we checked the security tapes. Your . . . uh . . . The guy pretending to be you—he was here."

The guy pretending to be me. Who's that? Who am I? There's a guy pretending to be Sobell, or a guy pretending to be . . . to be . . . Joe. Joe Gresser.

It was Sobell, the voice reminded him. *You were supposed to have him killed.*

"Shit," Gresser said. "You were supposed to have him killed."

"He got away. We didn't expect him to come here."

Enough of the fog parted to give Gresser a clear look at that concept, and cold fear seized his guts. Sobell, for real, here. Gresser stared at the diagram he'd been working on, seemingly since sometime in the last century. He'd seen Enoch Sobell knock out one of these in fifteen seconds, and something very unpleasant had happened right after that, hadn't it? Something that had required a shovel and a mop to clean up what was left of a man.

But wait. I'm Sobell. Right?

No, that wasn't right. Goddammit, why was that so hard to keep in his head?

"Mr. Sobell?"

Oh, I am *him.* Another momentary burst of clarity. *No, I'm* pretending *to be him. So the guy who was here was somebody pretending to be me pretending to—fuck! No, it was* him.

"Where is he now?"

"We don't know."

The panic rose again. "He's not in the building, is he?"

"No. No, sir."

"Just—just go find him, all right? And kill him, for Christ's sake!"

"Yes, sir."

Gresser hung up the phone. God, this had gotten complicated.

Don't worry about it. You have work to do.

Ah, right. The drawing. He got a fresh piece of that odd thick paper out of his *(Sobell's)* desk and started again. This was important work, he reminded himself.

Sobell—or a man pretending to be him, and let's not get too hung up on the confusing details, OK?—was out there somewhere, and there was almost nobody else who could stop him at this point. *Maybe* the guys would find and kill him on their own—and maybe not. He could find the man, though, and this irritating goddamn diagram was the key. If he could find the man pretending to be Sobell, he could kill him.

He felt strangely vulnerable, and he wasn't sure where the feeling originated. He was safe here, at the center of his *(Sobell's)* empire. That had been part of the plan, hadn't it? Wasn't that why he was here? Safety. Power. They were kind of the same thing, when you got right down to it. Yet he was practically teetering on the edge of panic, filled with a sense of urgency. Time would fix it, if he could hold on long enough. Long enough to ... what? *To grow.* The thought didn't seem to be his, but the truth of it was obvious.

Tie up the loose ends. Stay safe and protect himself, until he could assume full power at the head of his empire. Something about that didn't seem quite right, but his head was nowhere clear enough to figure out what.

He returned to his work.

Another set of orders hissed into his ear, another set of curves sketched on the paper. The strange fatigue in his back and shoulders built until he found himself leaning so far forward his face nearly touched the paper. Despite the comfort of the building's air-conditioning, sweat dripped from his face, fell in drops from slick, clumped strands of hair.

Then, when it seemed that he must at last collapse and give up the whole enterprise, he finished.

From the top desk drawer, he pulled a plastic bag full of faintly disgusting human detritus he'd gathered from the office. It contained a few strands of short hair, a fine whitish dust gathered from the seams of his *(Sobell's)* chair, and a wad of used Kleenex. He tipped the bag up and coaxed a single gray hair from the opening, placing it in the center of the drawing he'd labored over for so long.

Words came from somewhere, ugly, foreign words that meant no more to him than the babblings of an infant, but they wriggled inside his head and he knew he was to pronounce them aloud.

He said the words. Each one leapt from his tongue with a crack and a sizzle, and when he had completed the full incantation—

Nothing.

Again.

Once more, he urged the words from his lips, this time with an intensity and urgency lacking in the last round, propelled on by fear. Fear of what, he didn't stop to consider.

Once more, nothing.

Again, a voice whispered, and he began anew. This time, though, he read defeat under the whisper's rage. Whatever was supposed to be happening wasn't happening, and maybe it wouldn't.

He spat out the last word in a final, foul-sounding guttural heave of his throat.

Nothing.

Behind him, in a place between his shoulder and the nape of his neck, the whispering thing howled and screamed.

Chapter 26

Peanut butter on stale crackers. Not enough to go around, but Karyn hadn't eaten since breakfast, and Nail had spoken up loudly on her behalf. She bit off a piece, trying to choke down the queasy feeling kicked off by the thick, sticky texture and the cardboard taste of the crackers. She had to eat, she knew. It wasn't clear whether the dizziness she'd been experiencing was a symptom of her condition or just low blood sugar, but she hadn't had a real meal in a couple of days now, and regardless of the phantasms and half-assed prophecies that swam in the air before her, she needed some calories.

She took another bite with her eyes half closed to filter out some of the chaos she saw. Earlier, she'd tried closing them entirely, but that seemed like a good way to smear peanut butter over a third of her face. Amusing to the guys maybe, but not worth it.

"How are you doing?" Drew asked, sitting on the couch next to her. "You, uh, you don't look so good. I mean—that's not what I meant. I mean, are you sick?"

"Just overtired," she said.

"You sure?" he asked.

"Yeah," she said. *No. Not at all. Nothing is OK.* The visions were bad now. Everything existed in a state of flux between present and future, the future sometimes plain, sometimes bizarrely symbolic, and sometimes wholly uninterpretable. Right now, she saw the eventual fate of the house—roof collapsed, walls decayed, one wall wide open to the street. She could feel the wind blowing in, hot and dry and reeking of asphalt, and her hair blew across her face with a light, nervous touch.

At least her friends were whole. She hadn't had to listen to a talking corpse now for a good twenty minutes, though she occasionally got unsettling glimpses of their futures, too—Nail, his skin dry and wrinkled, a patch over one eye. Genevieve with a few new tattoos, the lines around her eyes deep as she wept into her hands. Anna, hard and humorless. Nothing to be done about any of that, and most of it was so far off it could change radically between now and then anyway. Or so she guessed. She hadn't had it this bad before, had never seen this far into the future, and had no idea what it meant.

She ate another couple of crackers, but she might as well have been chewing warm mud. It sat in her stomach in a heavy ball, roiling in slow waves and offering nothing to sustain her.

The talk in the room went around in obnoxious circles. She checked in every once in a while to see if anything new had been unearthed or discussed, but it was all depressingly constant. Anna would announce that they needed to wrest the bone from Greaser. Nail would point out that they didn't know where Greaser was. Anna'd say that she herself could find him, she could find anyone, given time—and Nail would counter that as soon as she went out in public, Sobell or the Brotherhood would waste her on sight. Genevieve agreed with Nail's assessment and kept touching the back of Anna's hand, like she was afraid Anna was going to simply disappear or something. Drew brooded in the corner, adding nothing.

While they talked, Karyn tried to tune out the craziness around her and concentrate on the problem of blind. She didn't know where to begin getting more, and she wasn't sure how well she'd be able to cope with even a few more days of this. She and Anna had been lucky and resourceful to find Adelaide and her nasty miracle drug back when, and that was without dozens or hundreds of people waiting to gun them down as soon as they stuck their faces out in public.

The problem was intractable and terrifying, and between the rapidly aging room and the ongoing argument around her, Karyn could barely focus on it. And, as if to tease her, every so often the discussion would wind down, the conversation would falter, and, just when it seemed possible that a moment of peace could be had, Anna would kick-start the whole thing again.

This time around, Anna was trying to convince Nail that it wouldn't hurt if she started calling some of her contacts, and Nail wasn't having any of it.

"Do you know what kind of people these are?" he asked. "They're thieves, for fuck's sake—and worse. They're just gonna sell us out."

"I don't have to tell them anything. I just need information."

Karyn tuned them out and, for once, turned to her hallucinations for solace. The house had regressed in time, rebuilt itself around her. The walls stood, whole and strong, and the interior was still marked with Genevieve's scrawlings at the base of the doors and windows. It might even be *now* in her head instead of tomorrow for a change. Nothing in the room told her otherwise.

"No, you don't have to tell them anything—but then they won't tell you shit. We're not talking about charities, you know?"

The phone rang, its old-fashioned bell shrill and clanging even from the phone's new home in the oven, and Karyn jumped.

"What is it?" Genevieve asked.

"So I lie," Anna said. "It's not that hard."

The phone rang again, and the front door swung open. Karyn checked the others—they were still caught up in their argument, and nobody'd noticed the door, so she assumed it hadn't actually opened.

"Are you OK?" Genevieve asked.

"That works once," Nail said, "and after that nobody believes a fucking thing you have to say."

"If ever there was a time to blow my cred, I'd say that's now."

In the doorway stood a silhouette, completely black

and featureless against the porch light across the street. As Karyn watched, it held out its hands, palms up, in an ambiguous gesture, either offering something or demonstrating that it carried no weapons.

The figure stepped over the threshold and abruptly disappeared. Karyn blinked and the vision was gone, the door closed—but the phone rang louder, screaming over the conversation in the room.

She stood. "Somebody's coming," she said. "Now, right now."

"What?" Genevieve asked. "How?"

Nail went for one of his guns and tossed another to Anna. "How much time we got?" he whispered.

Somebody knocked on the door. Inside the dark room, heads turned toward the door. The doorbell rang.

"I think it's cool," Karyn said.

Anna raised her gun toward the door. "How sure are you?"

"Not very."

Another knock, and then an exasperated voice, smooth and male, came through the door, barely muffled by the cheap wood. "I know you're in there. How long do we have to continue this charade before you let me in? Or I could call the police. I'm sure they'd love to have a conversation with you all, or at the very least draw a great fat lot of attention to this nondescript suburban shithole."

"Uh-oh. It's Sobell," Anna said.

Nail moved to the curtain and gently parted it a finger's width. "Two guys," he whispered. "I can take them now. Just say the word."

"Really, Ms. Ames, Ms. Ruiz, I'm sure we have more to gain working together than by remaining at odds. We have both been liberally fucked by the same party, and, frankly, I didn't even get a token lube first. I'd very much like to talk with you."

"Is this shit for real?" Nail asked.

Karyn nodded. "I think so."

Anna shrugged. "Let him in."

Nail stepped next to the door, undid the sorry security

chain, and turned the knob. He flung the door open and stepped back.

"There," Enoch Sobell said. He held his hands open in front of him in exactly the manner Karyn had seen in her vision. "Was that so hard?"

"Sit down," Anna said, gesturing with her gun toward the uncomfortable chair in the corner. She wished it had nails sticking out of it, for all the trouble this asshole had put them through.

Sobell did as he was told, though Anna thought she detected an ironic, amused smile on his face as he walked.

"Who's this?" she asked, flicking her gaze toward the guy with Sobell. He was a big man with close-cropped graying hair and square shoulders, who reminded her of a middle-aged football player just starting to get soft around the middle. Tough-looking, but not enough for her to take the gun off Sobell, even for a second.

"That is the entirety of my loyal army," Sobell said as he eased himself into the chair. Damned if his presence in the chair didn't elevate it from lumpy ass-breaker to something more like a throne, albeit one in hideously poor taste. "You can call him Mr. Brown."

"Hey," the guy said, accompanying the words with a lazy wave.

"You can sit on the floor. Put your hands in your lap. If you move them, I will shoot you." She hated the sound of the words coming out of her mouth.

"You got a fuck of a lot of nerve, coming here," Nail said, also training his gun on Sobell.

"If you say so," Sobell said. "You wouldn't be the first."

"What do you want?" Anna asked.

"How did you find us?" Genevieve asked at about the same time.

Sobell didn't even bother to look at Genevieve. "I'd like to clear up a misunderstanding," he said.

"I don't think we misunderstood anything," Anna said. She wished she knew how Sobell could face down both her and Nail, and their respective firearms, without showing a trace of anxiety. She was so nervous the grip of the gun dripped sweat.

Maybe he's bulletproof, she thought, and then dismissed it. *Bullshit. Focus, woman!*

"Perhaps not. Whereas I seem to have misunderstood quite a bit. The time seemed opportune to get some clarity in my thinking, before I killed a lot of the wrong people."

"And you think we can help you with that?"

"The clarity, or the mass murder?"

Jesus. Who actually admits to things like that? "The clarity. Let's go with that."

"Ah. Well, yes, actually. I was rather hoping you could tell me exactly what happened with the magic disappearing bone after you handed it over."

"After we—*what*?" Nail shouted. "You've been fucking shooting us and shit all day, and you already knew we made the drop? You asshole!"

"Cool it," Anna said, though a similar thought had occurred to her, adding rage to the fight-or-flee rush pounding through her body.

"No, I won't cool it. He's been fuckin' playing us this whole time. He knew about the demon at Mendelsohn's. Had *business* with it. You stop to think that if he hadn't been fucking around with that thing, Tommy might still be alive?"

"I don't know where you're getting your information, but I assure you I was not fucking around with the demon at Mendelsohn's. Thanks to your efforts, it got loose before I ever showed up," Sobell said. "I would have liked to speak with it, yes, but you all made sure that couldn't happen."

"We had nothing to do with that," Anna said.

"You'll pardon me if I'm not ready to take your word for it."

"You knew about the demon, though," Nail said, rather weakly.

"So did you. I'm not sure what your point is."

"My point is, you've been screwing around with us since the start. And now what? After a long day of trying to shoot the shit out of us, you're here to finish the job in person?"

"Actually, I haven't so much as lifted a finger against you," Sobell said. "I have been out of the loop, as they say, up until a short time ago, and my erstwhile lieutenant has run amok. *He* has been 'fucking shooting you and shit' all day, probably in an effort to delay the moment wherein I finally figure out what is going on."

"But you know Greaser took the damn thing now," Anna said.

Sobell folded his hands, crossed his legs, and leaned back in the chair. His grin wasn't even smug—it was a calm half smile that said, *Ah, at last a civilized discussion.* "Yes. I finally figured that much out, though it took an inexcusably long time. In any case, I'd be grateful if you could tell me what happened after you gave, ah, *Greaser* the bone."

Anna shrugged. "Nothing. He and his guys stayed put."

"Stayed put for a long time," Nail put in. "Way longer than they were supposed to."

"And then?"

"Then they left," Nail said.

"They left? You're certain?"

"Yeah. We watched until they took off."

Sobell nodded. "The burned wreckage of the vehicle was found in the parking garage you specified for the drop. Mr.—*Greaser* went back to set you up."

"We figured," Anna said drily.

"Still, it's unlike him to meddle with objects for the collection—he's picked up half a dozen for me over the years without showing the slightest interest in fucking around with them. You didn't give it to him wrapped in tissue paper, did you?"

"No!" Genevieve said, her professional pride apparently wounded. "The box was good, warded inside and out. We didn't even open it when we gave it to him."

"Greaser did," Anna said. "After we handed it over. He opened the box and had a look inside."

"Did he close it again?"

"Sure."

Her arm beginning to weary, Anna lowered the gun, though she glanced at Nail to make sure his was still at the ready. "Look, we know he took the damn thing. It pissed off everybody in the known universe. None of this helps us."

"Just assembling the facts, dear."

"Don't call me dear."

"Apologies. You'd stopped pointing that gun at me, so I thought we were getting close."

"Whatever," Anna said. "Enough of this shit. You don't get to come here and ask all the questions. We get a turn."

He shrugged. "Ask."

"OK. The bone. What did you want it for?"

Sobell cocked his head, brow knit in puzzlement. "For? Some things aren't *for* anything, child. Like a ten-foot-high stack of hundred-dollar bills or a wriggling pile of nubile whores, some things are worth having for their own sake." He favored them with an oily grin. "Actually, though, in this case, I was going to use it to jump-start my career in politics."

Blank stares and gaping mouths greeted this statement, and Anna felt her own jaw drop. "You what?"

"I assure you, even being a notorious crime lord wears thin after a while. I have other ambitions. Can I count on your support in November?"

"You're insane," Anna said.

Sobell merely shrugged. "It's been said, though not generally when people think I can hear them. However, this is beside the point. Do you have other questions, or can we get down to business?"

"What business?"

"Oh, boy," Nail muttered from somewhere behind Anna and to her left.

"I propose an alliance. Your crew, combined with my incomparably vast army"—he raised his eyebrows and glanced toward Brown—"and any other tricks I may have up my sleeve."

"An alliance to do what?"

"We need to repurloin that godforsaken bone before we all end up with even greater problems."

Anna looked right and left, checking the expressions on her companions' faces. Genevieve was listening with avid interest, of course, but Sobell had Nail's complete attention as well. Drew, too. Even Karyn seemed engaged rather than drawn into whatever strange world she now lived in. They were going to do this, Anna realized — they'd done everything but say yes.

"And how is stealing that thing — again — going to clear up any of this mess?"

"I'm so glad you asked. Rumor has it that, if you hold the Devil's jawbone, those who can hear you speak will believe any lie you tell them."

Anna thought that made a certain amount of sense. In any case, she could see how that would allow a dirtbag like Greaser to take over Sobell's operation, at least temporarily.

"Actually," Sobell continued, "although my preference is to recover the bone, at this point I'd be quite happy to simply destroy it."

"Whoa!" somebody said. Anna turned to see Drew standing, hands up as though he were trying to push Sobell away from him over a distance. "I don't think that's a good idea at all."

"Why ever not?"

"It's a piece of a *god*," Drew said. "What if you can't destroy it? What if you piss it off?"

"It's not a god," Genevieve said.

"It's not even a piece of a god," Sobell added.

Genevieve gave him a cocked half smile. "Thank you."

"Presumably if we destroy it, we break its power. Then I can go back to my riches, drugs, and multifarious sex partners, and you can go back to skulking in the undergrowth and doing work for people like me. I'll make sure you're well compensated, I assure you. You can probably take quite some time off skulking, if you so desire."

Drew stood with his mouth half-open, trying to cough up a reply that seemed lodged in his throat.

"That arrangement should be agreeable for all of us, no?"

"No!" Drew shouted, finally getting the word out. "The Brotherhood will kill all of us. How are you in any position to prevent *that*?"

"I'm not right *now*, obviously, but once I am again at the reins of my vast criminal empire, I should be able to whip something up."

Drew shook his head wildly from side to side. "You don't get it. It's not a thing or a relic or an artifact to those people. *It's their god.* Physically. Like, in the flesh. I mean—you know what I mean. When it was stolen, they were in the middle of trying to bring the damn thing to life."

"And?"

"And what? This is the Brotherhood *of Zagam*. They thought they were moments away from bringing their god to earth, and then poof! It was snatched away. They will overturn heaven and earth, kill dozens or hundreds, do whatever is necessary to get it back and finish the rite. They *will not stop*. You have no idea what these people are capable of."

"I have some idea. They're definitely capable of killing eight or ten of my hired thugs in a firefight. I can't imagine any escalation will deter them, if that's what you mean."

"See? This is crazy!"

"Nonsense. Once we have the bone, we have options. We can give it to them, though I wouldn't necessarily advocate that. We can just lie to them and make them go away—they'll have to believe us. If we destroy the bone, well, yes. Provided the Brotherhood doesn't simply become discouraged and go home, there's nothing for it then but a bloodbath. *C'est la vie.*"

"Jesus," Drew said.

"I'm impressed, if that's any consolation. You've clearly done your research."

"It's not research," Anna said. "He's one of them."

Karyn frowned. "No, he's not. He's with us."

"Whatever. He used to be one of them, anyway."

Sobell smiled in a casually sadistic way that reminded Anna of a kid frying ants with a magnifying glass. "How badly might they want him back?"

"No," Karyn said. "There's no leverage there, so put it out of your head."

"Pity." He studied Karyn for a moment. "I'm sorry, we haven't made formal introductions. You must be Ms. Ames."

"Yes."

"And what do you think of all this?"

Karyn's face remained blank, a gray oval in the dim light. Anna wondered what she was seeing now, whether it had any bearing on the current situation, or whether she was moving farther and farther away from everyone else's reality. Anna thought of Adelaide and closed her eyes briefly.

"I'm listening," Karyn said. "The Brotherhood was a problem we already had. So was Greaser and your thugs. I don't see how your being here is all that much help."

Sobell uncrossed his legs and put his hands in his lap, taking some time to consider. "I know where Greaser is," he said at last. "I know the layout of the building and the nasty tricks that are set up to deter people like you. If we can get to him, we can get the bone, and then—problem solved. Also . . ." He said a few low words under his breath and snapped his fingers. A naked blue flame flickered to life in his palm, casting a thin, sickly light over his face. "Like I said, I know a few tricks."

"Anna," Karyn said, "can I talk to you in private?"

Karyn was still looking at the world through half-slitted eyes, Anna noted, and her face was a tight, unmoving mask of control. Somebody who didn't know her might think she was holding back a mighty blast of anger, but Anna had seen this before, and she knew better. Karyn was hurting and she didn't want it to show.

"Yeah," Anna said.

"And we were making *such* progress here," Sobell complained.

"You guys can get acquainted until we get back. Try not to kill each other."

*   *   *

Karyn led the way out through the back door, and the two women went out to the wide concrete slab that stood in for a back porch. A breeze blew hot and dry, stirring the high brown grass of the lawn. It didn't cool Anna in the slightest.

Karyn put her fingertips to her temples.

"Pretty bad, huh?" Anna asked.

"Yes, ma'am." Karyn barked out a short laugh. "You know, I'm at the point where I don't even know if this headache is real or if it's just a premonition of a future headache."

"I don't suppose you can have a premonition of some aspirin to make it go away?"

That coaxed a tiny smile from Karyn's lips. "As soon as I figure out how, I promise I will get right on that."

"So what's up?"

Out here, the streetlights and the city light reflected off the low umbrella of yellow-brown pollution gave enough illumination to read Karyn's face, to see the faint twitching at the corners of her mouth and the subtle movements of her eyes. Anna liked what she saw even less than she had before. Karyn's eyes darted from place to place without stopping, and her shoulders were pulled in like she was huddling up, making herself small. The constant tension would become excruciating after a while if it wasn't already.

"I'm not getting anything bad off Sobell."

"What? How is that possible?"

"I mean, well, he's got bat wings and horns half the time, but other than that . . ."

"Holy shit! Don't you think—" Anna broke off as she saw a smirk flicker across Karyn's face and vanish. "You're fucking with me," she said.

"Yeah," Karyn said, laughing a little.

Anna felt herself smile in response. "Knock it off!"

"All right, all right. Really, I'm not getting anything off him. I can't tell if that's because there's nothing to get, or my condition's being fickle, or if he's got some serious shit locking that down so I can't read him."

"He can do that?"

"I don't have any idea. If anybody could, though, you'd think he'd be on the short list."

Anna turned in to the breeze, trying to get it to take some of the sweat from her skin. No such luck. "What do you think, then? About all this?"

"I don't know. But I have to tell you, I'm useless right now. Jumping at shadows of things that aren't even here yet." She looked down at the cement and made a face. "I can tell you there's probably going to be an earthquake here, a bad one, but I can't tell you if it will be tomorrow or fifteen years from now."

"You don't get any credit for that. There's always an earthquake here."

"The only reason I haven't freaked out yet is that I'm in a safe place that's more or less controlled. I *know* there's nothing here to be worried about, and even so I'm about one hair's breadth from climbing the walls at all times. How's it going to work out there, when it gets dangerous?"

"So you think we ought to do it then?"

"I told you, I don't know. I just thought you ought to know about my situation before you make any decisions, and I didn't want to talk about it in front of everyone."

Anna frowned. "What do you mean, before *I* make any decisions? This is your outfit."

Karyn took a step back from her, and Anna wondered what expression was on her own face that had caused that to happen. Once again, Karyn got very interested in the ground. "I walked out. I ditched you guys. It's not my outfit anymore."

"That's crap, Karyn. You're trying to walk out again right now and leave me with this shit." Anna could feel something rising through her chest, filling her head with gunpowder and gasoline—not anger, but *fury*, the same fury she'd felt when Karyn had stood there like a fainting schoolgirl and watched Tommy die, while Anna herself was up to the elbows in his blood. That time, she'd let it out, nearly scouring away her oldest friendship. This time . . .

She let out a hot, shaky breath. In a tight, trembling voice, she said, "This has always been your show. You don't get to walk out."

"It's always been the two of us," Karyn said. "Never just me."

"You don't get to walk out," Anna said. She was fully aware now that what she really meant was, *You don't get to leave me,* but no fucking way was she saying that out loud.

Karyn must have read something in her voice, though, because she paused, opened her eyes fully, and met Anna's gaze. And held it. "I don't even know what's real anymore—maybe half of everything I see, and maybe way less. If you want, I'll—you don't have to make all the decisions alone, but my judgment is unbelievably bad right now."

Some of the fury still burned in Anna's chest, but part of it had burned off, apparently releasing the kind of toxic fumes that made her eyes water. Rather than speak, afraid of how her voice might sound, she nodded.

"So now what?" Karyn asked.

"Do we take Sobell up on his offer or not?"

Karyn glanced skyward, tracking some phantasm across a long arc before returning to the question. "I don't know. Part of me hates the idea. You know we can't trust him. I think I believe Nail's guy—Sobell probably had other reasons he wanted us to go into Mendelsohn's. Other business he didn't see fit to share with us."

"Yeah. Can't really say that would surprise me."

"So working with him directly sounds like a good way to get screwed. On the other hand, we're *already* screwed, and I suspect he has more than a few 'little tricks' to help us out with."

"Oh? I thought you said in there that you didn't see how he'd add much."

"In front of him, yeah, that's what I said."

Anna grinned. "You want to be the bad cop, huh?"

"I want to set this up so we don't end up in his pocket. If that means one of us has to play bad cop, I'm game."

"Sounds good."

"Also"—Karyn hesitated—"if we can get some cash

out of him, maybe we can get back in Adelaide's good graces."

Anna nodded slowly. "Actually I was thinking the same thing."

"And it's gonna need to be a lot, especially once it's divvied up."

"Don't sweat that. I mean, yeah, we'll make a run at it, but even if we can't get that much, we'll still have my cut. We'll manage until the next job, if we survive this one."

Karyn shifted and crossed her arms. "That's not going to work forever. I don't want to be your charity case. I need to put some money aside. You know. In case."

"In case what?"

"In case."

Anna felt the urge to put a hand on Karyn's shoulder, but instead she just looked at her very directly. "I like Genevieve a lot, but no matter what happens with her or anyone else, I'm not going anywhere. Period."

The breeze picked up, sweeping warm air over her body and doing little to cool her down. When it dropped again, she was aware of how quiet the night was out here. The traffic from the interstate seemed far away, more like the distant sound of the ocean. She imagined she could hear her own pulse, and briefly feared that it would drown out anything Karyn had to say.

But when Karyn spoke her voice reached Anna with absolute clarity. "OK."

"I guess we're in, then," Anna said.

Karyn closed her eyes again, leaving them shut this time. "We probably ought to run it past the others—but, yeah. Basically. I don't know what else to do."

A 747 bound for LAX passed overhead. Anna wondered whether it tracked the same arc Karyn had watched a few minutes before. Karyn looked up.

"I'm about useless, though," Karyn said after the jet had gone. "Really."

"I don't know. I've been thinking about that, and I have an idea."

"Good, because I have an idea about our numbers problem."

"Numbers problem?"

"You know, the fact that there are maybe hundreds of them and seven of us."

"Oh?" Anna said. "Spill it."

The room had long since descended into an awkward silence when Nail heard the back door open. He hoped Karyn and Anna had worked their shit out, because this situation was in no way stable, and he was getting tired of holding a gun on Sobell and his security guy. It crossed his mind that the cleanest thing to do would be to shoot both of them and bury them in shallow graves in the desert, but he'd never shot anyone in cold blood before, and it held no appeal for him now. Better if Karyn had a solution, even if she was getting pretty flaky lately.

"Have you ladies reached a verdict?" Sobell asked as the two women stepped into the room.

"Yeah," Anna said. She wore an embarrassed grin, which immediately put Nail on alert. He'd never known Anna to be embarrassed about anything. "I'm up for it," she continued, "but Karyn says we already delivered your, um—what was it? Your 'stupid goddamned bone.'"

"Is that right?" Sobell asked. Nail swore he heard amusement under the man's voice.

"Yeah, that's about right," Karyn said. She crossed her arms and sat back in her previous spot on the couch. She closed her eyes. "It's not our fault you picked a lousy messenger."

Anna shrugged and gave Sobell a look that said, *See? Can't do a thing with her.*

Surprisingly, Sobell smiled. "Not a very sophisticated negotiation, ladies. But I can't fault the logic. Name your price."

"The cash part will be the same as the last time," Karyn said. "It's the same job, after all."

"I get the bone, you get two million dollars, correct?"

"Yeah."

"Need I point out that you're in as dire a predicament as I am? Call it one million, and be glad you have my assistance."

Anna and Karyn exchanged a glance. If Anna nodded, Nail couldn't tell, but Karyn seemed to find a decision on her face. "Deal," Karyn said.

"Shake on it, or you'll just take my word?"

Karyn was rubbing her head, and Nail swore she missed the question entirely. He didn't like that one bit. Anna stepped in without much of a hitch, though Nail doubted that Sobell missed the lapse.

"We'll take your word, thanks," she said.

"Great. Let's get started."

"That's not everything," Anna said.

"No?"

Karyn shook her head, apparently catching up to the conversation. "I need blind."

Sobell's bland smile didn't budge. "I'm sorry, but I have no idea what you're talking about."

"It's a medication. It helps with my condition."

"I don't really deal in pharmaceuticals."

"It dulls my perception. Keeps the future from squashing me where I stand. Do you know where to get some or not?"

"No."

There was a long pause, and Nail didn't miss the way Karyn's face fell, or the worried look Anna gave her. Not good.

Sobell folded his hands in front of him. "Do we have a deal, or what?"

Karyn looked to Anna, then nodded. "Yes."

Nail took a quick read of every face he could see. It was tough to make out details in the dimness, but he got enough. Genevieve was ready to go, practically jumping up and down in her seat. Anna had that determined set to her jaw that said she, too, was ready, and best get the fuck out of her way. Karyn was distracted, already looking at something past Sobell's head.

And Drew. The guy's mouth opened, closed, and opened again, and he glanced back at the door. Couldn't make up his mind whether to talk or run.

"Spit it out," Nail said.

"Who, me?"

"Yeah. You."

Drew shuffled his feet and took another look at the door. "Well, I was wondering, um . . ."

"You get a full cut," Anna said. "Two hundred Gs."

"Really?" Drew said.

For the first time since Sobell walked in, Nail let his gun drop. "Bullshit. I've been busting my ass in this outfit for years, and he walks in off the street for a full share?"

"It's always been one share per person," Karyn said.

"Besides," Anna put in, "he'll have earned it, if he can do what we need him to."

Drew whipped his head around to gawk at Anna. "Huh?"

"Let's hear it," Nail said. "This oughta be good."

Anna leaned against the wall, a smug smile on her face. "We're outnumbered. Greaser's got Sobell's guys, and the Brotherhood brought a small army to track us down. Only, if you think about it, the Brotherhood really doesn't give a shit about us one way or the other."

"Oh, no," Drew said.

"That's right. It's the bone they want. We can tell them where to find it—we'll pick up a distraction and some firepower at the same time. Except they have no reason to believe us." She clapped a hand on Drew's shoulder. "But they might believe you."

"That's insane. If they think I'm messing with them, they'll kill me."

"Better make it good, then." She turned back to Nail. "That worth a share?"

"Yeah. I think it just about is."

Anna clapped her hands together. "All right. Here's how this is going to work."

Chapter 27

"This is dumb," Genevieve said. "Karyn or Nail ought to be here. They're actually good at this shit."

"None of us is in a position to get everything we want," Sobell said. "I, for one, remain unconvinced that you aren't about to quietly knife me and leave my body in a Dumpster for the rats to fight over."

Genevieve shook her head. "No percentage in that."

"Admirable."

The two of them stood next to an empty parking attendant booth, staring across the way at Sobell's building. Nearby, a cheap plastic sign, zip-tied to a chain-link fence, buckled and flexed in the wind. This was a nice part of downtown, but that didn't preclude the presence of yet another overpriced parking lot, one of the thousands of flat spots that stood out like scabrous bald spots in the mostly vertical city. At least nobody would question them, if they didn't stand there for long.

From everything Genevieve could see, and everything she remembered, Sobell's building was a nightmare. Bad enough that the lobby was lit up like full daylight, but floodlights poured thousands of blue-white watts on the stairs out front as well, and the little stalks of cameras seemed to protrude everywhere, inside and out. "You must have a hell of an electric bill," she said.

"A trifle. You should see my monthly graft expenditure."

Genevieve chuckled.

"How many guards?"

"Usually two out front, but unless my eyes deceive me, they've staffed up since lunchtime. Look."

Sure enough, Genevieve could see at least four big Cro-Magnon bruisers behind the security counter. A tall, garish wall of pink-and-black marble towered behind them, and two wide corridors stretched back on either side—the halls to the elevator lobby.

"Four's workable," Genevieve said.

"Not four. Look to the sides of the door."

For an old guy, Sobell had incredible eyesight. If Genevieve squinted, she could just make out the shiny tip of somebody's shoe on the left side and something that might be an elbow on the right—men flanking the door on the inside.

"OK, six. That's not good."

"Eight," Sobell said. "Check the mirror."

The mirror of which he spoke was a tiny reflective circle, from here about the size of a dime held in an outstretched hand. "I'll take your word for it," she said.

"And they're all one button away from summoning the rest of Security. If a man were to show up on the front stairs with so much as an angry expression on his face, the guards could have a dozen more security personnel here inside of a minute."

"Shit."

"That was this morning," Sobell admitted. "By now, I have no idea what the security arrangement looks like. I rather doubt Greaser has relaxed it."

"The front door is out, then."

"Barring some unforeseen stroke of brilliance on your part, yes."

"All right. Let's see what's around—hey! Someone's coming out!"

A man had emerged from the hall. Genevieve couldn't make out his features from here, but he seemed like an older gentleman, maybe in his fifties. Salt-and-pepper mustache, bit of a gut, but he walked with a certain swagger. He triggered a sense of vague recognition, but Genevieve couldn't figure out where she'd seen the guy before.

Two of the security guards opened a set of glass doors for the guy and let him out. He nodded to them and headed down the steps toward a boring blue sedan illegally parked in front of a fire hydrant.

"Ah. Bill Mendez."

"Who?" Genevieve asked.

"Chief of Police of Los Angeles. Stand-up fellow," Sobell said. "Quite incorruptible. Or was, until a short time ago."

"What's he doing here?"

"Nothing that increases our chances of success, I wouldn't imagine."

The car pulled away, and Genevieve turned her back to the street, hunching her shoulders and pretending to study a sign on the attendant's booth.

"I don't suppose you can just walk in and order the guards to stand down?" she asked after the police chief's car had gone.

"Now, why didn't I think of that?"

"What?"

Sobell rolled his eyes heavenward. "No, I can't just walk in. I assure you, they will shoot me on sight. They've already tried."

"Oh. It was worth a shot."

"If that pun was intentional, *I* may have to shoot you."

"Not at all." Genevieve squared her shoulders. "Can we go around back?"

"Why not?"

"Jesus," Genevieve muttered, and she kicked a pebble across the sidewalk.

Karyn put her hand on the car's door handle and paused. "I don't feel good about this," she said.

Anna's reasoning had sounded good when she'd proposed this little side trip. *Think about it,* she'd said. *Adelaide is way gone. She's so far gone, there's no way she'd be able to go out in public without using blind. No way. She'd get mowed down by a bus the first time she tried to cross a street.*

Karyn had shaken her head. *I don't know. Maybe she*

just knows how to use it somehow. She lives with her condition better than I do.

If you mean that she's gone completely insane, then yeah, I guess so. But she's not stupid. She's got a stash. Think about how much we've paid her over the years—it's gotta be close to a million bucks, and she lives in a dripping wet hole in the ground. I bet she needs to buy the stuff, too. That's where all the money goes.

But she didn't have a stash, Karyn had protested. *Otherwise, she'd never have gone out when Drew and I came last time.*

Except you weren't going to pay her. Maybe she knew something, knew she'd be more likely to get paid if she brought those guys back with her. Maybe she was getting desperate, too. Look, she was screaming *about needing to go home, telling those fuckers she could help them, if only they would take her home. She's got a stash.*

Karyn had grudgingly accepted that *maybe* Anna's line of reasoning wasn't totally broken. Or maybe she had simply been grasping at the nearest convenient straw. At the rate the visions were worsening, she worried that she'd become completely disconnected from reality in a matter of days. An exploratory mission to check out Adelaide's stash was the only game in town. Now that they were here, though, Karyn just wanted to get the hell away.

Anna turned off the car. "Don't feel good about it, or you saw something?"

"Don't feel good. I didn't see anything special." That wasn't strictly true—she'd seen a thousand people, objects, and creatures on the way here that easily surpassed "out of the ordinary" and went straight on into "freakish and terrifying," but if any of it had particular significance, she couldn't suss it out.

"You want to call it off?" Anna meant it, Karyn knew, but her voice still held a frustrated anger. It said, *If you thought this was a bad idea, you should have said something sooner.* That was probably true, but Karyn didn't see what choice she had. She felt like she was losing her mind, and rapidly.

"We're not going to find anything here."

"You want to call it off?" Anna repeated, and this time the anger poked through the surface.

Karyn opened her eyes. The car she was in had become a rusty skeleton with a smashed-in windshield. In another half a second it became a faded junker, still running, but the dashboard had faded from the sun and the vinyl peeled from the seats and steering wheel. Outside, a fanged monkey led a strung-out woman down the street on a thin leash of iron chain. The symbolism was obvious enough, but Karyn had no way of telling what the woman was *now*. Already a hooker in need of a fix, or maybe just a woman on her way back from the late shift, years out from a possible encounter with the drug that would seize her life. Or, hell, maybe there was nobody there at all, and this person would come walking through, following her monkey, sometime tomorrow morning.

And that was only one thing. *Every*thing was affected.

"No," Karyn said. "Let's try it."

She opened the door and stepped out onto the curb. Her foot came down, turned strangely, and she stumbled. One arm flailed out and she caught herself against the car door, but her ankle cried out in protest.

"You all right?" Anna asked.

"Sure," Karyn said, but she checked the curb. It had eroded substantially here, chunks of cement broken away and gone, but it had felt smooth and rounded. She kicked at it, gently so as not to do herself any further damage—and her foot bounced off air.

"Jesus," she said, and she slumped against the car, back pressing against the window and head tipped back against the roof. "I don't believe this."

"What?" Anna came around to the other side. Concern warred with impatience in her eyes.

"I'm not even seeing the right ground anymore," Karyn said. She kept her voice under control, but it was a close thing. Reality—or maybe just her sanity—was collapsing around her, and a sudden surge of terror threatened to overwhelm her. Tears swelled at the corners of her eyes, but thankfully didn't fall. "I can't even walk without hurting myself, because my eyes are now feeding me complete bullshit." She rolled her head to the side and looked past Anna to the sidewalk. It had cracked and heaved in spots, creating great sloping ramps nearly as tall as she was that weren't actually there at all. What would happen, she wondered, if her sense of touch bought into that vision, too? Would she hurt herself, break herself against the ground, and not even know it? Or would she slip right out of this reality into a new one, defined by her own hallucinations?

"Take my hand," Anna said. "And close your eyes."

"This is ridiculous."

"Come on. I don't like being here any more than you do."

The words and, even more, Anna's tone made Karyn feel like a kid being dragged to the doctor's office. She closed her eyes, put out her hand, and pushed away from the car. "This is dumb," she said. "It'll be faster if you just leave me here, check for the stuff, and come back."

"Unh-uh. As soon as I leave you alone, one of the ten thousand happy assholes looking for us will come by. It's almost a guarantee."

"Oh, Christ. Let's just get this over with."

Anna walked forward. Karyn trailed a few feet behind her. The sidewalk felt rough and flat, as it should, and it made coarse sliding sounds as she shuffled her feet. She was tempted to open her eyes and have a look, but if the disparity between what she felt and what she saw was too great—if, for example, she found herself hip deep in a concrete slab or standing over a yawning hole—she thought she might just stop here and start screaming.

The toe of her shoe got hung up on an uneven chunk of sidewalk, and she stumbled. Anna's hand tightened on hers.

"This sucks," Karyn said.

"It's like a game. Something you'd do when you're a kid."

"That's been a long time," Karyn said. Anna made no reply.

The walk from the car to the building seemed impossibly long, the sidewalk a cratered, bombed-out landscape of treacherous cracks and holes. Anna pulled her in one direction, then another, presumably leading her around the worst of it, and announcing the unavoidable as they approached. "Hole. Ledge. Dip here." Karyn tripped a few times, but only in small ways. Anna was good at this. Even so, with no visual reference, no sight of the end, she seemed to walk forever.

"Funny," Anna said after an unusually wide detour. "This is usually your job."

"Wha —" Karyn began, but then she got it. "Cute."

"Maybe, but it's true." The sound of a heavy door swinging open on creaky hinges. "Threshold."

Karyn picked up her feet and came inside. The cooler temperature in here would have been welcome if it weren't for the dank stench. "Christ, I hate coming here."

"Me, too. Come on, and let's get it over with."

Anna started forward, but Karyn didn't move. All she could think of were all the reasons she hated this place, and it was ten times worse with her eyes closed. She felt, again, like she'd been reduced to childhood, afraid that a hand would reach out of the darkness and close around her arm, her ankle, her throat, and drag her to a secret, terrible place where monsters slept and lurked and ate. Especially ate.

"Karyn?"

"I'm ready. Go on."

Anna resumed her slow walk into the building. Karyn allowed Anna to pull her to the end of the corridor, then stopped again.

"What is it?" Anna asked.

Karyn opened her eyes.

Anna's flashlight shone in front of her. The staircase below looked intact, for a miracle, and the space beyond was the same wet blackness it had always been. Perhaps a beam or two had fallen in, but Karyn couldn't tell. The walls of the stairwell, though, had undergone a horrifying transformation. The cinder blocks were gone, replaced by a rippling, fleshy wall on either side — faces, thousands of them, growing together seamlessly at the edges. Each showed only the bottom of the forehead to the bridge of the nose—the eyes, in other words.

And all the eyes were closed.

Karyn swallowed a scream and breathed out. "It's OK," she said. "I think we're cool."

"You good?"

"Yeah." She walked down the middle of the stairs, holding her arms close and keeping well away from either side. A grim certainty filled her, that she would reach the very center of the staircase and all the eyes would open, fixing on her and sending her right over the edge of madness.

She snorted. *Take a lot more than that right about now.*

"Something funny?" Anna asked, her voice tense.

"Not a single thing."

Karyn reached the bottom without her fears coming to pass, and she stepped into the water. She shuddered at the cool, vaguely slimy feel as her shoe filled up.

Anna's hand touched her shoulder. "You all right?"

"Yeah."

"Want me to go first?"

"I'm good for now." She was, too. The darkness here shrouded everything, reducing even the most ominous of shapes to a shadowy, nonspecific bulk. For once in her life, Karyn found the unseen to be less frightening than what was visible in front of her.

She turned to her right, but the light that had been there earlier in the day had been extinguished. Anna pointed her flashlight in that direction. The beam attenuated into nothing but a faint shine on the dull surface of the water.

"Looks like there's a vacancy," Anna said.

"Thank God."

The water sloshed over Karyn's feet and wicked up the legs of her pants as she moved toward Adelaide's former den. She stopped twice, listening for any sound of movement, but nothing was audible over her breathing and a distant drip of water. The two women had made it about halfway along the length of the wall when Anna's light caught a pale shape floating under the surface of the water ahead of them. The flashlight wasn't much, but it got the job done. Karyn saw thin tendrils of hair floating off the shape, the hunch of naked shoulders, the knobbed row of vertebrae.

"You see that?" she whispered.

"See what?"

"Never mind." She pressed forward. As she approached the corpse, she saw another beyond it, then the obscure green-pale shapes of others beside it.

At least they're not moving. She shook her head. How bad must things have gotten if *that* thought was a source of consolation?

A few more steps, and she reached a point where the water became choked with bodies in various states of decay. Little chunks of waterlogged flesh floated in clouds around some of them, and Karyn's stomach roiled. She scanned the water ahead of her, becoming sick with dread and revulsion as she realized there was no way to go forward without pushing through the corpses.

"Ah, fuck," she said.

Anna looked over, no trace of revulsion on her face, no acknowledgment of the bodies at all. They weren't there, Karyn knew, but that fact had no power to calm her.

"You want me to go on ahead?" Anna asked.

"Sort of defeats the purpose, doesn't it?"

"If I find anything I can bring it back. It's not far."

Tempting, Karyn thought, and then she imagined waiting here in the dark until Anna got back. In the dark with corpses in the water just a few feet away and who knew what else. This kept getting better and better.

"No," she said. "But you get to go first."

Anna pressed forward. The bodies spun slowly away as she pushed through them, leaving enough of a path that Karyn could at least hope to follow without touching anything horrible. She picked her way through after Anna and tried to ignore the way the glimmering, rippling surface of the water gave false movement to the corpses below.

All I need now is—

She let out a half-stifled scream as the outflung leg of one of the rotating bodies bumped her ankle. Her body convulsed in a shudder that started at the base of her spine and rocketed up through her shoulders.

"You all right?" Anna asked.

Karyn's breath came rapidly, and she forced herself to slow down. *Be rational. There's nothing there. And, even if there was, it was just a little bump. Like a piece of driftwood or a floating toy or something.* Yet, even after the corpse's touch had gone, she couldn't shake the sense that it had left a foul, indelible stain on her pants.

Another corpse came spinning toward her, and her control broke. This time, a full-fledged scream tore its way out of her lungs, and she ran forward, barreling past Anna, shoving and stomping the floating bodies. Her scream echoed throughout the basement, accompanied by the violent sounds made by her splashing path through the dead.

Behind her, Anna swore and ran after.

Karyn reached the collapsed ceiling in moments, and she leaned against it, arms covering her face. *Not gonna cry. Just not gonna do it.* Something that bore a suspicious resemblance to a sob shook its way out of her body, but she closed her eyes, held her breath, and counted to ten, and that was the end of it. It felt like part of her was still hidden in a corner of her mind screaming and gibbering and turning mad circles, but that part was locked down. It could gibber to its heart's content.

"It's cool," Anna said. "That was pretty subtle—I don't think anybody heard us."

Karyn laughed, short but genuine. "Oh, good. I wouldn't want to embarrass myself or anything."

"Ready?"

"Yeah. You go first."

Anna ducked into the tunnel, and Karyn followed. A new smell lay on top of the dank, wet odor of the basement, like scum on brackish water, and Karyn wrinkled her nose. The smell was roadkill or spoiled meat left in the sun. Whether it was real or not, she had no way of knowing.

They emerged from the tunnel, and Karyn looked around the small room in the glow of Anna's flashlight.

The alcoves were empty, the shelves barren. The candles had burned down to puddles and gone out. "Where are the rats?"

"Gone. How should I know?"

A tightness eased in Karyn's chest. One less thing to worry about right now. She moved to the wall. A quick review of the shelves revealed nothing, so she started checking for cracks or gaps, running her fingers over the wall from the rocky floor to the low ceiling. After a moment, Anna joined her.

"Here," Karyn said. A block in the bottom corner was loose, surrounded by a narrow gap instead of mortar. She wedged her fingers into the gap and pulled. The block came away.

"I need a light," Karyn said.

Anna leaned over and shone the flashlight into the hole. Inside were a handful of candles and a couple of rocks. Karyn scooped it all out and looked through it. No containers, bags, or powders—nothing that even looked like a component of blind, or even like it might be useful for something else. She threw the mess on the ground and squeezed her fists in frustration.

"Shit!"

"Keep looking," Anna said, but Karyn noted the worry in her voice. If they couldn't find anything here, the crew would have to wing it without Karyn, a grim prospect given the odds. And if they didn't pull off the job, then what about Adelaide? They wouldn't have the money to pay her off, and then what? Find another source? How? Where? How long would that take? Karyn might be screaming mad by then. Almost surely would be.

"Relax," Anna said. "Breathe."

Karyn realized she'd been hyperventilating, again, and again she tried to take one slow breath at a time. "A little freaked out here."

"Me, too. Just keep looking."

The desperate panic Karyn had been trying to hold back strained its leash, bucked and twisted, and it was only an extreme effort of will that kept Karyn from either running as fast as she could in no particular direction or collapsing into a trembling heap. No blind. Not now, maybe not ever. She recalled first meeting Drew, when he'd thought she was a junkie looking for a fix. This wasn't all that different, when you boiled it down. In her case, it was medicine she needed to keep her head together, but she wondered just how desperate she might get if she couldn't find any.

Ha. Look at my whole life.

Not for the first time, she wondered what the stuff was made of, that it was so damn expensive. Part of her thought that was just Adelaide taking advantage of her, that the crazy woman had a little room somewhere with piles of hundred-dollar bills rotting in it, but Anna's explanation felt more true. Adelaide had been taking blind herself, at least sometimes, and it was nearly as expensive for her as it was for her customers. More expensive than any street drug Karyn could think of—more expensive, for that matter, than gold, at least by weight. *If I could get blind for a thousand dollars an ounce, I'd have bought a truckload by now.*

"Hell yeah," Anna said, interrupting her reverie. "Jackpot." From another little hidey-hole close to the ceiling, she pulled out a tightly rolled plastic sandwich bag. She held it up to her flashlight and unrolled it.

"This the stuff?"

Tiny chunks of a greenish-black fibrous material lined up along the bottom of the bag. There wasn't much, especially as far gone as Karyn was, but she felt tears of gratitude and relief spring to her eyes anyway.

She wiped them away and pocketed the bag.

"Yeah. Let's get out of here."

Drew directed them to an apartment complex on the opposite side of the city from the motel, though in an equally shitty neighborhood. Nail drove into the parking lot, reasoning that none of the Brotherhood had gotten a good look at his van the last time. He sure hoped that was true. He backed into a spot in case they needed to get out of here quickly.

Nail turned to Drew in the passenger seat and gave

him a quick once-over. Guy was scared green. "You ready for this?"

"You better be," Brown put in from the backseat before Drew could answer.

Nail frowned. Drew was rattled, no doubt about it, and you never wanted a rattled guy on your team at a time like this. You needed cool heads, or you needed to calm your guy down until his head cooled off. So of course Sobell's fuckwitted lackey here had to kick him while he was down. Nail had known plenty of guys like Brown in the service. They were boneheads destined to end up as drill sergeants forever. Useless in combat, no good at planning, but they knew how to follow orders and how to humiliate the poor bastards in their command. Nail had more respect for cockroaches.

"Fuck you, jack," Nail said, giving Brown the stink-eye in the rearview mirror. "I didn't ask for your opinion."

"We don't have time for hand-holding right now, so—"

"We don't have time for your bullshit right now. You earn your stripes?"

Brown stopped short. "My—what? Fuck you." He stuck out his jaw, obviously preparing for a full-scale pissing contest.

"Didn't get mine, neither."

"Then I guess—"

"Busted my sergeant in the mouth, though."

Brown's mouth hung open.

"That's right. That's why they threw my ass out." Pure fiction. He'd never hit a sergeant, and when he'd gotten out, it had been an honorable discharge—but if he was reading Brown right, it was the kind of thing the guy would respond to.

He wasn't wrong. There was a pause, and then a genuine, good-humored grin appeared on Brown's face. "Threw your ass out, huh?"

"Yep."

"Me too."

Imagine my surprise. "And here we are."

Brown nodded. "Pretty fucked up, if you ask me."

"True that. You suppose we can get this over with without you giving Drew here any more shit?"

Brown glanced at Drew. "Yeah. Sorry, man. I've just had the shittiest day."

"Yeah. Ain't we all." Nail dismissed Brown and returned his attention to Drew. Guy was sweating a bucketload, and by the look of him, he was about ready to re-release his peanut butter and crackers into the wild. "How you doin'?" Nail asked.

Drew swallowed, then sucked a long, hissing breath in through his teeth. "They're gonna kill me."

"They're not gonna kill you." *Probably.* "That isn't gonna help them any, and they may be crazy, but they're not stupid."

"It's the crazy part I'm worried about."

Nail just nodded. That was the part that worried him, too. Relying on the self-preservation instinct of a bunch of religious fanatics wasn't what he thought of as bulletproof strategy. But they'd talked it over, and this was all they had left to work with.

He let the minutes tick by. Brown's movements rustled in the backseat. Cars drove by. A naked guy, locked out of his room without clothes for whatever unfathomable reason, pounded on a nearby door with one hand and covered his junk with the other.

"OK," Drew said. "Who wants to live forever, right?"

"Oorah."

Nail took the lead with Drew right behind him and Brown bringing up the rear. He wished he had some body armor. How the hell had he never gotten around to picking up a Kevlar vest or something? A wide-open space, maybe thirty feet, gaped between the last car and the apartment door he was headed for, and if one of the creeps inside looked out their window and recognized him, he'd be the proverbial sitting duck. *Bang bang.*

Or maybe Drew had been mistaken, and this wasn't the Brotherhood's backup plan after all. That would be plenty embarrassing. Plus, they'd have to figure out how to track down the Brotherhood all over again.

The little group broke cover. Nail's body tensed up, like he thought he could stop bullets with his abs if he just flexed them hard enough. He knew better, of course, but the screaming fear of being out in the open did funny things to him.

They crossed a strip of sorry grass without attracting any unwelcome attention—or bullets—and Nail stepped onto the sidewalk in front of the unit. The scrape of his boot on the sidewalk was deafening. No shots were fired, though, and he stopped in front of the door. He bowed slightly and made a little "after you" gesture at Drew. Drew didn't seem to find that funny, but he stepped to the door.

"Oh, boy," Drew whispered, and he knocked. If Nail had thought their footsteps were loud, the knocks were like mortar rounds exploding. Even Brown, whom Nail wouldn't have placed among the top, oh, thousand or so brightest people he'd ever met, looked nervous.

"Open up," Drew said, and his voice barely shook at all. "It's me. Drew."

Nothing happened, and Nail couldn't hear a damn thing through the door.

Drew knocked louder. "It's me, guys." He leaned close to the door and spoke in a low voice. "I know who's got the relic."

Nail heard the dead bolt slide back. He took a step to the side, getting Drew between him and the widening crack in the door. It didn't hurt to be careful.

A face peered from the gap between door and frame. For a wonder, it wasn't even accompanied by the barrel of a gun. "Drew?"

"Yeah."

The guy's bulging eyes darted from Drew to Nail to Brown. He looked about twenty years old, unshaven, and scared out of his wits. "And you know where the relic is? For real?"

"Yeah."

"Oh, wow. We gotta go get Brother Martel." The guy

flushed. "Er, the Revered One." The guy turned and muttered something to somebody else inside the room. A moment later, he slipped out of the room followed by a man ten years his senior who looked at them all with a scowl of disapproval.

"Who are you?" he asked.

Nail stared him down. These guys didn't even seem to be armed. *Amateur hour here, folks.* "Friends. You want the bone or what?"

Both men flinched, and the younger looked around the parking lot nervously. "Quiet, man," he said.

The other man recovered his composure more quickly. "How about you tell us where it is, and we'll take care of the rest?"

"How about you take us to somebody in charge, so I don't get the idea you're gonna run off with the damn thing yourself?"

The look of horror on the man's face was too genuine to be a scam. "Do you — ? I can't . . . That's — that's blasphemy!"

Damn. We got the lowest of the low rent here. It was all Nail could do to keep from rolling his eyes. "All the same."

The older man, his face considerably paler than it had been a few moments before, nodded and pulled the door to his room shut. "OK. We'll go see the Revered One."

The expedition to see the Revered One was all of a dozen steps long, culminating in the door to the next unit over. The older of the two nimrods from the previous unit knocked twice, paused, knocked three more times, then knocked again.

Jesus. A secret knock and everything.

But it did the trick, and a brief recap of the previous scene was played out — the door opened, Drew announced that he knew where the "relic" was, and a superior officer was summoned. The only real difference was when the door swung wide open and Nail found himself with half a dozen guns aimed at him.

He didn't need to be told. He put his hands up, and Brown rapidly followed suit. Drew just frowned.

At the center of the bristling array of guns stood a thin man dressed in stained jeans, shitkicker work boots, and a red-checked flannel shirt. A scruff of ragged beard clung to his chin. *Sure don't look like much of a cult leader. Bet he's sweatin' his ass off in that lumberjack shit.*

"Drew," the man said. "You have news?"

"Yes, sir."

The man waved a hand, and his cronies lowered their guns.

"Then let's talk."

Nail followed Drew into the apartment's living room with heavy-duty misgivings. Six men and two women were camped out in this one room, and five of them were armed. The ones who weren't looked decidedly twitchy, with eerie grins plastered across their faces like they couldn't wait for the action to start. The Revered One, formerly known as Brother Martel, stood in their midst, his hands outstretched. No gun in evidence, but he had one, Nail was sure. Just wasn't waving it about at the moment. No need to.

"Who are your new friends, Drew?" Martel asked. It should have sounded menacing, or sarcastic at the least, but the guy delivered it with such grandfatherly charm that it seemed sincere. Nail started to get the cult thing, after all. Then the guy added in a low whisper, *"Friends,"* and the charm turned instantly to creepy.

"I probably ought to cover that," Nail said.

Martel's eyes flashed in irritation. "Oh?"

"Yeah. We, uh, haven't all been on the same side until just recently. I figure that's going to take some explaining."

The man waited.

"One of my, er, colleagues took your relic." There. It was out. The cult members looked to Martel and shifted their weapons, and Nail felt his body tense again.

Martel reached into his back pocket and pulled out a pair of beat-up channel-lock pliers. The green rubber grips had been ripped in places, and they were covered in dark stains. "I hope this isn't going to lead to a ransom demand," Martel said. He clacked the pincers together, but that wasn't the most unnerving thing about the exchange. Nail swore the man was mumbling under his breath between sentences—nothing Nail could make out, but enough to give him a serious case of the willies. "Surely you wouldn't be *that* stupid."

"No, sir," Nail said. He had a sense that showing any fear here would cause Martel to leap on him like a mad dog, and he kept his eyes trained on Martel's. "We don't have the relic anymore."

Martel waited, his hand convulsively working the pliers.

"We gave it to one of Enoch Sobell's men, who took off with it instead of delivering it."

Martel's grandfatherly facade cracked, revealing something baleful and angry beneath. "So. Sobell wants it, too. Is that supposed to explain why six of the faithful were killed earlier tonight? Six of the faithful? *The faithful?*"

Damn. Sobell ought to be here to explain this. I'd leave it to Brown if I didn't think he'd fuck it up. "I think that was all a misunderstanding. He wanted Anna—the woman. In any event, he contacted us. He's prepared to help you recover the relic."

"Lies. *Lies.* I can see right through your lies."

"No lies."

Martel narrowed his eyes for a moment and then grinned. With that grin, all traces of the avuncular were gone. "I see. Sobell's lackey has used the relic to displace him."

"That is my understanding."

"Well, then. Perhaps we can reach an arrangement after all." He muttered something inaudible. "An arrangement."

Chapter 28

Karyn sat in the passenger seat of Anna's car and picked a lump of blind out of the plastic bag. She let it rest in her palm, a chunk no bigger than a pencil eraser. It would taste like shit, she knew, acrid and eye watering, and she didn't even know how much of an effect this amount would have on her, as bad as the hallucinations had gotten.

"You gonna take it, or what?" Anna asked.

"Give me a minute, OK?"

Anna started the car. Karyn stared at the lump in her hand.

"It isn't going to bite you," Anna said.

"Don't be so sure." Karyn checked the landscape outside the car window again. It didn't look like L.A. anymore—it barely even looked like Earth. It was a jumble of structures and creatures and things that might have been either, some symbolic, some merely projections of their future selves, and maybe even some that appeared as they were right now. It was impossible to tell.

Karyn ate the tiny chunk of blind.

Anna pressed the gas, accelerating the car away from the broken-down building Adelaide called home.

Karyn watched the world outside as they passed by. Things hadn't calmed down yet, but it was early. The taste of the drug still coated her tongue like some foul turpentine. It would be long minutes yet before it worked. Even so, she fought a dim panic that, this time, it wouldn't do anything at all, fought the urge to take a handful from the bag and eat that, too. Anything to get some reassurance that she wasn't doomed to propel herself headlong into madness.

Still, though, she knew it would be a bad idea to take too much. Look what had happened last time. And, given her low supply and no certain source of more, moderation made sense.

She closed her eyes and leaned her head back against the headrest. Watching the craziness for signs of improvement would be akin to watching water and waiting for it to boil, only twice as maddening.

"How are you feeling?" Anna asked.

"Honestly? Like somebody put my brain in a blender, pureed it, and poured it back into my head. I think they slopped some on the floor when they did it, too."

"That good?"

"And better all the time."

"About what I said earlier . . ."

Karyn waited as the words trailed off. Anna obviously wanted her to cut in and say it was all OK, but Karyn didn't have that kind of energy right now. And, anyway, she wasn't sure it *was* all OK.

"If you gotta sit this one out, that's OK. I mean, I'll be OK with it."

Karyn considered that. On the surface it sounded great, but it wouldn't work. If somebody got hurt or killed, and she could have stopped it, she'd never forgive herself—and she had plenty of that flavor of guilt already, thank you very much. Besides, she needed the cash. After the job, if somehow they managed to find a new hookup, it would cost. She didn't think she could stand it if Anna came back from the job with a few hundred grand and handed her a big wad of money on the grounds that Karyn was her new favorite charity. Fuck that. Anna had been looking out for her since forever, but that was a bridge too far.

Unless, of course, the blind didn't work this time. Then she'd be a complete liability.

"We'll see," Karyn said. "As long as I can tell the ground from the sky, I'm in. Just, you know. That's not exactly guaranteed right now."

A sound of movement as Anna shifted position. "Yeah," she said quietly.

The rest of the trip passed in silence, and Karyn kept her eyes closed until Anna stopped the car and turned it off.

"Ready?"

Karyn opened her eyes. Outside, in the spotty light from the streetlamps, the suburbs hardly looked strange at all. *That doesn't mean anything. But it's a good sign.*

"Yeah."

It was another hour before Genevieve and Sobell returned, an hour Anna spent napping in the corner chair and Karyn spent fidgeting on the couch. It would be a good idea to catch some sleep, Karyn knew, but she'd never slept well before a job, even a well planned one, and this promised to be more half-assed than most. Given that it was three in the morning and they didn't even have a plan yet, "half-assed" might be an overstatement.

The blind had done some of its thing, but not enough. The structure around her still flickered from one state of decay to the next, and the strange images coming from Anna were as varied as they were incomprehensible. After thirty minutes of watching the scenery change, Karyn ate another couple of pieces of blind. *That's all for now. I need to be lucid when we do this.* Pity she wasn't sure yet when "this" would happen.

When Genevieve knocked on the door, there wasn't much of a door to knock on, just a rotting hole with a few boards standing up in it. Karyn heard the sound, though, even as she saw Genevieve whacking on air. She got up and crossed the room, wondering how she was going to open a door she couldn't exactly find. In the end, she had to close her eyes and run a hand along the edge of the door to find the lock and open it. She did find it, though, and she smiled a shaky smile of relief as the shape of the cool metal resolved itself against her hand. She turned the bolt. *Definitely getting better.*

Genevieve came in hurriedly, and Sobell strode in after her, coat flapping behind him. Genevieve shut the door and dropped to a crouch, messing with some of the glyphs near the floor. Sobell watched. His face was unreadable.

"What did you find out?" Karyn asked.

Sobell took off his gloves, folded them, and put them in his pocket. "Precious little."

Genevieve nodded miserably as she worked. "Place is locked down. Shitload of security guys out front. Fewer in back, but he says they can get a dozen or more to any part of the first floor in less than a minute. And they have the cops, too."

Anna was sitting up now, attentive in the corner. "They 'have' the cops? What's that supposed to mean?"

"Means the chief of police was paying a friendly visit when we stopped by. I guess that means when they call, the cops will come running."

"What else?"

"I've got an idea, but it sucks."

"I thought it rather inventive," Sobell said. "And interesting, if you're up for acrobatics and derring-do and whatnot."

"You gonna make me beg?" Anna asked.

"That could be fun," Genevieve said, a shadow of her usual smile on her face.

Anna wasn't smiling. "Come on, what is it?"

Karyn looked from face to face. Nobody seemed to be bleeding or sprouting new body parts or sporting any kind of funky aura. Would wonders never cease?

"Where's Nail?" Genevieve asked. "I'd like to run this past him first. It seems like the kind of thing that might be up his alley."

"I like it already," Anna said.

"He's not back yet," Karyn said. "Still out recruiting the Brotherhood."

Genevieve frowned. "Still?"

"Maybe they take a lot of convincing," Karyn said uncertainly.

"Great."

Anna crossed her arms. "He'll get back to us later. Come *on*. Let's hear this idea of yours."

"OK, OK. Here goes."

Genevieve sketched out her plan while Anna made pained faces and Sobell looked on, grinning sardonically. If Karyn was any judge of these things, she was right—the plan sucked. Unfortunately, she couldn't think of anything better.

Genevieve finished the rough outline and stood back, hands on her hips, waiting for a response.

"Magical defenses?" Karyn asked.

Sobell nodded. "Some, but of course I know what they are and where. I can take care of that part."

A tinny speaker spit out the opening strains of Queen's "Under Pressure," or maybe "Ice Ice Baby." Genevieve pulled her phone out and answered it. "Hello." A pause, during which her face fell from a nervous but excited grin to a sick grimace. "You sure?" she asked.

"Fuck yeah, I'm fucking sure!" somebody shouted through the phone, loud enough for Karyn and the rest of the room to hear. It sounded like Nail. He followed up with a few more choice words, too quiet to make out.

"All right," Genevieve said. She held the phone out to Sobell. "It's for you."

Sobell raised his eyebrows and cast a long, disparaging look at the phone, but he took it and pressed it to his ear. "Yes?" His expression betrayed nothing, but as Karyn watched, the skin of his forehead split open and peeled back, pouring blood down his face.

"I see. I will meet you shortly." He handed the phone back.

"Hello?" Genevieve said. "Shit." She put the phone in her pocket. "Oh, shit."

"What was that all about?" Anna asked.

"The Brotherhood."

"Huh?"

"Indeed," Sobell said. "It appears they do not fully trust your colleague."

"What does that mean?"

"It means they are amenable to participating in an assault on my office building, but only if I physically accompany them."

"Why you?"

"I can think of a number of reasons. Possibly they think your group is trying to use them to attack me, regardless of where the bone might be. If I am present, they can rule that out. Alternatively, they think I'll afford them some protection from my security staff—not a bad assumption, if you don't know what the hell is going on. Or perhaps they think we're less likely to use them as pointless cannon fodder if I am in their midst. In any case, it's a smart request."

"I can't feel good about that," Anna said.

"Truly, I'm touched."

Genevieve shook her head, almost violently. "No, this is fucked. Sobell knows the layout, he knows the rough security plan, and remember those magical defenses you were so worried about? He's the only one who can turn them off. I don't even know what's there."

"Unless you have another sort of diversion in mind, I don't know what choice we have," Sobell said. "We simply don't have the manpower to deal with the small army Greaser has stolen from me."

"We could, I don't know, blow something up. You know, like a distraction."

"That only works in the movies, I fear. The building isn't going to disgorge all its security personnel to come check out an explosion—my security chiefs have not been notably bright in the past, but they haven't been incompetent, either. I have no reason to believe that's changed."

"Jesus," Genevieve said.

"I suppose I'll have to tell you what I can, and give you some instruction on how to disable the more, ah, arcane defenses."

"You can do that?"

"I can teach it. Can you learn it? We haven't got a lot of time."

Genevieve hesitated. "All right. Let's do it."

The scene that followed did not fill Karyn with a great deal of confidence. First, Sobell grabbed up the phone book from the stand near the TV and produced a fountain pen from his pocket. He began by sketching a floor plan, right over a page full of Ramirezes, and then he launched into a mess of gobbledygook.

"Then you'll need to transect an inverted cadaver sigil with a Scythe glyph . . ."

Genevieve waited, mouth pursed tightly shut and eyes darting back and forth across the page, trying to follow the lines. It looked like she was waiting for a pause, but if one was coming, it would be a while.

This was going to be a mess, if Karyn didn't say anything. "Mr. Sobell!"

Sobell looked up from his phone book. "Yes?"

"She doesn't know what most of that stuff is."

One glance at Genevieve's face erased most of the cockiness from Sobell's expression. "Fuck," he said. "Fuckety-fuckety-fuck."

"Sorry," Genevieve mumbled.

"Never mind. I'll draw up the diagrams you'll need in the car."

"In the car?"

"Well, yes. You didn't think I'd drive myself to this fiasco, did you?"

"Uh, no. 'Course not." Genevieve shot a wide-eyed glance over at Karyn, who just shrugged. Not much to be done for it now. She just wished Sobell's head would stop gushing blood all over the place.

"Hey, Mr. Sobell," she said. "I think this might be really dangerous for you."

He gave her a bland, deadpan look loaded with enough sarcasm to fell an elephant. "Is that your professional opinion?"

"Yes, actually."

"I have been shot at by my own employees, robbed of my worldly riches, and betrayed by my otherworldly minions. Amazingly, I had already reached the conclusion that my continued good health comes with no guarantees tonight. Is there anything specific you'd like to add?"

She shrugged. "Watch your head."

"Of course. Ms. Lyle, shall we depart?"

"Hold up," Anna said. "Is there anything left to do here?"

Karyn shook her head.

"All right, then. Let's load up. We'll drop you off on the way," she said to Sobell.

Chapter 29

It didn't take long to load up—just a moment for everybody to check their weapons. Anna was strapped, Genevieve had her phone book, and Sobell had—whatever it was he had. Karyn went empty-handed. She'd contemplated arming herself, but fear of shooting the wrong thing made her hesitate, and it turned out they didn't have a spare gun, anyway.

Then it was into the car. Anna drove. Karyn rode shotgun, and Sobell and Genevieve climbed in back. Genevieve got out a key-chain flashlight and pored over the phone book, taking whispered instructions from Sobell even before Anna started the car. Karyn didn't take a great deal of confidence from the way Genevieve's eyes flicked back and forth and she kept fiddling with her lip stud. She was scared, and it was contagious.

Karyn turned to the window, leaning her head against the glass and letting the fog from her breath obscure the view. She didn't need to see the future to know that this situation was a mess and very little good was likely to come from it. She wondered about Nail. The big guy was hanging with the Brotherhood now, which didn't bode well. In the best case, they'd use him as screaming armor, cannon fodder vanguard of their attack, and in the worst case—well, it could get pretty bad. Nail could handle himself, but there were a lot of those guys.

Nobody else dies, please.

It didn't take long to get to the address Drew had

given them, but it was enough time for Karyn to turn herself into a nervous wreck. She folded her hands in her lap and willed herself not to chew her nails. Her fingers would start bleeding soon if she didn't lay off.

"Verily, a paragon of shitholes," Sobell observed as they pulled up. "How do these people select their accommodations?"

"Places that take cash and don't ask for identification," Anna said.

"Indeed."

"Light's on. Apartment one thirty-seven."

"Thank goodness they waited up for me." Sobell opened the door and got out. He leaned down. "I'll watch my head. See you at the office shortly." He slammed the door and strode across the parking lot, walking like he was ready to crush the cars themselves under his heels.

"Guy doesn't lack for balls," Genevieve said.

"Till they cut 'em off," Anna muttered.

Sobell walked straight to the door and knocked. The door opened, and he walked inside. Once he was gone from view, the door shut after him.

"That's that," Anna said. "Let's get moving." She backed up the car and pulled out.

When Sobell came in, Nail didn't know whether to be relieved or worried. He and Brown had been treated well enough so far, but Martel had made it very clear that they'd walked into captivity, at least for the short-term. Maybe Sobell's arrival would get that sorted out, and maybe it would mean Martel didn't need them anymore. Maybe that slippery bastard Sobell would find some creative way to sell them out.

Sobell nodded at him, the picture of calm confidence. Nail wished he felt the same way. He wasn't tied up, not yet, but he was seated on the edge of the bed with armed fanatics filling the available space around him. If he sneezed, one of these jumpy motherfuckers would probably shoot him by accident.

Sobell turned to Martel. There was something odd about the way Sobell looked at the man. His eyes had locked onto him among all the others, though when he'd walked in, there hadn't really been any reason to pick him out from the rest. Did he know the guy from somewhere? What was going on here?

The two men considered each other for what seemed like a very long time.

"Mr. Enoch Sobell," Martel said, spitting out the words as though they were something disgusting he'd eaten. *"Enoch,"* he whispered.

"At your service. I don't believe I've had the pleasure." He made no move to extend his hand, and he paid no attention to the small army that crowded the room. Martel was the only guy there, as far as he was concerned.

"Where is the relic?" Martel asked. Nail didn't like the avid gleam in his eyes or the way his face had become flushed and feverish. The way his hands twitched and flexed, seemingly of their own accord. This was a guy for which rational, considered action was rapidly becoming a nonoption.

"Ah, excellent. I was hoping I could discuss that with you. You see, that particular object has become a source of no small amount of trouble for me, personally." Sobell's voice was even, his face composed. Did he not see that Martel was on the verge of losing it, or was he just that cool? Even the other cult members in the room had begun trading anxious glances and adjusting their grips.

"Where is it?"

"One of my lackeys unexpectedly grew a spine and ran off with it. Frankly, I'd like to be rid of the, ah, object in question. I have a proposal for you."

Martel said nothing, but Nail could see his jaw muscles bunching and imagined he heard the sound of grinding teeth.

"You help me deal with my wayward minion, and I'll gladly relinquish the relic into your capable hands. Our goals are completely aligned in this matter."

Martel peeled his lips back like a growling dog. "Where is it? Where?"

"My office. Of course, there will be the security personnel to deal with, but you look like an intrepid lot. I expect you'll have little trouble with them."

Martel smiled, and Nail read genuine joy in his face. "Well, Mr. Sobell, that sounds more than fair."

"Splendid," Sobell said. "There *is* one other issue I was hoping I might discuss with you. One of a more personal nature. Potentially *very* lucrative for you."

"Oh?" Martel said, turning away from the other man. "Do tell."

Martel's body blocked Sobell's line of sight, but Nail saw him reach for the pistol on the dresser.

"Yes. Well," Sobell began. "I don't suppose we could speak pri—"

Martel's movement was fluid and almost casual. He picked up the gun, turned, and at a distance of less than a yard, shot Sobell in the head. The bullet caught Sobell in the right side of his forehead, snapping his head back and spraying blood across the room. Sobell collapsed.

Nail was already moving. When Martel grabbed the gun, Nail grabbed the guy to his own right, a slow brute brandishing a shotgun. He pulled, spinning the man around between him and most of the guns in the room, and he ripped the shotgun from the man's hand. The route to the door was blocked, but there was only one guy between Nail and the window. As shouting started behind him and somebody fired, he threw that guy to one side. Two more shots sounded from behind, and somebody screamed. Nail felt something hot tear into his side as he threw himself through the window.

The glass shattered, and Nail flew through the window frame and landed shoulder-first on the sidewalk. The shock knocked the wind out of him, but he scrambled, gasping, to his feet and stumbled away from the window.

More shouts came from the apartment.

The first guy out the door nearly ate a blast of buckshot, but Nail's shoulder screamed in pain as he brought up the gun, and he knew as he fired it was a clean miss. A chunk of cheap siding two feet left of the door disintegrated—but, somehow, the guy took a hit and fell back in the room.

"Run!" a familiar voice shouted, and Drew dove out the window, pistol in hand. Behind him, more noise and shots came from the room—sounded like Brown was in there, giving as good as he got.

Nobody else came out for a moment, and Drew picked himself up from the pavement. "Go!" he shouted. He reached Nail a couple seconds later and practically pushed him around the side of the building.

"Come on, come on! We gotta get out of here!" Drew said in a hoarse and ragged whisper. He shoved Nail toward the back, prodding him with something that felt like a barbed electric cattle prod.

"Ow, man! What the fuck?"

Drew looked down at his hand. It was covered in blood. "Oh, shit."

"Ah, shit. Guess they got me."

"Just move, OK?"

Nail nodded. Now that he noticed, his lower back hurt like somebody'd turned a goddamn weasel or something loose in there.

He leaned on Drew and limped toward the back.

"*Now* would be good," Genevieve whispered.

"Shut it, OK?" Anna fiddled with the lockpicks some more, trying to get the damn lock to cooperate. Security was lax here—not even close to the same league as Sobell's building—but that didn't mean somebody wouldn't come along eventually. Genevieve ragging on her didn't help.

You'd think she'd never done this before, she thought. She felt the last tumbler click into place, and she pushed the door open.

"Voilà."

She checked with Karyn, who nodded, and then she went in. Genevieve and Karyn slipped in right after her, Karyn taking pains to ease the door shut without making any noise.

They found themselves in a stairwell, illuminated by one white lightbulb on each landing. Everything—walls, ceilings, stair treads, and handrails—was coated in an utterly forgettable shade of gray paint, the goal, Anna supposed, being to bore any intruders to death.

"Come on," Genevieve said, shifting the bag on her shoulder. She headed up the stairs. The echoes from her footfalls were no louder than whispers, but to Anna they seemed about as subtle as a kick to the head.

Now who's got nerves?

She waited for Karyn to follow Genevieve, then brought up the rear.

The ascent was long, leaving Anna gasping as she huffed and puffed her way upward. *I thought I was in better shape than this.* Genevieve was even worse off, and she had to pause for a few moments at the eighth floor to get her breath. Anna didn't complain—just gave Genevieve a weak grin, squeezed her hand twice, and took the opportunity to stock up on oxygen herself.

They stopped on the twelfth floor, and Genevieve cautiously pushed open the door. "Looks clear," she said.

They came out on a wide, carpeted walkway surrounding a large atrium that ran up the center of the building. The offices were situated along the outside walls.

"Which one?" Anna asked.

"That way," Karyn said, pointing. "That's east."

The three of them walked to the office suite at the east end of the walkway, staying well away from the handrail. All it would take was one bored security guard looking up to ruin their night if they got sloppy.

A glass door set in a glass wall barred their entry into the office suite. Another few moments with the lockpicks cleared that obstacle away, and Anna swung the door open. She took two steps inside the office, and the whole place lit up, fluorescent ceiling lights flickering on in banks across the wide open space. She froze.

"Motion sensor on the lights," Karyn said.

Anna gave her a sheepish grin. "I knew that."

"Let's move. I don't know how often the guard does a walk-through, but I bet he'll check out the lights."

"There's a switch, too," Genevieve said. She stepped in and shut the lights down. Anna felt her pulse start falling back toward normal.

"Come on."

The office was a wide-open floor plan, cut into pieces with short dividers, barely higher than the desks they contained. The outside wall was blocked by offices, also with glass doors. Through the nearest, outside the window, Anna could see their target. She led the way over and went in.

Across the street, Enoch Sobell's building stood tall. Two floors down from where Anna stood, the ESE sign reflected the light from the street below, just like on the building's other three sides. It wasn't much to hang your hat on, but it ought to be enough.

"All right," Genevieve said. "All right." She didn't move, though, just kept staring out the window.

"Faster would be better," Anna said.

"Right." She put down the heavy bag and pulled out a few items—two vacuum cups with heavy-duty handles on them, and an industrial glass cutter. She also pulled out a huge coil of nylon rope.

Anna picked up the vacuum cups and stuck them to the window, pumping a few times to get the air out. It'd take a hell of a lot more than the weight of the glass to break them free now. While Genevieve messed with the rope, she scored the glass with the cutter. After she'd made a few wide, sweeping lines, she pounded lightly along them with her fist while Karyn held the vacuum cups.

The glass came free, neat as you please, in a big sheet about three feet square. Karyn pulled it out and leaned it against the wall, disengaging the suction cups. The building's windows were double-paned, so they'd have to repeat the process one more time to open the room to the outside.

No problem. One more go with the cups and glass cutter, and a second sheet of glass joined the first. A hot wind blew in the hole, ruffling Anna's hair, and she took a few steps back toward the corner. Despite her nerves and the urgency of the situation, she smiled. She was doing the one thing she was good at, right here with her best friend and her lover, and if she just kept thoughts of the next steps at arm's length, she actually felt good. Better than good. She touched Genevieve's shoulder with her fingertips. Karyn glanced over and gave her a tight, distracted smile. As good as a blessing, Anna thought.

At last, Genevieve finished securing the end of the rope around a nearby structural column. She'd had to punch a hole through the wall to do it, but the gleam of metal behind the sheetrock, the structural member holding up the ceiling here, helped fill Anna with confidence. *That* thing wasn't going anywhere. All she had to worry about was Genevieve's knot. She took reassurance from the fact that it was about the size of a big man's fist.

Genevieve gave the rope a couple of hard yanks. "OK, that oughta do it. Now, the tricky part."

"Yeah," Anna said. "It'll be a miracle if this works."

"Ease up, huh? I don't need the attitude."

"I know. Sorry."

Anna watched as Genevieve slid the whole coil of rope closer to the hole in the window. It was about four hundred feet of serious nylon climbing rope, taken from Nail's stash. Nail was usually the guy responsible for fucking around with this sort of thing, and he'd have tested the rope religiously. She hoped. In any event, he didn't like to keep damaged equipment around. It offended him.

Genevieve sat cross-legged next to the rope and used a Sharpie to draw a diagram on the matted surface of the cheap carpet right in front of the window. It must not have been her usual rigmarole, since she kept referring to a page torn out of the phone book as she worked. Anna didn't want to think about that.

At length, Genevieve finished the diagram and shoved the coil of rope on top of it with a grunt. She glanced quickly up at Anna and Karyn, then back to the work. Anna heard her let out a long, shaky breath.

"It's gonna be fine," Anna said.

"Shh."

Genevieve started chanting. For over a minute, Anna stood and watched, enduring the hot wind and the growing sense of concern that the night security guard would come by any time. Genevieve's chanting seemed to have no effect on anything, and Anna began to worry about that, too. If she fucked this up, the plan was DOA. Even Karyn was getting anxious, shifting her weight from one leg to the next and darting glances at the door.

After a long, nerve-racking wait, the end of the rope moved. It picked itself up, snakelike, and climbed out the hole. Genevieve's eyes widened, but she didn't break off the chant. The backs of Anna's arms and neck prickled with gooseflesh.

Anna and Karyn both walked to the window and watched as the rope paid itself out. Moments later, Anna saw the end of the rope appear clear across the way. The rope had wriggled across the street, and now the other end was slithering up the side of Enoch Sobell's office building. It was a profoundly unsettling sight, and suddenly the breeze coming through the hole didn't feel so warm at all.

This was the dangerous part. If anybody on the street saw this, they probably wouldn't be able to resist fucking with it. Anna prayed that the security cameras at the corners of the building weren't of high enough resolution for the rope to show up on them.

As Karyn and Anna watched, the rope climbed to the ESE sign across the way, twenty feet or so down from their position. It disappeared behind the sign and began hauling itself up. Soon, the coil had run out, and the rope began tightening. Anna wondered again how good Sobell's security cameras were, and how attentive his guards.

The U-shaped arc of rope got shorter and higher. No alarm sounded. No security personnel ran out into the street, pointing.

Then the rope was tight, a nearly straight length connecting the two buildings.

Genevieve stopped chanting. "Holy shit," she said. "It worked."

Nail slumped against a couple of trash bins in the alley behind the apartment building, breathing fast. Somebody had lit a fucking fire in his guts. Drew crouched next to him, on the verge of panic—basically a liability at this point. Any minute now, the people from the Brotherhood would come running, waving their guns around, and overrun the two men, but for some reason it hadn't happened yet.

Over the sound of blood rushing in his ears, Nail heard a car engine cough its way to life. Two more, maybe three, started up after it.

No way. It can't be this easy.

Drew heard it too, and hope dawned on his face. "I think they're leaving," he whispered.

"Fucking . . . great."

"How you holding up?"

"Guts aren't in my lap." Nail pushed himself upright and winced. "I guess the guy ahead of me slowed the bullet down some."

"Um. OK. I'm gonna go out and see if they're gone."

"Give it a minute, huh?"

Drew leaned forward, trying to peer around the trash bins. They weren't very big trash bins, and they were plastic besides. If somebody saw him, they wouldn't be much good for cover.

"Get down, dumbass!" Nail said.

"I don't see anybody."

There was surprisingly little blood, and no exit wound. Hurt like a motherfucker, but he'd had worse. Pulse was good, skin didn't feel clammy, best as he could tell, so at least he wasn't going into shock. Probably. Still, this was nothing to fuck around with.

"Okay," he said. "Take a quick look. Then we get the fuck out of here, if we can." *And find a fucking doctor.*

The alley was empty so far, as best as Nail could see from where he lay. Drew crept out, gun at the ready. His hands were shaking. *Boy's gonna get his ass killed. Mine, too.*

Drew walked down the alley, nearly to the end, and stopped. The apartment building stuck out, blocking off the view at the end, and he'd have to jog right to come around the end of that building. If somebody was waiting for him, that's where they would be.

Drew disappeared behind the little turn. Nail waited for shots.

Nothing.

Shouldn't the cops be getting here pretty soon? Nail wondered, and the thought surprised him so much he almost laughed aloud. *First time I can remember wishing for some cops.* If they were coming, though, they were taking their time. Or hell, maybe gunfire was so common down here that nobody'd bothered to call them. Wouldn't that be funny?

Yeah. Like a heart attack.

Still no sounds. A minute passed during which Nail's wound seemed to stiffen up, such that every breath grew more painful. Where'd the fucking bullet end up? Kidney? No, probably be bleeding worse if they'd hit a kidney.

Movement at the end of the alley. It was Drew. He walked quickly to Nail.

"It's clear," he said.

"Come on, then. Get me the hell out of here."

Once, in Dublin in the seventies, Enoch Sobell had gotten clipped in the head by a piece of debris from an exploding house. One moment, he'd been strolling down a calm street in an expensive neighborhood, enjoying the sun and the clear sky and, for once, not up to anything more complicated than stretching his legs. Then came a mighty roar, and something that felt like a meteorite the size of a school bus smashed into the back of his head.

The next time he was conscious, it was four days later and the pain was a constant, slightly muted screaming that turned into five-alarm agony if he did anything so foolish as to touch the back of his head in any way.

He should have been killed, they'd told him. He'd been standing a hundred yards or so from some rich muckety-muck's house when the IRA blew it up for reasons he neither understood nor cared to, and a quarter of a brick had hurtled in a straight line from beneath the window casement to a spot on the back of Enoch Sobell's head, somewhat on the left.

If not for having taken a few magical precautions, it would surely have killed him. Even so, the wound had hurt like a bastard and taken weeks to heal, and he'd had little patience for the IRA ever since.

His current injury made that earlier one feel like a paper cut.

My head. Ohhh, my fucking head. The top of my head's off, I know it. The whole top. Brain's probably got flies on it, laying eggs. And it's drying out, most certainly. What happens when your brain dries out? Is that a problem?

He instinctively moved his hands toward the pain, but caught himself before he did anything stupid. *Like prodding my exposed brain with my filthy bare hands. Idiot.*

He needed to get up. He wasn't entirely clear on what had happened over the last—how long?—but he could see nobody in the room other than a couple of lumps that were almost certainly dead bodies. That meant even more violence than the shot he'd taken to the head, which meant police, who, of course, were all in Greaser's pocket. If they found him here, he was fucked. *More fucked, rather.*

His head felt like somebody had taken an auger to it, drilled out a nice hole, packed it with gunpowder, and lit the fuse. At least when the IRA had blown him up, he'd gotten to spend four days in a coma and miss the worst of it.

Nonetheless, he sat up. The room spun and nausea seized his gut. A slow bead of thick blood oozed down his forehead. Sweat popped out over his whole body. With a grunt that came out alarmingly close to a wheeze, he used the dresser to pull himself to a kneeling position. The room not only spun now—it turned upside down and actively tried to shake him off. He gripped the edge of the dresser with both hands until his fingers ached.

Eventually the room settled down to a low, rolling motion. Sobell forced himself to stand. He had a bad moment when his unsteady feet buckled, nearly dropping him back to the ground, but sheer terror of the pain that would ensue if he bumped his head helped him regain his balance.

Breathing like he'd just run half a marathon, Sobell

stood and looked at himself in the reflection from a framed photo of a bland landscape.

So much for my rakish good looks. Still, it wasn't as bad as he'd feared. It only *felt* like the top of his head had come off. In reality, it appeared the bullet had entered just above his right eye, skidded along his skull, and traced a red-hot line beneath his skin about six inches long before exiting and blowing a hole in the wall. Part of his forehead hung down in a gruesome flap, and his head hurt like hell, but he'd gotten off lucky.

Nothing a couple of safety pins won't fix. His stomach convulsed at the thought. That wasn't, apparently, something he was ready to even joke about.

He straightened, and another bad dizzy spell sloshed through his head. Again, he steadied himself against the wall, and when the moment passed, he took a cautious step toward the door.

As expected, the room was over its quota for dead bodies—three of them. Two were men Sobell didn't recognize, presumably members of the Brotherhood. Brown was the third. His body leaned against the wall, eyes open, torso shot full of holes.

Sobell sighed. This had not been one of his finest moments. He'd badly misgauged the Brotherhood's motivations. Either rational self-interest wasn't among the Brotherhood's virtues—which he could well imagine— or they were playing a different game. Maybe they thought if they knew the location of the bone, they could get it themselves. Hell, maybe they were right.

He opened the door and walked out, one shuffling step at a time.

Nail didn't scream when Drew helped him up, impressing even himself. He *wanted* to scream, and if he'd been a hundred percent sure it wouldn't get him shot, he'd have cut loose with a roar that would have woken people up in Long Beach. He almost passed out instead, but after a blurry few moments during which he couldn't tell *what* the fuck was going on, he found himself on his feet, leaning against the building. A few moments after that, he was half draped over Drew, hobbling down the alley. A brief pause for Drew to check around the corner, and then they were out in the open.

The parking lot was almost empty. Sure enough, the Brotherhood had split.

"Fuck yeah," Nail said—and then he remembered. "Shit. Brown. He make it?"

Drew gave him a blank look. "Huh?"

"Brown. Is he alive?"

"I . . . I don't know."

"Come on. We gotta go check."

The blank look turned incredulous. "You gotta be shitting me."

"Nope. Never leave a man behind. Guy's a dick, but he pulled some Sylvester Stallone shit in there, and we'd probably both be dead if he hadn't."

"Unfuckingbelievable," Drew said, but he started hauling Nail toward the apartment.

A moment later, a figure lurched out of the apartment. Drew let out a terrified squawk and went for his gun before Nail put a hand on his arm and stopped him.

"Jesus!" Drew said.

Sobell took half a step and then slumped against the doorframe. "No, but that wouldn't be the first time I've been a victim of a case of mistaken identity."

"Brown?" Nail asked.

"Dead."

"Shit. We gotta get out of here."

"I'm shambling as fast as I can. This may look like a mere scratch, but, surprisingly enough, it's actually rather painful."

"Well, come on," Nail said. "We ain't got all day."

"No. I expect not."

Chapter 30

"Mr., uh, Sobell? Um, sir?"

Gresser tried to lift his head, but it wouldn't go. Something grabbed him by the hair and pulled his head up for him. He felt gratitude for that, despite the pain.

He was supposed to say something. Words. There were some words he needed, but he couldn't seem to find them. It had gotten hard to think. His back and shoulders hurt— well, no. They didn't hurt at all. But there was a strange stiffness to them, and they didn't want to move, and somehow that stiffness, that nonsensation of pain, was a source of constant distraction. And his hips, too. They didn't quite . . . go.

"Sir?"

The wide-eyed lieutenant stared at him, expecting some kind of response. But what did he want? Gresser wasn't Sobell, so why was this asshole bothering him? *No, wait. I am Sobell. Right?*

He wasn't sure, but he didn't have any words anyway.

A thin, bony hand, sticky with some kind of viscous fluid, crept around his head and seized his jaw.

Yes, he heard in his mind. The hand pulled his jaw open, puppetlike, and somehow the word came out.

"Yes?"

"A whole bunch of people just showed up down front. Like, twenty or so guys. They say they're looking for you." The young man, a broken-nosed bruiser who must have gone two-forty and probably made a habit of picking a fight with the biggest guy in any given bar, just for fun, shuffled his feet and kept his eyes down, daring only the briefest glances at Gresser.

"Who are they?" The hand worked his jaw again, and words came into his head and out his mouth at almost the same time. They sounded oddly doubled, as though he were speaking and whispering simultaneously.

"The Brotherhood."

Gresser had no idea who that was or what it meant, but he straightened in his chair. A sound of grinding, crunching things came from his spine, and he almost screamed before he remembered that it didn't hurt. "Good," he said. "Send them up."

"Shit. Looks like the distraction's arrived." Anna looked out the hole in the window where a bunch of cars had roared up and parked in front of Sobell's building. She couldn't see most of them from here, but from the look of the stragglers at the end, it wasn't the cops or Sobell's guys. Had to be the Brotherhood, then.

"Nail with them?" Karyn asked.

"I can't tell."

"We gotta go," Genevieve said. "Like, now."

"Yeah, yeah." Anna knelt and clipped her harness to the zip-line trolley. She didn't get to use this stuff often, but it was her favorite part of any job that needed it. Hell of a rush, and probably the next best thing to flying. She didn't feel great about the small crowd moving toward the front of the building, though, but there wasn't any time left to fuck around. She just had to count on all the spotlights out front wrecking their night vision.

"See you on the other side," she said, and she pushed herself out the window.

The harness caught, and the trolley took off, speeding down the length of rope. It was maybe a hundred feet across and twenty down—a good-sized drop that rocketed her forward. It was all she could do to keep an exultant yell smothered in her chest.

She made most of the drop and slowed as the rope started to sag toward the far end. By the time she reached

Sobell's building, she'd dropped enough speed that she was able to catch herself against the wall, legs absorbing the shock so well she barely made any noise above the squeak of rubber on glass.

She hung from the bottom of the sign. From here, she could see the complex mess of brackets and angle iron that held the sign in place, as well as the spot where the rope had coiled itself after it finished its work. She waved back at Genevieve and Karyn and pulled herself up behind the sign. Then she busied herself with more of the climbing gear. Unfortunately, the sign was too high above the nearest window to simply hang from the existing line—she'd need to set up a belaying system to get down where they could get in front of a window. Pain in the ass, really.

She set up the pulley and readied another section of rope.

Genevieve hit the wall a few moments later with too much speed and a muffled curse.

"Shh!" Anna whispered, looking down at where Genevieve twisted below her. "You OK?"

"Hit wrong. Twisted my ankle."

"How bad?"

"It'll be all right. Just hurts."

"Christ. Get up here, would you?"

Genevieve clambered up onto the bracket system next to her. Even in this light she looked pale. "Conjuring up monsters? Sign me up. Hanging from a rope a hundred feet above concrete? Not so much."

Anna hooked her to the new rope and tried on her best reassuring smile. "It's all right. Just a few more minutes, and you'll be on solid ground."

Below them, Karyn stopped herself against the glass. She was even quieter than Anna had been, so much so that Anna might not have noticed her if she hadn't been looking in that direction. A few moments later, and she joined them behind the sign.

Anna pulled on the rope holding Genevieve. "Ready?"

"I guess so," she said. "This seemed a lot less scary when I was thinking it up."

"You'll be fine," Anna said, touching her hand.

"I'm gonna hold you to that."

Genevieve slid off the bracket and rappelled down eight feet or so, favoring her ankle but not badly. Once she'd gotten situated, she pulled a roll of double-sided tape out of her satchel. She slapped it on the glass in four places, the corners of a square about four feet on a side. Then she got out a few pages from the phone book that Sobell had scrawled on and stuck one in place at each corner.

She looked up at Anna one last time, a question on her face. Anna shrugged and gave her the thumbs-up. What else did she expect? Anna didn't have any better idea than Genevieve of whether Sobell's shit would work as advertised. There simply wasn't anything else to go on.

Genevieve tapped the center of the square. The window blew inward in a soundless explosion, the draft of its passage pulling Genevieve in after it. She grabbed at the edges of the window frame, steadied herself, and looked up at Anna, eyes wide. Her mouth widened in a grin, and she returned the thumbs-up.

Moments later, the three of them were inside. The room was a small office, the pictures on the wall vague dark spots, a small desk pushed back against the corner. Powdered glass crunched like sand underfoot.

Anna checked her gun. "Ready?" she whispered.

Genevieve nodded.

Karyn closed her eyes, then opened them again. Her face was pale against the darkness. "Genevieve, you . . . Maybe you should stay here."

Anna cut in before Genevieve could do more than look puzzled. "What do you mean?"

"I mean maybe she should stay here. I think . . . I think this could be really bad for her."

"You think, or you know?"

Karyn studied the floor, kicked at the sand there, then looked back up. "I know," she said softly. "As much as I know anything."

Silence greeted this pronouncement. Anna looked

from Karyn's anguished face to Genevieve's worried grin. She thought of Tommy. Judging from Karyn's expression, she wasn't the only one. "Gen, maybe you should sit this one out."

"Right. And just how do you plan to get past the seventh seal and the magical gatekeeper at the end of level nine?"

"The what?"

"You know what I mean." She held up a sheaf of papers. "I'm only about halfway through the phone book here, so unless you've been hiding your light under a bushel, I'm all you got."

There was no answer for that, so Anna looked back to Karyn.

"Genevieve, can Anna and I have a minute alone?" Karyn asked.

"No." Genevieve shifted her weight, but she didn't back away. "You just told me I'm toast real soon, unless we do something about it, and now you want me to step out into the hall alone? No way."

"They're already in the building," Anna said. "We don't have a lot of time."

Karyn cast a despondent look out the window, where the rope still hung between the two buildings. The faint pull of wind dragged her hair across her forehead. "If she goes up there with us, she'll be in real danger." She took a quick look at Genevieve, then resumed staring out the window. "This shit comes true, Anna. Tell her to stay here."

"She doesn't *tell* me to do anything," Genevieve began, and Anna cut her off.

"It doesn't always come true," Anna insisted. "We can stop it this time, like we have a million times. This is what you *do*, Karyn. You see it coming, and you get us out of the way."

"Not every time." Karyn's face crumpled, and even in the low light reflected from the building across the way, Anna saw the bright bubble of tears threaten to burst.

She pulled Karyn to her. "I'm sorry," she said. "Tommy wasn't your fault. I never should have said those things."

Karyn's body convulsed with sobs, and Anna felt the hot streaks of tears wet her collar.

"I can't . . ." Karyn's words were lost in a fresh flood of sorrow, and she clung to Anna with a fierce desperation that Anna had never expected. Anna's heart felt like it was being wrung out like a wet dishcloth—but they didn't have time for this now.

"Later," Anna said. She gently pulled Karyn's hands from her. "We have to do this now. The others are counting on us."

The naked misery on Karyn's face was almost too much to bear, and Anna felt a rush of relief when she wiped her face and nodded. "Yeah. OK."

Anna turned to Genevieve. "You OK with this?" It would be OK, she thought. Karyn would keep her from getting hurt. That's what she did, for everybody. Except once.

Genevieve summoned up one of her wry grins. "Long as you two are in front."

"Ah. Home sweet home." Sobell stood at the front stairs of his building, doing his best to bask under the glare of the floodlights rather than wince. "I suppose I should be happier to see it."

"That's it, then?" Drew asked, the sound of hope unmistakable in his voice. He'd been anxious ever since they left Nail at the emergency room. Sobell couldn't blame him.

"That's it. Unless you'd care to stick around for the finale?"

Drew shook his head. "No, thanks. The Brotherhood—they're done after this? I won't have to worry anymore?"

"No more worries," Sobell said. He twisted his hand a certain way and spat out a nasty syllable. The spreading grin died stillborn on Drew's face, and he fell to the ground. His eyes were still open and frantic, darting left and right in rolling arcs, but he made no sound as Sobell leaned over him.

"I'm sorry, young man. Truly." One swipe from St. George's sword, and blood flooded forth from Drew's open throat, the pool spreading quickly to a shallow groove in the marble. Sobell stepped over it just as it reached the edge and spilled over. Drew gurgled, but scarcely moved—the paralysis was thorough.

Another short incantation. Nothing happened visibly, but the next unwanted visitor to attempt to cross that line would be the recipient of a particularly unpleasant surprise. And the next after that, and so on.

"So much for Bill Mendez and his boys," Sobell muttered. He dipped his index finger in Drew's blood and drew three runes on his own face—one on his damaged forehead, one below each eye—and then followed up with yet another incantation. He imagined he could hear the clamor of hungry, sharp-toothed mouths swell around him.

Is this the last one? The one where I finally step over the line, and they take me?

It seemed not. Nothing stirred in the flat, hot air.

He wiped his hand on his pants and walked to the front door.

The halls were empty, to judge by Anna's expression, but as far as Karyn could tell, there was a party on this floor. The lights were simultaneously on and off, bright and dark, and the corridors were choked with traffic. Men and women in suits raced down the halls, shuffling papers, muttering to themselves, shouting at each other, talking excitedly, or simply walking straight ahead at a rapid clip, as though they were late for an important meeting. She startled as a naked man and a woman with her skirt missing fell out of a side office, laughing.

"Are you OK?" Genevieve asked.

"Fuck you." Nothing was OK. She couldn't tell if what she was seeing was tomorrow or the day after or yesterday, or twenty-six possible Thursdays rolling around together in the Great Thursday Orgy, or all of them jammed together at once.

"Sorry."

Karyn glanced back. Half of Genevieve's face was gone, a ruin of blood and bone. Gunshot, probably. *How am I supposed to stop this? We're walking right into it.* In her mind, she saw Tommy on the ground, clutching his stomach and screaming, his eyes rolled up to look accusingly at her. It was a lie—his eyes had been gone, hadn't they?—but it felt like the truth.

Keep walking. Keep walking.

Anna stopped at the next intersection and peeked around the corner. Satisfied, she turned and waved at the others to follow. The hall ended after a few dozen steps. There was a door in the wall on the left and another on the right, but the space ahead was blank. It should have been the outer wall of the building—almost.

Anna motioned for Genevieve to do her thing. Then she looked to Karyn.

The cul-de-sac was light and dark, and people went in and out of the office doors on either side, but Karyn saw nothing else. She shrugged.

Anna nodded, then went back to the mouth of the hall, gun at the ready, while Genevieve got to work. Karyn turned slow circles and tried to watch everywhere, awaiting the inevitable. Maybe it would reveal itself in time—*it always has,* she reminded herself without much effect.

Genevieve's flashlight burned white-hot in the darkness, then vanished the next moment as the whole hall lit up. In the stretched oval of the light, weird characters took shape under Genevieve's marker. Tomorrow somebody would get a hell of a surprise when they came in to find the place vandalized, Karyn thought, but tomorrow was the least of anybody's concerns.

Genevieve will be dead by tomorrow, and, if this keeps up, I won't be sane. And Anna? What about Anna?

Karyn looked down the hall to where Anna leaned against the wall, listening. What about Anna? She was whole, for now, without a single bullet hole or bloody wound. Maybe she'd make it, then. And if Sobell was a man of his word—and survived—they'd be a million dollars richer. They'd get the nice apartment Anna wanted, and there'd be money for blind, if Karyn could convince Adelaide to keep providing it. It could all go back to normal.

Minus Tommy.

Yeah. Minus Tommy. And Anna would be a wreck. Between Tommy and Genevieve, Anna would probably never forgive her. *As if I'll forgive myself.*

"Holy shit," Genevieve said. "I don't believe that worked."

The wall had gone transparent, becoming a shimmering sheet of thinnest gauze, and Karyn could see plumbing and electrical conduits in the empty space behind it.

"Is that for real?" she asked.

"I sure hope so. Anna, come on!"

Anna came over. She reached a tentative hand forward into the wall, then through it. "Whoa. Feels like . . . nothing." She leaned her head in and shone her flashlight up the shaft.

"Ladder's on the right," she said. "Follow me."

Not a trace of blood in the front lobby, nor the scent of gunpowder, and Sobell's hopes found that, yes, there was yet another subbasement to which they could further descend. His shoes clicked loudly on the marble floor, and the sound echoed back to him off the towering slab before him. There had been no battle here, no winnowing of the enemy. The Brotherhood had surely arrived already, so the absence of any signs of violence could only mean they had been welcomed.

One lone guard stood at the front desk. The man wrinkled his brow in confusion as Sobell approached.

"Sir—I—you . . ." He trailed off and pressed one hand to his temple. Then he caught sight of St. George's sword and the blood that covered Sobell's hand and dripped from the broken blade. He went for his sidearm, fumbled it, and, by the time he'd rescued it from a fall to the floor, Sobell was on him. A moment later, his head tumbled from his shoulders. The gun fell from his lifeless hand, and his body collapsed to the floor a fraction of a second later.

"Tragic waste," Sobell muttered. He walked around the counter and back toward the elevators. He wondered if he was being observed. The main camera screens were out here behind the desk, but there was another set upstairs, just in case. Whether anyone was monitoring them now was unknowable. It probably didn't matter. The party was upstairs, and surprise would get him only so far with so many arrayed against him. In the end, he would have to trust in his magic, his wits, the spell woven around him, and the rusted-out relic in his right hand.

And, hopefully, that pack of thieves I hired for this job. The thought should have given him pause, but he grinned as he pushed the button to summon the elevator. He wouldn't trade his life now for the days of scrabbling in Belfast or San Francisco, but the old life had had a certain feral charm in its more desperate moments, and this certainly matched those days for desperation. He wondered whether he was really a gutter rat by nature and inclination.

"Perish the thought," he said.

The elevator doors opened, and he smiled at himself in the mirror as he stepped inside. A preternatural awareness lifted his senses, propelled him to a nearly transcendent state of consciousness. He was aware of the smooth cloth of his shirt settled on his shoulders, of the rough grip of the broken sword, of the dull curtain behind which he'd swept the screaming pain in his forehead, and a thousand other details. In a moment, the elevator would open, and he would go to war for what was his.

His smile widened. He shifted the sword to his left hand and straightened his tie with his right, smearing more blood on his shirt.

The elevator slowed, then stopped. Sobell stepped to one side as the doors opened—no sense in getting shot right off, after all. But nobody made a sound, and the elevator lobby was empty. He stepped out onto the highest floor the elevator went to, the level just below his office. The city twinkled through the windows, the view interrupted only a few times by the columns holding up the rest of the building.

He walked across the checkered floor to the spiral staircase. No sound drifted down to him from above, but then he hadn't expected any. The office above had been soundproofed to his rather demanding specifications, and even if an orgy of unprecedented dimensions and enthusiasm were taking place up there, he doubted he'd hear anything.

He readied a spell, speaking the incantation under his breath and then holding it in his mind, one word away from discharge. The noise of chittering, hungry mouths echoed in his ears and then fell silent, to be replaced by the sound of his panicked heart. But he was still here. *Not this time, then.*

He ascended.

He came up the stairs into the antechamber to his office. It, too, was empty of people, and the engraved black slabs seemed to tower ominously over him in a way they never had before. One more door. One more door, and he would be face-to-face with the miserable prick who'd taken his office—usurped his very throne, as it were. There were no signs of fighting anywhere, suggesting that Gresser had simply allowed the Brotherhood to come up, perhaps counting on the power of the jawbone to keep them from killing him and taking it.

Sobell pulled a pair of cheap convenience-store earplugs from his pocket, stuffed them into his ears. *If it was good enough for Ulysses . . .*

He opened the door.

Inside, nearly filling his office, dozens of men and women prostrated themselves before a figure that stood in front of his desk. His first impression of the figure was confused, jumbled, but then his mind arranged it into something, and his gorge rose.

Oh, Joseph. What have you done?

Anna went first up the ladder, followed by Karyn, then Genevieve. The shaft was narrow, not much wider than Karyn's shoulders, and she marveled that Sobell should have built himself such a tiny escape hatch. He wasn't a large man, it was true, but this must have been uncomfortable for him, if he'd ever had to use it.

It was five floors up, and by the time they reached the

top, Karyn's arms ached, her heart pounded, and her nerves were worn raw. Confined space or no, if she fell, she'd end up broken at the bottom of a forty-foot shaft—most likely with Genevieve crushed beneath her. At least there were no visions here. Nobody ever came to this place, a fact for which she could barely express the depth of her gratitude. It was hard on the body, but at least one part of her mind got a break.

Anna reached the top and stepped to the left of the ladder onto a narrow ledge that surrounded the shaft. Sweat dripped from her face. *But she looks OK,* Karyn thought. *She's OK.* Anna extended a hand and helped Karyn off the ladder. A moment later, Genevieve followed, limping more now on her injured ankle. In the wobbling light of Anna's flashlight, her face was still a bloody mess. Karyn looked away.

Anna held the flashlight while Genevieve checked another in Sobell's series of diagrams. A few more quiet words, a few lines on the sheetrock, and the wall faded to transparency. Beyond, Karyn saw a room full of softly lit alcoves, each of which contained an old, battered piece of junk. At the far end of the room, yellow light outlined a door.

Genevieve stepped through the wall. Anna and Karyn followed her.

The awful apparition before Sobell swung two heads in his direction when he spoke. The first was Joe Gresser's, and it barely twitched. Gresser was a wasted ruin of the man he had been. He still had the big, broad-shouldered frame, but the flesh had melted away, leaving him no more substantial than a coat rack, and his back hunched over like that of a man who had seen a hundred years come and go.

If Sobell had wondered where Gresser had wasted away to, he had to look no farther than the creature growing from his body. It was nearly skeletal, wrapped in a sticky, clinging skin of bilious yellow. One bony arm wrapped around Gresser's shoulder and torso, and the other caressed the big man's face, leaving slimy trails of mucus. A fat, grotesque umbilicus came from under Gresser's shirt and entered its side, looking like nothing so much as a loop of pale white intestine. The creature's head was nearly that of a human skull papered over with wet skin, the jaw somewhat more protuberant, the eyes slitted and baleful.

It pointed at Sobell. Gresser did the same, puppetlike.

"Kill him," Gresser said, and the creature's mouth moved with his.

OK, ladies. Don't let me down here.

Sobell spoke the last word of his spell, and the room exploded. A blazing white light detonated before him and a thunderclap ripped the air, sounding like the Devil himself had drop-kicked the earth. A dozen or more people dropped to the ground, screaming and clutching their ears or eyes, and even Sobell staggered for a moment, shocked by the force.

He moved a moment before those farthest from the epicenter recovered their wits.

It wasn't fast enough, he saw, as the bodies closed in around him.

Brilliant light suddenly outlined the door, accompanied by screams, and Karyn jumped. Anna dashed forward. She pushed the door open ever so slightly and held her eye to the crack. Karyn heard her gasp from across the room.

Before Karyn and Genevieve could reach her, Anna pulled her gun and kicked the door open.

Karyn nearly gagged. The *thing* before them wrapped around Greaser like a gruesome living backpack, its flesh stretched tightly over spindly bones. *What the hell is that?* she had time to wonder, and then Anna was firing.

Four loud, sharp bangs, and the bullets tore through the creature's back, passing into the body of the man it hung from. An unearthly scream came from Gresser's throat, and both figures fell back into the desk.

Anna stood, shocked and staring. Karyn saw a handful of armed Brotherhood standing against the wall to

Anna's right, no less shocked. Opposite them, at the other side of the office, a man with a spotty beard and angular features clutched Adelaide by the elbow.

"The bone! The fucking jawbone, you twit!" Sobell shouted from across the room, where he was being mobbed by angry cult members and security personnel. Part of an arm went flying.

"Anna!" Karyn shouted, and she pointed. The bony horror that had ridden Greaser pulled itself off the dying man with a horrid ripping sound and turned to face Anna.

It sprang at her before she could bring her gun up, jaws snapping at her face. She staggered backward and fell as it barreled into her.

A high-pitched, frantic scream sounded over the shouts—Sobell, barely recognizable: "KILL IT!" His arm swung free for a moment, and something—black, maybe a foot long—spun out from the crowd, arcing through the air.

"ANNA!" Genevieve screamed.

The scene doubled itself, and for once, Karyn saw future and present spread before her in a crystal clear tableau. *Nobody else dies on my watch,* she saw with wonder and terror.

The spinning thing cut through the air, tumbled end over end, and effortlessly sliced off a corner of Sobell's hard wooden desk before hitting the ground.

Anna screamed as the bony monstrosity clawed at her. It was making an awful wheezing, chittering sound now, and its jaw clacked and spittle flew.

Genevieve moved. Karyn saw it before it happened, saw the whole sorry mess play out in slow motion. Genevieve would rush forward for the sword fragment, or whatever it was, and then it would happen. The blast would tear through her head, shower the room with blood and brains, and leave Genevieve a corpse before she hit the ground.

And then, when the dust settled, it would be back to normal. Minus Tommy, of course. Just the two of them, plus Nail. Back to Anna looking out for her all the time, with the extra added bonus of Anna's grief and her own culpability in two deaths she could have stopped.

Or . . . the alternative. The horrible, unthinkable alternative.

It was so easy. Karyn took one step forward, right into what would become Genevieve's path, and twisted her body. Genevieve arrived a fraction of a second later, bounced off her, and went skidding to the side. Karyn fell forward. To her right, one of the Brotherhood—a confused, scared kid, probably no more than twenty—brought up his shotgun.

The gun didn't seem loud when it went off, not among all the chaos. Karyn felt a slight tug at her hip. She spun, falling to the floor with a thud.

On the other side of the room, Adelaide reeled back against the wall as shotgun shot sprayed her rib cage and shoulder. When she met Karyn's eyes, the look on her face wasn't pain. It was rage, pure hate—and shock. She, too, had seen the possible futures unfolding, and she had moved just a moment too late, perhaps lost in the myriad possibilities, perhaps never believing Karyn would really make that choice.

She wasn't going to die, Karyn didn't think, but even so, that was it. No more blind. Not from Adelaide. Maybe not ever.

Genevieve leapt over Karyn and scooped up the broken sword. There was a moment when she froze, terror on her face as she looked across the room at something Karyn couldn't see. Then she made a noise of horrified disgust and spun away. She crossed the room, stumbling a bit over her twisted ankle, and brought the weapon down on the monster's skull. Karyn saw the sword pass neatly through the creature's head, through cranium, spine, and jaw, and leave it cloven in two pieces.

The noise in the room abated, or maybe it just seemed far away. Karyn was having a great deal of difficulty breathing, and distantly she felt that that ought to be cause for panic. But there wasn't any pain. Anna was crawling out from under the dead pile of bones, screaming as tears poured from her eyes.

"It's OK," Karyn said, or tried to. No sound seemed to come out, but that didn't matter. She smiled. "I'm OK."

Everything was OK.

She closed her eyes.

The room was bedlam, insanity far beyond what it had been just moments before. To Anna's eyes, everything got weirdly calm for one second after Genevieve destroyed the bone—everyone paused, it seemed. Then shrieks and wails erupted from the Brotherhood, and a wall of bodies surged toward the desk, toward Genevieve, Anna, and Karyn.

"Fucking *kill them*!" Sobell shouted.

Kill them? They were outnumbered twenty to one! Then the dazed bruisers on Sobell's security staff recovered their wits, and the mass of people exploded with violence in all directions, and Anna understood whom Sobell had been yelling at. Security attacked the Brotherhood with fists, batons, and guns, and the room erupted into a cataclysmic brawl.

Anna jumped up from the floor, heaving the bony horror aside just as two of the Brotherhood vaulted the desk. She shot them both without a trace of hesitation and was running to Karyn's side before they even hit the ground. Genevieve backed up to meet her there, holding the weird metal fragment up as though she could ward off evil with it.

"Is she OK?" Anna asked, still not taking her eyes from the violence unfolding in front of her. Sobell had somehow managed to surround himself with a handful of his security people, who were backing him into a corner as they held off half a dozen enraged Brotherhood members. One went down with a knife in his ear, hands still clutching at the cultist in front of him. "Is she all right?"

Any answer she could have gotten was drowned out by her own gunfire as she pulled the trigger again and again. In seconds, the gun was empty, the slide racked back, but she still pointed it at the assembled throng of

Brotherhood and Sobell's people. The tendons in the back of her hand jumped as she convulsively squeezed the trigger over and over, her face twisted in a wordless cry of anguish.

Two bullets tore into the wood paneling next to her head.

Karyn was down, not moving, stretched out on the floor at an uncomfortable-looking angle. *Dead,* Anna thought. *She's dead.*

"Come on!" Genevieve shouted. "Now!" She dropped the piece of sword and grabbed at Karyn's arm. "*Anna!* Help me!"

Finally, Anna turned her head, registering what was going on around her. She reached for Karyn's other arm, and the two women pulled Karyn into the back room.

The last thing Anna saw before she pushed the door shut was Sobell, grinning out between the gap in a wall of his remaining people as the last of the Brotherhood fled or faced the guns. He looked awfully proud of himself.

Chapter 31

The apartment was practically empty. Nothing in the way. Nothing to trip on, if one's sense of reality became distorted and confused.

Nothing to pack. As always.

Anna walked through the living room in a numbed-out daze. She knocked on Karyn's door out of habit. There was no response, but she went in anyway.

Karyn lay on the bed. Her eyes were open, fixed on the doorway Anna had just come through. Her brow furrowed, as though she were trying to puzzle out some intense mystery.

"How you doing?" Anna asked. She got no answer. Karyn's gaze didn't move from the doorway, even though Anna now stood by the side of the bed. What was she seeing? *When* was she seeing? She had been unconscious for almost two days after the doctor stitched up the mess of shredded flesh just above her left hip, and when she finally woke up, Anna had been there holding her hand—and she'd been gone. Not catatonic. Functional, sort of, but nothing she said made sense. Everything was a non sequitur, an answer to a question nobody had asked.

Nothing she saw was *now* anymore.

Anna slumped against the wall. *Did she know?* Anna wondered, for maybe the thousandth time. Had she seen it coming? Had she known that she'd be trading her sanity for Genevieve's life? And, if so, *how long* had she known? Moments? Days? Anna had run through all the scenarios in the days since the disaster, then gone back and raked through her memories, looking for any little tic or word that might tell her something about how and when her oldest friend—her *only* friend, for so many years—had decided to plunge headlong into the insanity that had been her greatest fear for so long. Part of her couldn't help wondering if Karyn had kept so little stuff not because she was afraid of barking her shin on something she couldn't see, but because she'd known this was coming, known that one day it would fall to Anna to deal with her and all of her earthly possessions, and she didn't want to make it any harder than it had to be.

Oh, bullshit, Anna thought, but the numbness had cracked a little, and tears gathered in her eyes.

So it had gone since the night at Sobell's. It seemed that every few moments, she could feel the limp weight of Karyn's body in her arms, and she relived those last terrible seconds over and over again. The chaos behind Anna as Sobell's men regained their senses and the violence in the room ascended to a whole new level faded to a distant noise, buried beneath her own sobs as she and Genevieve pulled Karyn's body to the back room.

Each time the memory resurfaced, it triggered a mess of warring emotions. She wanted to be angry, rage over this last, deepest abandonment, knock over Karyn's shit and break it into pieces, and she wanted to curl up in a corner, weep for her friend, and never come out. She'd spent an entire day waiting for Karyn to wake up, not moving or saying a word, just lying in bed and going over the scattered moments that had somehow coalesced into a decade of fighting, fleeing, surviving, and more, emotions she couldn't put a name to—moments that simultaneously seemed more important than ever, yet hollowed out and empty now. The image that came back most was Karyn, standing on the civil administration building steps, cigarette in hand, matter-of-factly facing down insanity.

They'd *beaten* it, though.

It had come for her again, though—and it would keep

coming. And, dammit, Anna would beat it back again. Somehow. Alone, if she had to.

The doorbell rang, jolting her from her reverie. *Numbness,* she reminded herself. That was the order of the day, the only way to get through all the necessary bullshit that came next. She composed herself, then crossed the small apartment to open the door.

Genevieve stood there, looking about as exhausted as Anna felt. The light outside the door cast harsh shadows on her face. "You, um . . . ready to go?" she asked softly.

Anna opened her mouth, but no sound came out. A hard, painful lump had formed in her throat, and her eyes were beginning to sting again. She swallowed once, forcefully, closed her eyes. "Yeah. Let's—let's go." She didn't move, though, didn't open her eyes. She just stood there trembling, hands clenched into fists by her side.

The sound of movement—the sliding sound of jeans, the faint jingle of the chain running from Genevieve's belt loop to her pocket—and then Genevieve's arms were around her. Her body softened, and she leaned against Genevieve for support. She could feel the tears battering against that shield of numbness, slamming against it in waves like a furious ocean battering down a wall, and her shaking got worse.

Don't cry. Don't cry. No more goddamn crying.

"It's gonna be OK," Genevieve whispered.

Don't ever fucking tell me that, Anna wanted to say— but the numbness chose that moment to crumple.

Genevieve shut the door and held her while she wept.

The cash sat in a scattered pile on Sobell's desk, dumped as if by somebody who just didn't give a damn about it. Anna stood and watched Sobell's face over the heap. The wound in his forehead was a crusted black hole over which, for whatever perverse reason, he had not bothered to put a bandage. He grinned, but Anna thought she read deep fatigue underneath the bullshit.

Blood still stained the carpet in a dozen spots, some mere spatters, others great brown smears the size of a man's torso or larger. From where Anna stood, she could see the splotches on the wooden desktop where Greaser's life had run out. She wanted to take Genevieve's hand, take some comfort from it—but not in front of Sobell.

"Would you like to count it?" Sobell asked. "I'll wait."

She shook her head. In truth, she just wanted to get the hell out of there. The place made her feel cored out, a wasted shell filled with little but horror. She began clawing the bundles of cash into the duffel bag while Sobell waited. The money wouldn't have to stretch far—it was just four of them once more. Tommy was dead and Drew had been found dead alongside a couple of off-duty cops who had been summoned to the building for whatever mysterious purpose.

Nail would live, and he'd even gotten out of the hospital after a few days. He still looked like shit, but at least he'd chuckled when Anna had told him so.

Anna zipped the bag and hefted it to her shoulder. "We done?"

"There is one more thing," Sobell said.

"Yeah?"

"The four of you work for me now. Do what you want on your own time, but when I call, you should find your schedule miraculously clear. Understood?"

A dozen biting replies leapt to mind, but all the fight had been ground from her spirit. And, whatever else she might have learned, it was still unwise to make an enemy of Enoch Sobell.

"Yeah," she said.

"Excellent." He looked to Genevieve. "Ms. Lyle, might I have a word with you in private?"

Genevieve nodded. "I'll be right out," she told Anna.

Anna walked out.

Despite her punk-rock fuck-you attitude, or whatever the kids were calling it these days, Ms. Lyle was looking considerably the worse for wear, Sobell thought. He could sympathize. His head hurt like blazes, his most trusted and capable lieutenant was dead, his new lieutenant had also been killed, he had dead men scattered across the city, and even his vast resources would be hard-pressed to keep him from going to prison for *something* after this latest debacle. That was disappointing and inconvenient, and it would be an unwelcome distraction while he got about his real business.

"I have a question for you," he began. "I trust we are past the point where I need to make veiled threats and dire pronouncements on the price of bearing false witness?"

"Yeah. Way past." She would have chuckled at that at one point, he thought, but he supposed they'd all been through a lot since then.

Sobell stood and walked to the end of the room, near the main door. He opened an elegant wood cabinet to reveal a small flat-screen TV.

"The authorities have done a fair job of raiding the premises for evidence, despite the best efforts of my attorneys. To their disappointment, I'm sure, they've found that all the security footage has gone missing." He held up his hands to show how powerless he was. "Incompetent staff, I'm sorry to say."

"That's rough."

"There is one surviving tape," he said. Without taking his gaze from Genevieve's face, he flicked on the television.

She flinched. It was quick, so quick that he might not have noticed had he not been watching for it, but her lips pulled back in a moue of disgust that she immediately suppressed, not much different from the expression he'd seen on her face the night of the firefight.

Sobell turned to look at the screen. It showed a single still image from the night of the battle royale in his office. A dozen men and women were frozen in as many poses, running, falling, shooting, or shouting. In the top left quadrant, a face was caught in a clear three-quarters view. A man with angular features and a patchy beard.

Sobell put his finger to the screen. "This man. Who is he?"

"His name is Hector Martel," Genevieve said. "And he's not a man anymore."

"A demon."

"Yeah."

Sobell smiled. "Beautiful. Do you know which one?"

"Which—no. How would I?"

"You know him from somewhere."

Genevieve didn't look at him. She couldn't, it seemed, take her gaze from the screen. Her fingers absently pulled at a stud in her eyebrow as she stared. "Yeah, but—it was a while ago. He should be dead by now."

"How long?"

Genevieve was twisting the stud back and forth now in what had to be one of the more unpleasant nervous tics Sobell had seen in some time. "Few months."

Sobell closed the cabinet. Line of sight broken, Genevieve's attention drifted back to him.

"That's long, but not *that* long," Sobell said.

"I don't know. The only other guy I know who—who had that happen lasted about two weeks."

"Maybe so, but if Mendelsohn made friends with a demon, somehow, that would explain his sudden aptitude for conjuring up things he shouldn't be conjuring, as well as his untimely demise." Sobell pondered this for a moment. "What do you suppose it wants?"

"I don't know," Genevieve said. The stud pulled loose and slipped from her fingers, falling to the floor. "He saw me. Here, that night. He recognized me."

"I thought as much," Sobell said. The expression Sobell had seen on the man's face that night had been hard to mistake, even with all the chaos.

"This is not good."

"No, it's really not. I suspect that, in an otherwise innocent quest for material enrichment, you and I have both stepped in something nasty. Not to worry, though. Whichever demon it is, I'm sure it's entirely the forgiving sort." If it was, in fact, Forcas, he was entirely sure it was not. But Genevieve was right about one thing—a few months *was* a long time. Forcas, formidable as it may have been, probably wouldn't have had the wherewithal and discipline to keep a human body alive and relatively intact that long. That was worrisome, suggesting that

Forcas either had potent help or some other access to power it normally wouldn't.

Genevieve answered with a desperate-sounding moan.

"Nothing to be done for it now," Sobell said. "Tell me everything you know about him."

The scene was all wrong. Instead of a folding card table in empty apartment, they sat around a real dining table, a regular old slab of oak Americana, in a place that, Anna had remarked more than once, looked like Mr. Rogers's digs. Instead of four of them, there were three. Karyn sat alone in the living room, and Tommy's presence at the table had been changed out for Genevieve's.

There was the money, though. A huge pile of it, looking even more ridiculous here than it had on Sobell's desk. Anna and Genevieve had already divided it into four mostly equal stacks.

Across the table, Nail glanced from the cash to Anna, his face expressionless. His arms hung by his sides. This, too, was wrong. At this stage, he usually sat leaning back, arms crossed, a smug smile on his face. The proverbial cat that ate the canary.

"You guys want to . . . you know. Count it?" Anna said.

Nail made a disgusted sound in his throat. "No. Fuck that." Genevieve merely shook her head.

Anna looked to the living room, as though now that everyone was in position Karyn was going to wake up and resume her triple duty as leader, oracle, and friend. But she only sat, her lips moving soundlessly, eyes flicking left and right.

"Yeah," Anna said. "Fuck that."

They sat in silence. Nobody pulled out a deck of cards. Nobody reached for the booze. Nobody moved.

Eventually, Anna shifted. "Sobell says we work for him now. We can line up whatever we want on the side, but when he needs us, we come running."

"That's not all he says," Genevieve added. "We pissed off a demon when we broke up the party at Sobell's the other night. Probably killed another."

"What's that mean?" Nail asked.

"Means we're in the middle of some shit now."

"More than usual?"

"Yeah. I think so."

"Look, I don't really care about that," Anna said. "I'll keep Sobell happy because he might be useful, and because I think we might need the money. That demon shit—I can't do anything about that. Put him on the list of people we've pissed off."

"Long list," Nail said.

Anna ignored him. "Karyn is . . . She's out of commission. This is what she's been afraid of her whole life. I've got a pile of money here, and I'm going to blow every last dime, burn every last contact, and steal every goddamn thing in Los Angeles County if that's what it takes to get her straightened out."

"Fuckin' A," Nail said. "I'll drink to that."

"I'm in," Genevieve said simply.

And that was it. She hadn't even had to ask. Relief cut the bands of tension around her chest that had been keeping her breath shallow and short, and she felt a ghost of a smile on her lips.

"All right. Where do we start?"

Read on for a special preview of
Jamie Schultz's next novel,
SPLINTERED
Available in July 2015 from Roc.

"I hate this," Anna said. She twisted her body to look out the back window of the parked car. Street mostly dark, nobody moving. A pair of headlights swung by and vanished, as somebody made a wrong turn onto the street and then turned right back around. "I hate every damn thing about it."

Nail didn't say anything from the driver's seat, but Anna thought she could feel annoyance radiating from him anyway, and it wasn't hard to imagine what he was thinking. Something along the lines of "I heard you the first six times." She turned to face forward again, held still for almost ten seconds, and then started monkeying around with the car's side mirror. She caught a glimpse of the side of Genevieve's face watching out the window from the seat behind her, just a line highlighting the profile of cheek and a small arc of metal gleaming above the shadow of an eyesocket.

"What time you got?" Anna asked.

Nail made a slight skeptical smile and raised his eyebrows. "Two forty." A long pause, and then, with a smirk playing around the corners of his mouth, "Two forty-one."

"Not funny."

"The hell it ain't. I never seen you with nerves like this."

"I never fuckin' kidnapped nobody before, neither."

He shrugged. She wasn't sure if he was conceding the

point or indicating that it wasn't really a big deal. *You think you know a guy . . .*

He was right, though. She couldn't remember the last time she'd been so jittery. Ten years, maybe, back when she and Karyn had first gotten into their weird line of work, swiping items of usually dubious occult value from their so-called rightful owners. Maybe the first job, the first time she'd found herself standing in a stranger's house at night, wondering, *Hey, what if they were actually home? And armed?* Maybe not even then. Her heart raced like she'd downed a pot of coffee, and the acid-burning sensation in her gut wasn't too dissimilar, either.

"He's taking his time," she said.

"Yeah."

She checked the side mirror. Still nothing. No movement of any kind. There was an empty lot, overgrown with high weeds and strewn with bricks and other construction debris. Then a body shop, closed down with metal shutters at this time of night. Past that, Bobby Chu's party shack, a big metal building that pulsed with bass. Lights flashed through the seams, extending multicolored fingers out through the windows of the cars that crowded around.

"What's Van Horn doing here?" Anna asked.

"Depends what he needs, I guess," Nail said.

"I guess." Still, it wasn't quite in pattern. They'd found Van Horn and his creepy entourage three nights ago, and this was by far the lowest the group had crawled down the socioeconomic ladder. The last few nights, Van Horn had been visiting well-off criminals who were plugged in to the occult underworld in some way or other—one of them had, in fact, given Sobell the tip that had led the crew to Van Horn. Bobby was plugged-in, but not with the grade of crook that Van Horn or Sobell trafficked with. More like the kind of scum that grew on the rocks at the bottom of a lake.

I hate this, Anna thought, again, but at least this time she kept herself from singing that refrain aloud and aggravating Nail and Gen with it once more. Bad enough that Sobell had them doing every odd shit job under the sun, but it was escalating. She'd thought she'd drawn a sharp line the first time he'd told her to act as a bagman — *just this once, and then it's back to business as usual,* she'd said, her voice stripped down to a cold steel edge. He'd pretended to hear, or maybe she'd read acquiescence where none had existed, and then sent her out again the following week. The week after that, it had been another pickup job, except she knew it wasn't, not really, not when Sobell strongly suggested she bring Nail and maybe somebody else along. That was how he put it: *Far be it from me to instruct you in the finer points of your business, but I strongly suggest you bring that big fellow along. For the ride, as it were.* And the pickup job had turned into a beatdown when Ernesto "Spaz" Rivera chose to live up to his nickname. He freaked right out when he saw Anna coming—evidently, he'd been short on the cash, but rather than talk it out, he'd gone for intimidation and violence. Nail hadn't actually been necessary. Pepper spray, it turned out, was more than adequate for the likes of Spaz Rivera. That wasn't the last beatdown, either, and there had been a couple of other unsavory demands sprinkled in as well. It barely came as a shock when Sobell upped the stakes to kidnapping.

"I shoulda told him to fuck right off," Anna muttered.

"Who the hell is that?" Nail said.

"Huh?"

"There."

Anna followed his pointing finger to the barrels and tubs stacked against the side of the body shop. "I don't ... huh." No, there *was* somebody there. Hard to see in the shadows thrown by the streetlight, but there were at least a couple of people lurking among the trash. As she watched, one peeked around the corner at Bobby's place.

"Here he comes," Genevieve said.

"What?"

Nail looked over his shoulder down the sidewalk behind them. Anna angled the mirror until she saw the group leave Bobby's and walk out into the street. A dozen people, at least, throwing long dancing shadows in front of them as they jumped and spun and collided with one another. Somebody fell down hard, and the first sounds of the group reached the car—laughter, high and hysterical. Seconds later, the whole group erupted in the same sort of frenetic, desperate laughter as well, making an eerie chorus that grabbed Anna's spine at the base and twisted.

There was a ripple of motion to Anna's left as Nail actually shuddered.

"You okay, tough guy?" Genevieve asked.

He nodded. Anna studied his face for a moment, then slid down in her seat and resumed watching the mirror. It looked like the same drill out there as the last several nights. Van Horn walked in the middle, head down, fedora pulled low, hands in the pockets of his pin-striped pants. He wasn't close enough for her to see his face or hear him well, but if the past nights were representative, he was either grinning like a fool or whistling some creepy waltz-like, music box–sounding tune. Around him, a shifting, spinning cloud of chaos. Maybe half a dozen men and half a dozen women, and a more motley assortment couldn't easily be imagined. Two of them looked like Genevieve's crowd—lots of black, trenchcoats despite the scorching heat of August in Los Angeles, and lots of piercings. The others, not so much. There was a skinny black kid in a basketball jersey. An old white guy with a mustache, wearing a black suit. He'd look like a slimebag attorney, if only he weren't capering and shouting and stumbling down the street without any shoes on. A twentysomething hippie in what appeared to be a tie-dyed muumuu, tossing invisible handfuls of something at the group and laughing.

It looked like the membership had dwindled again. Seemed like every day, one or two of Van Horn's entourage disappeared. There had been fifteen or so to start with. Genevieve had joked that maybe the missing ones had been eaten by the others, and nobody had laughed. Anna had wondered if she and the crew could just wait until nobody was left and Van Horn was alone, but she eventually decided there was no guarantee that would ever happen, and Sobell was not a terribly patient man.

The mob got closer, and the shouting got louder, and Anna slid farther down into her seat. Even Nail did his level best to make himself small. They hadn't been noticed before, but Anna couldn't help feeling that, if Van Horn's deranged entourage ever did pay them any attention, a bad scene would follow.

In the mirror, Anna saw the guy in the suit stop. He weaved unsteadily on his feet, waved his hands in the air, then pointed at a trash bin that had fallen over in the mouth of an alley.

The trash ignited.

"Oh, shit," Genevieve said.

Van Horn spun on the lawyer type and, in a sudden move totally unlike the easygoing, down-on-his-luck businessman he'd seemed to Anna all week, clouted the other man viciously on the side of the head, shouting something Anna couldn't make out. The lawyer rocked, then fell back, tensed and half-crouched, and Anna could have sworn he was about to spring on Van Horn. She had the sudden crazy impression the man was about to attack Van Horn with his teeth, and then the rest of the entourage formed up, standing to Van Horn's left and right. The lawyer's legs uncoiled, like energy was leaking out through his heels. He laughed. Even from here, Anna could tell he was playing it off like a joke. "Hey, sorry, man. Just got carried away." That kind of thing.

Van Horn's entourage wasn't placated. They began spreading in a semicircle around the lawyer.

"They're gonna kill him," Genevieve whispered.